THE CHARMER

BY
KATE HOFFMANN

AND

HER SECRET FLING

BY
SARAH MAYBERRY

MILLS & BOON

THE CHARMER

BY
KATE HOFFMANN

All the characters in this book have no existence outside the imagination of
the author, and have no relation whatsoever to anyone bearing the same name
or names. They are not even distantly inspired by any individual known or
unknown to the author, and all the incidents are pure invention.

First published in Great Britain 2011
Harlequin Mills & Boon Limited,
Eton House, 18-24 Paradise Road, Richmond, Surrey TW9 1SR

© Peggy A. Hoffmann 2010

ISBN: 978 0 263 88052 6

14-0111

Harlequin Mills & Boon policy is to use papers that are natural, renewable
and recyclable products and made from wood grown in sustainable forests.
The logging and manufacturing processes conform to the legal environmental
regulations of the country of origin.

Printed and bound in Spain
by Litografia Rosés S.A., Barcelona

For all my readers, everywhere!

Kate Hoffmann has been writing for Mills & Boon since 1993. She's published sixty titles, most with the Blaze® imprint. Kate lives in south-eastern Wisconsin with her cats, Tally and Chloe, and her trusty computer. When she's not writing, she works with local school students in music and drama activities. She enjoys talking to her sister on the phone, reading *Vanity Fair* magazine, eating Thai food and travelling to Chicago to see Broadway musicals.

Dear Reader,

The Charmer marks my sixtieth title. It's difficult to believe I've reached that milestone. It seems like just yesterday I was sending off my first manuscript and hoping that a publisher might be interested!

I've loved writing stories for Mills & Boon readers and I hope to continue to do so for many years to come. I've been lucky to find a home here, now with the Blaze® line, and you've helped by watching and waiting for my stories—especially for the Quinns.

I also owe a special thanks to my ever-patient editor, Brenda Chin, who has been with me through most of these books and always helps me give you a story that you'll enjoy.

So, this book is for you, the readers. Thank you for all your support over the years, for your letters and e-mails, and for the opportunity to do work that I love so much. There are two more books coming, *The Drifter* in March and *The Sexy Devil* in May, making this another trilogy.

Happy reading!

Kate Hoffmann

Prologue

Angela@SmoothOperators.com
January 6, 5:30 a.m.
Heading out for my 7:00 a.m. interview on
Daybreak Chicago. Hope you all remember to
tune in. I'm a bit nervous, but excited at the same
time. Call in with questions! I'll post more later.

ANGELA WEATHERBY GLANCED up at her image in the
video monitors, squinting into the bright television
lights that illuminated the studio. She looked worried.
Quickly, she pasted a cheery smile on her face.

The chance to make an appearance on _Daybreak
Chicago_ had seemed like a good idea when it had first
been offered. But now, faced with the prospect of airing
her dirty romantic laundry, Angie wasn't so sure.

With her Web site, SmoothOperators.com, she could
be anonymous, just another jilted lover with a score to
settle. But on morning television, for all of Chicago to
see, she might come off looking like a first-class bitch,
out for revenge.

She glanced over at Celia Peralto, her Web master and best friend, who stood next to one of the cameramen. Ceci grinned and gave her a thumbs-up.

A sound technician approached her from behind and clipped a microphone to her collar. "Just tuck the wire under your hair," he advised, "and set the pack on the chair next to you." With trembling fingers, Angie did as she was told.

"Thirty seconds," the producer called.

"Just relax," the host said as she took her place in the opposite chair. "This isn't the Spanish Inquisition. Just a fun segment on single life in Chicago. And it's great publicity for your Web site—and for the book you're planning to write."

The book. Her publisher was expecting the manuscript in three months and though she had gathered all sorts of anecdotal research from her Web site, the book still had to be written.

"Good morning, Chicago! I'm Kelly Caulfield and I'm here with our next guest. About two years ago, Angela Weatherby founded a Web site called Smooth-Operators.com and it has become a national sensation. What began as a way for single girls in Chicago to network over their dating horror stories has evolved into something akin to the FBI's most-wanted list for naughty men."

"I wouldn't put it that way," Angela said. "These men aren't criminals."

"I suspect some Chicago bachelorettes would disagree. Through the Web site, women are helping each other avoid those men who make dating miserable for all of us. And the trend is spreading—the site adds new cities every week. So, tell us, Angela, what gave you the idea for your Web site?"

Angie shifted in her chair, then drew a deep breath. If she just focused on answering the questions, her nerves would eventually calm. "After a series of not-so-nice boyfriends, I felt there had to be a way for me to avoid guys who weren't interested in an honest and committed relationship. I started blogging about it and before long I had over a thousand subscribers. They added their stories and my friend and Web master, Celia Peralto, put their comments into a database. Now, you can check out your date before you even step out the front door. As of last night, we have files on almost fifty thousand smooth operators in cities all over the country."

"Don't you think this is unfair to the men out there? An ex-girlfriend might not be the most objective person to provide commentary."

"You'd check out the plumber you wanted to hire or the doctor you planned to visit, right? We offer information and leave it to our visitors to decide the truth in what they read. And I think we're doing a service. We've even unmasked a number of cheating husbands."

Kelly leaned forward in her chair. "Well, I looked up my cohost, Danny Devlin, and he wasn't very well reviewed on your site. Your rating system goes from one to five broken hearts, with five being the worst. And he's rated a four. Care to comment?"

Angela opened her mouth to reply, then snapped it shut. A glib answer here might turn the interview in a different direction. "Mr. Devlin is always welcome to defend himself. We're open to differing opinions. We just require that the discourse be civilized."

Kelly flipped to her next note card. "Well, that leads us to the book you're writing. Tell us about that."

Angela drew a deep breath and focused her thoughts. She'd practiced her pitch more than once in the mirror at home. "I hope the book will be a guide to the different species of smooth operators out there. Most of these men fall into one of ten or twelve categories. If women can learn to spot them quickly, maybe they'll save themselves a bit of heartbreak."

"And what professional credentials do you bring to the table?" Kelly asked.

"I have an undergraduate degree in psychology, a masters in journalism and experience as a freelance writer. And I've dated a lot of very smooth operators myself," Angie replied, allowing herself a smile. "I'm curious as to why they behave the way they do, as are most women."

"Let's take a few questions from callers," Kelly said. For the next three minutes, Angie jousted with a belligerent bachelor, commiserated with two women who'd just been dumped and fended off the evil glares of Danny Devlin, who had wandered back onto the set. When the six-minute segment was finally over, she sat back in her chair and breathed a sigh of relief.

"You were wonderful!" Kelly exclaimed, hopping out of her chair. "We'll have to have you back again."

"The switchboard went crazy," the producer said as she walked onto the set. "The most calls we've ever had in this time slot. Let's book another interview for next month. Maybe we can do a longer feature segment when the book comes out."

Angie stood up and unclipped the microphone. "That would be lovely," she murmured as she handed it to the sound technician. "Thank you. Is there anything else I need to do?"

"Get that book written," Kelly said. "And personally, I think Danny Devlin deserves five broken hearts. He dumped me by e-mail."

Angie crossed the studio to Ceci, then grabbed her arm and pulled her along toward the exit. "Let's get out of here," she said, tugging her coat on. "Before Danny Devlin corners me and demands that I take his profile off the site."

The early morning air was frigid and the pavement slippery as they walked through the parking lot. When they reached the relative safety of Ceci's car, Angie sat back in the seat and drew a long, deep breath. It clouded in front of her face as she slowly released it. "So, how was I? Tell me the truth. Did I come across as angry or bitter?"

"No, not at all," Ceci said. "You were funny. And sweet. And just a little vulnerable, which was good. You were likeable."

"I didn't seem judgmental? I want people to look at

the Web site as a practical dating tool. Not some orga-
nization promoting hatred of the opposite sex." She
glanced over at Ceci. "I really do like men. I just don't
like how they treat women sometimes."

Ceci smiled as she started the car. "Sweetie, if we
didn't like men so much, we wouldn't waste our energy
trying to fix them. Someone has to hold these guys ac-
countable."

"Did you get through to Alex Stamos?" Angela
asked, turning her attention to the next bit of research
for her book. "He's been ducking my calls for a week
now."

"I got his assistant. She says he's out of town for the
next few days on business, but he'll be sure to get back
to me when he returns. She also mentioned that she had
a few stories of her own about the guy."

"You made it clear that this interview would be
anonymous, didn't you?" Angie asked.

"I said that you wanted to give him a chance to set
the record straight," Ceci said. "But I think getting an
in-depth profile of each of these types might be kind of
tricky. Especially once they've seen the site."

"Maybe I shouldn't do the interviews and go with
my original plan."

"Absolutely not," Celia cried. "I think having a conversation with each of these types makes them real. Just
move on to the next guy on your list and catch up with
Stamos later."

Angie had been working as a freelance writer ever
since she got out of college. It had been a hit-and-miss

career and there were times when she barely had enough to pay the rent. The blog had just been a way to exercise her writing muscles every day, but once it took off, she was able to attract advertisers and make a reasonably constant paycheck from the Web site.

She sighed. Her parents, both college professors, had wanted her to become a psychologist, but when she finished her undergrad studies at Northwestern, she'd decided to rebel and try journalism.

This book would give her instant credibility as a journalist—and it might appease her parents as well as open a lot of doors. The advance alone was nearly gone, lost to car repairs and computer upgrades. Right now, every Tom, Dick and Mary was a blogger. But not many people could say they were a real author.

"You're right," she said. "I can work on Charlie Templeton. Or Max Morgan." But would they be willing to talk? She'd have to readjust her strategy. If the men weren't going to be identified in the book, then maybe a bit of subterfuge to get their stories wouldn't be entirely out of line.

1

ALEX STAMOS PEERED into the darkness, the BMW's headlights nearly useless in the swirling snow. He could barely make out the edge of the road, the drifts causing the car to fishtail even at fifteen miles per hour.

He'd done a lot of things to boost business at Stamos Publishing and as the new CEO, that was his job. But until now, he'd never had to risk life and limb to get what he wanted. His cell phone rang and he reached over to pick it up off the passenger seat. "I'm in the middle of a blizzard," he said. "Make it quick."

"What are doing in a blizzard?" Tess asked. "I thought you were leaving for Mexico tonight."

He had decided to put off his midwinter vacation for a few days. Business was much more important than a week of sun and windsurfing at his family's oceanside condo. "I have to take care of this business first. I'm leaving the day after tomorrow."

"Where are you?"

"The middle of nowhere," he said. "Door County."

"Isn't that in Wisconsin?"

"And you failed geography, little sister. How is that possible?"

Tess groaned. "That was in eighth grade."

"There's a new artist I need to see. He hasn't been returning my calls, so I decided to drive up and pay a personal visit."

"Well, I thought you'd want to know. *The Devil's Own* got a great review in *Publisher's Preview,*" Tess said. "And the distributors have been calling all afternoon to increase their orders. At this rate, we're going to have to go back for the second printing before the first is out the door, so I just wanted to let you know that I'm going to put it on the schedule for later next week."

Tess was head of production at Stamos Publishing. She and Alex had been working together on his new business plan for nearly a year and this was the first sign that it was about to pay off. Until last year, Stamos Publishing had been known for it's snooze-inducing catalog of technical books, covering everything from lawnmower repair to vegan cookery to dog grooming. But as the newly appointed chief executive officer, Alex was determined to move the company into the twenty-first century. And that move began with a flashy new imprint for graphic novels.

From the time he was a kid, walking through the pressroom with his grandfather, he'd been fascinated by the family business. While most of his peers were enjoying their summers off, he'd worked in the bindery and the production offices, learning Stamos Publishing from top to bottom.

His dream had been to make Stamos Publishing the premier printer in the comic book industry. That way, he could get all the free comic books he wanted. But as he got older, Alex began to take the business more seriously. He saw the weaknesses in his father's management plan and in the company's spot in the market and vowed to make some changes if he ever got the chance.

The chance came at the expense of his family, when his father died suddenly four years ago. His grandfather had come back to run the business, but only until Alex was ready to take over. Now, nearly all the extended Stamos family, siblings, cousins, aunts and uncles, depended upon him to keep the business in the black.

"I'm going to run forty thousand," Tess said. "I know that's double the first run, but I think our sell-through will be good."

"I guess we were right about the graphic novels," he said, keeping his concentration on the road. Though they weren't comic books, they were the next best thing. The edgier stories and innovative art had made them popular with readers of all ages. And Stamos was posed to grab a nice chunk of the market. "What else?"

"Mom is upset," Tess said. "One of her bridge club ladies showed her that Web site. The cool operators site."

"Smooth operators," he corrected. "What did she say?"

"That a nice Greek boy won't find a nice Greek wife if he acts like a *malakas*. And she also said the next time you come to Sunday dinner, she's going to have a conversation with you."

"Great," Alex muttered. A conversation was always

much more painful than a talk or a chat with his mother. No doubt he'd be forced to endure a few blind dates with eligible Greek girls, handpicked by the Stamos matriarch.

"Some people think that any P.R. is good P.R. I don't happen to agree, Alex. I think you need to do some damage control and you need to do it fast. I'm looking at your profile on this page right now and it's not good. These women hate you. Heck, I hate you, and I'm your sister."

"What do you suggest? I'm not about to talk about my love life in public."

"Who suggested that?"

Alex cursed beneath his breath. "The owner of the Web site called to interview me. Angela...I can't remember her last name. Weatherall or Weathervane."

"She wants to talk to you?"

"I guess. Either that, or she wants to yell at me. But I'm almost certain I've never dated her." He cursed softly. "What makes her think I'm the one at fault here? Some of these women are just as much to blame. They were ready to get married after three dates."

"You have had a lot of girlfriends. Listen, Alex, I know you're a nice guy. So why can't you find a nice woman?"

The car skidded and he brought it back under control, cursing beneath his breath. "I'll figure this out when I get back."

"So this artist must be pretty good for you to drive through a blizzard to see him."

"A little snow is not going to stop me," he replied.

"And this guy isn't just good, he's…amazing. And oddly uninterested in publication. The novel came through the slush pile and I figure the reason he's avoiding me is because he's got another publisher interested."

"So, you're just going to drive five hours in the snow and expect he'll want to talk business?"

"I'm a persuasive guy," Alex said. "My charm doesn't just work on the opposite sex. Besides, if I'm his first offer, then I have a chance to get a brand-new talent for a bargain-basement price. I'm not leaving without a signed contract."

The car skidded again and Alex dropped his phone as he gripped the wheel with two hands. He gently applied the brakes and slowed to a crawl as he fished around for the BlackBerry. But he couldn't find it in the dark. "I have to go," he shouted, "or I'll end up in the ditch. I'll call you after I check in."

"Let me know when you're settled," Tess replied.

Alex found the BlackBerry and tucked it in his jacket pocket, then turned his attention back to the road. He knew Door County was well populated, at least in the summer. But in the middle of a Wisconsin winter, the highway was almost desolate between the small towns, marked only by snow-plastered signs looming in the darkness.

Was he the only one crazy enough to be out during a blizzard? Alex leaned forward, searching for the edge of the road through the blowing snow. A moment later, he realized he was no longer in control of his car.

Without a sound the car hit a huge drift and came to a silent stop in the ditch.

This time, Alex strung enough curse words together to form a complete sentence, replete with plenty of vivid adjectives. He wasn't sure what to do. The car wouldn't go forward or backward. Even if he got the car back on the road, it was becoming impossible to see where the road was. He didn't have a shovel, so there wasn't much chance of getting himself out of the ditch.

Alex grabbed his gloves from the seat beside him and pulled them on. If he could clear some of the snow from beneath the wheels, he might be able to get back on the road. If not, he'd call the auto club for a tow. He grabbed a flashlight from the glove box, then crawled out of the car, his feet sinking into a three-foot drift.

Even with the flashlight, it was impossible to see through the blowing snow. Blackness surrounded him as he dug at the snow with his hands. But for every handful of snow he pulled away, two more fell back beneath the tire. Alex knew the only safe option was to wait in the car for help.

He pulled out his phone to call for a tow, but his gloves were wet and his fingers numb from digging in the snow. The BlackBerry slipped out of his fingers and disappeared into the snowdrift. "Shit," he muttered. "From one bone-headed move to the next." Was it even worth searching for the phone?

He decided against it, figuring the BlackBerry would be ruined anyway. As he struggled back to the door, headlights appeared on the road. For a moment, he wondered if the car would even see him in the blinding snow, but to his relief, the SUV stopped. He waded through the drift as the passenger-side window opened.

"Hi," he called, leaning inside. "I'm stuck."

A female voice replied. "I can see that."

Alex could barely make out her features. She wore a huge fur hat with earflaps and a scarf wound around her neck, obscuring the lower part of her face. In truth, she was bundled from top to toe, except for her eyes. "Can you give me a ride into town?"

"No," she said. "I've just come from town. The road is nearly impassable. I'm on my way home."

Her voice was soft and kind of husky…sexy. He felt an odd reaction, considering it was the only thing that marked her as a woman. "I'd call for a tow, but I lost my cell phone."

"Get in," she said. "I'll take you to my place and you can call from there."

"Let me just get my things from the car." By the time Alex retrieved his duffel, his laptop and his briefcase from the BMW, he was completely caked with snow. He crawled into the warm Jeep and pulled the door shut. "Thanks," he said. He glanced over his shoulder to find two dogs in the backseat, watching him silently, their noses twitching. The larger of the two looked like a lab mix and the smaller had a fair bit of terrier in him.

"What are you doing out on a night like tonight?" she asked.

"I could ask the same of you," Alex said with a grin. "I'm glad you were as brave as I was."

"Stupid is more like it. And I'm not driving a sports car," she said.

"It's not a sports car," he said. "It's a sedan." He glanced over at her. It was impossible to tell how old she was. And the only clue to her appearance was a lock of dark hair that had escaped from under her hat. "Do you live nearby?"

"Just down the road."

He settled back into the seat, staring out at the swirl of white in front of them. He couldn't see the road at all, but she seemed to know exactly where she was going, expertly navigating through the drifts. Before long, she slowed and turned off the highway onto what he assumed was a side road and then a few minutes later, into a narrow driveway, marked by two tall posts, studded with red reflectors. The woods were thick on either side, so it was easy to find the way through the trees.

A yard light was visible as they approached and, before long, Alex could see the outline of a small cabin made of rough-hewn logs. She pulled up in front and turned to face him. "The front door's unlocked," she said. "I'm just going to put the Jeep in the shed."

Alex grabbed his things from the floor and hopped out, then walked through another knee-deep drift to get to the front steps. As he stamped the snow off his ruined loafers, the dogs joined him, racing through the darkness to the porch.

He opened the door a crack and the animals pushed their way into the dimly lit interior. The cabin was one huge room, with a timbered ceiling and tongue and groove paneling. A stone fireplace covered one wall and windows lined the other. The décor was like nothing he'd ever seen before, every available space taken with bits and pieces of nature—a bird's nest, a basket of acorns, a single maple leaf in a frame on a bent-willow table.

He kicked off his shoes and stepped off the rug, but then froze as the dogs growled softly. They'd seemed so friendly in the car, but now they watched him suspiciously as he ventured uninvited into their territory.

"The phone is over there."

He turned to see her standing in the shadows on the other side of the kitchen. "Do they bite?" he asked.

"Only if I tell them to," she murmured. There was a subtle warning in her tone. It wasn't surprising, considering she just allowed a stranger into her home. For all she knew, he could be some deranged psycho—driving an expensive European sedan and wearing ruined Italian loafers.

"I won't make any sudden moves," he said.

She shrugged and walked out of the room, her heavy boots leaving puddles of water on the floor. Alex slipped out of his coat and tossed it over a nearby chair, then kicked off his shoes. When the two dogs approached, he held his breath. They sniffed at his feet, then each picked up a shoe and retreated back to the sofa with their prizes.

"Give those back," he pleaded. "No, don't do that. You can't eat those." Alex heard footsteps behind him and he spun around, coming face-to-face with a woman of peculiar beauty. He glanced around the room. "Hello," he said.

He slowly took in the details of her face. She wore dark makeup on her eyes and her shoulder-length hair was cut in a jagged way, with streaks of purple in the bangs. Was this the woman who had rescued him? He'd imagined the face that went with the voice, speculated about the body, but this wasn't at all what he'd expected.

"They eat shoes," she said, grabbing the loafers and handing them back to him.

Only when he heard her voice was Alex certain. This *was* the woman who had rescued him. But the instant attraction he felt was rather disconcerting. She was the exact opposite of women he usually pursued. He liked blondes, tall and willowy, surgically enhanced and trainer-toned. This girl was petite, with an almost boyish figure, and a quirky sense of fashion.

"Put them in the closet," she said, pointing to a spot near one door. "They don't know how to operate a doorknob…yet. They're still working on tearing strangers limb from limb."

Alex smiled, but she didn't return the gesture. She continued to regard him with a cool yet slightly wary stare. After he'd dropped his shoes in the closet, he surveyed his surroundings. "Nice place. Do you live here alone?"

"No," she said. "There are the dogs. And two cats. And I have two horses down in the barn."

"A regular Noah's Ark," he teased. She gave him an

odd look and he decided be more direct. "So, you're not married?"

"Are you?"

"No," he said, chuckling. Crossing the room, he held out his hand. "I'm Alex Stamos." He waited, growing impatient with the long silence between them. "Now, you're supposed to tell me your name."

"Tenley," she said, refusing his gesture.

"Is that your first or last name? Or both. Like Ten Lee?"

She shook her head. "I haven't had dinner yet. Are you hungry?"

"I could eat, Tenley," Alex said. Odd girl with an odd name. Yet, he found her fascinating. She didn't seem to be interested in impressing him. In truth, she didn't seem the least bit fazed by his charm.

Strange, Alex thought to himself. Women usually found him utterly mesmerizing from the get-go. He slipped out of his jacket and draped it over a nearby chair. His pants were damp and his socks soaked through.

"You should probably call for a tow. Or your car is going to get covered by the drifts. The phone is over there."

"I'll call the auto club." He paused. "I don't have the phone number. It's on my BlackBerry, which is in the snowbank."

"I'll call Jesse. He has the garage in town." She walked over to the phone and dialed. Alex watched her from across the room, studying her features. She really was quite pretty in an unconventional way. Alex drew a slow breath. She had a really nice mouth, her lips full and lush.

When she turned to face him, he blinked, startled out of a brief fantasy about the body beneath the layers of winter clothes. "He won't be able to get to you for a while," she said. "Maybe not until the morning."

"Did you tell him that wasn't acceptable?"

This caused a tiny smile to twitch at the corners of her mouth—the first he'd managed. "No. He's busy. There are more important people than you stuck in the snow. You're safe and out of the storm. Your car can wait. Now, if it's acceptable to you, I'll make us something to eat."

Alex cursed beneath his breath. He hadn't gotten off to a very good start with Tenley. And hell, spending the evening in her company, sharing an intimate dinner, was far more intriguing that sitting alone in his room at the local bed-and-breakfast. "Can I give you a hand?" he asked, following her to the kitchen.

HE SAT ON A STOOL at the kitchen island, his elbows resting on the granite counter top, his gaze following her every move. The tension between them was palpable, the attraction crackling like an electric current.

What had ever possessed her to bring this man in from the storm? She thought she was doing a good deed. He probably would have survived just fine on his own. She could have come home, called the sheriff and let law enforcement ride to the rescue. But now it looked like she'd be stuck with him for the rest of the night.

Tenley was accustomed to a solitary existence, just her, the dogs, the cats, the horses and those occasional demons that haunted her dreams. Having a stranger in the house upset the delicate balance—especially a stranger she found so disturbingly attractive.

In truth, she wasn't sure how to handle company. Since the accident almost ten years before, she'd made a habit of isolating herself, always maintaining a safe distance from anything that resembled a relationship. It was just easier. Losing her brother had sapped every last bit of emotion out of her soul that she didn't have the energy or the willpower to engage in polite conversation. And that was what people expected in social situations.

"Stop staring at me." Tenley carefully chopped the carrot, focusing on the task and trying to ignore Alex's intent gaze. She felt her face grow warm and she fought the urge to run outside into the storm to cool off.

There was work to do in the barn; the horses had to be fed. She didn't have to stay. But for the first time in a very long time, Tenley found herself…interested. She wasn't sure what it was, but his curious stare had her heart beating a bit quicker and her nerves on edge. From the moment he'd offered his hand in introduction, she'd felt it.

Maybe it was just an overreaction to simple loneliness. She had been particularly moody this winter, almost restless. In years past, she'd been happy to hide out, to take long walks in the woods, to spend time with her animals, indulging in an occasional short-lived affair. But this winter had been different. There had been no men and the solitude had begun to wear on her.

She handed him a carrot to munch on, using the opportunity to study him more closely. Alex Stamos. For some reason, the name sounded familiar to her, but she couldn't put her finger on why. He was here on business. Maybe he was one of those real estate developers from Illinois, interested in building yet another resort on the peninsula. She'd probably seen his name in the local paper.

And she didn't understand this sudden attraction. Tenley was usually drawn to men who were a little rougher around the edges, a bit more dangerous. She usually chose tourists who were certain to leave at some point, but she had indulged with a number of willing single men from some of the nearby towns. Her grandfather called them "discardable," and Tenley had to agree with his assessment.

Tenley looked down at her vegetables. There weren't many women who'd kick Alex Stamos out of their bed.

Tenley glanced up again, to find him still staring. She drew a deep breath and met his gaze, refusing to flinch. For a long time, neither one of them blinked.

"I like this game," he said. "My sister and I used to play it when we were kids. I always won."

"It makes me uncomfortable," Tenley said. "Didn't anyone ever tell you it wasn't polite to stare?"

He shrugged and looked away. "Yeah, but I didn't

think that applied in this case. I mean, it's not like you
have a big wart on the end of your nose or you've got
two heads. I'm staring because I think you're pretty.
What's wrong with that?"

"I'm not pretty," she muttered. She grabbed an onion
and tossed it at him, then shoved the cutting board and
knife across the counter. "Here, cut that up."

She didn't invite this attraction. In fact, over the past
year, she'd done her level best to avoid men. The last
man she'd invited into her bed hadn't been just a one-
night stand. She'd actually found herself wanting more,
searching for something that she couldn't put a name
to.

She knew the risks. Physical attraction led to sex
which led to more sex which led to affection which ul-
timately led to love. Only love didn't last. It was there
one day and gone the next. She'd loved her brother,
more than anyone else in the world. And when he'd
been taken from her, she wasn't sure she'd ever recover.
She wasn't about to go through that again.

"I'm wondering why you wear all that makeup. I
mean, you don't need it. I think you'd look prettier
without it."

"Maybe I don't want to look pretty," Tenley murmured.

Alex chuckled at her reply. "Why wouldn't you want
to look pretty? Especially if you are?"

The question made Tenley uneasy. She didn't tolerate curious men, men who wanted to get inside her
head before they got into her bed. What business was

it of his why she did what she did? He was a complete stranger and didn't know anything about her life. Why bother to act as if he cared?

She turned and tossed the chopped carrots into the cast-iron pot on the stove. Maybe the town's speculation about her would come true. She'd slowly devolve into an eccentric old spinster, living alone in the woods with only her animals to talk to.

"Do you like peppers?" she asked, turning to open the refrigerator.

"Do you ever answer a direct question?"

"Red or green? I prefer red."

"You don't answer questions," Alex said. "Red."

Tenley gave him a smile. "Me, too. They're sweeter." She handed him the pepper, then grabbed a towel from the ring beneath the sink. Bending over the basin, she quickly washed the makeup off her face, wiping away the dark liner and lipstick with dish soap.

When she opened her eyes again, she found an odd expression on his face. "Better?"

"Yeah," he said softly, his gaze slowly taking in her features. "You just look...different." He paused. "Beautiful."

She swallowed hard, trying to keep herself from smiling. "Thank you," she murmured. "You're beautiful, too."

The moment the words were out of her mouth, she wanted to take them back. This was what came from spending so much time alone, talking to herself. She expressed her thoughts out loud without even realizing it.

He opened his mouth, then snapped it shut. "Thanks."

"I'm not just saying that. You are. Objectively, you're very attractive." Oh, God, now she was just digging a deeper hole. "I just noticed, that's all. I'm not trying to…you know."

"I don't know," he said. He picked up the pepper and walked around the island to the sink, then rinsed it off. "But you could try to explain it to me."

There was no going back now. "The way you're looking at me. I just get the feeling that you're…flirting."

He turned and leaned back against the edge of the counter. "I am. Is there something wrong with that?"

"It's not going to work. I—I'm not interested in…that."

"What?"

"Sex," she said.

He frowned, then shook his head. "Is that what you think I'm doing? I was just having some fun. Talking. I didn't mean to—"

"I didn't want you to think that I was—"

"Oh, I didn't. I guess, I'm just used to—"

"I understand and I don't mean to—"

"I do understand," he said softly. He took a step toward her and she held her breath.

This was crazy. She wanted him to kiss her. With any other man, she would have already been halfway to the bedroom. But Alex was different. All these strange feelings stirred inside of her. She longed for his touch, yet she knew how dangerous it would be. Need mixed with fear and she wasn't sure what to do.

But then Alex took the decision out of her hands. He smoothed his hand over her cheek and bent closer. An instant later, his lips met hers and Tenley felt a tremor race through her body. He lingered over her mouth, taking his time, waiting for her to surrender.

With a soft sigh, Tenley opened beneath the gentle assault. A delicious rush of warmth washed through her body. Lately, she hadn't felt much like a woman. It was amazing what one kiss could do to change all that.

She pushed up on her toes, eager to lose herself in the taste of him. It didn't matter that they'd just met. It didn't matter that she knew nothing about him. He made her feel all warm and tingly inside. That was all she cared about.

He drew back slightly, his breath warm against her mouth. "Maybe we should get back to dinner," he suggested.

With a satisfied smile, Tenley stepped out of his embrace. They did have the entire night. With the blizzard raging outside, there was no way he'd be able to get into town. "There's white wine and beer in the fridge and red wine in the cabinet above. Pick what you want."

"What are you making?" He stood over her shoulder and peered into the cast-iron pot steaming on the stove. "It smells good."

"Camp supper," she said. "It's just whatever's at hand, tossed into a pot. There's hamburger, potatoes, peppers, carrots and onions. I think I'll add some corn."

It wasn't gourmet. Cooking had never been one of her talents. In truth, Tenley wasn't really sure what she was good at. Right about the time she was ready to find out, her life had been turned upside down. Her grandfather was an artist and so was her father. And her mother was a poet, so creativity did run in her veins.

But like everything else in her world, she'd been too afraid to invest any passion in her future for fear that it might slip through her fingers. So she chose to help her grandfather further his career by running his art gallery. At least she knew she was good at that, even though it was more of a job than a passion.

Alex retrieved a bottle of red wine from the cabinet and set it on the counter. She handed him a corkscrew and he deftly dispatched the cork and poured two glasses of Merlot. "This is a nice place," he said.

"It belonged to my grandparents. My great-grandfather built it for them as a wedding gift. After my grandmother died, my grandfather moved into town, and I moved here."

"What do you do?"

"I was just going to ask you the same thing," Tenley said, deflecting his question. "What brings you to Door County in the middle of a blizzard? It must be something very important."

"Business," he replied. "I'm here to see an artist. T. J. Marshall. Do you know him?"

Tenley's breath caught in her throat and for a moment she couldn't breathe. This man had come to see her grandfather? How was that possible? She was in charge of her grandfather's appointments and she didn't remember making one for— Oh, God. That was where she knew his name. He'd left a string of messages on her grandfather's voice mail. Something about publishing a novel. Her grandfather already worked with a publisher and he didn't write novels, so she'd ignored the messages. "I do. Everyone knows him. What do you want with him?"

"He sent us a graphic novel. I want to publish it."

Tenley frowned. Her grandfather painted landscapes. He didn't even know what a graphic novel was. She, however, did know. In fact, she'd made one for Josh Barton, the neighbor boy, as a Christmas gift, a thank-you for caring for her animals. "Do you have it with you?" she asked, trying to keep her voice indifferent.

"I do."

"Could I see it?"

"Sure. Do you like graphic novels?"

"I've read a few," she replied.

"This one is incredible. Very dark. The guy who wrote this has got some real demons haunting him. Or he's got a great imagination. It's about a girl named Cyd who can bring people back from the dead."

Alex walked across the room to fetch his briefcase. Tenley grabbed her glass of wine and took three quick gulps. If this was her work, how had it possibly gotten into Alex's hands? Perhaps Josh had decided to start a career as an artist's agent at age fourteen?

Alex returned with a file folder, holding it out to her. "The story is loaded with conflict and it's really edgy. It's hard to find graphic novels that combine great art with a solid story. And this has both."

Tenley opened the folder and immediately recognized the cover of Josh's Christmas gift. She sighed softly as she flipped through the photocopy. What had he done? He'd raved about the story, but she'd never expected him to send a copy to a publisher. It had been a private little gift between the two of them, that was all. Josh had shared his love of the genre with her and she'd made him a story of his very own. She'd never intended it for public consumption.

Tenley had always had a love-hate affair with her artistic abilities. Though establishing her own career in art might make sense to the casual observer, Tenley fought against it. She and her brother had always talked about striking out on their own, leaving Door County and finding work in a big city. She'd wanted to be an actress and Tommy had been interested in architecture.

But after the boating accident, Tenley had given up on dreams. Her parents had been devastated and their grief led to a divorce. There was a fight over where Tenley would live and in the end, they let her stay in Door County with her grandparents while they escaped to opposite coasts.

They still encouraged her to paint or sculpt or do anything worthy with her art. But putting herself out there, for everyone to see, made her feel more vulnerable than she already did. There were too many ways to get hurt, and so many expectations that could never be met. And now, the one time in years that she'd put pen to paper had brought this man to her door. What were the odds?

"This is interesting," she murmured. "But I think someone is messing with you. T. J. Marshall paints landscapes. This isn't his work."

"You know his work?"

"Yes. Everyone does. He has a gallery in town. You must be looking for another T. J. Marshall."

"How many are there in Sawyer Bay?" he asked.

Two, Tenley thought to herself. Thomas James and Tenley Jacinda. "Only one," she lied.

"And you know him. So you can introduce me. Tell me about him. How old is he? What's his background? Has he done commercial illustration in the past?"

What was she supposed to say? That Tenley Jacinda Marshall was the T. J. Marshall he was looking for? That she was twenty-six years old, had never formally studied art or design, and had spent her entire life in Door County? And that she'd never intended anyone, outside of Josh Barton, to see her story?

"I know this will sell. It's exactly what the market is looking for," Alex continued. "A female protagonist, a story filled with moral dilemmas and great pictures."

Was he really interested in paying her for the story? It would be nice to have some extra cash. Horse feed and vet care didn't come cheap. And though her grandfather paid her well, she never felt as if she did enough to earn her salary. Still, with money came responsibility. She liked her life exactly the way it was—uncomplicated.

"I think I'll make a salad," she said.

He reached out and grabbed her arm, stopping her

escape. "Promise you'll introduce me," Alex pleaded, catching her chin with his finger and turning her gaze to his. "This is important."

"All right," Tenley said. "I will. But not tonight."

He laughed. "No, not tonight." He bent close and dropped a quick kiss on her lips, then frowned. "Are you ever going to tell me anything about yourself?"

"I don't lead a very exciting life," Tenley murmured, as he smoothed his finger along her jaw. A shiver skittered down her spine. His touch was so addictive. She barely knew him, yet she craved physical contact. He'd come here to see her, but somehow she knew that revealing her identity would be a mistake—at least for the next twelve hours.

"You rescued me from disaster," he said. "I could have frozen out there."

"Someone would have come along sooner or later," she said.

They continued preparations for dinner in relative silence. But the thoughts racing through Tenley's mind were anything but quiet. In the past, it had always been so simple to take what she wanted from a man. Physical pleasure was just a natural need, or so she told herself. And though she chose carefully when it came to the men who shared her bed, she'd never hesitated when she found a suitable sexual partner.

This was different. There was an attraction here she'd never felt before, a connection that went beyond the surface. He was incredibly handsome, with his dark hair and eyes, and a body that promised to be close to perfection once he removed his clothes. He was quite intelligent and witty. And he seemed perfectly capable of seducing her on his own.

It might be nice to be the seduced rather than the seducer, Tenley thought. But would he move fast enough? They only had this one night. Sometime tomorrow, he'd find out she was the artist also known as T. J. Marshall. And then everything would change.

"Would you like some more wine?" Alex asked.

Tenley nodded. "Sure." The bottle was already half-empty. Where would they be when it was gone?

THEY HAD DINNER in front of the fire. The sexual tension between them wasn't lost on Alex. By all accounts, the setting was impossibly romantic—a blazing fire, a snowstorm outside and the entire night ahead of them. With any other woman, he could have turned on the charm and had her within an hour. But there was something about Tenley that made him bide his time. She wasn't just any woman and she seemed to see right through him.

In the twelve years he'd been actively pursing women, Alex had honed his techniques. He'd found that most women were turned off by a man who wanted jump into bed after just a few hours together. Though he usually felt the urge, he'd learned to control his desires. He never slept with a woman on the first date. Or the second. But by the third, there were no rules left to follow.

Now he was finding it difficult putting thoughts of

seduction out of his head. He wasn't sure he was reading the signs correctly. Though he found Tenley incredibly sexy, he wasn't sure they were moving in that direction. One moment she seemed interested and the next, she acted as though she couldn't care less.

Though the conversation between them was easy, it wasn't terribly informative. He'd learned that Tenley had lived in Door County her entire life and that the cabin had belonged to her grandparents. Her father was an artist and her mother, a poet. Though she didn't say for certain, he gleaned from her comments that they were divorced. When he asked where they lived, she'd quickly changed the subject.

She kept the conversation firmly focused on him, asking about his business, about his life in Chicago, about his childhood. She seemed particularly interested in the market for graphic novels and his interest in publishing them.

"My grandfather started the company in 1962," Alex explained. "He used to do technical manuals, then started a line of how-to books, right about the time everyone was getting into home improvement. He retired and my father expanded our list to include other how-to titles. *How to Groom a Poodle, How to Make a Soufflé, How to Play the Ukulele.* Real page-turners."

"And then you came along with an idea for graphic novels."

"I've read comic books since I was a kid. But they're not just comic books anymore. They're an incredible mix of graphic art and story. They've turned some of the best ones into movies, so they're starting to move into mainstream culture."

"And this book by T. J. Marshall? Why do you like it?"

"It's…tragic. There's this heroine who, after a brush with death, discovers she can bring people back to life. But she's forced to choose between those she can save and those not worthy. The power only works for a short time before it's gone again. And there's this governmental agency that's after her. They want to use her powers for evil."

"And you liked her—I mean, *his* art?"

"Yeah," Alex replied. "The drawings have an energy about them, a rawness that matches the dark emotion in the story. I find it pretty amazing that someone could be such a great writer and an incredible artist, too."

"So you just want to publish it? Just like that?"

Alex shook his head. "No. There are some things that need to be addressed. The story needs to be expanded. There's a subplot that has to be fleshed out. I've got minor questions about the character, some inconsistencies in the backstory. And we'd want to explore a story arc for a sequel or two, maybe make it a trilogy."

She frowned. "A trilogy?"

"Yeah. We'd want to publish more than one novel. The real success in publishing is not in buying a book, but in building a career."

"So it pays a lot of money?"

"Not a lot. It would depend on how the books sold. But we have a great marketing department. I think they'd do really well. Well enough to provide a comfortable living for the artist."

Tenley quickly stood and gathered up the remains of their dinner. He got to his feet and helped her, following her into the kitchen with the empty bottle of wine. Though he hadn't quite figured out her mercurial mood changes, he was finding them less troublesome. She just moved more quickly from one thing to the next than the ordinary person, as if she became bored or distracted easily.

"Can I help you with the dishes?" he asked, standing beside her at the sink.

"Sure," she murmured.

He reached across her for the soap, his hand brushing hers. The contact was startling in its effect on his body. A current raced up his arm, jolting him like an electric shock. Intrigued, he reached down and took her hand in his, smoothing his fingers over her palm.

"You have beautiful hands," he said, examining her fingers. It was as if he knew these hands, knew exactly how they'd feel on his face, on his body. Her nails were painted a dark purple and she wore several rings on her fingers and thumb.

Alex slowly pulled them off, setting them down on the edge of the sink. It was like undressing her in a way, discovering the woman beneath all the accoutrements. He drew her hand up to his lips and placed a kiss on the back of her wrist.

Her gaze fixed on his face, her eyes wide, filled with indecision. Alex held his breath, waiting for a reaction.

He kissed a fingertip, then drew it across his lower lip. The gesture had the desired effect. She leaned into him and a moment later, their mouths met.

Unlike the experiment that was their first kiss, this was slow and delicious. She tasted sweet, like the wine they'd drunk. He pulled her close, smoothing his hands over her back until her body was pressed against his. Kissing her left him breathless, his heart slamming in his chest.

He ran his hands over her arms, then grasped her wrists and wrapped them around his neck. A tiny sigh slipped from her throat and she softened in his embrace, as if the kiss were affecting her as much as it was him.

Alex had made the same move with any number of women, but it had never had this kind of effect on him. What was usually carefully controlled need was now raw and urgent. He wanted to possess her, to get inside her soul and find out who this woman was. She was sweet and complicated and vulnerable and tough. And everything about her drew him in and made him want more.

Maybe that was it. He'd learned well how to read women, to play on their desires and to make them want him. But Tenley was a challenge. She didn't react to his charm in the usual ways. Yet that wasn't all he found so intriguing. She lived all alone in the woods, with a bunch of animals. Where was her family? Where were the people who cared about her? And how did a woman as beautiful as Tenley not have a boyfriend or a husband to take care of her?

He sensed there was something not right here, something he couldn't explain. Alex felt an overwhelming need to reveal those parts of her that she was trying so hard to hide. She'd rescued him out on the road, but now he suspected that she was the one who needed saving.

The diversion was short-lived. The phone rang and, startled by the sound, Tenley stepped back. Her cheeks were flushed and her lips damp. "I—I should get that."

Alex nodded as she slipped from his embrace. She hurried to the phone and picked it up, watching him from beneath dark lashes. He leaned back against the edge of the counter and waited, certain they'd begin again just as soon as the call was over. But when she hung up, she maintained her distance.

"Jesse towed your car into town," she said.

"Good."

"But not before the snowplow hit it. He says it's not real bad. It'll need a new back bumper and a side panel. And a taillight. And a few more things."

Alex groaned. "Can I still drive it?"

"No. I don't think so."

"Great," he muttered. "How the hell am I going to get around?"

"I guess I'll have to drive you," Tenley said. "You're not going to be going anywhere tonight anyway, so it's not worth worrying about. Jesse says the wind is just blowing the roads closed right after they plow them." She crossed back to him. "I—I should go out and check on the horses."

"I'll come with you," Alex suggested.

"It's late. You're probably tired. You can have the

guest room. It's at the end of the hall. There are towels in the closet outside the bathroom. Just help yourself."

With that, she fetched her boots from a spot near the back door, then pulled on her jacket. A moment later, she stepped out into the storm. Alex opened the door behind her and watched as she disappeared into the darkness. The cold wind whipped a swirl of snow into his face and he quickly closed the door and leaned back against it.

What had begun as a simple business trip had taken a rather interesting turn. But he wasn't sure whether he ought to take his chances and hike into town, or spend the night under the same roof as this utterly captivating and perplexing woman.

He grabbed his duffel and walked to the guest room. When he finally found the light switch, he was surprised to find two cats curled up on the bed. The two calicos were sleeping so closely, he couldn't tell where one ended and the other began. Neither one of them stirred as he dropped the bag on the floor. But when the dogs came bounding into the room, they opened their eyes and watched the pair with wary gazes.

"Time to go," he said, picking them each up and gently setting them on the floor. They ran out the door, the dogs following after them.

Alex shut the door, then flopped down on the bed. He closed his eyes and let his thoughts drift back to the kiss he'd shared with Tenley. Though he hadn't had any expectations of further intimacies, he wished they hadn't been interrupted. With each step forward, he found himself curious about the next.

Though he'd enjoyed physical pleasure with lots of women, this was different. Everything felt…new. As if he were experiencing it for the first time. He groaned softly. He wanted her, in his arms and in his bed. But wanting her was as far as he would go. He was a guest in her house and wasn't about to take advantage, no matter how intense his need.

He'd come here to do a job, to sign T. J. Marshall to a publishing contract. It wouldn't do to get distracted from his purpose.

2

THE WATER WAS SO COLD and black. Even with her
eyes open, she couldn't see her hand in front of her
face. *Stay awake, stay awake.* A voice inside her head
kept repeating the refrain. Or was it Tommy? Was he
saying the words?

Her nails clawed at the fitting on the hull of the boat
as it bobbed in the water. *Stay with the boat. Don't try
to swim for shore.* Though she wore a life jacket, Tenley
knew that sooner or later her body temperature would
drop so low it wouldn't matter. She wouldn't drown.
She'd just quietly go to sleep and drift out into the lake.

"Tommy!" She called his name and then felt his
hand on hers. "I'm sorry. I'm sorry." She grasped at his
fingers, but they weren't there. He wasn't there. He'd
decided to swim for it, ordering her to stay with the
boat. "I'll be back for you," he called. "I promise."

How long had it been? Minutes? Hours? Tenley
couldn't remember. Why was she so confused? She
called his name again. And then again. Over and over
until her voice was weak and her throat raw.

The sound came out of nowhere, a low rumble, like

the engine of a boat. It was Tommy. He'd come, just as he'd promised. But as the roar came closer, Tenley realized it wasn't a boat at all but a huge wave, so high that it blocked out the moon and the stars in the sky. She held her breath, waiting for it to crash down on top of her. Where had it come from?

A ton of water enveloped her, driving her deep beneath the surface. The breath burned in her lungs and she struggled to reach the cold night air. Maybe it was better to let go, to stop fighting. Was that what Tommy had done? Was he safe at home, or had the black wave taken him as well? No, she wouldn't. She couldn't. She—

Tenley awoke with a start, sitting upright in her bed, gasping for breath. For a moment, she wasn't sure where she was. She rubbed her arms, only to find them warm and clad in the soft fabric of her T-shirt. She was safe. But where was Tommy? Why wasn't he—

A sick feeling settled in her stomach as she realized, yet again, that Tommy was gone. There were times when she had such pleasant dreams about their childhood. They'd been the best of friends, twins, so much alike. As the only children of a poet and an artist, they'd grown up without boundaries, encouraged to discover all that nature had to offer.

Back then, they'd lived on the waterfront, in the apartment above her grandfather's studio. The sailboat had been a present from her grandfather for their thirteenth birthday and every summer, she and Tommy had skimmed across the harbor, the wind filling the small sail and the sun shining down on them both.

But as they got older, they became much more daring. Their adventures had an edge of danger to them. Diving from the cliffs above the water. Wandering into the woods late at night. Sailing beyond the quiet confines of the harbor to the small islands just offshore.

They'd both known how quickly the weather could shift in the bay and how dangerous it was to be in a small boat when the waves kicked up. But they both loved pushing their limits, daring each other to try something even more outrageous.

A shiver skittered through her body and Tenley pulled the quilt up over her arms. It had been her idea to sail out to the island and spend the night. Even though the wind had been blowing directly into shore and they'd gotten a late start, they'd tacked out, the small Sunfish skimming over the bay at a sharp angle.

But sailing against the wind had taken longer than she'd anticipated and by the time they'd reached open water, it was nearly dark. Tommy had insisted that they head back toward the lights, but Tenley had been adamant, daring him to go on. A few minutes later, a gust of wind knocked the boat over.

It was usually easy to right the boat in the calm waters of the harbor, but in the bay the currents worked against them, exhausting them both. Tenley could see the outline of the island and suggested they swim for it. But in the dark, it had been impossible to judge how far it was. In the end, Tommy had left to get help.

They'd found her clinging to the boat, four hours later. They'd found his body the next morning, washed up on a rocky beach north of town. Tenley shook her head, trying to rid herself of the memories. It had been nearly a month since she'd last dreamt of him. In many ways, she'd longed for the nights when the dreams wouldn't haunt her. But sometimes, the dreams were good. They were happy and she could be with her brother again.

She threw the covers off her body and stood up beside the bed, stretching her arms over her head. The room was chilly, the winter wind finding its way inside through all the tiny cracks and crevices in the old cabin. Outside, the storm still raged.

Tenley rubbed her eyes, then wandered out of the bedroom toward the kitchen. She rarely slept more than four or five hours at night. For a long time, she'd been afraid to sleep, afraid of the nightmares. But she'd learned to cope, taking the good dreams with the bad.

The dogs were curled up in front of Alex's door and they looked up as she passed. Tenley stirred the embers of the fire and tossed another log onto the grate. As she watched the flames lick at the dry birch bark, her mind wandered back to the kiss she'd shared with Alex in the kitchen.

She'd been tempted to let it go on, to see how far he'd take it. The attraction between them was undeniable. But she wasn't sure she wanted to act upon it. She preferred uncomplicated sex and Tenley sensed that sex with Alex might be like opening a Pandora's box of pleasure.

Restless, she got up and began to pace the perimeter

of the room. She had no idea what time it was. Tenley had
given up clocks long ago, preferring to let her body
decide when it was time to sleep and when it was time to
wake up. Besides, since Tommy's death, she'd never
slept through an entire night so what was the point of a
schedule?

Tenley grabbed a throw from the back of the leather
sofa and wrapped it around her, then slowly walked
down the hall to the guest-room door. Dog and Pup
were still asleep on the floor, pulling guard duty, defending her safety. Perhaps the dogs knew better than
she did about the dangers that lay beyond the door.

"Up," she whispered, snapping her fingers softly.
They both rose, stretched, then trotted off to her
bedroom. Holding her breath, Tenley opened the door
and peeked inside.

Alex's face was softly illuminated by the bedside
lamp and Tenley crossed the room to stand beside the
bed. His limbs were twisted in the old quilt, a bare leg
and arm exposed to the chilly air in the room. Tenley
let her gaze drift down from his handsome face and
tousled hair, to the smooth expanse of his chest and the
rippled muscles of his belly.

An ache deep inside her took her breath away and
she felt an overwhelming need for physical contact,
anything to make her feel again. She'd pushed aside her
emotions for so long that the only way to access them
was to lose herself in pleasure. Until now, all she really
required was a man who wouldn't ask for anything
more than sex. But now, watching Alex sleep, she

yearned for a deeper connection, a way back from the dark place where she'd lived for so long.

Was he the light she was looking for? Tenley rubbed her eyes with her fingers. Then reaching out, she held her hand close to his skin, surprised at the heat he generated. If she were warm and safe, she could forget the dream, forget the guilt. All she needed was just a few minutes of human contact.

A shiver skittered through her and without considering the consequences, she lay down beside him, tucking her backside into the curve of his body. Tenley felt him stir behind her and she closed her eyes, waiting to see what might happen.

He pushed up on his elbow and gently smoothed his hand along her arm. She glanced over her shoulder to find a confused expression on his face. Slowly, she rolled onto her back, their gazes still locked. Then, Tenley slipped her hand around his nape and gently pulled him closer, until their lips touched.

The kiss sent a slow surge of warmth through her body as he gently explored her mouth with his tongue, teasing and testing until she opened fully to his assault. With a low moan, he pulled her body beneath his. They fit perfectly against each other and Tenley arched into him, desperate to feel more.

The memories of the nightmare slowly gave way to a tantalizing pleasure. Alex ran his hand along her leg and beneath the T-shirt, then stopped suddenly, as if surprised that she wore nothing beneath. Giving him permission to continue, she slipped her fingers beneath the waistband of his boxers, searching for an intimate spot to explore.

But as the touching grew more intense, the clothing they wore seemed to get in the way. Frantic to feel his naked body against hers, Tenley sat up and tugged her T-shirt over her head, then tossed it aside. She heard his breath catch and she smiled. "It feels better without clothes."

He grinned, then skimmed his boxers off, revealing the extent of his arousal. Unafraid to take what she wanted, Tenley wrapped her fingers around his hard shaft and gently began to stroke him. The caress brought a moan from deep in his throat and his fingers tangled in her hair as he drew her into another long, deep kiss.

"Am I awake or am I dreaming?" he asked, his lips soft against hers, his voice ragged.

"You're dreaming," she whispered.

"It doesn't feel like a dream," he countered. He cupped her breast with his palm and ran his thumb over her nipple. "You're warm and soft. I can hear you and taste you."

"Close your eyes," Tenley said. "And don't open them until I get back."

She crawled off the bed, but he grabbed her hand to stop her retreat. "Don't leave."

"I'll be right back. I promise. Close your eyes."

He did as he was told and Tenley hurried out of the room to the bathroom. She rummaged through the cabinet above the sink until she found the box of condoms, then pulled out a string of plastic packets.

When she returned to the room, he was sitting up in bed, waiting for her. She held up the condoms. "I think we might need these."

He chuckled. "All of those?"

Tenley felt a blush of embarrassment. It had been a while since she'd had a man in her bed. Once might not be enough. "Yes," she said. "All of them."

"I think you might be overestimating my abilities," he teased.

"And you might be underestimating mine," she replied.

When she got close to the bed, he grabbed her hand and yanked her on top of him. "Tell me what you want. I'll do my best to comply."

She wanted to lose herself in the act, to let her mind drift and her body take flight. She wanted to forget the past and the present and future and just exist in a haze of pleasure. She wanted the warmth and touch of another human being. And most of all, she wanted that wonderful, exhilarating feeling of release with a man moving deep inside her.

She tore a packet off the strip and opened it, then, with deliberate care, smoothed it down over his erection. Without any hesitation, Tenley straddled his hips and lowered herself on top of him. When he was buried to the hilt, she sighed. "This is what I want," she murmured, her eyes closed, her pulse racing.

"Me, too," he whispered.

ALEX HADN'T BEEN prepared for how good it would feel. Maybe because it had all been so unexpected.

He'd always taken his time charming a woman, knowing that once he got her to bed, his interest would soon wane. But from the moment Tenley had lain down beside him, Alex knew something remarkable was about to happen.

This wasn't some game he was playing, a diversion that he found interesting until something better came along. This was pure, raw desire, stripped of all artifice and expectations. He closed his eyes and sighed, reveling in the feel of her warmth surrounding him.

He didn't care what it meant or where it would go after this. All he knew was that he wanted to possess her, even it if was just for an hour or two on a snowy January night.

His fingers tangled in her hair and he drew her to his mouth. Though she didn't possess any of the attributes he normally found attractive in a woman, he couldn't seem to get enough of her. Her skin was pale, but incredibly soft. And her breasts, though small, were perfect. She was everything he'd never had before—and never wanted. Alex smoothed his hands over her chest and down her torso to her hips. Then he sat up, wrapping her legs around his waist and burying his face in the curve of her neck.

Tenley moved against him, her head tipped forward and her eyes closed. Her hair fell across her face and he reached up and brushed it aside, watching as desire suffused her features. Though he wanted to surrender to his own passion, Alex found it far more fascinating to watch her.

The intensity of her expression made him wonder what was going through her mind. She seemed lost in her need, searching for release in an almost desperate way. He reached down between them and touched her. A soft cry slipped from her lips and Alex knew he could give her what she wanted.

Her breath came in deep gasps and he focused on the sound, trying to delay the inevitable. And then, she was there, dissolving into spasms, her body driving down once more, burying him deep inside her.

It was all Alex could take, watching her orgasm overwhelm her. He surrendered to the sensations racing through his body and a moment later, found his own release.

Tenley nestled up against him, her arms draped around his neck, her lips pressed to his ear. "Oh, that was nice," she whispered.

"Umm," he replied, too numb to put together a coherent sentence. "Very nice."

She drew back, a wicked smile curling her lips. "You want to do it again?"

"No, not quite yet," he said with a chuckle. "Just let me catch my breath for a second." Alex wrapped his hands around her waist and pulled her down beside him, dragging her leg up over his hip. "This is a nice way to spend a snowy night." She shivered and Alex rubbed her arm. "Are you cold?"

Tenley shook her head. "Would you like some hot chocolate? I feel like some." She crawled out of bed and walked to the door, naked. "Are you coming? It makes a really good nightcap."

With a groan, Alex rolled out of bed. First, incredible

sex and then hot cocoa. He didn't know much about her, but she was a study in contradictions. Grabbing the quilt off the bed, Alex wrapped it around himself and followed her to the kitchen.

The room was dark, lit only by the flames flickering in the fireplace. She opened the refrigerator and he stood and stared at her body, so perfect in the harsh white light. "You are beautiful," he said.

"No," Tenley replied. "You don't have to say things like that to me. I don't need reassurance. I wanted that as much as you did."

"I'm just telling you what I think," Alex said. "You don't take compliments well, do you?"

"No," she said. "They make me…uncomfortable."

"Personally, I love compliments," he teased.

She poured milk into a pan and set it on the stove. The burner flamed blue and she turned it to a low simmer. "I think you have nice eyes," she said. "And I like your mouth."

"Thank you," he replied. "I like your mouth, too."

"Thank you," she said.

"See, that wasn't so bad."

"The key to making good hot chocolate is in the chocolate. You have to use real cocoa and sugar, not those powdered mixes."

He sat down on a stool and wrapped the quilt more tightly around him. "I was always of the opinion that marshmallows were the key. You can't use the small ones. You have to use the big ones. They melt slower."

Tenley opened a cabinet above the stove and pulled

out a bag of jumbo marshmallows, then tossed them at him. "I totally agree. Bigger is better."

"Oh, another compliment. Thank you."

She giggled. "You're welcome." Tenley turned back to the stove and Alex got up and circled around the island to stand behind her. He wrapped the quilt around her, pulling her body back against his. Just watching her move had made him hard again.

She tipped her head as he pressed his lips to her neck. "Why do you smell so good? What is that?"

"Soap?" she said. "Shampoo."

"I like it." The women he'd known had always smelled like a perfume counter. But Tenley smelled clean and fresh. He closed his eyes and drew a deep breath, trying to commit the scent to memory. "I'm glad you came into my room," he whispered.

She turned to face him, then pushed up on her toes and gently touched her lips to his. "It's too cold to sleep alone." Tenley brushed his hair out of his eyes and smiled. "Cocoa. I need cocoa."

After she'd retrieved a container from a nearby cabinet, Tenley measured out the cocoa and stirred it into the milk, before adding a generous handful of sugar. Then she picked up the pan and poured the steaming drinks into two huge mugs that were nearly full of marshmallows.

"Let's sit by the fire," she said, grabbing the mugs.

Alex followed her, spreading the quilt out on the floor in front of the hearth. She seemed just as comfortable naked as she did clothed, stretching out on her stomach and offering him a tempting view of her backside.

"What are you doing here?" he asked.

She took a sip of her hot chocolate, then licked the melted marshmallow from her upper lip. "Relaxing?"

"That's not what I meant. I meant, here, all alone, in this cabin. Why isn't there someone here with you?"

She rolled over and sat up. "Like a roommate?"

"Like a man," he said.

"I like being alone. I don't really need a man." She paused. "Not that I don't enjoy having you here."

The words were simple and without a doubt, the truth. "I can always head back out into the storm, if you'd rather be alone," he offered.

"No. It's nice to have company every now and then."

"Someone to talk to?"

"Someone to touch," she said. Tenley reached out and placed her hand on his chest. "Aren't there times when you crave physical contact?" She paused. "Never mind. I suppose you just go find a woman when that happens, right? Men have it easy. No one questions your need for sex."

"And they question yours?"

"Not they. Me. I guess that comes with being a female. We aren't supposed to want it like men do."

"And do you want it?" Alex asked.

"I'm not afraid to admit that I enjoy it," she said. "Sex makes me feel…alive."

"Good to know," Alex said. He took her mug from her hand and set it down on the floor, then cupped her face in his hands. "You are the strangest girl I've ever met."

"Weird strange?"

"Fascinating strange," he replied.

He gently pushed her back until she lay on the quilt. Tenley stretched her arms over her head, her body arching sinuously beneath his touch. Taking his time, he traced a line from her neck to her belly with his lips.

He knew how to bring a woman to the edge and back again, and he wanted to do that for Tenley. His fingers found the damp spot between her legs. She responded immediately, her body arching, her breath coming in shallow gasps.

And when his mouth found that sensitive spot, she cried out in surprise. But Alex took his time. He'd always been a considerate lover, but sex had been about his pleasure first. It wasn't that way with Tenley. He wanted to make it memorable for her.

After he was gone, Alex needed to know he would be the standard by which other men in her life might be judged. It was silly, but for some strange reason, it made a difference to him. He wanted her to remember what they shared and continue to crave it.

Her fingers slipped through his hair and he felt her losing control. Alex slowed his pace, determined to make her feel something that she'd never experienced before. Her drew her close, tempting her again and again. She whispered his name in a desperate plea to give her what she wanted.

The sound of her voice was enough to arouse him and to Alex's surprise, he found himself dancing near the edge. He shifted, the friction of the quilt causing a delicious frisson of pleasure to race through him. Gathering his resolve, Alex brought her close again. But this time, it was too much for her.

When he drew back, she couldn't help herself. Tenley moaned, her body tense. An instant later, her orgasm consumed her, her body trembling and shuddering. It was enough to drive him over the edge. Startled, Alex joined her.

He rolled over on his back. This was crazy. He felt like a teenager, with nothing more than his imagination and a little friction standing between him and heaven. Throwing his arm over his eyes, he waited for the last of his own spasms to subside.

"That was a surprise," he murmured. Alex rolled to his side and kissed her hip.

"I've never really liked surprises, until now."

Alex knew how she felt. From the moment she'd rescued him from the snowbank, he'd learned to expect the unexpected from Tenley. He closed his eyes and pressed his face into the soft flesh at her waist. Forget the vacation. Spending time with Tenley was all the adventure he needed.

TENLEY OPENED her eyes to the early morning light. An incessant beeping penetrated her hazy mind and she pushed up on her elbow to survey the room.

After making love in front of the fire, they'd wrapped themselves in the quilt and fallen asleep on the floor. She couldn't remember the last time she'd slept so soundly and for such a long stretch of time.

She sat up and glanced over her shoulder at Alex. He

was a beautiful man, tall and lean and finely muscled. And he knew what he was doing in bed—and on the floor, too. A shiver skittered through her as she remembered the passion they'd shared.

She'd never experienced anything quite so powerful. Usually she used sex to forget. But she remembered every little detail of what she'd shared with Alex, from the way his hands felt on her skin to the taste of his mouth to the soft sound of his voice whispering her name. She felt safe with him, as if she didn't need to pretend.

It had taken so much energy to keep her emotions in check and now, she finally felt as if she might be able to let go, to find a bit of enjoyment in life…in Alex. Tenley didn't know what it all meant, but she knew it felt right.

As she studied his features, she wondered about the women he normally dated. A man like Alex Stamos wouldn't lack for female company. There were probably hundreds of women waiting outside his door, hoping to enjoy exactly what she had last night.

The beeping continued and she crawled around him to find his watch lying on the hearth. Tenley picked it up and, squinting in the low light, tried to turn off the alarm. But when she couldn't find the right button, she got to her feet and carried it into the kitchen. With the soft curse, she opened the refrigerator door and put it inside.

This is exactly why she hated clocks. Simple, inanimate objects in control of a person's life! Was there anything more obnoxious? Well, maybe television.

She didn't own one of those either. She preferred a good book. Although, there were times when she wished she could watch a movie or check out the weather station.

Rubbing her arms against the cold, Tenley returned to their makeshift bed, ready to slip back beneath the covers and wake him up slowly. It was so easy to relax around him, to just be herself without any of the baggage that came along with her past. Everyone within a thirty-mile radius of Sawyer Bay knew about her past. She couldn't walk down the streets of town without someone sending her a pitying look.

She knew what they were saying about her. That she'd never recovered from the tragedy. That she deliberately pushed people away because she blamed herself. It was all true. Tenley was acutely aware of what she'd become. But that didn't make it any easier to forget her part in what had happened. Nor did she feel like changing just to make everyone else more comfortable. It was simply easier to keep people at a distance.

Alex was different. For the first time in her adult life, she wanted to get closer. If Tenley had the power, she'd make the storm go on for another week or two so they could be stranded in this cabin a little longer. There would be quiet afternoons, making love in front of the fire. And then never-ending nights, when sleep could come without dreams.

There was a way to keep him close, Tenley mused. If she accepted his proposal to publish her graphic novel then they'd have an excuse to see each other every so often. Maybe he'd make regular trips up to Door County to see her and they could enjoy these sexual encounters three or four times a year.

Tenley smiled to herself. It was the closest she'd ever come to a committed relationship. But in that very same moment, she realized the risk she'd be taking. Cursing softly, she turned away and walked through the cabin to her room.

"Don't be ridiculous," she muttered to herself as she pulled on her clothes. She and Alex Stamos had absolutely nothing in common, beyond her novel and one night of great sex. What made her think he'd even want a relationship?

He probably had his choice of women in Chicago. Why would he choose to carry on with her? It was a prescription for heartbreak, Tenley mused. She'd make the mistake of falling in love with him, living for the times they could be together, and one day, he'd tell her it was over.

She'd learned how to protect herself from that kind of pain and it wouldn't do to forget those lessons now. Alex was a momentary fling, just like all the other men in her life. She could enjoy him for as long as he stayed, but after that, she'd move on.

As for her novel, it would be best to put an end to that right away. Though a little extra money might be nice, she certainly didn't need the pressure to produce another story.

Tenley tiptoed back out into the great room and found her boots and jacket near the back door. The dogs were waiting and, when she was bundled against the cold, she slipped outside, into the low light of dawn. She bent down and gave them both a rough scratch behind the ears. Pup, the larger of the two, gave her a sloppy kiss on the cheek. And Dog pushed his nose beneath her hand, searching for a bit more affection.

"Go," she said, motioning them off the porch. They ran down the steps and into the snow, leaping and chasing and wrestling with each other playfully. The wind was still blowing hard, the snow stinging her face. She tipped her head back and looked into the sky, still gray and ominous.

A memory flashed in her mind and she remembered the sky on the day she and Tommy had set off on their sail. The image was so vivid it was like a photograph. A storm had taken her brother away. And now another storm had brought Alex into her life. The forces of nature were powerful and uncontrollable.

Was that what this was about? Was nature giving her back what she'd lost all those years ago? She drew a deep breath of the cold air. She'd never believed in fate or karma but she couldn't help but wonder why Alex had suddenly appeared in her life. A few minutes one way or the other, a different day or time, and they never would have met at all. Another shiver skittered down her spine and she started off across the yard.

The barn was set fifty yards from the house, a simple wooden structure painted the traditional red. Attached to one corner was a tower that rose nearly three stories off the ground. Her grandfather had built it as a studio, with four walls made of windows to take in the views of the woods and the bay.

Tenley slogged through the snow to the barn door and retrieved a shovel. She cleared off the stairs to the studio, then stepped inside to escape the icy wind. The stairwell was as cold as the weather outside, but when she opened the door to the room at the top of the stairs, it was pleasantly cozy.

Dropping her jacket at the door, she walked to the wall of windows facing the lake. The snow was still coming down so hard, she wasn't able to see more than a hundred yards beyond the barn.

With a soft sigh, she sat down at the huge drawing table in the center of the room. Her grandfather's easels had moved to town with him, but he'd left his drawing table, in hopes she'd find a use for it.

She and her grandfather had always been close. After Tommy's death, he'd been the only one she could stand to be around. And after her grandmother had died, Tenley had taken over the duties of running the business end of the gallery, a job her grandmother had done since their wedding day.

She did most of her business over the phone and, when customers came in the front door, her grandfather usually greeted them. He hated the details of running the gallery and she avoided the customers. It had been a good arrangement. If she weren't working for him, he'd have to hire someone at a much higher salary. All Tenley needed was enough to buy food and clothes and feed for her animals.

She sifted through the sketches scattered over the surface. Her work was a mishmash of genres and media. A pen-and-ink drawing of a hummingbird, a pastel landscape, a watercolor self-portrait. She'd never been to art school, so she'd never really discovered what she was good at.

Grabbing a cup filled with black markers, she sat down at the table. Taking a deep breath, she sketched a scene with her heroine, Cyd. She imagined it as a proper cover for the novel, something that would set the mood for the story inside.

There was a generous portion of Tenley in her character. She was an outsider, a girl who had known tragedy in her life, one who was graced with an incredible power. But with that power came deep moral dilemmas. Tenley often wondered what it would be like to change the past, to alter the course of history.

What would her life be like if she hadn't teased her brother into sailing to the island? Or if the weather hadn't turned on them? What if they'd stayed home or left earlier? Where would she be today?

Tenley closed her eyes and tried to picture it. Would she be married, happily in love with a man, surrounded by their children? Or would she be living in some big city, working as an artist or a writer? She'd always thought about becoming an actress.

Perhaps her parents wouldn't have divorced and maybe her grandmother wouldn't have suffered the stroke that killed her. Maybe the townspeople of Sawyer Bay would admire her, rather than pity her. Snatching up the drawing, Tenley crumpled it into a ball and tossed it to the floor.

She couldn't change the past. And she didn't want to change the future. There was a certain security in knowing what her life was, in the sameness of each passing day. "I'm happy," Tenley said. "So leave well enough alone."

She grabbed her jacket and pulled it on, then headed back down to feed the horses. The dogs joined her in the barn, shaking the snow from their thick coats. As she scooped feed into a bucket, the horses peeked over the tops of their stall doors.

"Sorry, ladies. No riding today. But after breakfast, you can go outside for a bit." The two mares nuzzled her as they searched for a treat—a carrot or an apple. But Tenley had left so quickly she'd forgotten to bring them something. "I'll be out later," she promised.

On her way back to the house, Tenley decided to walk up to the road and see if it had been plowed. The woods kept the snow from drifting too high, but it was clear they'd had at least sixteen or eighteen inches since it began yesterday morning.

By the time she reached the end of the driveway, Tenley could see they'd be stuck in the cabin for another day. A huge pile of snow had been dumped across the driveway and beyond it, the road was a wide expanse of bare pavement and three-foot drifts.

In truth, she was happy to have another day with Alex. If they spent it in the same way they'd spent the night before, then she wouldn't have reason to grow impatient with the weather. Tenley smiled as the dogs fell into step beside her. "We'll keep him another day," she said.

The cabin was quiet when she let herself back in. She stripped off her jacket and boots, then shimmied out of her snow-covered jeans. The dogs were anxious to eat and they tore through the great room in a noisy tangle of legs and tails.

"Ow! What the hell!" Tenley looked up to find Pup lying across Alex's chest, his nose nudging Alex's chin.

"No!" she shouted. "Come here!"

Pup glanced back and forth between the two of them, then decided to follow orders. Alex sat up and wiped his face with the damp quilt. "Funny, I expected someone of an entirely different species to wake me up."

"Sorry. If you want to get some more sleep, you should probably go to your room. Once the dogs are up, they're up."

"What time is it?" He glanced at his wrist. "I lost my watch."

She opened the refrigerator and pulled it out. "It wouldn't stop beeping."

Alex got to his feet and walked naked to the kitchen, then took the watch from her grasp. He strapped it onto his wrist, silencing the alarm. Then, he looked at the clock on the stove and noticed it was almost noon. "Is that right?" he asked, rechecking his watch.

She shook her head, trying to avoid staring at his body. "No. I don't like clocks. There isn't any need for them here."

Alex frowned, raking his hand through his hair. "What about when you have to be somewhere on time?"

"I never have to be anywhere on time. I get there when I get there."

Alex chuckled. "I wish I could live like that," he murmured.

She glanced over her shoulder at him. He was so beautiful, all muscle and hard flesh. Her fingers twitched as she held out her hand. "You could. Here, give me your watch."

"No. This is an expensive watch."

"I was just going to put it back in the refrigerator."

He thought about the notion for a second, then smiled and slipped it off his wrist. "When in Rome."

She opened the fridge and put it inside the butter compartment. "You've been liberated. Doesn't that feel good?"

"How do you know when to get up in the morning?"

"I usually get up when the sun rises," she explained. "Or when the dogs wake me."

"Don't you have to be to work at a certain time?"

She shrugged. "I keep my own hours." She opened a cabinet and pulled out two cans of dog food. "Here, make yourself useful. The can opener is in that drawer."

"I thought I had made myself pretty useful last night," he murmured.

Tenley felt a warm blush creep up her cheeks. "You want to talk about it?" she asked.

"You…surprised me. I wasn't expecting…"

"Neither was I," she said. "I was curious."

"About me?"

She nodded. "Sure. You seemed like you were interested."

"I was," he said. "Am. Present tense. But I'm even more curious about something else."

"What's that?"

"Whether it might happen again?"

A tiny smile curved the corners of her mouth. "Depends upon how long this storm lasts." So it wouldn't be just a one-night stand. Tenley wasn't sure how she felt about that. She wanted to spend more time with him, even though she knew she shouldn't. But she liked Alex. And he lived in Chicago, so sooner or later, he'd head back home.

A brief, but passionate affair, one that wouldn't be dangerous or complicated. As long as she kept it all in perspective. It wouldn't last long enough to become a relationship. And if it didn't become a relationship, then she couldn't possibly get hurt. Still, she had to wonder what he was thinking about it all. Why not just ask? "What if it does happen again," she asked. "And again. What would that mean?"

He gave her an odd look. "It would probably mean we'd have to go out for condoms?" he teased. Alex paused, then shrugged, realizing that she didn't find much humor in his joke. "It would mean that we enjoy each other's company. And that we want to get to know each other better?"

"Then it wouldn't be a relationship?" she asked.

"It could be," he said slowly.

"But if we didn't want it to be?"

Alex drew a deep breath. "It will be whatever you want it to be," he replied. He glanced over his shoulder, clearly uneasy with the turn in the conversation. "Maybe we should check out a weather report so we can plan our day," Alex suggested. "Where's your television?"

That was it, Tenley thought. She knew exactly where he stood and she was satisfied. Neither one of them were ready to plan a future together. Still, if she did ever want a man in her life, someone who stayed more than a few nights, Alex would be the kind of guy she'd look for. "I don't have a television," she said.

He stared at her in astonishment. "You don't own a television? How is that possible? What about sports and the news?"

"There's never a need. I have a radio. They do the weather every hour on the station from Fish Creek. It's over there in the cabinet with the stereo. But you really don't have to check the weather. The storm is going to last for a while."

"How do you know that?"

"The barometer. Over there, by the door. It hasn't started going up yet. When it does, the storm will start to clear."

"Does that mean you can come back to bed?"

"Maybe we should try a real bed?" she suggested. Tenley tugged her sweater over her head and let it drop on the floor. Then she turned and walked toward her bedroom, leaving a trail of clothes behind her. The storm wouldn't last forever, so they'd best put their time to good use.

3

ALEX WASN'T A meteorologist, but from what he could see outside, the storm showed no signs of weakening. Though he had business to attend to, he was content to spend the day with Tenley, sitting in front of a warm fire with a comfortable bed close at hand.

Without his watch, he could only guess at the time, probably early afternoon. But Tenley was right. It didn't matter. He didn't have anywhere important to be. T. J. Marshall could wait.

He rolled onto his side and watched Tenley as she slept. He'd known her for less than a day, yet it seemed as though they'd been together for much longer. In truth, he'd spent more time with her than he had with any single woman over the past ten years. And considering he'd never spent a complete night in a woman's bed, this was another first.

He thought about their earlier discussion. She'd made it very clear she wasn't interested in anything more than a physical relationship. And he'd agreed to her terms. But Alex was already trying to figure out whether there was more between them than just great sex.

He reached out and smoothed a lock of hair from her eyes. She didn't possess the studied perfection of most of the girls he'd dated. Everything about her was much more natural, more subtle. She was...soft and sweet.

Yet she also had an edge to her, an honesty that caught him off guard at times. There wasn't a filter between her thoughts and her mouth, just a direct line. But he was beginning to enjoy that. Though she didn't answer every question he asked, when she did, he could trust that he was getting the truth.

Alex stretched his arms over his head. He needed to call the office or see if he could get an Internet connection. He smiled to himself. She didn't have a television. She probably wouldn't find a home computer particularly useful either.

He slipped out of bed and walked to the bathroom, deciding to grab a shower. He flipped on the water in the shower stall and waited for it to warm up, then looked at his reflection in the mirror. He needed a shave first.

Alex shut off the water, then retrieved his shaving kit from the guest room. After plucking a razor and a can of shaving cream out of the leather case, he rinsed his face off and continued to stare into the mirror. He was exhausted, but it was a pleasant exhaustion, a sated feeling that he hadn't felt in...a long time? Ever. He'd never felt this way after making love with a woman. In truth, intimacy always left him restless.

Alex heard the bathroom door creak behind him and a few seconds later, he felt her hands smooth over his back. She rested her cheek on his shoulder and watched him in the mirror.

"I thought you were asleep," he said. "I was just going to catch a quick shower and shave." He slowly turned and she smiled. "What do you want?"

"Nothing," she said. "What do you want?"

"I need a shave," Alex replied.

She reached around him for the can of shaving cream he'd set on the edge of the sink. "I can help with that." Tenley sprayed some cream on her palm, then patted it onto his face.

"Are you sure you know what you're doing?"

"No," she said. "But I do shave my legs. It can't be much different. Hand me the razor."

Alex grabbed it and held it over his head. "Be careful. We're a long way from emergency medical care. And this pretty face is all I have."

She took the razor from his hand, then stepped closer. "You are full of yourself, aren't you?" Her hips pressed against his and he slipped his arms around her waist to steady them both. Slowly, she dragged the blade over his skin, her brow furrowed in concentration.

Alex held his breath, waiting for disaster, but Tenley took her time. And as she worked at the task, he found himself growing more and more aroused. There was something about her taking on this mundane part of his life, even if it was as simple as shaving, and making it erotically charged.

With a low moan, he moved his hands down to her hips, his shaft growing harder with every second that passed. Was it possible to want her any more than he already did? Every time he thought his need might be sated, he found himself caught up in yet another sexual encounter, more powerful than the last.

"Quit squirming," she warned. "I'm almost finished."

"Finished?" He chuckled, running his hands up to her breasts. "Look what you started."

"It really doesn't take much, does it?" Tenley teased.

"From you, no." Why was that? Alex wondered. Why did every innocent touch seem to send all the blood to his crotch? What kind of magical power did she hold over him?

"You know," she murmured, "we're lucky we're snowed in."

"What do you mean?"

"Because if we have to take care of your little problem every time it pops up, we'd never get out of the house."

"We could always take a shower together and see how that goes. Maybe it will just disappear."

"I know exactly how to get it to disappear," she said. "Come on." Tenley grabbed his hand and pulled him out of the bathroom, bits of shaving cream still on his face. "You'll love this."

They walked through the house, both of them stark naked. Then she opened the coat closet and rummaged around inside until she pulled out a pair of boots. "Here, put these on."

"Oh, wait a minute. Is this going to get kinky? You want me to be the lumberjack and you're going to be the... I don't know, what are you going to be?"

"Just put them on."

"Why?"

"Do it," Tenley said. She grabbed her own boots from the mat beside the back door and tugged them on, then flipped a switch beside the door. A red light blinked. "Ready?" she asked, her hand on the door.

"For what?"

"Just follow me." Tenley yanked the door open, then stepped outside onto the back porch.

Alex gasped. "What the hell are you doing? You're naked. You'll freeze to death."

"Not if I run fast enough," she cried. With that, she scurried across the porch to the steps, then carefully waded through the drifted snow.

If this was Tenley's idea of fun, then Alex was going to have to expose her to more interesting events—concerts, ball games, nightclubs. Drawing a deep breath, he walked through the open door and pulled it shut behind him. She stood waiting, her hair blowing in the wind, her skin pink from the cold.

"You have to move fast, before you start to feel the cold," she cried.

"I already feel it." He glanced down to notice that the erection she'd caused had subsided and the effects of the cold were beginning to set in. "Tenley, come on. I don't want to play in the snow."

"Follow me," she called. She headed toward a small log building. When she turned and waved to him, her foot caught on something beneath the snow and she disappeared into a snowdrift.

With a sharp curse, Alex took off after her. By the time he got there, she'd already picked herself up and was laughing hysterically, snow coating her hair and lashes and melting off her warm body.

"What the hell are you laughing about?"

"I picked a bad time to be a klutz," she said. Tenley grabbed his hand and led him to the tiny log hut, then opened the door. She reached inside and pulled out two buckets. "Here, fill these with snow." She grabbed two for herself and scooped them into a nearby drift.

By this time, Alex could barely feel his fingers, much less the other appendages on his body. But when the buckets were filled, she led him inside the hut. To his surprise, it was warm and cozy inside.

Cedar benches lined three walls and a small electric stove was positioned in the center. "Wow. A sauna."

Tenley set the buckets next to the stove and stretched out on one of the benches. "My grandfather built this for my grandmother. She was Finnish and she grew up with one of these. Her family was from northern Michigan. They didn't have indoor plumbing so this is the way they took a bath. Except they'd cut a hole in the ice afterward and jump in."

"We're not going to do that are we?"

"No, we'll just roll around in the snow. It works the same way."

"And this is what your family does for fun?"

"Yes. What does your family do?"

He chuckled. "We don't roll around naked in the snow. We…eat. And argue. Occasionally, we play board games or watch movies. I grew up with typical suburban parents. My mother would be shocked to hear I was running around without any clothes on."

She smiled. "I was raised a bit differently. My parents were very open-minded. Free thinkers. They taught us that being naked was perfectly natural."

"Hey, I'm all for nudity. In warm weather."

"You'll love it. I promise. It's invigorating. And relaxing." She made a sad face at him. "Don't be such a baby. You city boys don't know what you're missing."

"Believe me, there is no way I'd ever miss this."

Tenley crawled across the bench and stood in front of him. Then she gently pushed him back. "Sit," she said. "Relax. Take a load off."

Alex did as he was told, leaning back against the rough wall of the cabin. Tenley knelt down in front of him, running her hand along the inside of his thighs. "You're very tense," she said.

"It was freakin' cold out there."

"Relax," she said, smoothing her hands over his belly and then back down his legs. Alex watched her as she explored his body, her touch drifting down to his calves. She tugged off the boots and tossed them aside, then massaged his feet.

This was definitely worth the run through the cold, he mused, tipping his head back and closing his eyes. "Those Finns have the right idea," he said.

She pushed his legs apart and knelt between them, pressing her lips to his chest. Alex knew what was coming, but the rush of sensation that washed over him came as a surprise. Her lips and tongue were sweet torture, making him hard and hot in a matter of seconds. He wondered if it might be dangerous to become aroused in such a warm environment, then decided that if he died as a result, he'd go out a happy man.

He'd experienced this same pleasure with other women before, but he'd always focused on his own enjoyment, taking what was offered without thinking much about his partner. But as Alex watched Tenley seduce him with her mouth, he realized that she wasn't just any woman. The pleasure with her was more intense, more meaningful, because she was the one giving it.

He never understood how a guy could be satisfied spending his whole life with just one woman. But he was beginning to see how it was possible. Tenley was like a dangerous drug, alluring and addictive. The more he had of her, the more he needed.

Though he tried to delay, Alex's release came hard and quick. One moment he was in control and the next, he was caught in a vortex of incredibly intense pleasure. When he finally opened his eyes, he found Tenley staring up at him, a satisfied smile on her face.

"I told you saunas could be relaxing," she said.

"I will never doubt anything you say. Ever. Again."

"ARE YOU HUNGRY?" Tenley asked.

Alex distractedly rubbed her stockinged feet as he read, his long legs stretched out in front of him. Tenley sat on the opposite end of the leather sofa, trying to finish *Madame Bovary,* but she found her study of Alex much more intriguing. She'd been focusing on a tiny scar above his lip, wondering how it got there.

"No, I'm fine," he murmured.

They'd returned from the sauna and snow bath, tumbled into bed for another round of lovemaking, then taken a quick shower together. After a long and leisurely breakfast at two in the afternoon, Alex had rebuilt the fire and they'd settled in, listening to the wind rattling the windows and the drifting snow hissing against the glass.

"I should probably go check on the horses," she said. "I was going to let them out for a while."

He glanced up at her. "Don't you ever just sit still? Chill out. Just be with me."

"So, you liked the sauna?" she asked. Though it took every ounce of persuasion to get him out there, Tenley considered the activity a success. Alex, naked, in any environment, was fun.

"It was just about the best thing I've ever experienced," he said, his gaze still fixed on the book he was reading.

"We could play a game," she said. "Do you like Scrabble?"

He snapped the book shut. "Do I have to have sex with you again, to calm you down? Because if that's what it's going to take, I will. Just say the word. I'm willing to make the sacrifice."

Tenley giggled. "I'm just not used to sitting around. I don't read in the middle of the day. I read before bed because it puts me to sleep."

"If I weren't here, what would you be doing?" Alex asked.

"Clearing the driveway. I have a small tractor with a front-end loader. After that, I'd shovel the walk out to the barn. Then I'd probably get the dogs and take a hike out on the road, to see if it was plowed. Or maybe brave the storm and drive into town for some dinner."

"Is the road clear?" Alex asked.

"No."

"Does it make sense to plow the driveway right now?"

"No."

"Why don't we just talk, then. Have a conversation. I'll ask you a question and you answer it. And then you ask me a question and I'll answer it."

Tenley really didn't like the suggestion. After all, there were a few things she was hiding from him. She wasn't quite ready to tell him she was T. J. Marshall. Though it would certainly make for some interesting conversation, it might change everything between them.

She tried to imagine his reaction. He probably wouldn't be thrilled at her deception. He might wonder what other lies she'd told. But he would have to be happy he'd found her and they'd developed a relationship of sorts. He liked her. How could he be angry for long?

She could always test the waters, Tenley thought. Throw a tiny bit of truth out there and see how it went. "I suppose you're anxious to get into town," she ventured. "I mean, since you have business."

"That can wait," Alex said. "There's not much I can do about it in the middle of this storm."

"The snow should quit in a few hours," she said. "The barometer is starting to rise. Then I can dig us out and you can be on your way." She paused, waiting for his response.

"There's no hurry," he said.

"So you'd like to stay another night?"

He squeezed her foot. "If you'll have me. I'm not too much trouble, am I?"

"No," she said. She drew a long breath, steeling herself for what would come next. "You can meet my grandfather tomorrow morning."

His hand froze on her foot and his brow furrowed. "You want me to meet your family?"

"You came here to see T. J. Marshall, didn't you? That's my grandfather."

Alex gasped, his eyes going wide. "Wait a second. Why didn't you tell me that earlier?"

She shrugged. "I didn't think it made a difference. Does it? Make a difference?"

"You're Tenley Marshall?"

"Yes."

He leaned back into the sofa and raked his hand through his hair, shaking his head. "I just don't understand why you wouldn't have said something."

"Because I thought you might be one of those guys who doesn't like to mix business with pleasure? Because I'm the one who rescued you and I found you attractive? Mostly because I wanted to see what you looked like naked and I figured if you knew who I was, you wouldn't take off your clothes."

Alex thought about her explanation for a moment, then sighed. "I guess I understand. Is there anything else you're keeping from me?"

She shook her head. If she didn't say the word *no,* then it wasn't a full-fledged lie, was it? "My grandfather didn't create that book, though. I run his gallery. I know his work. And that's not his."

"I don't get it. Why would someone send it in under his name? It doesn't make sense."

Tenley jumped off the sofa. "I'm going to take care of the driveway before it starts to get dark. If the weather clears we could drive into town and see about your car."

"Are you that anxious to get rid of me?" he asked.

"No," she said. In truth, Tenley wished she could keep him for the rest of the week. Maybe even for the rest of the month. It was nice to have a man around, if only for the good sex. And the sex was really good. "But we don't have much to eat for dinner. The snow isn't going to plow itself. Besides, it will give you a chance to relax and read."

"I'll come with you," he said. "I can help."

"No, you're the guest. I'll be in soon. You can feed the dogs if you like." She hurried over to the kitchen and retrieved two cans of dog food from beneath the sink.

"You never told me their names, either."

"Dog," Tenley said. "And Pup. The little one is Dog and the big one is Pup," she said.

"Unusual names."

She slipped her bare feet into her boots, then tugged on her jacket. "They just wandered in one day and that's what I called them. Once they decided to stay, I didn't see any reason to give them new names since they seemed quite happy with Dog and Pup."

"Do you always take in strays?" he asked.

"I took you in, didn't I?" She sent him a flirtatious glance, hoping that it might smooth over any ruffled feathers. He chuckled. So she hadn't completely messed things up between them. If this revelation didn't upset him, maybe he'd be fine learning that she was the artist behind the graphic novel he wanted.

She zipped her coat up and pulled the hood tight around her face, then grabbed her gloves from her pockets. Sooner or later, he'd discover the whole truth. And after that, she'd have to try to explain her entire life to him. She could barely make sense of it herself.

Her novel meant money to him. And he'd assume she'd want a share of the financial windfall. But Tenley wasn't sure she wanted to turn a silly little scribble into a job. She wasn't a decent artist. People would criticize and she didn't think she'd be able to take that. Hell, there were a million reasons she could give him to go back to Chicago and leave her alone. But there was only one that made any sense to her.

She was starting to imagine a future with him. Not marriage or children, but a relationship, a connection that went beyond what they shared sexually to something resembling affection and trust. She'd already wondered what it might be like to have him present in her life, to speak to him every day on the phone, to see him on weekends…to make plans.

With a soft sigh, she trudged down the hill toward the shed. "I've spent less than twenty-four hours with the man," she muttered to herself. "It's a little early to confuse good sex with a relationship."

But would she even know a relationship if it dropped out of the sky and landed at her feet? She'd never been in love, never wanted to be with anyone for more than a night or two. Maybe after a second night together, she'd want him to go away.

Tenley waded through a huge drift, then grabbed the shed door and slid it open. Her Jeep was inside, still coated with snow from the night before. The small tractor sat beside it. All these thoughts about the future were beginning to drive her a bit crazy.

Maybe it was time to heed the warning signs, to put a little distance between them. If they spent another night together, there was no telling how she'd feel in the morning. She might just fall in love with Alex Stamos. And Tenley knew that was the worst thing she could possibly do to herself.

ALEX PEERED OUT the window, watching as Tenley maneuvered the tractor around the small yard, scooping up snow and dumping it against the trees. He wasn't quite sure how to take her news. Had he known she was T. J. Marshall's granddaughter, he'd have played things a whole lot differently.

Getting the artist under contract was his first priority. Everything else fell to the bottom of his to-do list. Still, even if he'd wanted to, Alex suspected it would have been impossible to resist Tenley's advances. She did crawl into bed with him, so he wasn't completely to blame.

The only way this could go south is if he and Tenley parted on bad terms. Alex cursed beneath his breath. What if she'd already fallen in love with him? If he didn't handle this right, she could sour a deal with her grandfather before it even began.

Alex stepped away from the window and crossed to the fireplace. Holding his hands out to the warmth, he contemplated the possibilities. If he had to choose between Tenley and the book contract, the choice would have to be— His breath caught in his throat.

No, it wasn't that easy. His first instinct wasn't to put business first. He wanted to choose Tenley. The notion startled him. He'd never made a woman the priority in his life. Beyond his sisters and his mother, women were pretty much a temporary distraction. Work always came first.

Alex shook his head. Maybe it was time to start thinking about business. He crossed the room to the phone, then picked it up and dialed the office. When the receptionist answered, he asked for his sister's extension.

"Where have you been?" she asked. "I've been ringing your cell and it kept bouncing through to your voice mail. I've called all the hospitals up there thinking you got into some kind of accident."

"I'm sorry. I lost my cell in a snowbank and I spent the night with the Good Samaritan who rescued me from the ditch. My car got hit by a snowplow and I haven't had a chance to talk to this artist yet. So, I'm going to be here for a while."

"Sounds like you've had a very exciting twenty-four hours," she said.

"You wouldn't believe it," he said. "I need you to overnight another cell phone to me. Send it to the Harbor Inn in Sawyer Bay. Then find a place for me to rent a car. And have them deliver it to the inn. On second thought, rent an SUV. Once I get into town, I'll try to find a wireless network and I'll pick up my mail."

"What's your number at the inn?" Tess asked.

"I'm not there yet. I probably won't be until to-morrow morning."

"Where are you?"

"I'm staying with this…with T. J. Marshall's grand-daughter."

"Oh, that's nice," Tess said. "So things are going well?"

"That's debatable," he said. "And a very long story to tell. But, I should be at the inn sometime tomorrow. I'll call you then."

He set the phone down, then picked up his book from the sofa. *Walden* was one of his favorite books and obviously one of Tenley's as well. She had written notes in the margins and he found drawings at the ends of chapters. Frowning, he walked over to the bookshelves that flanked the fireplace.

He'd noticed the eclectic selection of literature and was quite impressed. But the books hadn't been hers originally. Most of them held copyrights from the 1950s and earlier. The library had probably belonged to her grandfather.

He plucked out a copy of *Jane Eyre* and flipped through it, noticing the notes and drawings. If he looked hard enough, he could see hints of the artist who had drawn Cyd. Alex grabbed another book, *The Catcher in the Rye,* and opened it, only to find a drawing of a young girl on the title page.

The parallels were there to see. In the eyes and in the hands. T. J. Marshall had drawn these sketches and he'd drawn the graphic novel. But according to Tenley, her grandfather only painted landscapes. She'd been adamant that the novel wasn't his work.

Something wasn't right. He wasn't getting the whole story, and Tenley was standing in the way. She worked at her grandfather's gallery. Was she afraid that publishing an edgy graphic novel might hurt his reputation as a serious painter? If that was the case, they could publish under a pseudonym.

Alex needed to meet this man and make his proposal. If the roads were clear, then he'd have Tenley take him into town. If not, he'd go tomorrow morning. But he was definitely not sleeping with Tenley tonight. There was every chance that she was deliberately distracting him.

"Definitely not," Alex repeated. He grabbed the copy of Thoreau and sat down on the sofa. But as he tried to pick up where he'd left off, Alex's thoughts kept returning to Tenley. Sleeping in separate rooms seemed like a good plan, but in reality, he'd have a serious problem staying in his room. And if she crawled into bed with him, then all bets were off.

No, he'd have to get back to town tonight. If Tenley wouldn't take him, then he'd call a cab. Perhaps the inn had a shuttle service.

Over the next half hour, Alex tried to focus on reading, but he found himself walking back and forth to the window, peering out at Tenley as she ran the tractor up and down the driveway. He'd never known a woman who could drive a tractor. But then, he wondered if there was anything Tenley couldn't do for herself. She seemed like the kind of woman who didn't need a man.

When she parked the tractor near the shed and started back toward the house, Alex returned to the sofa and opened his book. She burst through the door, brushing snow off her jacket and stamping her feet on the rug.

"Get your things together," she said. "The road is plowed. I'll take you into town." She opened the closet door and pulled out a down jacket. "Wear this. You'll need something warm. And find a hat. It's still windy."

With that, she turned and walked back outside, slamming the door behind her. Alex stared after her. "I guess I will be sleeping alone tonight, after all." He wouldn't have to worry about controlling his desires. Somehow, he'd rather that the decision had been his.

Alex went back to the guest room and gathered his things, then found the pair of boots he'd worn out to the sauna. When he was dressed against the cold, Alex walked out onto the porch, expecting to find Tenley waiting there with her SUV. But the woods were eerily silent.

He hiked down to the shed, calling her name, the sound of his voice echoing through the trees. As he passed the barn, he noticed her inside. She was working with one of her horses.

"I'm ready," he said, dropping his duffel on the ground.

"I'll just be a few minutes."

"Tenley, I don't want you to think that I'm angry with you. I can understand why you might want to protect your grandfather's reputation."

She gave him a perplexed look. "All right," she said. "You have business to do and sleeping with me is probably just a distraction. It's better that you go."

"You're not a distraction," he said, contradicting what he'd been thinking earlier. "I don't regret the time we spent together. Or anything we did. Do you?"

She smiled and shook her head. "No. I liked having sex with you."

He caught her gaze and held it. Was that all it had been to her? Just sex? "Do you want me to stay the night?"

"You don't have to," she said. "The roads are plowed."

"That's not the point," Alex countered. "I'm asking if you want me to stay another night."

"Have you ever taken a sleigh ride?" she asked, striding out of the barn, the horse following her. She handed him the reins. "Hold these."

"What does that have to do with anything?"

Tenley smiled. "Minnie needs exercise and the roads are perfect. They're covered with snow so they're nice and smooth. It'll be fun." She walked to a large sliding door on the side of the barn and pulled it open to reveal a small sleigh. Then she took the reins from his hands and deftly hitched the horse to the sleigh.

"Hop in," she said, leading Minnie toward him. "You can toss your things in the back."

When they were both settled in the sleigh, a thick wool blanket tucked around their legs, Tenley snapped the reins against Minnie's back and the sleigh slid out into the yard. The horse took the hill up to the road without breaking stride and before long, they were skimming over the snowy road at a brisk pace.

The horse's hooves were muffled by the hard-packed snow. Alex drew a deep breath and let it out slowly, listening to the hiss of the runners beneath them. He glanced over at Tenley, the reins twisted in her hands, her gaze fixed intently on the road.

She was amazing. He'd had more new experiences with her in the past twenty-four hours than he had in the past year of his life. How could he ever forget her? And why would he want to? He scanned the features of her face, outlined by the afternoon sun.

It was all so breathtaking—her beauty, the sparkling snow, the blue sky and the crisp silence of the winter evening. She glanced over at him. But this time, she didn't smile. Their gazes locked for a moment and he leaned over and dropped a kiss on her lips. "This is nice."

"My grandfather used to take my brother and me out after snowstorms. We'd bundle up and my mother would make us a thermos of hot cocoa and off we'd go. We'd sing and laugh and my face would get so cold it would hurt. It's one of my favorite childhood memories."

"I can see why. It's fun. Does he live around here?"

"My grandfather lives in town. I told you, he has a gallery—"

"I meant your brother," Alex corrected.

An odd expression crossed her face. Alex wasn't quite sure how to read it. She looked confused and then sad. Tenley shook her head. "No. He died."

Alex was shocked by her reply. He'd come to believe he knew most of the basic facts about Tenley. But what he'd pieced together obviously still had a lot of holes. Very big holes. "I—I'm sorry. I didn't mean to—"

"No, it's all right. Nobody ever mentions him around me. I'm just not used to talking about him." She pasted a bright smile on her face. "People think I'm…fragile. I'm not, you know."

"I can see that," Alex replied. "I don't know a single woman who can drive a sleigh *and* a tractor. Or run naked through the snow."

"People also think I'm crazy," she said. "You'll probably hear a lot of that when you're in town."

He slipped his arm around her and pulled her body against his. "I like crazy." Alex paused. "I'm going to see your grandfather tomorrow. I'm hoping to convince him to let me publish his novel."

"I know," she said.

"And then, after he's signed a contract with me, I'm going to come back out here for another sleigh ride."

They passed the rest of the trip in complete silence. As they drove into town, Alex was struck by the fact that he'd spent an entire day away from what he considered the conveniences of civilization. There were people driving on the streets and lights that seemed a bit too bright and clocks confirming what the sun had already told him— the day was coming to an end. And it was noisy.

He fought the temptation to grab the reins from Tenley and turn the sleigh around. Their time together had been such a nice respite from his real life, much better than a week at his family's beach condo in Mexico.

They wove through the narrow streets of town, snow piled high and nearly obscuring their view of the white clapboard buildings. She pulled the sleigh to a stop. "I don't know where you were planning to stay," she said. "But this is the nicest place in town. Ask Katie for the big room at the top of the stairs. It has a fireplace."

He caught sight of the sign hanging from the porch. "Bayside Bed and Breakfast," he said. "I had a reservation at the Harbor Inn."

"This is better. Katie Vanderhoff makes cinnamon rolls in the morning." She twisted the reins around a ring near her feet, then jumped out of the sleigh.

Alex followed her around to the back, then grabbed his things from the luggage box. "Thanks for everything. For saving me from the storm, for taking me in and feeding me."

"No problem," she said.

This wasn't going to be easy, saying goodbye to her. Alex didn't like the prospect of spending the night alone in bed. Nor did he want this to be the end. "Let's have dinner tomorrow. I'm going to be staying another night and you probably know of a nice place."

She hesitated, then nodded. "Sure. I'll talk to you tomorrow." Tenley turned to walk toward the sleigh, but Alex didn't want her to leave.

He dropped his things onto the snowy sidewalk, then caught up to her and grabbed her hand. He pulled her against him, his mouth coming down on hers, softly at first, then urgently, as if he needed to leave her with something memorable. Alex searched for a clue to her feelings in the softness of her lips and the taste of her tongue.

She surrendered immediately, her arms slipping around his neck. Time stood still and, for a few moments, Alex felt himself relax. She still wanted him, as much as he wanted her. So why the hell were they spending the night apart?

"Stay with me," he said.

"I can't. I have to take Minnie back. And if I stay here, the whole town will know by tomorrow morning. They already spend too much time talking about me." She pushed up on her toes and kissed him again. "I'll see you tomorrow."

With that, she hopped back into the sleigh and grabbed the reins. The horse leaped into a brisk walk when she slapped the reins against the mare's back and

Alex watched as she disappeared around the corner. A sense of loneliness settled in around him.

Suddenly exhausted, Alex picked up his things and walked up to the porch. When he got inside, he rang the bell at the front desk. A moment later, an elderly woman stepped through a door and greeted him.

"I need a place to stay," Alex said. "I'm told that I should ask for the big room at the top of the stairs."

"Have you had friends that have spent time with us?" she asked.

"No. Tenley Marshall suggested this place."

The woman blinked in surprise. "You're a friend of Tenley's?"

"Yes. Is the room available?"

She nodded. "How is Tenley? I haven't seen her recently. She used to work for me when she was a teenager. But that was before all that sadness." She drew a sharp breath and shook her head, then forced a smile. "I'm glad to know she has a friend."

Alex frowned. Though he wasn't one to pry into other people's private affairs, he believed he had a right to know a little more about the woman who had seduced him. "Yes," he said. "I heard about all that. You'd think after all this time—how long has it been?"

"Oh, gosh. Ten years? She was fifteen or sixteen. They were a pair, those two. Joined at the hip from the moment they were born. And you've never seen such beautiful children. That black hair and those pale blue eyes. You'd never recognize her now with all that silly makeup."

"I think she's beautiful," Alex said, feeling the need to defend Tenley.

She blinked in surprise. "Well, that's lovely." A smile slowly suffused her entire face. "Let's get you registered and then I'll show you your room."

Though he was tempted to ask more, Alex decided to bide his time. He didn't want to give the town gossips any more to chat about.

4

TENLEY CAREFULLY maneuvered the sleigh down the narrow streets to the harbor. Before long, the salt trucks would be out and the snow would melt away, making it impossible to use the sled. They could have brought her truck, but Tenley had wanted time to talk to him, to tell him the entire truth.

Unfortunately, she hadn't been able to figure out a way to adequately explain her reasoning. Forced to come up with an alternate plan, she decided to enlist her grandfather's help. But she needed to talk to him before Alex had a chance to introduce himself. She drew to a stop in front of her grandfather's gallery, then tied the reins to the mailbox.

"What kind of gas mileage do you get with that rig?"

Tenley turned to find the town police chief, Harvey Willis, hanging out the window of his cruiser. He waved and she returned the gesture. "Oats and hay," she said. "And an occasional apple."

"Drive safe," he said. "And get that thing back to your place before dark or I'll be giving you a citation. It doesn't have lights on it." He chuckled, then continued up the road from the harbor.

Her grandfather answered the door after only thirty seconds of constant ringing. He carried a paint-stained rag and wiped his fingers as Tenley greeted him.

"You brought the sleigh out. Give me a few minutes and I'll get my jacket."

"No, we need to talk," Tenley said.

"We can talk and ride," he said.

She nodded, impatient to get to the subject at hand—Alex Stamos. When her grandfather returned, bundled against the cold, Tenley helped him into the sleigh, then handed him the reins.

"Oh, this brings back fine memories," he said, urging the horse into a slow walk. "How long has it been since we've had a ride? Last year, we barely had snow. And the year before that, I spent most of the winter in California with your father. Three years? My, time really does fly."

"Grandpa, I need your help. There's this man—"

"Is someone giving you trouble, Tennie? It's not Randy, is it? Is he making a pest of himself again?"

"No. It's not Randy." Randy Schmitt had been pursuing her since high school and she'd been fending off his affections for just as long.

Tenley fiddled with the fingers of her gloves, searching for a way to enlist her grandfather's help. It wasn't difficult to predict his reaction to her dilemma. But she couldn't think of any way to make Alex's offer sound insignificant.

"I made a little comic book for Josh as a Christmas gift. Just a story with some pictures to go with it. And he loved it so much, he sent it to a publisher in Chicago. Now that publisher has come here, hoping to put the work under contract."

"Tennie, that's fabulous! I didn't realize you were working on your art."

She groaned. "I don't have any art. This was just…doodling. Crude illustrations. The problem is, Josh told the publisher the book was done by T. J. Marshall. And the publisher, his name is Alex Stamos, thinks that's you. So tomorrow, he's going to come by the gallery and try to convince you to sell him the rights to the book. And you're going to tell him you're not interested."

Her grandfather scowled, his eyes still fixed on the road ahead. "Why would you want me to do that? This is your chance to do something on your own. Tennie, you have to grab an opportunity like this. Not many artists can make a living off their talents."

Tenley shook her head. "But I don't have any talent. And I'm just too busy with my work at the gallery."

"You can do both."

"I've never really thought about a career as an artist," she said.

"You've never really thought about a career, period," he said, drawing the horse to a stop at the corner. "Everything went to hell before you had a chance to decide what you wanted to do with your life. You've been afraid to be passionate about anything, Tennie. Afraid if you showed any interest, it would be taken away. But your talent can't be taken away. It's in your genes."

She really had no excuse. Her grandfather was right. But she'd never wanted a career as an artist. She wasn't prepared. "I love my life exactly the way it is."

He shook his head. "No, you don't. Every day, I look at you trying to avoid living, trying to keep things on an even keel. You hide out in that old cabin. You hide behind that makeup and that silly hairdo. You dress yourself in black, as if you're still in mourning. Everything you do is meant to push people away. It's time to take a chance."

He was talking about her art, but what her grandfather said applied to Alex as well—or to men, in general. Reward didn't come without risk. She slipped her arm through his and rested her head on his shoulder. "I don't mean to be such a mess," she said.

Her grandfather laughed. "You've always been a bother. But that's why I love you, Tennie. We're not so different, you and I. I was lucky to find your grandmother. She was a sensible woman and she put me in my place. And I loved her for it. I'd like to think there's someone out there who can do the same for you. Someone who can bring you balance."

Tenley sighed, her breath clouding in front of her face. "Do you ever wonder what he would have been like? He would have changed as he got older. I always try to imagine what kind of man he would have become."

"I know one thing. He would have been mad as hell to see you wasting away in that cabin. He would have told you to get off your butt and make something out of your life."

"He would have," Tenley said with a weak laugh. She gave his arm a squeeze. "Would it be all right if we cut our ride short? I have some things I need to do."

"Sure, sweetheart." He handed her the reins. "I'm going to walk from here. I need some exercise. And I want you to think about what I've said. Carpe diem. Seize the day, Tenley Marshall."

He jumped down to the ground, then knocked on the side of the sleigh. Tenley clucked her tongue and sent Minnie into motion. Though she could have taken a quick way out of town, she decided to ride past the inn.

She slowed the sleigh as she stared up at the window of Alex's room. What was he doing now? Was he lying on the bed, thinking about the time they'd spent together? Was he reliving all of the most passionate moments between them?

She fought the urge to park her sleigh and climb the trellis to the second-story porch that fronted his room. But someone would see the sleigh and question what she was doing at the inn. There'd be all sorts of speculation. Though small-town life could be nice, there was a lot of bad with the good.

"Get up, Minnie," she called. "Let's go home."

Tomorrow would be soon enough to tend to her future. For now, she wanted a quiet place to think about the past twenty-four hours.

THE WHITE CLAPBOARD inn was as quaint on the inside as it was on the exterior. Two huge parlors flanked the entry hall and a wide, open staircase led to the second floor and Alex's room.

Tenley had been right about the choice. The room, furnished with a mix of real and reproduction antiques, was spacious, but cozy. It overlooked a wide upper porch with two sets of French doors that could be thrown open in the warm weather.

After checking in, he'd walked down to a small coffee shop and had dinner, then spent a half-hour looking for a place to buy a new pair of shoes for his meeting with T. J. Marshall. The only men's shop in town was closed and wouldn't open until ten the next morning, so Alex decided to return to his room.

An attempt to kick back and relax only made him more restless. He felt imprisoned amongst the chintz curtains and the overstuffed furniture, used to the soothing mix of rustic charm and natural comfort in Tenley's cabin.

Alex opened the French doors and let the cold wind blow through his room, breathing deeply as he tried to clear his head. Maybe Tenley had it right all along. Maybe people weren't supposed to live with all those silly conveniences like televisions and clocks and microwave ovens.

Though he'd only spent a day with her, Alex sensed something inside him had changed. He looked at his surroundings with a greater awareness of what was necessary for happiness and what could be discarded. And in his mind, Tenley was standing with the necessities.

He looked over at the bed, to the pages of the novel that he'd spread over the surface, the papers fluttering. Tenley. Something had been nagging at him since he'd left her place, something he couldn't quite put his finger on. He locked the doors against the wind and then crossed the room.

His thoughts focused on the drawings he'd found inside her grandfather's books, the little sketches that seemed familiar in a way. Gathering up the pages, Alex stretched out on the bed and began to read the novel again, carefully studying each illustration before moving on.

The haze of desire that had clouded his thoughts slowly cleared and Alex realized instantly what had been bothering him. The heroine in the story was Tenley. A girl who'd lost her family in a tragic accident and who had discovered a way to bring them back to life. Cyd was Tenley. But it was more than that.

The story was so personal, so rooted in the heroine's viewpoint that it could never have been written by a man. Nor had it been illustrated by Tenley's grandfather. She'd done the drawings. And she'd written the story.

He rifled through the pages until he found a close-up of Cyd's hand. The rings that Tenley wore were exactly the same as Cyd's. The shape of the hands, the long, tapered fingers and the black nail polish. Hands just like those that had touched his body and made him ache with need.

"Oh, hell," he muttered, flopping back against the

pillows. This was all his fault. He'd made some rather big assumptions about T. J. Marshall—pretty sexist assumptions—that had been completely wrong. He was looking for an artist by that name from Sawyer Bay and he'd found one. But he'd never considered that the *T* in T.J. might stand for Tenley.

Alex tried to rationalize his mistake. He'd been blinded by desire, anxious to believe everything she said and even things she didn't say. "The surprises never end," he said.

Tenley had never claimed to be a conventional girl, but what artist wouldn't want to make a living from their work? There were thousands upon thousands who struggled to make ends meet every day. And he was offering her a chance to do what she loved and get paid to do it.

Alex carefully straightened the pages, then put them back in his briefcase. As he closed it, he noticed the phone and considered calling her and demanding the truth. But if she'd gone to so much trouble to hide herself from him, then he'd have to proceed cautiously. She'd be the one to sign the contract, so his approach would have to change.

Her number was in the phone book under Tenley J. Thomas J. followed immediately after, and below that, the Marshall Gallery. Had he bothered to look in the phone book, he might have figured this out sooner. And maybe he wouldn't have made the mistake of sleeping with her.

Or maybe not, Alex mused. She would have been

awfully difficult to resist, all soft and naked, her hands skimming over his body. He punched in the digits of her number, casting aside the images that raced through his head, then waited as her phone rang. He wasn't sure what he intended to say or how he intended to say it. But that became a moot point when she didn't answer. "She's probably outside, chopping wood or rebuilding the engine on her Jeep," he muttered.

Irritated, Alex stripped off his shirt and tossed it onto a nearby chair, then discarded his khakis and his socks. The simplest way to occupy his mind was to lose himself in his work, but he preferred to think about Tenley instead. Perhaps a hot shower would clear his head.

He strode to the bathroom and turned on the water, waiting for it to heat up. Then he skimmed his boxers off and stepped inside the tiled stall. Bracing his hands on the wall, he let the water sluice over his neck and back, his eyes closed, his mind drifting.

Tantalizing images teased at his brain and he thought about the sauna, about the two of them naked and sweating, of Tenley's mouth on his shaft and the orgasm that followed. Alex groaned. Just the mere thought brought an unwelcome reaction.

If he got hard every time he thought of her, then he needed to find something else to occupy his mind. He reached for the faucet and turned off the hot water, forcing himself to bear the sting of the cold. It wouldn't take much to ease his predicament and Alex considered taking matters into his own hands. But surrendering wasn't an option. He was the one in control of his desires, not her.

He tipped his face up into the spray, waiting for the water to have an effect on his body. But his mind once again drifted to thoughts of Tenley. What would they be doing at this very moment if he'd spent the night in her cabin? Would they be curled up in front of the fire, drinking hot cocoa? Maybe they'd already be sound asleep, naked in each other's arms, after a long afternoon of mind-blowing sex.

Alex slowly began to count backward from one hundred, challenging his body to bear the cold shower. He needed to stop thinking about sex. Even if he wanted to return to her bed, he didn't have a car. There was no way to get back to her cabin. Hell, he didn't even know where her cabin was.

Finally, after his erection had completely subsided, Alex shut off the water and grabbed a towel from the rack above the toilet. His skin was prickled with goose bumps and he shivered uncontrollably. But his erection was gone.

Alex shook his head, then stepped out of the shower and wrapped the towel around his waist. As he walked back into the room, his ran his hands over his wet chest. But when he glanced up, he jerked in surprise. "Geez, you scared me."

Tenley sat on the edge of the bed, dressed in her parka and fur hat, her big boots dripping water on the hardwood floor.

"How the hell did you get in here?"

She pointed to the French doors. "I climbed up the trellis and came across the porch."

"Those doors are locked."

She shrugged. "They are. But you can jimmy the lock with a library card." Tenley reached in her pocket and pulled out her card. "It's good for more than just books."

Alex stared at her from across the room, afraid to approach for fear that he wouldn't be able to keep his hands off her. Why was she here? Had she missed him as much as he'd missed her?

"I didn't want to sleep alone tonight," she said. "I thought maybe I could sleep here."

"Just sleep?"

Tenley nodded. "I like sleeping with you. When I sleep with you, I don't dream."

Alex knew once they crawled into bed, there'd be a lot more than sleeping on the menu. "Tenley, I think you and I both know that we can't be in the same bed together and just sleep."

"We could try," she said.

Every instinct in Alex's mind and body told him to show her the door. He had an obligation to treat her as a business prospect and the last time he checked, that didn't include losing himself in the warmth of her body. "I'm not even remotely interested in doing that," he said.

Her eyes went wide and he saw the hurt there. "You aren't?"

Alex knew he was risking everything, but suddenly business didn't matter. He could live without her novel, but he couldn't go another minute without her body. "If you spend the night here, I won't hold back." He paused, then decided he might as well be completely honest. Then the ball would be in her court. "I'm going to see your grandfather tomorrow. If he isn't the one who made that story, I'm not going to give up. I'm going to find that person, whoever he—or *she*—is."

She stood, her expression unflinching, and shrugged out of her jacket, letting it drop to the floor at her feet. Then she kicked off her boots and dropped them in front of the door. She still wore the goofy hat with the earflaps. Alex reached out and took it off her head, then set it on the desk.

He hadn't seen her in a few hours, but the effect that her beauty had on his brain was immediate and intense. His gaze drifted from her eyes to her lips. Alex fought the temptation to grab her and pull her down onto the bed, to kiss her until her body went soft beneath his.

Slowly, she removed each piece of clothing, her gaze fixed on his, never faltering. When she was left in just her T-shirt and panties, Alex realized that he hadn't drawn a decent breath since she'd begun. A wave of dizziness caused him to reach out and grab the bedpost.

His fingers twitched with the memory of touching her body as he took in the outline of her breasts beneath the thin cotton shirt. He looked down to see his reaction, becoming more evident through the damp towel. Tenley noticed as well, her gaze lingering on his crotch.

Who were they trying to fool? There was no way they'd crawl into bed together and not enjoy the pleasures of the flesh. Alex untwisted the towel from his waist and it dropped to the floor. Then he pulled her into his arms, tumbling them both back onto the bed.

This was dangerous, he thought to himself as he drew her leg up along his hip. To need a woman so much that it defied all common sense was something he'd never experienced in the past. It wasn't a bad feeling, just a very scary situation. How much was he willing to give up to possess her? And when would it be enough?

TENLEY STARED at the landscape of the harbor at Gill's Rock. "It's lovely," she said, nodding. "The colors are softer than those you used on the painting of Detroit harbor. Are you going to have prints made?"

"Definitely. The prints of Fish Creek harbor sold well. I'm thinking we ought to do some smaller ones and sell the whole series as a package."

"Are there any harbors left to do?"

"After Jackson, I think I'm done with them," her grandfather said. "I'm going to move on to barns. Or log buildings."

"You could start with the cabin."

"I was thinking of doing that. But there's a nice barn on Clark's Lake Road that I've always wanted to paint." He stepped back, studying his painting intently. "Light-houses, harbors, barns. The tourists love them and I do give them what they love."

Tenley knew the compromises that her grandfather had to make over the course of his life. Though he might have wanted to become a serious painter and have his work hang in museums, he'd come to accept his talent for what it was—good enough to provide for

his wife and a family and more than enough to tempt
the tourists into buying.

"By the way," her grandfather said, "I like the new
look. All that stuff on your eyes…I never understood
that. You're a pretty girl, Tennie." He paused. "No,
you're a beautiful woman."

Tenley threw her arms around his neck and gave
him a fierce hug. "I have to run over to the post
office. I think your paints are here. And I'm going to
mail these bills, too. Do you have anything you want
to put in?"

Her grandfather scowled. "Is there a reason you're
so anxious to leave?"

"No. I just have work to do."

"I thought you said that guy from the publishing
house was going to stop by."

Tenley wasn't sure what Alex had planned for the
day. She'd slipped out of his room at dawn, leaving him
sound asleep, his naked body tangled in the sheets, his
dark hair mussed. To her relief, she'd managed to crawl
back down the trellis and get back her Jeep without
anyone seeing her, minimizing the chances for gossip.

"He might. He didn't make an appointment, so I
don't know what time he plans to show up. If he comes,
tell him I'll be back soon."

"Tenley, I am not going to make excuses for you. The
man has come all the way from Chicago. The least you
could do is talk to him."

Oh, she'd done a whole lot more than talk to him
already, Tenley mused. If her grandfather only knew the

naughty things he'd done to her, he'd probably lock the front door of the gallery and call Harvey Willis to escort Alex out of town. "I'll only be a few minutes, so—"

The bell above the gallery door jingled and she heard someone step inside. Tenley forced a smile. "There he is," she said. Clutching the envelopes in front of her, she wandered out of the workroom and into the showroom. Alex stood at the door, dressed in a sport jacket, a crisp blue shirt and dark wool trousers. His hair was combed and he'd shaved and he looked nothing like the man she'd left that morning.

"Hello," she said, unable to hide a smile. There were times when she forgot just how handsome he was. Boys like Alex had always been way out of her league. They dated the popular girls, the girls who worried about clothes and hair and…boobs. They always had boobs. Tenley glanced down at her chest, then crossed her arms over her rather unremarkable breasts.

"Hi. I'm here to see T. J. Marshall."

Tenley swallowed hard. It was now or never. Her grandfather wouldn't take part in the subterfuge, so Tenley was faced with only one choice. She cleared her throat and straightened to her full height. "I'm T. J. Marshall. At least, I'm the one you're looking for."

He didn't seem surprised. "Yeah, I kind of figured that out on my own." He crossed the room and held out his hand. "Alex Stamos. Stamos Publishing."

Hesitantly, she placed her fingers in his palm. The instant they touched, she felt a tremor race through her. He slowly brought her hand to his lips and pressed a kiss to her fingertips. "I missed you this morning," he whispered. "I woke up and you weren't there."

"See, that wasn't so difficult."

Tenley jumped at the sound of her grandfather's voice. She tugged her hand from Alex's and fixed a smile on her face. "Alex Stamos, this is my grandfather, Thomas Marshall. Also known as T.J. Or Tom."

Alex held his hand out. "It's a pleasure to meet you, sir. You have a very talented granddaughter. Did she tell you we're interested in publishing her graphic novel?"

"I've always thought she had talent. She used to draw little sketches in all my books. Drove me crazy. I thought she might be an illustrator someday. She never did like books without pictures." He chuckled softly. "Well, it's a pleasure, Alex. I'll leave you two to your business."

When they were alone, Alex reached out for her hand again, placing it on his chest. "Why did you leave?"

"I figured I'd better get out of there or the whole town would be talking."

Alex gave her fingers a squeeze. "So, what do you think they'd say if I took you to breakfast? There's a nice little coffee shop down the street from the inn."

"You didn't stay for the cinnamon rolls?"

He shook his head. "Hmm. Cinnamon rolls. Tenley. Cinnamon rolls. Tenley. The choice wasn't tough."

"All right," she said. "But you're buying."

"I wouldn't have it any other way."

Tenley grabbed her jacket and they stepped out into

the chilly morning. "How did you figure it out?" she asked as they headed away from the harbor.

"I was flipping through some of those books your grandfather mentioned. There were drawings in the margins. At first I thought they were just crude scribblings, but then I came across one that looked very familiar."

Tenley knew she ought to apologize. But that might prompt a discussion of her motives and even she wasn't sure why she'd kept her real identity a secret from him. "I didn't intend to deceive you. I just didn't want anything to… I wanted to be able to… I wasn't ready…" She shook her head, feeling her cheeks warm with embarrassment. "It's sometimes easier not to get too personal. At least, that's always worked for me in the past."

"So, I'm just one in a long line of uninformed men?" he asked.

Her breath caught in her throat. "No! You're not like anyone I've every known. I thought if you knew, you wouldn't want to sleep with me." She cursed softly. "I wanted you and you wanted me. All that other stuff is just…business."

"I have rules about mixing business with pleasure. Very strict rules."

"You haven't mixed the two. Not yet."

"What are you talking about?"

She straightened. "I haven't agreed to do business with you, Alex, so all we've had is the pleasure part. You haven't broken any rules…yet."

Alex laughed, shaking his head. "Whatever made me think this was going to be easy? God, I thought I'd come up here, do my little presentation, charm you and get you to sign on the dotted line."

"You have charmed me," she said.

"Yeah, I've heard I have a way with women," he muttered. "But do me a favor. Don't say no until I've told you the plan. Consider my offer and if you don't like it, then I'll—I'll make you another offer." He stopped and grabbed her arms, turning her to face him. "But be assured of one thing, Tenley. You are going to sign with me."

"You must have a lot of confidence in that charm of yours," Tenley said.

"It worked on you, didn't it?"

"I think you're forgetting who seduced whom." She started walking again, then turned back to him. "Maybe I should hire an agent. Just to make sure I get the best deal."

"At least agent would make sure you didn't pass on a great deal. He'd say, don't be stupid. Sign the contract."

In truth, Tenley *was* interested in how much her novel might bring. After talking with her grandfather, she'd begun to see the wisdom in his words. She'd be silly to turn down a chance to make money from her art. But she had no idea what a project like hers was worth. There was the money to discuss—and a few other conditions.

"But an agent will take fifteen percent," he added. "You don't need an agent. I'm going to give you a good offer." He caught up to her as they turned down the main street, toward the inn. "I had a nice time last night. Did you sleep well?"

Tenley nodded. "I did."

"I'm going to stay another night," he said.

"I thought you'd be leaving today."

Alex took her hand and tucked it into the crook of his arm. "Nope. I'm going to stay until I convince you to sign with us. And after that, we're going to go over all the things that need to be done with your story to make it better."

When they reached the coffee shop, Alex opened the door for her and stepped aside for her to enter. The shop was filled with all the usual customers. Morning coffee was a daily ritual for a number of the folks in town, choosing the same seats every day.

Her entrance caused a quite a stir, with everyone turning to watch as the hostess seated them in a booth near the front windows. She handed them menus and asked about coffee. Alex ordered a cup and Tenley asked for orange juice.

"Why is everyone staring?" Alex whispered.

"I don't usually come in here," Tenley said. "It's like Gossip Central. If you want the town to know your business, you just mention it during breakfast at The Coffee Bean. Here, information moves faster than the Internet."

They ordered breakfast, Tenley choosing a huge platter with three eggs, bacon, hash browns, a biscuit and three small pancakes. Alex settled for toast and coffee.

"Not hungry?" she asked.

"I usually have a bigger lunch," he said. "So, I think we need to talk business."

"Let's not," Tenley said, slathering her biscuit with honey. She took a huge bite and grinned at him. "Sex always makes me hungry. I find that my appetite is in direct proportion to the intensity of my orgasms. This morning I am really, really hungry. You should be, too. We did it three times—no wait, four times, last night. That has to be some kind of record."

Alex glanced around. "Do you really think this is an appropriate topic for breakfast conversation?"

Tenley slipped her foot out of her boot and wriggled her toes beneath his pant leg. "You know what I like the best? I like the way you look, right before you come. Your lip twitches and you get this really intense expression on your face. I love that expression."

She loved the way his body tensed and flexed as he moved inside of her, she loved the feel of his skin beneath her fingers and the warmth of his mouth on hers. Tenley loved that she could make him lose touch with reality for a few brief moments. There weren't many things that she did well, but seducing Alex was one task at which she excelled.

Alex cleared his throat. "Stop."

"Why?"

"Because I don't like being teased, especially in public."

She took another bite of her biscuit and then held it out to him. "You should eat more. You're going to need your energy. We should go skiing. Have you ever been cross-country skiing?"

"Never," Alex said.

"Or skating. There's a nice rink in Sister Bay. And you can rent skates. Do you know how to skate?"

"I used to play hockey when I was a kid. But I'm not much for the cold. I prefer warm-weather activities. I like windsurfing. I go hiking. I like to water-ski."

"We have all that here. Just not now."

"Tenley, I want to talk about this contract."

"Always about business," she muttered. "I find business very dull. And if you're trying to charm me, you're not doing a very good job. If I want to go skating, then you should be happy to take me."

"I don't have anything to wear," he said.

"We have stores here. You'll need some long underwear and a decent pair of boots. And some good gloves. Those leather gloves won't last. We'll go shopping after breakfast."

It was nice to have a playmate, both in and out of bed. Alex made a good companion. He was funny and easygoing and he seemed to find her amusing. And he made her shudder with pleasure whenever he touched her. What more could a girl want?

She grabbed a piece of bacon from her plate and slowly munched on it. With Tommy's death, she'd lost her best friend. Since then, she hadn't tried to find a new one. Alex was the first person she really wanted to spend time with.

"All right," he said. "We'll talk business at dinner."

"At my place," she said. "I'll cook."

"You're not going to distract me again," he said. "I want you to promise. And I think it would be better if we went out."

Tenley shrugged. "We'll see."

"If you don't promise, I'm going to kiss you, right here and now." He glanced around. "What would the gossips say about that?"

"Go ahead," Tenley said. "I dare you." In truth, she wanted him to accept the challenge. She wanted to shock everyone watching, to make them wonder just what poor, pitiful Tenley Marshall was doing with this sexy stranger.

When he didn't make a move, she leaned across the table, took his face in her hands and gave Alex a long, lingering kiss. She didn't bother to look at the crowd's reaction. Tenley chose to enjoy the look on Alex's face, instead. "I don't make a dare unless I'm willing to back it up."

He licked his lips, then grinned. "Bacon," he murmured. Reaching out, he snatched a piece from her plate. "Maybe I'm hungrier than I thought."

5

ALEX CURLED INTO Tenley's naked body, pulling her against him and tucking her backside into his lap. He usually didn't spend a lot of time outdoors during the winter. But since he'd come to Door County, he'd realized just how delicious it felt to spend the day outside in the cold and the evening getting warm in bed.

Though this had begun as a business trip, it was slowly transforming into one of the best vacations he'd ever had. Previous vacations had always been solitary escapes, a time to get away from his social life and focus on himself. But his time with Tenley was making him question why he hadn't enjoyed those holidays in the company of a woman.

Perhaps because he didn't really know any women who shared his interests. The girls he dated weren't really interested in hiking the mountains or rafting river rapids. But Tenley had probably experienced more of those things than he had. "Are you awake?" he whispered.

"Umm. Just barely."

"What do you think of rock climbing?"

"Right now?" she asked.

"No, in general."

"It's difficult to do in the winter," she said. "Cold hands, slippery rocks, big boots. But there are some nice spots around here if you come back in the summer. We could go." She rolled over to face him. Her hands smoothed over his chest and she placed a kiss at the base of his neck. "You should try kayaking. And hiking at Rock Island is fun. But that's all summer stuff. We could snowshoe. Have you ever been snowshoeing? I'll take you tomorrow if you'd like."

"Interesting," he said.

"It is." She sighed, then rolled on top of him, stretching her naked body along the length of his. "And then there's sex. Sex is a year-round thing in Door County." Her lips found his and she gave him a sweet kiss.

Was it possible she was the perfect woman? He'd always imagined his ideal mate to be tall and blonde and eager to please. And though Tenley did excel in the bedroom, she did it on her own terms. There was no question about who was in control. Maybe he'd been looking for the wrong perfect woman.

"Is there anything you wouldn't try?" he asked.

"Scuba diving," she said. "Being underwater scares me. It would be like drowning alive."

Well, there it was. She wasn't perfect. Alex loved scuba diving. "Interesting," he said.

"You know what would be *really* interesting? If you'd get up and make dinner for us."

"Don't you think you're taking this slave-boy thing

a bit too far? Just because I want that contract, doesn't mean you can take advantage of me."

She sat up and clapped her hands, her face lighting up with amusement. "Oh, a slave boy. I've always wanted one of those. I think that's a wonderful idea." Tenley crawled over the covers until she was stretched out alongside him, her head at his feet. She wiggled her toes. "Rub my feet, slave boy."

Alex let his gaze drift along her naked body. Would he ever get enough of her? Though he'd only known her for a few days, he'd come to think of her body as his, as if he were the only one smart enough to see what an incredible woman she was.

Grabbing her foot, he rubbed his thumbs against her arch. "How's that?"

"Oh, that feels so nice."

He pressed his lips to a spot beneath her ankle. "How about that?"

"That's nice, too. But don't stop rubbing."

"So, let me tell you about what we can do for your novel."

"Please don't. I just want to relax. Talking about business makes me nervous."

"Do you plan to fight me on this every step of the way? If this is some plan to drive me crazy so I'll leave, it's not going to work."

"Would sex work?" she asked.

"Sex?"

"Yes. If I seduced you right now, would you be satisfied?"

"I'm always satisfied when you seduce me." Alex picked up her other foot. "What are you afraid of, Tenley? Most artists would jump at the chance to sell their work."

"I don't really know what I'm doing," she said. "I didn't go to art school. I haven't studied writing. I have no technique, no style. I'm afraid if I have to produce something, I'll just…freak out."

"You don't seem like the type to freak out. Besides, some of the greatest writers and artists never went to college. So that excuse doesn't fly. What else?"

"That story was personal. What if I only have one story in me? And now that it's out, there's nothing left."

"No problem. We'll cross that bridge when we come to it. For now, we'll focus on the novel you have written. Anything else?"

"Are you going to work on this book with me?"

"Yes. You'll also have an editor to work with once the contract is signed. But if you want me to stay involved, I will. This imprint is my idea, so I am going to have my fingers in it until it gets up and running."

"So, you and I will be…business associates? And we'll pretend that we've never seen each other naked. And that we've never touched each other in intimate ways."

He chuckled. "That's going to be very difficult to forget."

She sat up, crossing her legs in front of her and resting her arms on her knees. "But how will it work, when I see you? Don't you think it will be strange?"

Alex saw the confusion in her eyes. "Because we've been lovers? I don't know. I guess we're just going to have to make it up as we go along."

To be honest with himself, Alex hadn't really thought about the end of their affair. He wasn't sure why it had to end. The passion they'd shared was real and intense, not something that could be tossed aside without a second thought.

Was Tenley worried she was about to become another notch on his bedpost? Like all those other women who'd registered their complaints on that silly Web site? Sure, he didn't have the best reputation, but where was it written that a guy couldn't change?

"Tenley, I want to get to know you better. I don't want to think this will be over when I go back to Chicago."

A tiny smile twitched at her lips. "Me neither."

"Then let's do it. Let's get to know each other. You start. Ask me any question and I'll answer it. Go ahead."

She regarded him shrewdly. "All right. Do you want to have sex with me all the time, or are there times when you're thinking about something else?"

Alex laughed. This was one instance when he wasn't afraid to be honest. "When you're in the room, I'm pretty much thinking about the next time I'll see you naked. And when you're not close by, I'm thinking about the next time I'll be with you—so I can take off your clothes and see you naked."

"Men think about sex a lot, don't they? Women aren't supposed to think about it."

"Do you?"

"Yes," she said, her voice filled with astonishment. "All the time. When I see you dressed, the first thing I want to do is take your clothes off. I like the way you look. I like your skin and your muscles and your eyes and your hair."

"My turn. Tell me about your favorite fantasy."

Her face softened and her expression grew wistful. "That one is easy. I'm at work and I'm sitting at my desk and the bell above the door rings and there he is. All grown up. He still looks the same, but he's bigger. And it's like it never happened, like he was just gone for a few hours, running errands or having lunch."

He'd expected a sexual fantasy, at least that was what he thought they were talking about. But from the look on her face, he could see the emotional toll the confession was taking. He wanted to stop her, to tell her she misunderstood, yet he was curious to know the truth.

"Your brother?"

She nodded. "I used to have that dream all the time. It would be the only thing that kept the nightmares from becoming unbearable. I'd wake up and I'd be so happy. Sometimes, it was different. I'd be somewhere and I'd see him on the street and I'd run after him. Or I'd be hiking and find him sitting in the woods, all alone."

"What happened, Tenley? How did he die?"

She bit her bottom lip. Her voice wavered when she spoke. "Tommy drowned. In a boating accident," she said. "I'm getting hungry. I think you should fetch us some dinner."

He kissed her gently, satisfied that she'd told him enough for now. "I'm not much of a cook."

"There's a bar in town that makes the best pizza. We can order one and you can go pick it up. And while you're gone, I'll feed the horses and make a fire. Then after supper, we'll take a walk down to the bay."

"That sounds good to me," he said, dropping a kiss on her lips. "And then we'll talk about your book."

"What if I just say 'yes' right now? Then do we have to talk about it tonight?"

"Are you saying yes?" Alex asked.

Tenley nodded. "Yes. Yes, you may publish my silly book, Alex. Yes, I'll sign your contract. As long as we don't have to talk about it for the rest of the night."

Alex held out his hand. "Deal." He paused. "Don't shake unless you mean it. A verbal agreement is legal and binding."

She shook his hand. "Deal. Green olives, green peppers, sausage and mushrooms. And get the eighteen-inch. With extra cheese. And hot peppers on the side."

"Can I get dressed first?" he asked.

Tenley rolled over onto her stomach, her legs crossed at the ankles. "As long as I can watch. But do it really slowly."

He got up and began to retrieve his clothes from where they were scattered on the floor. Tenley followed his movements, a brazen grin on her face. "Stop staring at me," he teased, repeating the words she'd said to him their first night together.

"In the summer, I live without clothes."

"Really?"

"I walk down to the bay and climb down the cliffs and take off all my clothes and lie on the rocks in the sun. Sometimes sailboats go by and see me, but I don't care."

Alex could picture her, walking through the forest like a wood nymph, her long, pale limbs moving gracefully through the lush undergrowth. He'd be back in the summer to see that, making a silent promise to himself.

"Why don't you come with me to this bar? We'll eat there. Maybe have a few drinks. Then we'll come back and I'll help you feed the horses."

"Would this be a date?" Tenley asked.

"Yes," Alex said. "This would be a date."

"Then I accept," she said. She jumped up and ran from the bedroom to the bathroom. "I'll have to make myself pretty."

"No," he said. "I like you just the way you are." There was nothing at all he'd want to change about Tenley. And Alex found that fact quite amazing.

TENLEY GRABBED the pitcher of beer from the bar and walked over to the table she and Alex had chosen. He followed behind her with two empty glasses and a basket of popcorn. Before she sat down, he pulled her chair out for her and Tenley sent him a playful smile.

"Your mother taught you well," she said.

"My great-grandmother," he corrected. "She was from the old country. She learned English by reading Emily Post and she somehow got the idea that all

Americans had to act that way. Usually Greek families are loud and boisterous. We're loud, but unfailingly polite. You should hear our conversation around the table at Easter."

"My parents didn't believe in social conventions. They let us run wild. We were allowed to say and do anything we wanted. As I look back on it, I'm not sure that was good. It's cute in children, but people think it's weird in adults."

"I think you turned out just fine," Alex said.

Tenley loved the little compliments he paid her. She'd often thought a good boyfriend would work hard to make her happy. And Alex seemed to do that naturally, as if his only thought was to please her. "Do you have a girlfriend?" she asked.

The words just popped out of her mouth and an instant later, she wanted to take the question back. Yet her curiosity overwhelmed her. How could a guy like Alex be single? He was smart and funny and gorgeous. And there were a lot of women in Chicago who would consider him a great catch.

"No," he replied. "I don't really get into long-term relationships. I date a lot of different women, but no one seriously."

"I see," Tenley said. Though it was exactly what she wanted to hear—he was unattached—she wasn't sure she liked the fact that he dated "a lot" of women. Was she just the latest of many? "But do you sleep with them?"

"On occasion," he said in a measured tone. "What about you?"

"I don't sleep with women, especially women who've dated you. Although there was a rumor going around town that I preferred girls."

"Do you?" Alex asked.

"I started the rumor. I got tired of every single man in town asking me out. I don't think there's anything wrong with liking girls. You love who you love. I guess if you're lucky enough to find that, it shouldn't make a difference."

"I guess not," Alex said. "I've been thinking that I might be missing out. Maybe I should try the whole relationship thing. See how it goes."

"I wouldn't be any good at that," Tenley said. "I have too much baggage. Everyone says so. They say my last name should be Samsonite."

Alex laughed, but Tenley had never found the comment particularly funny. She couldn't help how she felt. Putting on a sunny face and pretending she was happy seemed like a waste of energy.

But this was the first time she'd been out in ages, and she was with a man she found endlessly intriguing. And tonight, they'd go home and crawl into her bed and make love. Tenley had to admit, for the first time in a long time, she was genuinely happy.

"Who is that guy over there?" Alex asked, pointing toward the bar. "He's giving me the evil eye."

Tenley glanced over her shoulder, then moaned. "Oh, that's Randy. He's in love with me."

"Really?" Alex's eyebrow shot up. "He doesn't seem like your type."

"He thinks he's in love with me," Tenley corrected. "He's had a crush on me since high school and every year about this time, he asks me out to the Valentine's Day dance at the firehouse. And every year, I say no."

"You'd think he'd get the message," Alex said.

"He's kind of thick-headed," Tenley explained. She looked at Randy again, then quickly turned around. "He's coming over here. Maybe we should leave."

"No!" Alex said. "We have just as much right to be here as he does. Besides, I'm hungry and they haven't brought our pizza yet."

"Hello, Tenley."

She forced a smile as she looked up. He really wasn't such a bad guy. Except for the fact that he was in love with her. "Hello, Randy."

He shifted nervously, back and forth on his feet. "How have you been doing? I haven't seen you in a while. I heard you had breakfast at the Bean this morning. I thought you didn't like that place."

"News travels fast." Randy had probably heard about the kiss as well, but Tenley wasn't going to get into that. "Randy, this is Alex Stamos. Alex, Randy Schmitt."

Alex got to his feet and held out his hand, but Randy refused to take it, turning his attention back to Tenley. "Can I talk to you for a second?"

"Randy, I'm not sure that—"

"Just for a second. Over there." He pointed to the far end of the bar.

Tenley looked at Alex and he shrugged. "All right." She pushed back in her chair and stood. "Just for a second."

Randy held on to her elbow as they wove through the patrons at the restaurant. Tenley was aware of the gazes that followed them and she knew what they were thinking. It was the opinion of most of the folks in town that Randy was just about the only man who'd be interested in marrying Tenley Marshall. Though Tenley had never given him any encouragement, he persisted with his belief that they were destined to be together.

In truth, Tenley felt a bit sorry for Randy. It must be horrible to love someone who couldn't love you back. She'd made sure to harden her heart against love, but Randy wore his on his sleeve.

"What are you doing with that guy?"

"It's not what you think," she said. "He's just a friend."

"A friend you kiss at the breakfast table. And rumor has it that he spent the night out at your place. Jesse said he pulled the guy's car out of the ditch after you took him home. Now, I can understand that a girl like you might be attracted to a big-city guy like him, but he's all wrong for you, Tenley. He won't make you happy the way I will."

"Randy, you have to give this up. I don't love you. I'm not going to suddenly change my mind one day and marry you. You need to find someone else."

"I know those flatlanders," he said. "They flash around their money and think they can take whatever they want."

His attitude wasn't uncommon. Though the locals appreciated the money that tourists brought in, they didn't like them encroaching on their territory—especially their women.

"Randy, I'm going to go back and sit down. I suggest you finish your beer and go home."

"Hell, no! I've been waiting around for you all these years, thinking that sooner or later, you'd get your act together and see what's standing right in front of you. I'm the one who loves you, not him. He'll go back to Chicago and I'll be here. You'll see."

"But I don't love you," Tenley insisted. "I'm sorry." Frustrated, she turned to walk away. But Randy grabbed her arm and wouldn't let go.

"If you'd just give us a chance, I know I could—"

"Hey, buddy, let her go."

Tenley closed her eyes at the sound of Alex's voice. One moment, he'd been watching them from the table and the next, he was behind her. "I knew we should have had pizza at home," she muttered.

Alex grabbed Randy's wrist. "I mean it. Let her go."

"Get the hell out of here," Randy snarled. "You can't tell me what to do. I'm not your goddamned buddy, buddy."

"I will tell you what to do when you're making an ass out of yourself. She's not interested. Didn't you hear her?"

The next few seconds passed in a blur. Randy slapped at Alex's hand and accidentally hit Tenley in the head. Alex shoved Randy, Randy took a swing at Alex, and Tenley reacted. Without thinking, she drew back her fist and hit Randy squarely in the nose.

Blood erupted from his left nostril as he stumbled

back and knocked down a waitress with a tray full of drinks. "I'm sorry, I'm sorry," Tenley cried. "I didn't mean to do that." She held on to Alex to keep him from jumping on top of Randy, yet at the same time tried to help Randy to his feet.

"Tenley Marshall, I'm going to have to take you in." Harvey Willis stepped into the middle of the fight, his considerable girth creating a wall between Alex and Randy. The police chief's napkin was still stuffed in his collar and he was holding his fork in his right hand.

"This was not her fault," Alex protested. "She was just defending herself."

"You pipe down or I'll take you in, too. She wasn't defending herself, she was defending you. Now, I can understand how that might piss Randy off, seeing as how you're not from around here. But punching a guy in the face is assault. And doing it in a restaurant full of people is just bad manners."

"I don't want to press charges," Randy said, holding his flannel shirt up to his nose.

"Well, we'll sort that out down at the station. Tenley, you'll come with me. Your flatlander friend can follow us. Randy, you can walk off the pitcher of beer you drank. The exercise will do you good. Let's go." He nodded to the bartender. "They'll be back later to settle up, Bert. And pack up my pizza for me. I'll send Leroy back to get it."

Tenley struggled into her jacket as she walked out the front door. Harvey's cruiser was parked out front in a No Parking zone. "You can get in front," he said. "I don't think you're going to try any funny business, are you?"

"No," Tenley said. "I don't know why you're blaming me for this. You saw Randy start it. He just won't give up."

When they were both in the car, Harvey turned to her and shook his finger. "Tenley Marshall, you know how that man feels about you. Still, you decide to parade your out-of-state boyfriend in front of him and the whole town. How do you think he's supposed to react?"

"Alex Stamos is not my boyfriend. And I've made it perfectly clear to Randy that I don't have feelings for him. *And,* this is the big one, I didn't realize Randy was there. Had I known, we would have gone somewhere else."

"Well, since this Alex fella has come to town, people have been worried for you. You're not acting the way you usually do."

Tenley's temper flared. "Maybe if everyone would just mind their own business, I could get on with my life."

"Is that what you've been doing? I just think it's a little funny you've been hiding away like a hermit for years and then he rolls into town and you're suddenly a social butterfly. He seems to be the slick sort and you're falling for his tricks."

"Let's go," she muttered. "I'd really like to take care of this before it causes any more gossip."

"Oh, well, I think that horse is out of the barn already," Harvey replied.

They drove the three short blocks to the police station and by the time Tenley got out of the car, Alex was standing at the door, waiting for her, pacing back and forth. "Is she going to need a lawyer?" he asked. "Because if you're going to charge her with anything, then I want to get her a lawyer."

"Oh, just pipe down," Harvey said. "We're going to fill out a report, she's going to pay a fine and then you'll be on your way. We don't tolerate physical violence here, unlike what goes on in the big cities."

"He's the one who grabbed her first. She was trying to get away when I stepped in. And then he took a swing at me."

"I know. I saw the whole thing. So did half the town. But Tenley drew blood, so she's going to have to pay the fine."

As they walked into the lobby, Tenley turned to Alex. "Wait here. I'll be out in a few minutes. And don't start things up again with Randy. He's drunk and he has at least fifty pounds on you. Besides, Harvey treats outsiders a lot more harshly than townies."

True to Harvey's word, the matter was dispatched by filling out a short report and paying a small fine. Since Tenley didn't have fifty dollars in her wallet, Harvey agreed to let her come in the following morning with the money.

By the time they finished, Randy had arrived and was sitting glumly in the reception area across from Alex, staring at him with a sulky expression. Harvey motioned to him and he approached Tenley with a contrite smile. "I don't want to press charges," he insisted.

"Randy, my boy, you need to move on with your life," Harvey said. "Tenley's not interested. There's nothing more pathetic than a guy who won't take no for an answer. You bother her again and I'll toss your ass in jail. By the way, Linda Purnell has been in love with you for going on three years. If I were you, I'd give her a second look." He paused, then directed his gaze at Alex. "As for you, I'm going to be watching you. You keep your nose clean and you and me won't have any problems."

Alex stood and held out his hand to Tenley. "Thank you. We'll just be going now."

When they got outside, Alex dragged her toward his rented SUV. "What the hell was that?"

Tenley laughed. "Next time, when I suggest pizza at home, maybe we should just stay home and forget all this dating stuff."

"No," Alex said stubbornly. "Tomorrow night, we're going on a damn date. And you're going to wear a pretty dress and I'm going to take you to a nice restaurant, and we're going to have a pleasant evening that doesn't involve jealous ex-boyfriends and bloody noses."

"He was not my boyfriend," Tenley insisted.

Alex yanked open the passenger-side door. "Well, I *am* your boyfriend, and if we have to drive to Green Bay to get some privacy, we will."

ALEX STARED OUT the window of the tower studio, taking in the view of the bay beyond the trees. Tenley was seated at the drawing table, a pad of paper in front of her. "All right," she said. "I'm ready. Fire away."

"This isn't supposed to be painful," Alex said. "We're working together on this. To make your novel better."

"Why don't you just give me the list and I'll look it over and we can discuss it later."

"Because I want you to understand what we need before you sign the contract. So there are no misunderstandings."

"Take off your shirt," she said.

Alex cursed beneath his breath. "I'm not going to let you change the subject again, Tenley. Whenever you don't want to do something, you try to seduce me."

"I'm not going to seduce you, I want to try drawing you. So take off your shirt. And the rest of your clothes while you're at it."

"Tenley, this isn't going to get you—"

"Slave boy, you're not listening. I feel the need to draw you and you're supposed to do everything in your power to please me."

This was getting to be a pattern with the two of them, although Alex really couldn't be too upset. What man would grow impatient with a woman who wanted sex as much as he did? They did have the entire day to work on her novel. He could give her an hour or two of forced nudity as long as it was followed by more pleasurable activities.

"First of all, we need to have an understanding," he said. "This can't end up like one of those sex videos that everyone gets to see. This is for your own private viewing pleasure. Agreed? This will not end up on the Internet."

Hell, he'd had enough trouble from scorned girl-friends. Adding naked drawings to the mix would probably send his mother right over the edge.

"I won't even give you a face. Unless people recognize other parts of you, you'll be completely anonymous."

Reluctantly, Alex stripped out of his clothes, then stood and waited while Tenley gathered the things she needed. When she was ready, she took a deep breath. "All right. Turn around and brace your hands against that post. And lean into it."

He did as she ordered. With his back to her, all he could hear was the occasional rustle of paper and a few soft curses from Tenley. His arms were beginning to grow stiff and his shoulders tight when she finally spoke again.

"There. I think I'm done."

He turned around and she held up the sketchpad. Though Alex didn't know a lot about art, he knew the drawing was beautifully rendered, every muscle perfectly shaded. "Wow."

"You're hot," she said. "I'm not sure I got your butt right. But it's a decent first attempt."

"Tenley, it's better than decent. It's very good."

"You really think so?" She stared at the sketch. "You know, I've been thinking maybe I should take some classes. The university in Green Bay has an art program."

With any other woman, he might have turned on the charm and lavished compliments to soothe her insecurities. But as he grew to care about Tenley, Alex realized that they needed to have honesty between them.

"There are great art schools in Chicago, too," he said. "And you're good enough to get into a top-notch program, Tenley. Sure, you haven't had a lot of experience, but you do have talent."

"I couldn't move," she said distractedly, her attention still focused on her sketch. "My grandfather is here. He needs my help. Besides, I have my cabin and my animals. I couldn't bring them to Chicago."

Though Alex had considered what the future might hold for them, he'd never really appreciated her ties to this place. She was living in a paradise and he couldn't blame her for not wanting to leave. He'd only spent a few days here and he didn't want to leave either. What was Chicago compared to the beauty of this place?

"They have seminars at the Art Institute. You could come for a few days. Meet everyone at the office. Maybe do some publicity shots. You could stay with me."

"I want to try another pose," she said, changing the subject. "Turn to the side and lean back against the post." She stared at him for a long moment. "Put your right leg forward a bit and then hold on to the post with your left hand."

For the next hour, she sketched, posing him in different positions and then quickly completing the drawing. She tossed aside the pencil for charcoal and then switched to pastels.

"All right," she finally said. "You can get dressed."

"You're finished?"

Tenley stared at the drawings scattered across her table. "I think I can do this," she said breathlessly. "I'm not as bad as I thought I was."

"You're sure you want me to get dressed?"

Tenley grinned. "Yes. Well, only if you want to. If you prefer to work like that, then you can stay naked."

"We're going to work now?"

"Yes," she said in a gloomy voice. "You're going to tell me what's wrong with my novel and I'm going to try to fix it." She jumped up. "You do need to get dressed. It's too distracting having you sitting around here naked." She walked over to him and smoothed her hand from his belly to his cock.

Alex groaned as he closed his eyes, waiting for the involuntary reaction that came from her touch. Though he wanted nothing more than to make love to her, he had a choice to make. She was willing to talk business now. So sex would have to wait until later.

Turning away from her touch, Alex pulled on his boxers and jeans and then slipped into his shirt, not bothering to button it. "All right. The first thing, and this is going to be big—we're going to have to redraw everything. Your friend has the original, but even that is a little too rough. We're going to print at a high resolution, so everything has to be very clean."

"That's going to take a long time. I'd have to draw it oversized in order to get it just perfect."

"No, we'll scan it into a computer and have our graphic artist clean it up. But there are some parts that will need additional drawings and changes to the story."

Tenley took a deep breath. "Why don't we start with those changes first?"

Alex pulled up a stool and sat down next to her. He grabbed her hand. He pressed a kiss to the back of her wrist. This was actually going to happen. Tenley was going to sell her book to him and he was going to make her famous. He was also going to make her a lot of money. But it wasn't that thought that thrilled him. It was the fact that he and Tenley would always have a connection.

Over the next two hours, they worked together, going over the editor's notes, discussing the production process, arguing about the plot and drawings needed to flesh out the story.

For the first time since Alex arrived, he saw Tenley excited about the possibility of her novel being published. And he was grateful he was the one to make it happen. It was so easy to make her happy. It didn't require a huge bank account or a fancy apartment or the promise of a comfortable life or social status, things the other women he knew were always searching for.

Tenley responded to kindness and encouragement. Something terrible must have happened to make her so unsure of herself, Alex mused. Though he only knew the barest details of her brother's death, he was determined to learn more.

He wanted to know every tiny detail of her life, everything that made her the woman she was. He wanted to be the man who understood her the best. He wanted to be the man she turned to when she felt frightened or overwhelmed or lonely.

Making himself indispensable to Tenley Marshall was a huge task. But Alex was afraid of the consequences if he didn't. For it was becoming more and more evident that Tenley needed to be a permanent part of his life.

6

TENLEY RUBBED her eyes, then pinched them shut. She knew she ought to just set the work aside and get some sleep, but every time she closed her eyes, doubts began to plague her.

It was simple to feel good about herself when Alex was standing behind her, cheering her on. But without him, all her insecurities rushed back. How would she ever do this on her own? Nothing she drew would ever be good enough. She'd always find fault.

Tossing the drawing pad on the floor, she flopped back into the leather sofa. This was entirely his fault. Until she'd taken him home during the storm, she'd been perfectly happy with her life. She found her work at her grandfather's gallery satisfying and her free time was spent in relaxing pursuits, not frantically trying to make something out of nothing.

Grabbing the throw from the back of the sofa, she lay down and tucked it up around her chin, staring at the dying embers of the fire. She felt caught in a familiar dream. Tommy was on the phone and he was trying to tell her where he was. She'd scribbled down the directions, but they'd be wrong, so she'd start, again and again and again, never getting it quite right.

Her heart would begin to race and her hands would sweat as she became more and more frantic. Finally, faced with her ineptitude, he'd hang up. She felt tears press at the corners of her eyes. Would she ever be able to let go of what had happened? Somehow, Tenley knew her guilt over her brother's death was holding her back. She couldn't change the past, but was she strong enough to change her future?

Alex had put his trust and faith in her abilities as an artist and a writer. He claimed she had a real talent. Tenley had heard those words a million times from her parents and from her grandparents, but she'd never believed them. They were merely trying to make her whole again.

But Alex was a stranger, someone who didn't know about her past. He could be objective. She pushed up on her elbow and stared at the crumpled paper scattered on the floor. She'd just have to try again.

"Tenley?"

She sat up and watched as Alex wandered through the kitchen and into the great room. "I'm here."

"What time is it? What are you doing up?"

"I was just working. Trying to figure out these new scenes for my story."

He stood in front of her, his naked body gleaming in the soft light from the fire. He ran his hand through his hair, then sighed. "Is everything all right?"

"Sure," she said. Tenley felt emotion well up in her throat, but she swallowed it back. "Everything is fine."

He sat down beside her, slipping his arm around her shoulders. "Sweetheart, don't worry about this. I don't expect you to finish it in one night. Or one month. You can take your time. I'll wait."

A tear slipped from the corner of her eye and she quickly brushed it away before he could see. But from his worried expression, Tenley could tell she hadn't been quick enough. "Sorry," she said, shaking her head. "I'm just exhausted."

"Talk to me."

"It's nothing. I'm just having a little meltdown. I'm tired and cranky and frustrated."

"Go ahead," he said. "You can melt in front of me if you want."

Another tear slipped from her eye, but this time she let it run down her cheek. "Really?"

He nodded, then pulled her closer. Tenley sobbed as the tears suddenly broke through her defenses. Nuzzling her face into his naked chest, she let them fall, the emotion draining out of her with each ragged breath.

For Alex's part, he simply sat beside her, smoothing his hand over her hair and whispering soft words against her temple. She clung to him as tightly as she could, as if his presence would somehow save her from her feelings. Then, slowly, the sadness dissolved, replaced by relief and resignation. She'd allowed her emotions to overwhelm her and she'd survived.

"Better?" he asked.

Tenley nodded. "God, I feel like such a dope. Look at this mess. I couldn't sleep and I just worked myself into a panic." She pressed her hand against his chest and looked up into his eyes. "I don't know why you like me. I'm a mess."

"You're not a mess," he said.

"I've made so many mistakes in my life, Alex. I let so much slip away. I should have listened to my parents. I should have gone to college. I should have studied art. Everything would have been different."

"But maybe not better," Alex said.

"What do you mean?"

"That story you wrote came from your life as it was, from the pain you felt at the time. If you'd done things differently, that story might never have come out."

She sniffled, brushing at her damp cheeks. "I don't know. I tried to be strong, but it was so much easier to just avoid thinking about it. I didn't want to make my parents happy, I didn't want to plan for my future. I just wanted to grieve. And I did, in the only way I knew how."

"That was the right thing for you to do, Tenley. You have to let these things take their natural course. You can't be something you aren't."

"My life should have begun when I graduated from high school or college. But it feels like it's beginning now. And that scares me. I'm twenty-six years old."

"It doesn't scare me. You can hold on to me as long as you need to."

"You're a really nice guy," she murmured, pressing a kiss to his chest. "Did anyone ever tell you that?"

"No. I think you're the first."

Tenley laughed. "Really?"

"You're the only one that matters," he said in a quiet voice. Alex took her hand and pressed a kiss to her palm. "Come on. Leave this for later and come back to bed."

Tenley shook her head. She'd only lie awake and stare at the ceiling until dawn. She needed something to occupy her mind. "I won't be able to sleep."

"I know what will relax you," he said. Alex stood and pulled her to her feet. "A nice, hot bath."

"You're going to give me a bath?"

"Well, I thought we'd give each other a bath. Then we'd go back to bed and sleep until we couldn't sleep anymore."

Intrigued by the suggestion, Tenley followed him to the bathroom and sat on the toilet seat as he filled the old claw-foot tub. She fetched her shampoo and soap from the shower stall and grabbed a washcloth from the rack on the wall.

When the tub was full, Alex undressed her, pulling her T-shirt off over her head and skimming her pajama bottoms to the floor. He held her hand as she stepped over the edge and slowly settled herself.

Then she leaned forward and held out her hand. "There's room for you, too."

Alex stepped in behind her, her body tucked neatly between his thighs. She leaned back against his chest and closed her eyes. "This is perfect."

"Yeah, it is," he said. "I need to get a bathtub at my apartment. A big one, just like this."

"Tell me about your place," she said.

"I live in a two-flat in Wicker Park," he said. "I have the second and third floor and I have tenants who live downstairs. It's an old house, built at the turn of the century. But I've renovated it inside. It's comfortable, but it's not as nice as this." He ran his hands through her hair. "This is like a home. It's warm and cozy. I like it here."

"When do you have to go back?" she asked.

"I was supposed to leave for a vacation in Mexico on Wednesday, but I missed my flight. I was planning to be gone through Monday, so I guess I'd have to leave Monday night?"

"That gives us four more days," she said.

"And three more nights," he said. "Doesn't seem like a long time, does it?"

"I'm sorry you had to miss your vacation," Tenley said.

"I'm not. This is the best vacation I've ever had."

She turned over, pressing her palms to his chest as she looked into his eyes. When she'd first met Alex, he'd been so charming, it had been difficult to believe anything he said. But now, as she lay in his arms, Tenley saw the real man beneath the charm, the sweet, considerate, affectionate guy that every girl wanted.

"I could fall asleep in this tub."

"Don't do that. You'd wake up all wrinkled." He scooped water into his hands and poured it over her hair, smoothing the damp strands away from her face. "There. I like you just like this."

"How is that?"

"With your hair out of your face, so I can see your

pretty blue eyes and your perfect nose." He bent closer and kissed her, tracing the shape of her mouth with his tongue. "And your lips."

"Do you realize that we've only known each other for just over three days?" Tenley asked.

"No, it's been longer than that," he said.

"Monday night. It's Friday morning."

He seemed stunned by the revelation. "That's... amazing." Alex drew in a sharp breath, then grabbed her hips. "Sit up. I'll wash your hair."

Tenley chuckled. "Slave boy has returned."

"Your wish is my command," he said, grabbing the bottle from the floor next to the tub. He tipped her head back and rubbed a small amount of the shampoo into her hair. "I think I need to get some of this. So when I'm back home, I can smell it and think of you."

It was difficult to imagine what her life would be like once he left. He'd changed everything for her. He'd carved out a place in her world and he fit perfectly. She had four days and three nights to prepare herself—to convince herself she could live without him.

It would be difficult to do when every moment they spent together seemed to be more perfect than the last. But Alex had taught her one thing. She was a lot stronger than she'd thought she was.

ALEX PUSHED OPEN the front door of The Coffee Bean and scanned the crowd inside, looking for Tenley's grandfather. He'd stopped by the gallery, only to find a note on the door indicating that Tom had gone to breakfast. Alex didn't know Sawyer Bay well, but he knew the best place for breakfast was The Coffee Bean.

Tom was sitting at a table with Harvey Willis, the two of them in deep discussion. Alex hesitated before he approached, knowing that the town police chief didn't have a high opinion of him.

"Morning," Alex said.

Harvey grinned. "Well, there he is. Were your ears burning? You've been the subject of some wild speculation 'round town."

"I'm sure I have," Alex replied.

Harvey got to his feet and indicated his empty chair. "Have a seat. It's all warmed up for you. Tom, nice talking to you. Thanks for the donation. Your pictures always bring a pretty penny in our raffle."

"Thanks, Harvey. I'll talk to you later."

Alex rested his hands on the back of the chair. "Mind if I sit?" he asked.

"Not at all. I've been expecting a visit from you. Would you like some coffee?" He twisted in his chair. "Audrey, bring us another cup of coffee, would you?"

The waitress nodded, then hurried over with a full pot and another menu. "What can I get you?"

Alex scanned the choices, then pointed to the Lumberjack Breakfast. It was what Tenley had ordered the last time they dined at The Coffee Bean. He was beginning to understand her point. After the previous night's activities in her bed, he was ravenous.

"So, I suppose you're here to discuss Tenley," Tom

said. "You're worried she might not want to go through with this?"

Alex shook his head. "No. She's agreed to the contract. We're going to publish her novel."

Tom grinned and clapped his hands. "I knew it. I knew something was going on with her."

"Going on?"

"Tenley has had a very hard time of it these past years. Lots of sadness in her life."

"Tell me about that," Alex said. "I know her brother died, that he drowned. And that it made her shut herself off to everyone around her. But that's all I know."

Tenley's grandfather took a slow slip of his coffee. "I'm not going to tell you anything. If Tenley wants you to know, she'll tell you. And if she does talk about it, then I think she's really ready to move on." He sighed. "If you feel a need to know, anyone in town can fill you in. Or you can read about it in the old newspapers at the library. May 15, 1999. That's when it happened." He paused. "But if I were you, I'd want to know her side of the story first. If she trusts you enough to tell you, then I think you might be the kind of man she needs in her life."

"I think I want to be that man," Alex said. "But I'm a little worried. I've gotten to know Tenley—her feelings can shift in the blink of an eye."

"Are you in love with her, Alex?"

He was surprised by the direct question. But then, it was clear where Tenley had gotten her plainspoken curiosity. "I don't know," he admitted. "I've never been in love before. I'm not quite sure how it's supposed to feel."

"I'd appreciate it if you'd be very careful with her heart. It was broken once and I'm not sure she'll be able to survive having it broken again."

"I won't hurt her," Alex said. "I can promise you that. But I can't guarantee she won't break my heart."

"She's a piece of work, isn't she?" Tom chuckled. "Oh, you should have seen the two of them. They were a pair. When they were born, their parents put them in separate cribs and they screamed until they were together again. After that, Tenley and Tommy were inseparable. When they started to talk, their words were gibberish to everybody else. They had their own language. No one understood it except the two of them." He reached into his back pocket and pulled out his wallet. "See. There they are. This was their tenth birthday."

Alex examined the photo. Tenley hadn't changed much. The dark hair and the pale blue eyes, the delicate limbs. "She was cute."

"After Tommy died, my son and his wife couldn't handle the grief. They grew apart, separated, and then decided to divorce. Tenley was uncontrollable, angry, lashing out at anyone who tried to get close. They ended up leaving, but she just flat-out refused. So she lived with her grandmother and me. I thought it was good she wanted to get back to her normal life, but that's not what happened. A few years later, I found out the reason she stayed was because she thought he might come back.

That the body they found wasn't really his and that he was alive."

"She's been waiting all this time?"

"She has. But I think she's stopped waiting for Tommy. I think maybe she's been waiting for you. Or someone like you. Someone she could trust. Someone who could give her the same confidence that her brother gave her. I think you've done that for her, Alex. And no matter what happens between the two of you, you need to respect that."

Alex had always shied away from commitment in the past, but this time, he wanted to make all the promises necessary to ensure Tenley's happiness. "I care about her. But if publishing this novel is going to hurt her in some way, I'll turn around and go back to Chicago today."

"No," Tom said. "I think you might be the best thing that's ever happened to her."

Alex smiled. "She's a very talented artist. And an incredible storyteller. I just want readers to see that."

"She and her brother used to draw cartoons all the time. After he died, she just stopped drawing. This is a big step for her. Don't do anything to mess it up, all right?"

"You can trust me," Alex said.

Tom's eyebrow arched up and he fixed Alex with a shrewd stare. "Can I? Will you stick with her, even when she's trying her damnedest to push you away? Because she will, you know. She'll find some excuse to run away and do everything to make you hate her."

"I think I can deal with that," he said, frowning. "I've used that technique myself on occasion." How many women had he charmed then ignored when he grew bored with the relationship? Except for the motivations, what Tenley did wasn't much different.

"You're taking on trouble," Tom warned. "But I'd venture to say the reward will be well worth the battle." He held up his coffee cup in a mock toast. "I wish you luck, young man."

They passed the rest of their time discussing Tenley's novel and what kind of opportunities publication would offer her. Alex was glad for Tom's insight into Tenley's behavior. Though there were moments when he thought he knew her well, he realized she was like a puzzle. Each individual piece was simple to understand, but it was how the pieces fit together that complicated matters.

When they were finished, Tom paid the bill, then invited Alex back to his studio, anxious to show him photos of Tenley's childhood. But Alex begged off. Tenley had closed herself in the studio at the house, determined to work on her new drawings. And Alex was anxious to see her progress.

But before he went back, he had to pick up his new phone from the Harbor Inn, call the office, then check out of his room at the bed-and-breakfast and move his things to Tenley's cabin. He and Tenley would spend the rest of his vacation together.

He walked back to the inn, where he'd parked the rental, then decided to surrender to his curiosity. He'd

seen a sign on Main Street for the local library. It was
past ten, so it would probably be open.

As he drove through the snow-covered streets, Alex
wondered if it might be best just to let it go. Would it
make a difference knowing the whole truth about
Tenley's past? It might help him understand her insecurities a little better. And it could explain why it took
her all these years to work through her grief.

He parked the SUV in an empty spot on the street
and walked the short distance to the library, a small
building that looked like it might have once been a
bank. A young woman, not much older than Tenley,
greeted him from the circulation desk.

"I'm interested in looking at some old newspapers,"
he said. "From this town, if possible. Back about ten
years ago."

"That would be the Sawyer Bay Clarion," she said.
"They stopped publishing it two years ago, but back
issues can be found in the periodical section. If you
want one from any further back than fifteen years, I'll
have to go down to the basement and fetch them."

"Thanks," Alex said. He wandered to the back of the
building and found the huge books on a shelf near a big
library table. May 15th, 1999. He laid the book on the
table and flipped through the yellowed pages. The paper
was a weekly, so he found the article in the issue dated
May 19th.

The headline was huge. LOCAL BOY DROWNS IN
BOATING ACCIDENT. The words sent a shiver
through him. Tenley had lived through this tragedy. As

his gaze skimmed the story, he was stunned to learn that she'd nearly died as well. She'd been clinging to the overturned sailboat for four hours before she'd been found. Her brother hadn't been so lucky.

"It was a tragedy."

Alex glanced over his shoulder to find the librarian standing behind him. "I guess you found what you came for."

"Yes. Did you know them?"

"I went to high school with them both. They were a few grades younger than me, but everyone knows everyone in this town. I think it was the most tragic thing that ever happened in this community. Everyone loved them so much."

"I can't imagine what she went though. But why would they have gone out in bad weather?"

"They were always doing crazy things," she said. "Always getting in trouble. Some folks said it was bound to happen, one of them getting hurt. It's the way they were raised. No one ever said no. There was no discipline. Children need boundaries."

"She blames herself," he said.

"I heard she was the one who talked her brother into going outside the harbor. They were always challenging each other. Dares and double dares and triple dares. Everything was game to them." The librarian shook her head. "She never forgave herself. That's why she's… different."

He slammed the book closed. "I like different," Alex said in a cool tone. He nodded at the librarian and headed back toward the door. "And you can tell everyone in town, if they're wondering."

As he walked back to his SUV, he thought about what it must have been like for Tenley. He was close to his two sisters and couldn't imagine how he'd feel if anything ever happened to one of them. It would be like a part of his soul had been cut away. Not only had Tenley lost her twin brother, she'd probably blamed herself for the breakup of her parents' marriage.

Suddenly, the burden of her happiness seemed like too much to bear. What if he couldn't be the man she needed? What if he failed her in the end? This was all moving so fast. Alex wasn't sure he was ready for it to go any further.

Maybe he shouldn't have pried into the past. It might have been better to remain comfortably oblivious. He got behind the wheel, then turned the key in the ignition. Alex wasn't sure what the future held for the two of them. But if this was love, then he sure as hell was going to give it a chance.

"HAVE YOU SEEN Alex?" Tenley distractedly flipped through the mail, separating the envelopes into bills to be paid and checks to be cashed.

"I did," her grandfather said. "We had breakfast this morning at The Coffee Bean. Had a nice chat. Although I've never seen anyone eat as much for breakfast as he did. Except for you."

Tenley smiled. "I think I'm going to take him snow-shoeing tonight. I love the woods after dark."

"Maybe he's over at the inn."

"He said he had to check in with his office. I hope nothing's wrong." She paused. "You don't think he had to go home, do you?"

"Without telling you? I don't think he'd do that."

"But what if there was an emergency? He could have tried calling me at home and I wasn't there."

"Then he would have called here. Or stopped before he left town. Don't worry, Tennie, he's not going to disappear."

The bell above the door rang and she smiled. "That's probably him. I'm just going to drop these at the post office and then I'm going. I promise I'll finish all this up next week."

"We're not exactly going crazy with customers these days," her grandfather said. "Maybe you should think about taking a week or two off. A trip to Chicago might be nice. There's a new impressionist exhibit at the Art Institute."

"I was going to drive into Green Bay. I'm thinking about enrolling in some classes this summer."

"I think that's a fine idea, Tennie. They've been trying to get me to come in and teach a class in acrylics. We could drive in together."

She gave her grandfather a quick kiss, then hurried out into the showroom, anxious to see Alex. But when she walked through the door, it was Randy who was waiting for her. Tenley stopped short. "What are you doing here?"

He gave her a sheepish shrug. "I came to apologize for the other night."

"You don't need to apologize."

"I do," Randy said. "And I'm sorry for being such a pest. But I've loved you for as long as I can remember. I've never said that to you and right now, I'm pretty sure it won't make any difference, but I had to say it."

"I'm sorry," Tenley said, shaking her head. "I don't feel the same way."

"And you may hate me for this, but I don't care." He held out a manila envelope. When she refused to take it, he set it on a nearby table. "I think you should know about this guy from Chicago. I did a little research on the Internet and he's not everything you think he is."

"Take it back," Tenley demanded, a defensive edge in her voice. "I don't need to see it." Cursing softly, she crossed the room and picked up the envelope, then shoved it at Randy. But he refused to touch it. Tenley ripped it in half and then in half again. "Go," she ordered. "Before I punch you in the nose again."

Randy slipped out the door and Tenley glanced down at the scraps in her hands. Her fingers were trembling and she wanted to scream. What right did he have to interfere in her life? People in this town spent too much time worrying about others. They ought to spend more time worrying about their own lives.

"Wasn't that Alex?"

Tenley spun around, her heart skipping a beat. "No."

"A customer."

"It was just Randy Schmitt. He wanted to drop something off for me." She held up the scraps. "It wasn't important." Tenley shoved the papers into her jacket pocket, then picked up the mail that she'd dropped on the floor. "I'll see you later. If Alex stops in, tell him I went home."

Tenley hurried out the door, anxious to leave all thoughts of her encounter with Randy behind. As she strode up the sidewalk to the post office, she passed several people she knew. They smiled and said hello and Tenley returned the greeting.

Usually people avoided her gaze, knowing she wouldn't respond. But things had changed over the past few days. Whatever they thought was going on between her and Alex suddenly made her "normal" again.

The odd thing was, she felt normal. She wanted to smile, even though she was still furious with Randy. In truth, lately, she found herself smiling for no reason at all. She picked up her pace as she walked and the next person she passed, Tenley made it a point to say hello first.

When she got to the post office, she made polite conversation with the postmaster and when she walked out, she held the door open for Mrs. Newton, the English teacher at the high school.

By the time she got back to her Jeep, parked beside the gallery, Tenley felt as if she'd accomplished something important. Though Sawyer Bay could be a difficult place to live, it also had its advantages.

She reached in her jacket pocket for her keys, but found the scraps of Randy's envelope instead. She pulled them out and searched for a trash can that wasn't covered with snow. In the end, she got in her car and set them on the seat beside her.

But her curiosity got the best of her. What had Randy found that warranted a personal visit and a plain manila envelope? All manner of possibilities came to mind. Alex Stamos was a criminal, a happily married man, a porn star.

Well, porn star wouldn't be that difficult to believe considering his prowess in bed. But criminals usually didn't run publishing companies. And she was pretty confident that Alex wasn't married. Maybe he'd been married in the past?

Though that really wouldn't change her feelings for him, she had to wonder why he wouldn't have mentioned it. She picked the papers out of the envelope and spread them out on the seat, piecing them together one by one.

They were pages printed off a Web site called SmoothOperators.com. From what Tenley could see, the pages were a file on Alex. Beneath each screen name was a paragraph describing Alex—most of them in very unflattering terms. As she read through them, Tenley realized that these were written by women Alex had dated—and dumped.

As she flipped through the pages, she was stunned at the sheer number of women who had something to say about him. He appeared to be a serial dater. He was known as "The Charmer," a nickname that appeared on the top of each page alongside his photo.

"'Modus operandi,'" she read. "'The Charmer finds more excitement in the chase than he does in what comes later. After he gets you into bed, it's bye-bye and onto the next girl. He can't seem to settle on just one mate because he feels compelled to make every woman fall in love with him. He'll love you and leave you, all in the same night.'"

This didn't seem like the Alex she knew. But then, did she really know him at all?

"'Stay away from this man,'" she read.

If this was Alex, and the picture proved it was, then perhaps she ought to be more careful. Maybe there wouldn't be a future for them after all. Tenley scanned the photos of the women next to the screen names. Every single one of them looked as if they'd stepped out of the pages of a fashion magazine. If they couldn't capture Alex's heart, what made her think she could?

She closed her eyes and leaned back into the seat. Who was she kidding? She and Alex had enjoyed a vacation fling, an affair that was meant to have a beginning and an end. When she'd found him, she'd been willing to settle for just one night. Now, she'd have almost an entire week.

It would have to be enough. After he left, she'd move on with her life. And if they saw each other again, they could enjoy a night or two in bed—no strings, no regrets. Tenley quickly picked up the scraps and shoved them into the glove compartment.

At least her relationship with Alex proved one thing. She was ready to fall in love. And someday, maybe she'd find a man like him, a man who made her feel like she could do anything and be anyone she wanted to be.

7

THE WOODS WERE SILENT around them. Alex held his breath, listening, waiting for some sound to pierce the night air. But there was nothing, just the dark sky and the bare trees and the moonlight glittering off the snow.

"Wow," he murmured. "In all my life, I'm not sure I've ever heard complete silence." He reached out and found her hand in the dark. "There's always some sort of noise in the city, even when it's quiet. It hums."

"Shh! Hear that?"

He listened and heard the flutter of wings behind them. "What is that?"

"Owl," she said. "Probably got a mouse. There are all kinds of things moving in the woods at night. In the summer, it's like a symphony of sound. But in the winter, the snow muffles everything."

He could barely see the features of her face in the moonlight, but he could hear the smile in her voice. "What if we get lost?" he said. "Will you protect me from the bears and the wolves?"

"We won't get lost. I know every inch of these woods. Every tree. I grew up here." She turned on the flashlight and began walking again, her snowshoes crunching against the snow. Alex followed her until she stopped at a large tree.

"See," she said, pointing to the trunk. Her gloved finger ran over an arrow carved into the tree, the head pointing down.

"Did you do that?"

Tenley nodded. "Underneath all this snow and about a foot or two of dirt is an old cigar tin. My brother and I buried a time capsule on our eighth birthday. We were going to dig it up when we turned eighteen."

"Did you? Dig it up?"

Tenley shook her head. "I didn't have the heart. I can't even remember what we put inside. Maybe this summer, I'll come here and find out."

"What was he like?"

"He was…like me. In every way. It was like we shared a brain. We knew what the other was thinking all the time. I could look at him and know the next words that were going to come out of his mouth. Some people say twins have a psychic connection. When I come out here sometimes, I can feel him. Does that sound crazy?"

"No," Alex said.

"I just wish I could go back and fix the mistakes I made."

"What mistakes?" Alex knew the answer to his question, but he wanted her to tell him. And to his surprise, she started talking. Maybe it was the fact that she couldn't see him in the dark or that they were out in the cold, alone.

"It was my idea to go out that night," she began. "I dared him to sail out to the island. He said no, but I wouldn't let it go. I kept picking at him and picking at him until he agreed."

"It's not your fault, Tenley. You were just a kid. You didn't know."

"I did. That's the point. I knew it was dangerous. So did he. But I wanted him to admire me. I wanted him to think I was the most important person in the world. I wanted proof that he loved me the best."

"But he did. You were important to him."

"I wasn't. Not anymore."

"I don't understand."

He heard her draw a ragged breath. "Tommy had a girlfriend. He told me all about her, how much he liked her. How he was going to ask her to go sailing with him that weekend. I knew she'd be afraid to go outside the harbor. But I wasn't afraid. I had to prove to him that I was better than she was."

Alex reached out for her, but she pulled away, stepping back into the darkness. "Tenley, what happened was an accident. You didn't cause it. There's a million and one ways that bad things can happen. A million and one reasons why they do. You didn't create the bad weather, the cold water or the wave that turned over the boat."

"We were out there because of me," she said, bitterness suffusing her tone. "Because I was jealous of some silly girl with blond hair and pretty clothes."

He saw the tears streaming down her face, glittering in the moonlight. Alex wanted to take her into his arms and make everything better. But he knew how much it had cost her to tell him. By trying to brush it away, he would only trivialize her feelings. "What if you had been the one to die that night? What if Tommy had lived? And he'd tortured himself the same way you've been doing? How would you have felt about that?"

"Angry," she said. "But I wouldn't blame him. He'd never do anything to deliberately hurt me."

"Don't you think he knew that about you? Don't you think he realized how much you loved him? He wouldn't want you to spend the rest of your life mourning his death. Hell, I don't know Tommy. But if he was anything like you, he'd tell you to stop acting like such a baby and get on with your life."

Tenley sat down in the snow. "I feel like I'm ready to let it go. But I'm afraid if I do, I'll forget him. And then I won't have anyone."

He squatted down in front of her, reaching out to cup her face in his gloved hands. "You'll have me," Alex said.

"No, I won't. You're leaving in a few days."

"I don't live that far away, Tenley."

"Don't," she murmured, brushing his hands away. "Don't make any promises you can't keep. I'm fine with what we've had. I don't need anything more."

This was it, Alex thought. Her grandfather had warned him it was coming, but he hadn't expected her to turn on him for no reason—and so soon. "What if I do? Need more, I mean."

"I'm sure you'll find plenty of girls eager to take care of your needs."

"Do you think that's what this is about? Sex?"

She stumbled to her feet and brushed the snow off her backside. Then she shone the flashlight in his face. "That's all this was *ever* about. We enjoy each other in bed. There's nothing to be ashamed of."

"I don't believe you," Alex said. "I refuse to believe you don't feel something more."

"What I feel doesn't make a difference. Come on, Alex, be reasonable. We can pretend that we'll see each other again, we might even make plans. But once we're apart, the desire is bound to fade. I can deal with that. Don't worry, I'm not going to fall apart on you."

Alex felt a surge of anger inside of him. She sounded so indifferent, but he knew it was a lie. He had seen it in her eyes, had felt it in the way she touched him. They shared a connection that couldn't be broken with just a few words and a wave goodbye.

"We should go back," she muttered. "I'm getting cold."

He knew what would happen when they returned to the cabin. Tenley would find a way to smooth over their discussion and she'd lure him into bed. And once again, he'd be left certain he was falling in love with her, yet completely unsure of her feelings for him.

Alex had to wonder if he'd ever know how she truly felt. Would she ever be brave enough to admit that she needed him? Or that she wanted someone to share her life? Maybe Tenley was right. Maybe they both ought to just move on.

She pointed the flashlight out in front of them and

retraced their steps in the snow. Alex had no choice but to follow her. They walked for a long while in silence, but when he saw the lights from the yard, Alex suddenly regretted giving up his room at the inn.

He wasn't angry with her. He knew why Tenley was pushing him away. But Alex wondered if she could ever fully trust him. Or trust any man. He found it odd that her insecurities didn't come from a series of bad relationships, but from never having experienced a relationship at all.

She'd obviously had sex before. She was far too comfortable in bed. But he suspected she treated sex the same way she treated a hike or a ride in her sleigh—a pleasant activity to pass the time and nothing more. Truth be told, that was the way he'd always approached it as well—until he'd met her.

From the moment he'd first touched her, Alex felt something powerful between them. And sex became more than just physical release—it became a way to communicate his feelings for her. For the first time in his life, he was actually making love.

"I think I'm going to work for a while," Tenley said. "I'll be in later. Don't wait up."

"Fine," he said.

They parted ways on the porch, Alex watching as she walked toward the barn. He ought to pack his bags and leave. Let her see how much she liked her life without him in it. Maybe, with some time apart, she'd actually realize what they'd shared was special.

He unbuckled his snowshoes, then stepped inside to

find the dogs waiting. "Go ahead," he said, moving aside. They bounded out into the snow in a flurry of flying feet and wagging tails. He watched them play. Dog and Pup.

She hadn't even bothered to name her dogs. Was she afraid they were going to leave her, too, someday? He wasn't sure what the two cats were named, if they even had names. And as far as she was concerned, he was probably just…Guy or Dude.

Alex had cast aside more women than he cared to count. Why couldn't he bring himself to do the same with Tenley? Instead of being apathetic, he found himself angry. He'd made a difference in her life and she refused to acknowledge it. They were better people together than they were apart.

He saw the light go on in the tower studio and stepped into the shadows of the porch. Tenley appeared in the window overlooking the cabin. He watched as she moved about, remembering the previous afternoon and how she'd talked him out of his clothes.

Alex shook his head, wondering how this would all end. Hell, he couldn't believe it had begun in the first place. Had he not ended up in that snowdrift, none of this would have happened. Eventually, he would have tracked down Tenley, made his proposal and been on his way. On any other day, he might have looked right past her, unaware of the incredible woman she was.

But something had brought them together, some great karmic design, some strange twist of fate. And he had to believe that same force would keep them together, even though she was doing her damnedest to drive them apart.

"IT'S BETTER THIS WAY," Tenley murmured to herself. She paced back and forth across the width of the studio, her nerves on edge, her mind spinning endlessly. She wasn't supposed to fall in love. She'd never meant for it to happen. But now that it had, Tenley needed to find a way to stop herself.

Though she'd heard of people who'd fallen in love at first sight, Tenley never believed it was possible. Lust at first sight, maybe. But love took time to grow. How could you possibly love someone you didn't know?

"That's right," she muttered. "You can't love Alex. You don't even know him."

She pressed her hand to her heart. It wasn't love. But it sure felt like something she'd never experienced before. And she'd never been in love in her life.

Tenley stopped in front of the table and picked up the new drawing she'd done for the second chapter. It was as close to perfect as she could make it and it was good. Even she was proud of the effort, and Tenley was her own worst critic.

The fact that she was able to believe in herself as an artist was Alex's doing. She owed him a huge debt of gratitude. But did she owe him her heart? It seemed to be the only thing he wanted from her. Tenley's heart was a mangled mess, shattered in a million pieces and stuck back together again with duct tape and school paste and chewing gum.

Who would want a heart like that, a heart so close to breaking again? A heart that wasn't strong enough to love. Tenley sat down in her chair and cupped her chin in her hand. Slowly, she flipped through her story.

And it was her story. Cyd was everything she'd wanted to be—strong, determined, blessed with powers that could alter the past. But as she looked at the pictures she'd drawn, Tenley saw that Cyd was just ink on paper. Every move she made was part of an intricate plot planned out ahead of time. She had all the answers.

Real life was a different matter. Tenley had no control over the plot. There was no plan. Nothing was black and white. Instead, she was left to navigate through a world filled with shades of gray.

Did she love Alex or didn't she? The answer wasn't that simple. Perhaps she had the potential to love him. Maybe there was a tiny part of her that loved him already. But if asked for a yes or no answer, Tenley couldn't give one.

She shoved the papers back and stood, the walls of the studio closing in around her. Grabbing her coat, Tenley ran down the stairs and out into the cold night. She wrapped her arms around herself and tipped her head up to the sky, staring at the stars.

What came next in her story? Would she let it unfold in front of her? Or would she try to manipulate the plot? Though it might be nice to possess a superpower or two, Tenley suspected there was no power in the world that could make Alex love her if he didn't want to. She had to be prepared to let him go and to do it without any regrets.

The snow crunched beneath her boots as she walked back to the cabin. The great room was lit only by the fading fire and the light from above the kitchen sink. Pup and Dog came out to greet her and she gave them both a pat on the head. Tenley tiptoed down the hall and peeked into her bedroom. A stab of disappointment pierced her heart when she saw Alex wasn't waiting in her bed.

The door to the guest room was closed and she could only assume he was sending her a signal. She wasn't welcome. Tenley walked back to the kitchen, her wet boots squeaking on the wood plank floor. She kicked them off at the door and shrugged out of her jacket, tossing it over the back of the sofa.

A survey of the refrigerator yielded nothing interesting to eat, but she felt compelled to munch in an effort to take her mind off the man sleeping in her guest room. They'd spent the past four nights in each other's arms. It didn't seem right, sleeping all alone.

Tenley grabbed an apple from the basket on the counter, then walked back to her bedroom. She took a huge bite, then tossed the apple on the bed and began to remove her clothes. But in the end, exhaustion overwhelmed her and she flopped down, face-first on the sheets, still half-dressed. She found the apple and took another bite, then carefully considered her options.

She could do the sensible thing, crawl beneath the covers of her own bed, close her eyes and pray she'd fall asleep before giving in to her impulses. Or she could do the reckless thing and strip off all her clothes, walk into the guest room and get into bed with Alex. Or she could lie here and think of other options.

The cats were curled up on her pillow and she rolled over and pressed her face into Kittie's fur. Kattie opened her eyes and watched Tenley for a moment, then nuzzled her face into her paws and went back to sleep. This was what she'd be reduced to after Alex left—searching for affection from her pets.

She'd survived on their love before he'd walked into her life. So why did the prospect seem so unsatisfying now? "I love you," she murmured to the cats. "I do." But they didn't open their eyes. "I know you love me. You don't have to say the words. I can tell by the way you're lying there that you love me." She paused. "God, am I pathetic."

With that, Tenley sat up and raked her hands through her hair. Then she grabbed a book from the pile on her bedside table. But as she flipped through the pages, one by one, she couldn't find anything that might occupy her mind. She could bake some cookies. Or clean the fireplace. Or scrub the bathroom floor. Tenley drew a deep breath. Or she could walk into Alex's room and do what she really wanted to do—make love to him for the rest of the night.

She crawled out of bed and tiptoed to his door, then slowly opened it, wincing at the squeaky hinges. The room was dark, the only light coming from the hall. Tenley stood next to his bed, then silently knelt down beside it, her gaze searching his face.

There were times when his beauty took her breath

away. Men weren't supposed to be beautiful, but she could look at Alex with an artist's eye and see the perfection of his long limbs and muscled torso. This was the kind of man the Greeks sculpted in ancient times, the epitome of the human form, from his well-shaped hands to his lovely feet.

She thought back to the sketches she'd made of Alex. For the first time in her life, she'd felt like an artist. And she'd understood the need for a muse. Drawing Alex brought out her passion for her art. When she looked at his naked body, everything she saw through her eyes came out on the sketchpad.

Her fingers clenched and she longed for a pencil and pad, wanting to capture this scene in front of her. The frustration she felt earlier was gone and now she felt nothing but regret for her sharp words. He didn't deserve them. Alex had been nothing but kind and encouraging. No matter what those other women claimed, he'd been a perfect gentleman.

Tenley didn't know how much longer this would last. She suspected the feelings might fade once he returned to Chicago. But they still had three more days together. The least she could do was put aside her insecurities and make their moments together count for something.

Holding her breath, Tenley crawled into bed beside him, still dressed in her jeans and long-sleeved T-shirt. She felt him move behind her and then his arms circled around her waist and he pulled her against his body. His soft sigh tickled the back of her neck and a moment later, he pressed his lips to the same spot.

Tenley smiled, holding on to his hands and allowing her body to relax. He didn't need to say a word. Just his touch was enough to know that she'd been forgiven. And though Tenley wanted to strip off her clothes and make love to him, there was something wonderful about just being in his arms, lying next to him in his bed.

They had three more days and two more nights. There would be plenty of time to reignite the passion between them. She closed her eyes and waited for sleep to take the last of her tensions from her body.

But the noise in her head refused to quiet. Tenley drew a deep breath and then let it out slowly, before turning in Alex's embrace. Facing him, she smoothed her hands over his features, memorizing the feel of them in the dark.

When he brushed his mouth against hers, Tenley realized he was awake. She touched her lips to his and slowly the kiss grew deeper and more passionate. But there was an edge of desperation to each caress they shared, as if they both knew that the clock was ticking down on their time together.

With each soft sigh and each whispered word, Tenley grew more frantic to feel him inside her. When he began to undress her, she impatiently tore off her shirt and kicked out of her jeans. Once she was naked, Alex pulled her beneath the sheets, into the warmth of his body.

He was already hard and as he moved against her, his shaft pressed into the soft flesh of her abdomen. This was all she needed in life, this wonderful warm feeling of anticipation. Alex could smooth his hands over her skin and she'd lose herself in a wave of sensation.

There was more at work here than just physical attraction. She ached for that moment when she felt most vulnerable, when their souls seemed exposed. At that instant, the past melted away and Tenley felt alive and aware. Though she'd had men in her bed, not one of them had ever made her feel a fraction of what Alex did.

She reached for the box of condoms on the bedside table, surprised to find just one left inside. He smiled as she smoothed it over the length of his shaft, his breath coming in soft, short gasps.

He rolled her beneath him, then pulled her leg up alongside his hip. Probing gently, he found her entrance and in one sure motion, he slipped inside of her. Tenley groaned at the thrill that raced through her body.

There was nothing in the world that had ever felt this good. And Tenley knew this was what it was like to want a man so much her body ached for his touch and her soul cried out for his love. If this was all she had in the world, she could be happy forever.

But happiness didn't always last. It could be snatched away in the blink of an eye. At least she knew when the end would come. And she'd be prepared.

THE RINGING WOKE Alex up from a deep sleep. He opened one eye, searching for the source. It wasn't his watch. That was still in the refrigerator.

"What is that?" Tenley murmured, turning her face into the pillow. "Turn it off."

"I can't find it. Where's the clock?"

"It's not an alarm clock. I don't have an alarm clock."

Alex sat up and searched the room, then noticed the sound was coming from his pants, which were tossed over a nearby chair. He stumbled out of bed and picked them up, then found the new BlackBerry in his pocket. He pushed the button and put it to his ear.

"What?"

"It's Tess. I'm sorry to call you so early but we have a huge problem. The new press just went down and we're in the middle of the Marberry project. It's Saturday and none of the techs are answering their phones. We're supposed to deliver this job on Monday and we've still got to run it through bindery. I need you to come home."

"Aw, hell." Alex rubbed his face with his hand, trying to clear the sleep from his brain. "It's going to take me a while. I can probably make some calls from the road. I'm going to call Marberry first and see if we can't push back delivery. How much of a hit can we take on our price?"

"Five percent at the most. But don't offer him a discount on this job. Tell him we'll discount the next one. At least we know we'll get him back as a customer, then."

"Do you have to talk so loud?" Tenley groaned. Alex sat down on the edge of the bed and put his pillow over her head.

"Who is that?" Tess asked. "Oh, my God. Are you with a woman? Good grief, Alex, send her home, get in your car and point it toward Chicago. I'll see you in…five hours."

"I've got to pick up my car from the garage and they won't open until eight or nine. It'll take me at least six hours to get back, so schedule a meeting with the production team at three. We'll get this sorted out."

Tess hung up and Alex flopped back down on the bed, the phone still clutched in his hand "I have to go," he said.

Tenley pushed up on her elbows, her hair sticking up in unruly spikes. "Go where?"

"Back to Chicago. We've got an emergency with one of our presses at the Elgin plant."

"No," Tenley moaned. "You're supposed to stay until Monday."

Alex rolled over and drew her into his embrace. "I know. Maybe I can come back. I'll take care of business and if everything's all right, I can drive back late tonight. I could be back here by midnight."

She closed her eyes and for a long time didn't speak. Alex thought she'd fallen asleep again. But then, she opened her eyes. "You have to go," she said. "We only had a few days left anyway. It's all right."

"No, I'll come back," Alex insisted.

Tenley shook her head, then pressed her finger to his lips. "No. It's better this way. You need to get back to work. And I need to work on the novel. I can't do that with you here."

"How about next weekend? I could drive up on Friday night." All Alex needed was a promise that there would be a next time. He didn't want to leave without knowing exactly where they stood.

Tenley reached out and smoothed her hand over his cheek. "Alex, we both knew, going in, how difficult this would be. You're down there and I'm here. Throw in the whole business thing and it gets too complicated. I'd like to believe we're both smart enough to see that and save ourselves the pain of trying to make a relationship work."

Alex couldn't believe what he was hearing. He'd never been dumped in his life and this sounded suspiciously like the big heave-ho. He brushed the hair out of her eyes and turned her face up to his. But all he saw in her eyes was complete honesty. Had he misread the depth of her feelings for him?

"So this is it?" he asked.

"I know you've done this before," Tenley said with a small smile. "A guy like you doesn't stay single for as long as you have without breaking a few hearts. It's easy."

"This doesn't seem easy to me," he said.

"It will get better." She leaned forward and brushed a kiss across his lips. "At least I didn't break your heart and you didn't break mine. I think we both got out of this feeling pretty good."

She was right. Still, he wanted her to want him to stay, so much that she would grasp at any chance to see him again. That was what women did. They got all crazy and clingy and demanding. But then, Tenley hadn't ever acted like the women he'd dated. So it would make sense she'd just cut him loose without a second thought.

"You're sure about this?"

"Absolutely sure," she said.

He frowned. "So, I guess we'll be talking to each other about the novel. You'll work on the changes. And when they're done, we'll discuss them."

"Yes. If I have any questions, I'll call you."

Alex sat up and swung his legs off the bed. Then he ran his hands through his hair. This just didn't seem right—hell, it didn't *feel* right. Every instinct in his body told him not to leave her like this, to make it clear he wanted more than what they'd already shared.

She slipped her arms around him from behind and rested her chin on his shoulder. "I am going to miss you. I like having you here when I wake up."

"That's a good reason to see each other again, isn't it?"

She crawled out of bed and pulled him to his feet. "Come on. Get dressed. I'll make you something to eat while you pack. And I'll call the garage and tell them you're coming for your car."

Tenley grabbed her T-shirt from the floor and tugged it over her head. "Wait a second," Alex said. "Not so fast." He pulled her against his body and kissed her, smoothing his hands up beneath her shirt until he found the soft flesh of her breasts.

Tenley giggled. "Wanted to cop one last feel?"

"Hey, I'm a guy. I have to have something to think about on the ride home."

Tenley dragged her T-shirt back over her head and threw it on the bed. "All right. I'll cook breakfast in the nude. That should give you plenty to think about for the next two or three days." She gave him a devilish smile, then walked out of the bedroom, a tantalizing sway to her hips.

Alex poked his head out the door and watched her as she moved down the hallway. Tenley had the most incredible body. And she didn't even work at it.

He gathered the clothes he'd left in Tenley's room and took them back into the guest room, then dug through his duffel for something comfortable to wear. He found a clean T-shirt, pulled it over his head, then stepped into his last pair of clean boxers. His missing jeans were mixed in with Tenley's laundry and he tugged them on, then searched for his socks.

"Scrambled or fried?" she called from the kitchen.

"Just toast," Alex called. "And coffee. Really black." He might as well get back to his regular routine as soon as possible. Besides, he wouldn't be spending the day and night with Tenley, so there wasn't much need for extra energy.

When he got out to the kitchen, he found Tenley standing at the counter, sipping a cup of coffee, still completely naked. She handed him a mug and then retrieved his toast from the toaster.

"I like this," he said, letting his gaze drift down the length of her body. "If a guy had this every day, he'd never get to work in the morning."

"It's a lot better in the summer," Tenley said. "I'm freezing."

Alex gathered her up in his arms and pressed a kiss to the top of her head. "You are, by far, the most interesting woman I've ever met, Tenley Marshall. I'm not going to forget you, even if you do make breakfast with your clothes on. Go get dressed."

She ran back to her bedroom and reappeared a minute later in flannel pajamas and slippers. She sat down next to him at the end of the island, sipping her coffee and waiting for him to finish his toast.

"I did have a wonderful time," she said with a warm smile. "I'm glad I stopped and rescued you."

"I'm glad you did, too." He reached out and slipped his hand through the hair at her nape. Gently, Alex pulled her forward until their lips met. He knew it might be the last time he kissed her, so he tried to make it as sweet and perfect as possible. When he finally drew back, Alex looked down, taking in all the small details of her face, committing them to memory.

There was a time when he thought her odd, but now, Alex was certain she was someone so special, so unique that he might never meet another woman like her again. He drew a steadying breath, then stood. The longer he waited, the more difficult this was going to be.

"I have to go. Now. Or I'm never going to leave."

Tenley nodded. "All right." She hugged him hard, then pushed up on her toes and gave him a quick kiss. "I'll see you, Alex."

He wanted to gather her in his arms and show her what a real goodbye kiss should be. But in the end, Alex took one last look, smiled and turned for the door. "I'll see you, Tenley."

The trek out to his rental car was the longest walk of his life. Every step required enormous willpower. When he looked back, she was standing on the porch in her pajamas, the cold morning wind blowing at her dark hair. He waved as he drove past the house to the driveway. And all the way to town, Alex tried to come up with an excuse to send him back to the cabin.

Tenley was right. They'd been caught up in a wildly enjoyable affair, but that was all it had been. Passion had turned to infatuation and he'd mistaken it for love. Love didn't happen in four days or even four weeks. And though his interest in other women had always faded quickly, Alex knew that his feelings for Tenley would be with him for a very long time. He would never, ever forget Tenley Marshall.

"YOUR PERSPECTIVE is off here."

Tenley studied the drawing, then nodded. "You're right. I always make that mistake." She cursed softly. "This is why I should have gone to art school. People will see things like that and know I'm an amateur."

"No, they won't. This is highly stylized, Tenley. You can break a lot of rules. In fact, in this kind of work, you can make up your own rules. It's your universe. I'm just pointing out some areas you might want to consider," her grandfather said.

"Right," she murmured.

It had been three days since Alex had walked out of her life. He'd called twice, but she'd ignored his calls, knowing it would be easier if they didn't speak for a while. Still, she'd listened to the sound of his voice on her voice mail over and over again.

She'd been working on the novel nonstop, but her progress had been cursed with fits and starts. With only her own resources to depend upon, Tenley found herself second-guessing the decisions she made. Her first impulse was to call Alex and discuss her concerns with him. But she realized that if she wanted to be an artist, she'd have to stand on her own. Or fail.

Though failing had once been a viable option, the more time she spent on the novel, the more Tenley wanted to make it work. This was a great story, a story that was so tightly woven into her own that she had trouble separating herself from Cyd. She'd grown to like the girl. She was strong and resourceful and determined. She was a survivor.

Yet even with a new story swirling around in her head, Tenley still couldn't keep her thoughts from wandering to Alex. She hadn't thought it would be this difficult. Once he was gone, she assumed her life would get back to normal. Sure, she'd think about him occasionally, but thoughts of him would soon fade.

In reality, she'd become obsessed with remembering. Each night, before she fell asleep, she'd go through each image in her head, lingering over them like a photo album. Yesterday, she'd actually made a drawing of Alex in the perfect state of arousal and she was quite taken with it, until she realized it was bordering on pornography.

On the floor in front of the fire, in the sauna, in the

studio, in his room—everywhere she turned there were reminders of him.

"Tenley!"

"What?" She stood up, spinning around to find her grandfather standing behind her, his arms crossed over his chest.

"How long are you going to be like this?"

"Like what?"

"Your young man has been gone for, what, three days?"

"Yes, three days."

"And when is he coming back?"

"He's not. And he's not my young man. He's just a guy I knew for a while."

"I see. And how long do you plan to mope around?"

"I'm not moping. I'm just distracted. I have a lot of things on my mind and not enough time to think about them all. Speaking of which, if you don't go through those bills of sale and mark the inventory numbers on them, I'm going to have a lot more to be crabby about than Alex Stamos."

"This arrived for you today." Her grandfather held up a large envelope. The logo for the university in Green Bay was emblazoned on the corner.

Tenley took it from his hand. "Thanks."

"So you're going to start school?"

"Yes," she said firmly. "This summer. I'm going to take a writing class, too."

"Why not spread your wings a little further, Tennie? Check out some other schools. The Art Institute in

Chicago has a great school. You could go down there and stay for the summer, really immerse yourself in something new."

Though the Art Institute might have a fabulous school, Tenley knew why her grandfather was pushing that choice. It would give her the opportunity to re-kindle her relationship with Alex. The thought had crossed her mind more than once. But she wanted to simplify her life, not make it more complicated. "I can't do that. I have responsibilities here. I have my dogs and cats and horses to care for. And I don't have the money to stay in Chicago for the summer. If I go to Green Bay, I can drive back and forth."

"I'll give you the money," her grandfather said.

"No, you won't. You don't have the money to give me."

"No?" He laughed. "I have a lot of money. Money you don't even know I have. I've put it all in a trust for you. I don't think you should have to wait for me to kick the bucket before you can use it. So I'm going to give it to you now."

"I can't take your money," Tenley said. "You should spend it on yourself."

"I intend to. In fact, now that you're planning on attending school, I might just go somewhere warm for the winter."

"You hate California," she said.

"I was thinking about Greece."

Tenley gasped. "Greece? Since when?"

He picked up a paintbrush and examined it closely.

"I've always wanted to go to Greece. Your grandmother hated to fly, so we couldn't go. And after she died, I had you to watch out for. But now that you're moving on, I think I should do the same."

Emotion welled up inside of her. She'd never meant to be a burden on her grandfather. She was supposed to care for him, not the other way around. "I'm sorry. I didn't realize that you— You should go. Oh, it would be wonderful. Think of all the things you could paint." With a sob, she threw her arms around her grandfather's neck. "Thank you for being so patient with me. I'm sorry it took me so long to figure things out."

He patted her back. "Not to worry. It all worked out in the end. You found a man and that's the only thing that matters."

"I didn't find a man," Tenley said stubbornly. "Alex went back to Chicago. He's gone."

"What difference does that make? If he's the one you want, then a few hundred miles won't matter. When I met your grandmother, she was living in the Upper Peninsula. and I was living in Minot, North Dakota. We managed to find a way to make it work."

"I don't want to make it work," Tenley said. "I'm not ready to be in love."

Her grandfather shook his head and chuckled. "It's not like you can prepare for it. It just happens and when it does, you have to grab it and hang on for dear life. It doesn't come along that often."

Tenley took her drawings and put them back inside her portfolio, then zipped it up. "Well, I don't want to be in love. Not right now. I have too many other things I have to do. It would just get in the way."

He reached out and placed his hand over hers. "Tennie, I really don't think you have a whole lot of control over that. Don't get me wrong, I've always admired your resolve. But on this one you're wrong." He tapped her portfolio. "Good work. When you're done, I think a trip to Chicago might be in order. It'll give you a chance to check out the school at the Art Institute."

"What would you do without me during the summer?"

"I was thinking I'd hire one of those college students who are always wanting to intern at the gallery. Someone who's not so much trouble."

Tenley giggled. "You're not going to get rid of me with insults." She picked up her portfolio and walked to the door. "If I go to Chicago for the summer, you'd have to take care of my dogs and cats. They'd have to move in with you. And we'd have to board the horses."

He held out his hands. "A small price to pay for your happiness."

She zipped up her coat and walked out the door into the chilly afternoon sun. Once, her days had been spent in a holding pattern, just waiting for something to push her forward again. Alex had done that for her. He'd given her a reason to move on and for that, she'd be forever grateful.

Someday, she'd tell him that. Someday in the distant future—when she'd be able to look at him and not wonder if she'd given up too soon.

8

TENLEY HAD BEEN to the Art Institute several times when she was younger. As she walked down the front steps, looking back at the classic facade, she let the memories wash over her. Her parents had been together and Tommy was still alive. They'd rushed up the front steps, racing each other to the door, hoping to see everything in just one day. And while her mother and father lingered over the paintings, she and Tommy found their favorite spots.

Tenley had been fascinated by the miniatures, like little dollhouses with each tiny piece of furniture perfectly reproduced. Tommy was drawn to the Greek and Roman coins, comparing them to his collection of Indian head pennies at home.

It had been one of the last times they'd traveled together as a family. But to her surprise, the memory didn't cause the usual ache in her heart. Instead, she felt only a tiny bit of melancholy as she recalled the affection they'd all had for each other. Tommy had lived a short life, but he had been well loved.

Maybe that was what life was all about—searching

for a place to feel accepted. Since Alex had left, Tenley had made the decision to walk away from the past and begin again. Though she was excited at the prospect, she was also a bit frightened.

She'd spent the afternoon strolling through galleries, studying the artists and wondering if they'd ever had the same doubts she was having. To pacify her grandfather, Tenley had met with an admissions specialist for the Art Institute school and, in the end, decided to apply for a three-week session in June and another in August. Six weeks away from home during her grandfather's busiest season would be difficult, but he'd assured her he could get along with temporary help.

Housing was offered by the school, but it didn't allow for pets. So Dog and Pup and her two cats were going to have to live at her grandfather's place while she was gone. Josh could take care of the horses, moving them over to his family's farm to make it more convenient, and she'd drive home on the weekends to make sure everything was running smoothly.

Yet, even though she tried to focus on the business at hand, her thoughts constantly shifted to the real reason she'd come to Chicago—Alex. They'd spoken several times since he'd left, mostly about the novel. But sometimes they drifted into conversation about their time together.

Though neither one of them wanted to make the first move to rekindle their romantic relationship, there always seemed to be a tension simmering right below the surface—as if the thoughts were there, waiting to be expressed.

Tenley stepped to the curb and held up her hand to hail a cab. A few seconds later, a taxi pulled up and she got inside. She reached into the pocket of her portfolio for Alex's business card and gave the cabbie the address.

Though she'd come to Chicago to see Alex, her excuse for the trip was a meeting she'd scheduled with her editor. She'd finished the requested revisions and had completed the new artwork for the changes. Rather than sending them via courier, Tenley had decided to deliver them personally.

Marianne Johnson, her editor, felt it important they meet, but Tenley was really hoping to take a few moments to say hello to Alex. It had been nearly three weeks since he'd left and even though she thought of him every hour of every day, she was beginning to forget the tiny details that had fascinated her so. The closest thing she had to a photograph was the picture from the Smooth Operators Web site. And then she had her drawings, but none of those had a face with the body.

All she needed was a few seconds to recharge her memory. As the cab wove through the late-afternoon traffic, Tenley tried to imagine how it would be. She'd stand at his door and say a quick hello. He'd ask her to come in and sit down, but she'd beg off, explaining that she had a meeting scheduled with her editor. He'd ask her to dinner and she'd tell him she was driving back that night. He'd say the traffic was bad until later and she ought to wait.

All she really wanted to know was that she and Alex could deal with each other as business associates. The past was the past. It might not have been so important before, but in the past few weeks, Tenley had begun to imagine building a career as a graphic novelist. She'd already come up with four or five new ideas for stories.

The headquarters for Stamos Publishing was located in the South Loop in a huge brick building that had been modernized with new windows and a gleaming entrance. One corner was constructed entirely of glass, revealing a printing press in full operation.

Tenley paid the cabbie, then hopped out of the car, clutching her portfolio to her chest. She'd left her Jeep parked in the lot at the hotel, her bags in the trunk, preferring to let someone else do the driving while she was in town. Later tonight, she'd pick it up and head home.

She checked in at the front desk and was given a badge to clip onto her pocket. A few seconds later, Marianne Johnson burst through the door, a wide smile on her face. "Tenley! Gosh, it's a pleasure to finally meet you." She held out her hand. "How was your drive down? The weather looked good."

"I actually came down yesterday afternoon. I went to the Art Institute this morning and spent most of the day there."

"Wonderful! First, I want to take you by Alex's office. I know he's in and I'm sure he wants to say hello."

"Oh, I don't want to bother him," Tenley said, suddenly succumbing to an attack of nerves. What if he wasn't thrilled to see her? What if they had nothing to say to each other? She'd built this meeting up in her mind for three weeks, ever since Alex had left Door County. And now that it was here, she wanted to run back home.

"It's no bother. When I told him you were coming, he insisted we stop by. Come on."

They wove through a warren of hallways, past small offices and large conference areas, all occupied by production personnel. Marianne took her back to the pressroom and explained to her that her novel would be printed at their new plant in Elgin and that she would be invited to do a press check once the process had begun.

By the time they stepped inside the elevator, Tenley's heart was slamming in her chest and she could barely breathe. What if she couldn't speak? What if everything she said sounded stilted and contrived?

"Our sales and marketing offices are up here," Marianne said, after they arrived at the second floor. "We're so excited about publishing your novel. I think this new imprint is going to be the best thing that's ever happened to this company."

Unlike the production offices, the second floor was quiet, the hum of the printing presses barely audible. Marianne took her through a set of glass doors, then smiled at the receptionist. "Alex wanted us to stop in," she explained.

Tenley took a deep breath. She'd brought a new outfit for the occasion. She wore a hand-woven jacket with a bright chartreuse turtleneck, a short black skirt and leggings underneath. Lace-up ankle boots and a studded belt finished off the ensemble. In her opinion, it was edgy and cool and it made her look like a real artist.

"Alex? I've got Tenley here."

Marianne stepped aside and directed her through a wide doorway. Tenley pasted a smile on her face and walked in. The moment their eyes met, she felt as if she'd been hit in the chest with a brick. Her heart fluttered and her breathing grew shallow and she felt a bit light-headed. "Hello." It was all she could manage.

"Hello, Tenley. Come on in. Sit down."

His voice was warm and deep and caused a shiver to race through her body. "Oh, I can't stay. Marianne and I have a meeting. And then I have to get back on the road. I've got a long drive home tonight. I just wanted to say hi." She gave him a little wave and a weak laugh. The words had just tumbled out of her mouth so fast she wasn't sure what she'd said. "Hi."

"Don't be silly. Your meeting with Marianne can wait." He glanced over at the editor. "Right?"

Marianne nodded. "Sure. Just give me a call when you're through." The editor disappeared down the long hallway, leaving Tenley standing alone in the door. Wasn't this how she'd imagined it? What was next?

"Come on in. Sit," he said, pointing to the chair on the other side of his desk. "God, you look…incredible."

"It's the new clothes," Tenley said. "Now that I'm an artist, I have to start dressing like one."

"They suit you," he said. "But then, everything looks good on you. I seem to remember a funny hat with earflaps. I liked that hat."

"I didn't bring it along. I didn't want to look like a complete bumpkin."

"So, are you really going back tonight? Because you can't. We have to have dinner. I'll take you out and show you the town." He reached for his phone and punched a button. "Carol, can you make a reservation for Tenley Marshall at the Drake? Confirm it for late arrival on our account."

Tenley shook her head. "I can't. I have to get back. I promised my grandfather."

"One of the suites would be good," he said to his secretary. When he hung up the phone, he nodded. "Just in case you don't want to go. You'll stay for dinner, right?"

"Sure. The traffic will probably be crazy until later on, anyway. So, yes, I'll stay for dinner."

"Good. We have a lot to catch up on. I can't believe you're here."

"I am," she said, slowly lowering herself into the chair. She set her portfolio on the floor, fumbling with the handles. Why had conversation suddenly become so difficult? She couldn't think of a single thing to say to him. He looked the same, maybe a bit more polished. He wore a finely tailored suit and a white dress shirt that showed off his dark features. If he'd picked out his clothes to please her, they were certainly doing the trick. He was as handsome as ever. "How have you been?"

"Good," he said. "You know, this is crazy. Good, fine, you look great." He circled around the desk, then stood in front of her, pulling her to her feet. Without hesitation, Alex cupped her face in his hands and gave her a gentle kiss. "That's better."

"I remember that," Tenley murmured, her gaze dropping to his lips.

"So do I." For a long time, they stood silently, staring at each other. And then, he blinked and glanced at his watch. "It's almost four. Let's go now and we'll have a few drinks before dinner and—"

"I have to see Marianne," she said, grabbing her portfolio.

"Right."

"But I won't be long. I'll come back at five and we'll go then."

"Sure," Alex said, following her to the door. "Her office is down there on the right. Name's on the door."

Tenley nodded and started down the hall. At the last minute, she glanced over her shoulder to find him watching her. "Stop staring at me," she said.

Alex laughed out loud and Tenley hurried down the hall, enjoying the sound. It hadn't gone badly. It could have been worse. They were able to be in the same room without jumping into each other's arms and tearing clothes off. And though the kiss was a bit more than what friends might share, they'd been a lot more than friends.

If this was all it was, Tenley could be happy. There was no anger or regret between them. Only good memories and a warm friendship. She could move on from there.

When she got to Marianne's office, she walked in, only to find another woman sitting in her guest chair. The woman jumped up and held out her hand. "Hello," she said. "I'm Tess Stamos. And you have got to be Tenley Marshall."

"Yes," she said.

"I'm Alex's sister. I work here, too. I loved your novel, by the way. It's about time women start kicking butt in those books, don't you think?"

"I do," Tenley said.

Tess was tall and slender, with dark hair and eyes. She appeared to be a few years older than Tenley, but she had a confidence that made her seem just a bit intimidating.

"So, you saw Alex? He's been going crazy all day waiting for you to come. He usually doesn't let a woman get him so rattled. You must be special."

"We're friends," Tenley said.

Tess observed her with a shrewd look. "I think you're more than that. Alex has even mentioned you to my mother, which means he's willing to put up with her nagging just so he can talk about you around the dinner table. But please, don't break my brother's heart or I will have to chop you into tiny pieces and run you through the printing press. I can do that, you know. I'm head of production."

With that, Tess Stamos waltzed out of the room, leaving Tenley with nothing to say except, "She was…nice."

Marianne circled her desk and took Tenley by the arm, guiding her toward a chair. "Don't let Tess bother you. She deals with loud printing presses and stubborn press operators all day long. She's used to speaking her mind."

As they went over the new drawings and story changes, Tenley's thoughts were occupied elsewhere. She'd expected a warm welcome, but there was something more going on. This wasn't just a casual visit, at least not for Alex. He'd been anticipating her arrival and had even told his sister about her. But then, as a new author, she would naturally be the subject of conversation around the office.

There was no need to read anything into Tess's words. Nothing had changed. Everybody was simply being kind and solicitous, just good business practice.

And at dinner tonight, she'd restrain herself, putting aside all the memories of their passionate encounters at her cabin. She was determined to make this relationship comfortable, to redraw the lines and follow the rules this time.

And though her heart ached a little bit for what they'd lost, Tenley could bear it. She was stronger now and able to look at the attraction between them with a practical eye. Though it would always be tempting, in the end, it just wasn't meant to be.

ALEX GUIDED THE SEDAN down Lakeshore Drive, impatient to get to the restaurant so that he could turn his full attention to the woman sitting beside him. It felt so good to have her back in his orbit again. Though they hadn't touched since he'd kissed her, just knowing he could reach out and make contact made him happy.

"How's your grandfather?" he asked.

"He's good. He says hello. He's working on a new series of paintings. Barns."

"And how are things in town? Is Randy giving you any problems?"

Tenley shook her head. "Actually, we're dating now. He just wore me down and I had to say yes. We're planning the wedding for June."

Alex frowned, then noticed the teasing smile twitching at the corners of her lips. "I'm very happy for you."

"What about you?" Tenley asked. "Have you been dating anyone?"

Alex was surprised by the question, but even more surprised by his answer. "Tenley, it's only been three weeks. I'm not interested in dating anyone."

"I just thought a charming guy like—"

He suddenly realized what she was getting at. "Oh, wait. I know where this is going. You looked me up on the Internet, didn't you? And you came up with that silly Web site."

"SmoothOperators.com. I didn't, Randy did. He gave me the full report."

"When?"

"Before you left. He dropped by the gallery when I was working."

"Damn, he doesn't give up, does he?"

"He's dating Linda Purnell now. So, yes, he has given

up. Unless he's carrying a secret torch for me." She glanced over at him. "Why haven't you started dating again?"

"Because I haven't met anyone half as interesting as you." In fact, Alex hadn't even bothered to go out since he got back to Chicago. He spent most of his evenings at the office, getting back to his apartment in time to catch the end of a basketball game or a hockey match. The rest of the night, he spent staring at his Black-Berry, trying to convince himself that not phoning Tenley was a good thing.

"I know what you mean. There aren't that many interesting single guys living in Sawyer Bay. Though prospects improve in the summer."

Alex reached out and grabbed her hand, lacing his fingers through hers. It felt so good to touch her. "We could skip the restaurant," he said. "We're just a couple blocks from the Drake. We could order room service and spend some time alone."

She smiled weakly and Alex immediately regretted his suggestion. He was moving too fast. And it was obvious her feelings for him had changed.

"I don't think that's a good idea," she said.

"You're probably right. Best to maintain a professional relationship. But it worked out pretty well for us when we did it the first time."

"Yes, but that was just for fun."

Alex watched the traffic as it slowed in front of him for the light. What did she mean by that? Was that all he'd been to her, just a few nights of fun?

Maybe all this distance was simply her way of letting him down easy.

As they drove along the lakeshore, Alex pointed out the major landmarks. Acting as tour guide kept the conversation light and interesting. But in his head, he was cataloguing all the questions that needed answers. Why couldn't she love him? She didn't really believe that ridiculous Web site, did she?

They were so obviously compatible, both in and out of bed. He loved talking to her. She didn't babble like most of the women he'd dated. And she wasn't obsessed with her looks or her clothes. Over time, Alex had realized that it was the little things that he found so attractive.

Tenley didn't wear makeup, at least, not anymore. From the moment she got up in the morning until the time she went to bed, she never once looked in the mirror. She combed her hair with her fingers. She wore clothes that were comfortable and shoes that didn't kill her feet.

And she read books. She didn't watch silly television shows or buy fashion magazines. She had a stack of classics on her bedside table. She was smart and talented and witty.

"And when you have a free moment, you go out and do something useful with your time," he muttered, "rather than going to get your nails done."

"What?"

Alex glanced over to find Tenley watching him with an inquisitive expression. Had he said that out loud?

"Nothing," he said. "Here we are." Thankfully, the parking valet provided a distraction. He opened Tenley's door for her and helped her from the car, then circled around to grab the keys from Alex.

When they got inside, Tenley excused herself and headed toward the ladies' room. Alex waited outside and watched as two women went in and came out before Tenley. What was she doing in there? He reached for the door and pulled it open. "Tenley?"

"What?"

"Is everything all right?"

He heard a sniffle. "Yes?"

Alex stepped inside, then locked the door behind him. He heard the tears in her voice. She was locked in the center stall and he rapped on the door. "Come on, Tenley, open up. I don't want to have to crawl under."

He heard the latch flip and he pushed the door open. She sat on the toilet, her eyes red, a wad of toilet paper in her hand.

"Go away," she said.

"No." Alex reached down and took her hand, then pulled her out of the stall. "Why are you crying?"

"I don't know." This brought a fresh round of tears and she turned away from him and sat down on a small chair in the corner. "God, I hate crying. I feel so stupid."

"Are you upset with me?"

"No." She paused and wiped her nose. "Yes. Maybe. You just make it so difficult."

"What?" He pulled her into his arms and smoothed his hands along her waist. "I don't mean to."

Alex's fingers found her face and he tipped her gaze up to his. Her eyes were red and watery and he brushed a tear away with his thumb. He didn't have the words to make her feel better because he didn't know what was wrong. So Alex did the only thing he knew would take her mind off her troubles. He kissed her.

But what began as a sweet, soothing kiss, slowly turned into something more. Her mouth opened beneath his and he took what she offered. How many nights had he lain in bed, thinking about this, about the next time he'd touch her and kiss her and make love to her? This wasn't exactly the setting he'd imagined, but at this point, it didn't matter. Tenley was back in his arms again.

He grabbed the lapels of her jacket and pushed them aside, desperate to find a spot of bare skin to touch. They stumbled back against the sinks and Alex picked her up and set her on the edge of the counter, stepping between her legs.

She had too many clothes on and there wasn't enough time. He glanced over his shoulder and considered the stall for privacy, but decided against it. The door was locked. If someone knocked, they'd have to stop. But until then, he—

"No," she said, pressing her hands against his chest. "Don't do this."

Alex was stunned and he immediately stepped away. "What is it?"

She pulled her jacket back up and slid off the counter. "I can't do this. I—I have to go." Tenley hurried to the door and pulled on it, but it wouldn't open. "I need to go."

"Tenley, wait. I'm sorry. I didn't— It's just been such a long time and I—"

She finally realized the door was locked and when she turned the knob, it opened. He followed her out into the lobby, but she headed back out to the street.

"Tenley." He took her hand. "Where are you going?"

"I have to go home. I can't stay here."

"Don't. I promise, I won't kiss you again."

She raised her hand for a cab, but he pulled it down. A cab screeched to a halt in front of the restaurant. Christ, he could wait all day for a taxi and now, when he didn't want one, there were ten available. She pulled the door open.

"Wait," Alex said to the driver. "We're not through."

"Go," Tenley said.

"No! Wait." He reached into his pocket for his wallet, ready to pay the driver to do as ordered.

But Tenley pulled the door shut. "Go, now!" she shouted at the driver.

Alex could do nothing but curse as the taxi roared off down the street. The valet stood at his desk, observing the entire scene with a dubious expression.

"Bad date?" he asked.

"Yeah, you could say that."

"Well, at least you didn't buy her dinner." He grinned. "Do you want your car?"

Alex nodded. He sat down on a bench, his breath coming in gasps, clouding in front of his face in the cold air. What the hell had happened? Where was the woman who'd crawled into his bed and seduced him on the night they met? Or the woman who ran into the snow stark naked?

Something had happened to the free-spirited Tenley he knew three weeks ago. How could someone have changed so fast? He reached for his cell phone. She'd spent the previous night in a hotel and left her car parked there. Maybe if he tracked her down, he might catch her before she left.

Alex stared at his phone, then shook his head as he realized the impossibility of that task. The bottom line was Tenley didn't want to be with him. Whatever they'd shared had faded. And he'd just killed what was left of it with his behavior in the bathroom.

When the valet returned with his car, Alex gave him a fifty-dollar bill and slipped behind the wheel. He'd made only one mistake in his life and Alex suspected he'd never stop regretting it. He'd left Tenley that morning after his sister had called.

He should have stayed. He should have lived up there with her until he was absolutely certain she was in love with him. He knew her heart was fragile and yet he thought they'd just be able to pick up where they'd left off in a week or two. Only in the meantime, Tenley had erected a wall around herself, too high and too thick for him to broach.

He'd missed his chance with her and there was absolutely nothing he could do about it.

TENLEY LOOKED at her reflection in the mirror, trying to see herself as others might. Gone was the streak of purple in her hair. Gone was the dark eye makeup and the deep red lipstick, the black nail polish.

She smoothed her hands over the bodice of the red vintage dress. She'd found the garment in a trunk in her grandfather's attic and had thought the shawl collar and wide skirt made it a classic design. When she'd brought it down, her grandfather had grown all misty, remembering the night her grandmother had first worn it.

In her ongoing effort to get out more, Tenley had invited her grandfather to the Valentine's Dance, held at the fire hall in town. The dance was one of the biggest events of the winter season. Everyone attended. Jimmy Richter's Big Band came in from Green Bay to play and the Ladies Auxiliary made cake and pink punch. Anyone who was single was invited to attend, from teenagers to retirees.

Tenley suspected her grandfather had ulterior motives for accepting the date. Rumor had it he and Katie Vanderhoff had been seen together at Wednesday-night bingo for the past four weeks in a row. Though he might have wanted to ask Katie to the dance, Tenley knew the potential gossip would have scared him away. Considering the suitability of the match, the gossips would have had them married off before they stepped on the dance floor.

Tenley heard a knock on her door and she took one last look in the mirror. "You can do this," she murmured. "It's just a silly dance."

But it was more than that. Since her trip to Chicago, almost two weeks had passed. She'd begun to see her life in a different light. She wanted to find someone to love her, a man who might make her feel the way Alex did. But Tenley knew it would take time. She wouldn't fall in love in a week or even a year. There were too many things in her past that kept her from surrendering so easily.

But she had felt something with Alex and she was certain she could find that again if she only got out there and started looking. She had made one vow to herself. No more one-night stands. Sex for fun was a part of her past. From now on, she intended to act a bit more circumspect.

She grabbed her coat from the bed, then hurried to the door. The dogs tried to follow her outside, but she slipped out without them. "Sorry," she said.

Her grandfather stood on the porch, dressed in his best suit, his hands behind his back. He slowly brought out a plastic box and Tenley was delighted to find a corsage there. "It's an orchid," he said. "I used to buy your grandmother white orchids all the time. She loved them because they lasted so long."

Tenley took the box from his hand. "I'll put it on in the car. It'll freeze out here." She hurried down the steps and hopped inside her grandfather's Volvo. Shivering, she rubbed her hands together and then held them close to the heat. "Are you really sure you want to do this?" she asked.

"Your grandmother died four years ago. I think it's time I got out there and met some ladies. Not that I want to get married again, but I would like to have some company if I decide to see a movie or dine out."

He'd combed his bushy hair and shaved off the usual

stubble that covered his cheeks. "You look very hand-some," Tenley commented. "All the ladies will want to dance with you. I heard you've been spending time with Katie Vanderhoff."

He grinned. "Maybe. It's those damn cinnamon rolls. I stop by for coffee in the morning and she feeds me one of those and I think I'm in love. That's how your grandmother won my heart. With her apple pie."

"Well, you'll have to be sure to ask her to dance. Just make sure I get the first and the last one."

Tenley flipped the visor down and looked at her reflection in the mirror. Her hair looked silly, all curled and poufed up. As soon as she got to the dance, she'd take it down.

"You look very pretty," her grandfather said, steering the car onto the road. "No more blue hair. Or was it purple? I can't remember."

"I've decided to be perfectly normal for one night. I'm even wearing underwear."

"I don't need to hear about that," her grandfather said, wagging his finger, "although, I am glad to hear it. I wouldn't want to have you twirling around on the dance floor wearing nothing beneath your skirt. And I do love to twirl a girl."

By the time they got to town, Tenley was nervous. She'd been off the social radar for so long she knew her appearance would cause a lot of speculation. Everyone in town knew about Alex and her romance with him. But as far as they understood, that was still going on, long distance.

If they asked, she would have to tell them the truth— she and Alex had parted as friends. Friends who didn't speak to each other. Friends who couldn't possibly be in the same room without wanting to tear each other's clothes off.

The dance was already well under way when they arrived. Her grandfather grabbed her coat and hung it up, then held out his arm gallantly, a broad smile on his face. "You look lovely. Absolutely lovely. I wish your grandmother could see you. You look just as pretty as she did on the night we met."

"Thank you," Tenley said. "Are you ready?"

"I am. Are you?"

She nodded. They walked toward the entrance to the hall and stopped at the ticket table. Harvey Willis's sister, Ellen, was selling tickets and complimented them both on their snazzy attire.

The interior of the firehouse had been transformed. The trucks had been moved outside for the night and lights had been strung from the overhead beams. A small stage was set up on one end and the band was already in the midst of their rendition of "Moon River."

To Tenley's relief, there were plenty of familiar faces in attendance. If no one asked her to dance, she'd at least be able to chat. But as she scanned the room, her gaze came to rest on a face she hadn't expected to see.

Her fingers dug into her grandfather's arm as she gasped. "He's here," she whispered.

"Who's here?"

"Alex. He's standing right over there."

"Oh, look at that," her grandfather said. "Now, doesn't he look handsome. And what's that he has in his arms? Looks like roses."

"Did you know about this?" Tenley asked.

"Well, he did call a few days ago. Wanted to know if the dance was on Saturday or Sunday night. I just told him what he wanted to know. I also mentioned you'd be attending." He unhooked Tenley's hand from his arm and gave her a little push. "Go on. Talk to him before some other girl snaps him up."

Tenley slowly crossed the hall. Everyone was watching, even some of the guys in the band. Her knees felt weak and her head was spinning, but she held her emotions in check. She was not going to break down and cry. Nor was she going to throw herself into his arms.

She stopped in front of him, swallowing hard before speaking. "What are you doing here?"

"I heard you were planning on attending and I didn't want to give any of these single guys a chance to charm you."

"How did you know about the dance?"

"You mentioned it. You said Randy asked you every year."

"You remember that?"

He nodded. "I remember everything you said to me."

She glanced over her shoulder at her grandfather and found him grinning from ear to ear.

"I brought you something," Alex said. He handed her the roses. "I'm sorry there's so many of them, but I asked for the nicest bouquet and this is what they gave me." He took them from her arms. "Here, we'll just put them down."

"Thank you," she said.

"And there's candy and a card, but I thought I'd save that until later. They're out in the car."

"Gee, all you forgot was the jewelry," she teased.

"Ah, no. I didn't forget that." Alex reached into his pants pocket, but when he didn't find what he was looking for, he patted down his jacket pockets. "Where did I put that?"

"I don't need any more gifts, Alex. The flowers are fine."

"No, you'll like this one," he said. "At least, I hope you will. Here it is." He held out his fist, then opened it.

Lying in his palm was a ring...a diamond ring...a very large diamond ring. Tenley gasped, her gaze fixed on it. It was the most beautiful thing she'd ever seen, a pale yellow heart-shaped diamond, surrounded by tiny white diamonds.

"What does that mean?" she asked. Was this a proposal? And if it was, did he really expect her to accept with all these people watching her? Or maybe that was why he'd done it here, so she couldn't refuse. "Alex, I don't think this is a good idea. You know how I—"

"Tenley, don't talk, just listen. Yes, I know how you feel. And I understand your hesitation. Your experiences in life haven't made it easy for you to open yourself up to loving someone. But what we shared that week in your cabin was something special and I don't want to let that go."

"Is this a proposal?"

"It's whatever you want it to be," Alex said. "You decide. All I know is I don't want to lose you. I want you to be mine, for now and for as long as you'll have me. I want you to be my valentine, Tenley."

"But I—"

"Don't say no. You can't say no. Because I'm going to keep coming back every weekend and every holiday until you say yes. I'll buy a place up here and I'll come over every morning and take you to breakfast. And I'll sit on your sofa every night and rub your feet. We'll go for walks in the woods in the winter and we'll take our clothes off and lie in the summer sun."

He took her hand and slipped the ring on her finger. "I'm giving this to you so that you understand I won't change my mind. For as long as you wear that ring, I'm completely yours."

"But how are we going to do this? You live in Chicago and I live here."

"I'm not sure. At first, I'll come up on the weekends. And maybe you can come down and visit. We'll figure out all the details later, Tenley. We don't have to decide everything right now. All we have to do is make a commitment to try."

He was making it so easy for her to say yes. And she wanted to say the word, to throw herself into his arms and tell him it was quite possible that she did love him. Not just possible, very probable.

"I was thinking about spending some time in Chicago. There are some classes I want to take at the Art Institute this summer."

He smiled. "Really? Because that's just a quick train ride from where I live. You could stay with me. I could take you out and show you the city. You could even bring the dogs and cats. I've got plenty of room for all of you." He dropped down on one knee and held her hand. "Say yes, Tenley. Tell me you're willing to try."

"Yes." The word came out of her mouth without a second thought. "Yes. I am willing to try. And I will be your valentine."

Alex stood up and pulled her into his arms, lifting her off her feet and twirling her around on the dance floor. The crowd around them erupted in wild applause and Tenley looked up to find everyone in the hall watching them. A warm blush flooded her cheeks and she buried her face in the curve of Alex's neck.

"We're causing a scene," he said.

"I know. Don't worry. It will give them something to gossip about tomorrow morning."

"Are you all right with that?"

She nodded. "I think I can handle it."

Alex set her back on her feet, then took her face in his hands and kissed her. That brought even more applause and a few moments later, the band broke into their rendition of "My Funny Valentine." Alex swept her out onto the dance floor.

She'd never really danced before, but Alex seemed to know exactly what he was doing. She followed his lead and before long, they looked like experts. Everything always seemed so much easier when he was around.

Life, love—and dancing.

Epilogue

ANGELA TACKED an index card on her bulletin board. "The Charmer," she said. "I've discovered ten archetypes of the typical male seducer. Once women learn to identify each type, then they'll be prepared to judge their relationships more objectively."

"So, who are you planning to interview for this chapter?" Ceci asked.

"I wanted to interview Alex Stamos. He seemed to fit the type perfectly. But when I called him last week, his sister told me that he's been involved with a woman for nearly two months. That doesn't fit the pattern."

"Do you think he could be in love?" Ceci asked.

"No," Angela said. She paused. "Well, maybe. But that would be an aberration. The majority of these men never change."

"Yeah, but we'd like to believe they could," Ceci said.

"Well, I'll just have to find another man to interview. The Charmer is the most common of the archetypes. It shouldn't be too difficult."

Angie sat down at her desk and picked up the description she'd been working on. "The Charmer is all talk. He knows exactly what to say to get what he wants and he enjoys wielding this power over women. He will often delay a physical relationship, waiting until it's your idea to hop into bed together. While you're certain that sex will take the relationship to a more intimate level, he knows it signals the end. He quickly moves on after blaming you for getting too serious, too fast."

"Sounds good," Ceci said. "But it would be nice to believe that, given the right woman, any guy could change his bad behavior." She sighed. "Kind of makes me wonder what happened to all those guys I dumped because I thought they were hopeless causes."

In truth, Angela had been wondering the same thing. Was she wrong about these men? Could you teach an old dog new tricks? Or were some of these men just lost causes? "I suppose we have to be optimistic," she murmured. "If not, we might as well just give up now, because the bad ones far outnumber the good ones."

"I guess I'd really like to know how much time you should give a guy before you cut your losses and move on," Ceci said. "I've been with Lance for three months and he still refuses to call me his girlfriend."

Angela gave her friend a weak smile. "There are always exceptions to every rule. We've just got to figure out a way to find those exceptions."

Angela stared at the index card. Alex's change of heart certainly didn't bode well for the theories she planned to present in her book. But for every one guy who left the single life behind and fell in love, there were a hundred more serial daters out there breaking women's hearts.

She was on a mission to make a point. And if Alex Stamos wasn't the man she thought he was, then she'd find another Charmer to take his place. After all, she could spot a smooth operator a mile away.

* * * * *

HER SECRET FLING

BY

SARAH MAYBERRY

First published in Great Britain 2011
Harlequin Mills & Boon Limited,
Eton House, 18-24 Paradise Road, Richmond, Surrey TW9 1SR

© Small Cow Productions Pty Ltd. 2010

ISBN: 978 0 263 88052 6

14-0111

Harlequin Mills & Boon policy is to use papers that are natural, renewable
and recyclable products and made from wood grown in sustainable forests.
The logging and manufacturing processes conform to the legal environmental
regulations of the country of origin.

Printed and bound in Spain
by Litografia Rosés S.A., Barcelona

This one is for all my female friends—the passers of tissues, the sharers of chocolate, the givers of hugs. Having a laugh with my mates is one of the small, perfect pleasures in life.

And, as always, no words would be written if it was not for Chris cheering me on from the sidelines and Wanda coaching me from the finish line. You both rock—thank you for your endless patience.

Sarah Mayberry is an Australian by birth and a Gypsy by career. At present she's living in Auckland, New Zealand, but that's set to change soon. Next stop, who knows? She loves a good department-store sale, French champagne, shoes and a racy romance novel. And chocolate, naturally.

Dear Reader,

What happens when a one-night stand becomes more than it should be? That's the question that was the seed for *Her Secret Fling*. Two consenting adults have a good time and agree that's all it was—then life intervenes and forces them to get to know each other. And, surprise surprise, they like what they discover— after some twists and turns along the way, naturally.

There's a scene towards the beginning of the book that was in my mind from the moment I started imagining this story. I call it "man versus machine," and if you're reading this after finishing the book, you'll know what I'm talking about. If you're reading this letter first... well, you'll know what I'm talking about pretty soon! I hope it tickles your funny bone as much as it did mine.

Most of all, I hope you enjoy reading about Jake and Poppy's story as they work their way around to realising they need each other and that loving someone is a gift, not a burden. I love to hear from readers, so please drop me a line at sarah@sarahmayberry.com if you feel the urge.

Until next time,

Sarah Mayberry

1

WHATEVER YOU DO, don't throw up.

Poppy Birmingham pressed a hand to her stomach. The truth was, if her breakfast was destined to make a reappearance, that hand was hardly going to make a difference. She let her arm drop. She took a deep breath, then another.

A couple of people frowned at her as they pushed through the double doors leading into the *Melbourne Herald*'s busy newsroom. She was acutely aware that they probably recognized her and were, no doubt, wondering what one of Australia's favorite sporting daughters was doing hovering outside a newspaper office, looking as though she was going to either wet her pants or hurl.

Time to go, Birmingham, the coach in her head said. *You signed up for this. Too late to back out now.*

She squared her shoulders and sucked in one last, deep breath. Then she pushed through the double doors. Immediately she was surrounded by noise and low-level excitement. Phones rang, people tapped away at keyboards or talked into phones or across partitions. Printers whirred and photocopiers flashed. In the background, huge windows showcased the city of Melbourne, shiny and new in the morning sunshine after being washed clean by rain overnight.

A few heads raised as she walked the main aisle, following the directions she'd been given for the sports department. She tried to look as though she belonged, as though she'd been mixing it up with journalists all her life. As though the new pants suit she was wearing didn't feel alien when she was used to Lycra, and the smell of stale air and coffee and hot plastic wasn't strange after years of chlorine and sweat.

The rows of desks seemed to stretch on and on but finally she spotted Leonard Jenkins's bald head bent over a keyboard in a coveted corner office. As editor of the sports section on Melbourne's highest circulating daily newspaper, Leonard was the guy who assigned stories and had final say on edits and headlines. He was also the man who'd approached her six weeks ago and offered her a job as a columnist.

At the time she'd been thrown by the offer. Since she'd been forced into retirement by a shoulder injury four months ago she'd been approached to coach other swimmers, to work with women's groups, to sponsor a charity. A chain of gyms wanted her to be their spokesperson, someone else wanted her to endorse their breakfast cereal. Only Leonard's offer opened the door to new possibilities. For years she'd known nothing but the black line of the swimming pool and the burn of her muscles and her lungs. This was a new beginning.

Hence the urge to toss her cookies. She hadn't felt this nervous since the last time world championships were in Sydney—when she *had* thrown up spectacularly before her first heat.

She stopped in front of Leonard's office and was about to rap on the open door when he lifted his head. In his late fifties, he was paunchy with heavy bags under his eyes and fingers stained yellow from nicotine.

"Ah, Poppy. You found us okay. Great to see you," he said with a smile.

"It's good to be here."

"Why don't I introduce you to the team first up and show you your desk and all that crap," Leonard said. "We've got a department meeting in an hour, so you'll have time to get settled."

"Sounds good," she said, even though her palms were suddenly sweaty. She was hopeless with names. No matter what she did, no matter how hard she tried to concentrate on linking names to faces, they seemed to slip through her mental fingers like soap in the shower.

She wiped her right hand furtively down her trouser leg as Leonard led her to the row of desks immediately outside his office.

"Righteo. This is Johnno, Davo and Hilary," he said. "Racing, golf and basketball."

Which she took to mean were their respective areas of expertise. Johnno was old and pock-faced, Davo was mid-thirties and very tanned, and Hilary was red-haired and in her early thirties, Poppy's age. They all murmured greetings and shook her hand, but she could tell they were keen to get back to their work.

"This mob around here," Leonard said, leading her around the partition, "keep an eye on motor sport. Meet our resident gear heads, Macca and Jonesy."

"All right. Our very own golden girl," Jonesy said. He was in his late twenties and already developing a paunch.

"Bet you get that all the time, huh?" Macca asked. He smiled a little shyly and ran a hand over his thinning blond hair. "Price of winning gold."

"There are worse things to be called," she said with a smile.

Leonard's hand landed in the middle of her back to steer her toward the far corner.

"And last, but not least, our very own Jack Kerouac," he said.

Poppy's palms got sweaty all over again as she saw who he was leading her toward.

Jake Stevens.

Oh, boy.

Her breath got stuck somewhere between her lungs and her mouth as she stared at the back of his dark head.

She didn't need Leonard to tell her that Jake Stevens wrote about football, as well as covering every major sporting event in the world. She'd read his column for years. She'd watched him interview her colleagues but had somehow never crossed paths with him herself. She knew he'd won almost every Australian journalism award at least once. And she'd read his debut novel so many times the spine had cracked on her first copy and she was now onto her second.

He was wonderful—the kind of writer who made it look effortless. The kind of journalist other journalists aspired to be.

Including her, now that she'd joined their ranks.

"Heads up, Jake," Leonard said as they stopped beside the other man's desk.

Not Jakey or some other diminutive, Poppy noted. His desk was bigger, too, taking up twice as much space as those of the other journalists.

Jake Stevens kept them waiting while he finished typing the sentence he was working on. Not long enough to be rude, but enough to make her feel even more self-conscious as she hovered beside Leonard. Finally he swiveled his chair to face them.

"Right. Our new *celebrity columnist*," he said, stressing the last two words. He looked at her with lazy, deep blue eyes and offered her his hand. "Welcome on board."

She slid her hand into his. She'd only ever seen photographs of him before; he was much better looking in real life. The realization only increased her nervousness.

"It's great to meet you, Mr. Stevens," she said. "I'm a big admirer of your work—I've read your book so many times I can practically recite it."

Jake's dark eyebrows rose. "*Mr. Stevens?* Wow, you must *really* admire me."

The back of her neck prickled with embarrassment. She hadn't meant to sound so stiff and formal. Her embarrassment only increased when his gaze dropped to take in her business-like brown suit and sensibly heeled shoes, finally stopping on her leather satchel. She felt like a schoolgirl having her uniform inspected. She had a sudden sense that he knew exactly how uncomfortable she was in her new clothes and her new shoes and how out of place she felt in her new environment.

"I suppose you must have interviewed Poppy at some time, eh, Jake?" Leonard asked.

"No. Never had the pleasure," Jake said.

He didn't sound very disappointed.

Leonard settled his shoulder against the wall. "Big week-end. Great game between Port and the Swans."

"Yeah. Almost makes you look forward to the finals, doesn't it?" Jake said.

The two men forgot about her for a moment as they talked football. Poppy took the opportunity to study the man who'd written one of her favorite novels.

Every time she read *The Coolabah Tree* she looked at the photograph inside the back cover and wondered about the man behind the cool, slightly cocky smile. He'd been younger when the photo had been taken—twenty-eight or so—but his strong, straight nose, intensely blue eyes and dark hair were essentially unchanged. The seven years that had passed were evident only in the fine lines around his mouth and eyes.

The photo had been a head shot yet for some reason she'd

always imagined he was a big, husky man. He wasn't. Tall, yes, with broad shoulders, but his body was lean and rangy— more a long-distance runner's physique than a footballer's. He was wearing jeans and a wrinkled white shirt, and she found herself staring at his thighs, the long, lean muscles outlined by faded denim.

There was a pause in the conversation and she lifted her gaze to find Jake watching her, a sardonic light in his eyes. For the second time that morning she felt embarrassed heat rush into her face.

"Well, Poppy, that's pretty much everyone," Leonard said, pushing off from the wall. "A few odds and bods on assignment, but you'll meet them later. Your desk is over here."

He headed off. She glanced at Jake one last time before following, ready to say something polite and friendly in parting, but he'd already returned to his work.

Well, okay.

She was frowning as Leonard showed her the desk she'd occupy, wedged into a corner between a potted plant and a pillar. It was obviously a make-do location, slightly separate from the rest of the sports team. Pretty basic—white laminate desk, multiline phone, a computer and a bulletin board fixed to the partition in front of her.

"Have a bit of a look-around in the computer, familiarize yourself with everything," Leonard said, checking his watch. "I'll get Mary, our admin assistant, to fill you in on how to file stories and all that hoopla later. Department meeting's in forty minutes—in the big room near the elevators. Any questions?"

Yes. Is it just my imagination, or is Jake Stevens an arrogant smart-ass?

"No, it all looks good," she said.

It was a relief to be left to her own devices for a few minutes. All those new faces and names, the new environment, the—

Who was she kidding? She was relieved to have a chance to pull herself together because Jake Stevens had rattled her with his mocking eyes and his sarcasm. He'd been one of the reasons she took the job in the first place—the chance to work with him, to learn from the best. Out of all her coworkers, he'd been the least friendly. In fact, he'd been a jerk.

Disappointing.

But not the end of the world. So what if he wasn't the intelligent, funny, insightful man she imagined when she read his book and his articles? She'd probably hardly ever see him. And it wasn't as though she could take his behavior personally. He barely knew her, after all. He was probably a jerk with everyone.

Except he wasn't.

Two hours and one department meeting later, Poppy was forced to face the fact that the charming, witty man she'd imagined Jake to be did exist—for everyone except her.

The first half of the meeting had been a work-in-progress update. Everyone had multiple stories to file after the weekend so there was a lot of discussion and banter amongst her new colleagues. She didn't say anything since she had nothing to contribute, just took notes and listened. Jake was a different person as he mixed it up with the other writers. He laughed, he teased, he good-naturedly accepted ribbing when it came his way. He offered great ideas for other people's stories, made astute comments about what their competitors would be covering. He was like the coolest kid in school—everyone wanted him to notice them, and everyone wanted to sit next to him at the back of the bus.

The second half of the meeting consisted of brainstorming future stories and features. With the Pan-Pacific Swimming

Championship trials coming up, there was a lot of discussion around who would qualify. Naturally, everyone turned to her for her opinion—everyone except Jake, that is.

He didn't so much as glance at her as she discussed the form of the current crop of Australian swimmers, many of whom had been her teammates and competitors until recently.

"Hey, this is like having our own secret weapon," Macca said. "I love that stuff about what happens in the change rooms before a race."

"Yeah. We should definitely do something on that when the finals are closer. Sort of a diary-of-a-swimmer kind of thing," Leonard said. "Really get inside their heads."

"There's plenty of stuff we could cover. Superstitions, lucky charms, that kind of thing," she said.

"Yeah, yeah, great," Leonard said.

Her confidence grew. Maybe this wasn't going to be as daunting as she'd first thought. Sure, she was a fish out of water—literally—but everyone seemed nice and she understood sport and the sporting world and the commitment top athletes had to have to get anywhere. She had something to contribute.

Then she glanced at Jake and saw he was sitting back in his chair, doodling on his pad, clearly bored out of his mind. A small smile curved his mouth, as though he was enjoying a private joke.

It was the same whenever she spoke during the meeting—the same smile, the same doodling as though nothing she had to say could possibly be of any interest.

By the time she returned to her desk, she knew she hadn't imagined his attitude during their introduction. Jake Stevens did not like her. For the life of her, she couldn't understand why. They'd never met before. How could he possibly not like her when he didn't even know her?

She'd barely settled in her chair when her cell phone beeped. She checked it and saw Uncle Charlie had sent her a message:

Good luck. Come out strong and you'll win the race.

She smiled, touched that he'd remembered this was her first day. Of course, Uncle Charlie always remembered the important things.

She composed a return message. She'd bought him a cell phone a year ago so they could stay in touch when she was competing internationally, but he'd never been one hundred percent comfortable with the technology. She could imagine how long it had taken him to key in his short message.

The sound of masculine laughter made her lift her head. Jake was talking with Jonesy at the other man's desk, a cup of coffee in hand. She watched as Jake dropped his head back and laughed loudly.

She returned her attention to the phone, but she could still see him out of the corner of her eye. He said something to Jonesy, slapped the other man on the shoulder, then headed to his own desk. Which meant he was about to walk past hers.

She kept her focus on her phone but was acutely conscious of his approach. When he stopped beside her, her belly tightened. Slowly she lifted her head.

He studied her desk, taking in the heavy reference books she'd brought in with her: a thesaurus, a book on grammar and the Macquarie Dictionary in two neat, chunky volumes. After a short silence, he met her eyes.

"You do know that *A* to *K* comes before *L* to *Z*, right?" he asked. He indicated the dictionaries and she saw she'd inadvertently set them next to each other in the wrong order. He leaned across and rearranged them, as though she might not be able to work it out for herself without his help.

"My hot tip for the day," he said, then he moved off, arrogance in every line of his body.

She was blushing ferociously. Her third Jake Stevens–inspired blush for the day. She stared at his back until he reached his desk, unable to believe he'd taken a swipe at her so openly. What an asshole.

He thought she was a stupid jock. That was why he'd been so dismissive when he met her and why he hadn't listened to a word she'd said in the meeting. He thought she was a dumb hunk of muscle with an instinct for swimming and nothing to offer on dry land. Certainly nothing to offer in a newsroom.

She knew his opinion shouldn't matter. It probably wouldn't, either, if it didn't speak to her deepest fears about this new direction she'd chosen.

She'd finished high school, but only just. She read a lot, but she wasn't exactly known for her e-mails and letters. For the bulk of her life, she'd measured her success in body lengths and split seconds, not in column inches and words. Even her parents had been astonished when she accepted this job. She could still remember the bemused looks her mother and father had exchanged when she'd told them. Her brother had laughed outright, thinking she was joking.

She picked up her phone again and stared at her uncle's text:

Come out strong and you'll win the race.

God, how she wished it was as easy as that.

She was filled with a sudden longing for the smell of chlorine and the humid warmth of the pool. She knew who she was there, what she was. On dry land, she was still very much a work in progress.

Who cares what he thinks? He doesn't know you, he knows nothing about you. Screw him.

Poppy straightened in her chair. She reached out and deliberately put the *L* to *Z* back where it had been before Jake Stevens gave her his *hot tip for the day.*

She'd beaten some of the toughest athletes in the world. She'd conquered her own nerves and squeezed the ultimate performance from her body. She'd stood on a podium in front of hundreds of thousands of people and held a gold medal high.

One man's opinion didn't mean dick. She was smart, she was resourceful. She could do this job.

JAKE PULLED THE CORK from a bottle of South Australian shiraz and poured himself a glass. He took the bottle with him as he moved from the kitchen into the living room of his South Yarra apartment.

Vintage R.E.M. blasted from his stereo as he dropped onto the couch. His thoughts drifted over the day as he stared out the bay window to the river below. He frowned.

Poppy Birmingham.

He still couldn't believe the stupid pride on Leonard's face as he'd introduced her. As if she was his own private dancing bear. As if he expected Jake to break into applause because a woman who had never put pen to paper in her life had scored the kind of job it took dedicated journalists years to achieve.

He made a rude noise as he thought about the brand-new reference books she'd lined up on her desk. Not a wrinkle on the spine of any of them. What a joke.

He took another mouthful of wine as his gaze drifted to his own desk, tucked into the corner near the window.

He should really fire up his computer and try to get some words down.

He smiled a little grimly. Who was he kidding? He wasn't going to do any writing tonight, just as he hadn't done any real writing for the past few years. It wasn't as though his publisher was breathing down his neck, after all. They'd stopped doing that about five years ago, two years after his first novel had made the bestseller lists, won literary prizes and turned him into a wunderkind of the Australian literary scene.

He'd missed so many deadlines since then, they'd stopped hassling him. Now the only time he was asked when his next book was due out was when he met people for the first time— mostly because they assumed he'd written second, third, fourth books that they simply hadn't heard about. After all, what writer with any ambition to be a novelist wrote only one book and never completed another?

Ladies and gentlemen, I give you Jake Stevens.

He offered a mock bow to his apartment and poured himself another glass of wine.

Like a needle in the groove of a record, his thoughts circled to Poppy Birmingham. He'd never interviewed her, but he'd interviewed plenty like her. He knew without asking that she'd discovered a love of swimming at an early age, been talent scouted by someone-or-other, then spent the next twenty years churning up various pools.

She'd sacrificed school, boyfriends, family, whatever, to be the best. She was disciplined. She was driven. Yada yada. She could probably crack walnuts with her superbly toned thighs and outrun, outswim and out-anything-else him that she chose to do.

She was a professional athlete—and she had no place on a newspaper. Call him old-fashioned, but that was how he felt.

He leaned back on the couch, legs straight in front of him,

feet crossed at the ankle. His stereo stacker switched from REM to U2—the good angry old stuff, not the new soft and happy pop they'd been serving up the last decade.

He swirled the wine around in his glass, shaking his head as he remembered Poppy's brown suit and how wrong she'd looked in it—like a kid playing dress up. No. Like a transvestite, a man shoehorning himself into women's clothing.

Honesty immediately forced him to retract the thought. He might not approve of her hiring, but there was nothing remotely masculine about Poppy. She was tall, true, with swimmer's shoulders. But she was a woman, no doubt about it. The breasts and hips curving her suit had been a dead giveaway there. And she had a woman's face—small nose, big gray eyes, cheekbones. Her mouth was a trifle on the large size for true beauty, but her full lips more than made up for that. And even though she kept her blond hair cropped short, she didn't look even remotely butch.

He took another mouthful of wine. Just because his new "colleague" was easy on the eyes didn't make what Leonard had done any more acceptable. A smile curved his mouth as a thought occurred—if Poppy was anywhere near as inexperienced a writer as he imagined, Leonard was going to have his hands full knocking her columns into shape. It felt like a fitting punishment for a bad decision.

JAKE WALKED TO WORK the next morning, following the bike path that ran alongside the Yarra River all the way into the city. A rowing team sculled past. He watched his breath mist in the air and kept his thoughts on the interview he wanted to score today and not the words he hadn't written last night.

He was the first one in, as usual. He shrugged out of his

coat, hung it and his scarf across the back of his chair then headed for the kitchen to fire up the coffee machine.

Someone had beaten him to it. Poppy Birmingham stood at the counter, spooning sugar into a mug. He counted four teaspoons before she began to stir. That was some sweet tooth.

She glanced over her shoulder as he reached for the coffee carafe, obviously having heard him approach.

"Good—" Her mouth pressed into a thin line when she saw it was him and the rest of her greeting went unsaid. Her dark gray eyes gave him a dismissive once-over. Then she turned back to her sickly sweet coffee.

She was pissed with him because of his gibe about the dictionary yesterday. Probably couldn't conceive of a world where athletic ability didn't open every door. Because he was a contrary bastard, he couldn't resist giving her another prod.

"Bad for you, you know," he said.

She glanced at him and he gestured toward her coffee.

"All that sugar. Bad for you."

"Maybe. But I'll take sweet over bitter any day," she said. She picked up her mug and exited.

He cocked his head to one side. Not a bad comeback— for a jock.

He picked up his own mug and followed her. He couldn't help noting the firm bounce of her ass as she walked. Probably she could crack walnuts with that, too. He wondered idly what she looked like naked. Most swimmers didn't have a lot happening up top, but she clearly had a great ass and great legs.

She sat at her desk. He glanced over her shoulder as he passed. She'd started writing her debut article already. He read the opening line and mentally corrected two grammatical errors. As he'd suspected last night, Leonard was going to have his work cut out for him editing her work into something publishable. Thank God it wasn't Jake's problem.

Then Leonard stopped by his desk midmorning and changed all that.

"No way," Jake said the moment he heard what his boss wanted. "I'm not babysitting the mermaid."

Leonard frowned. "It's not babysitting, it's mentoring. She needs a guiding hand on the tiller for a few weeks while she finds her feet, and you're our best writer."

Jake rubbed his forehead. "Thanks for the compliment. The answer is still no."

"Why not?" Leonard asked bluntly.

Jake looked at the other man assessingly. Then he shrugged. What the hell. What was the worst thing that could happen if he told his boss how he really felt?

"Because Poppy Birmingham doesn't deserve to be here," he said.

He wasn't sure what it was—his raising his voice, a freak flat spot in the background noise, some weird accident of office acoustics—but his words carried a long way. Davo and Macca looked over from where they were talking near the photocopier, Hilary smirked and Mary looked shocked.

At her desk, Poppy's head came up. She swiveled and looked him dead in the eye. For a long moment it felt as though the world held its breath. Then she stood and started walking toward him.

For the first time he understood why the press had once dubbed her the Aussie Amazon—she looked pretty damn impressive striding toward him with a martial light in her eye.

He crossed his arms over his chest and settled back in his chair.

Bring it on. He'd never been afraid of a bit of truth telling.

2

POPPY HAD PROMISED HERSELF she'd speak up if he did something provocative again. She figured broadcasting his antipathy to all and sundry more than qualified.

Leonard looked as though he'd swallowed a frog. Jake simply watched her, his arms crossed over his chest, his expression unreadable.

She offered Leonard a tight smile. "Would you mind if I had a private word with Mr. Stevens?"

Her new boss eyed her uncertainly. His gaze slid to Jake then to her. She widened her smile.

"I promise not to leave any bruises," she said.

Leonard shrugged. "What the hey? Tear him a new one. Save me doing it."

He headed to his office and Poppy turned to face Jake. His mouth was quirked into the irritating almost smile that he'd worn every time she spoke during their meeting yesterday. She wanted to slap it off his face. She couldn't believe that she'd once thought he was good-looking.

"What's your problem?" she asked.

"I don't have a problem."

"Bullshit. You've been taking shots at me since I arrived. I want to know why."

He looked bored. "Sure you do."

"What's that supposed to mean?"

"You don't want to hear what I really think. You want me to be awed by your career and treat you like the department mascot like everyone else," he said.

She sucked in a breath, stung. "That's the last thing I want."

"Well, baby, you sure took the wrong job." He turned away from her, his hands returning to his keyboard. Clearly he thought their conversation was over.

"I'm still waiting to hear what you really think," she said. She crossed her arms over her chest. She figured that way he might not notice how much she was shaking. She didn't think she'd ever been more angry in her life.

He swiveled to face her. "Let me put it this way—how would you feel if your ex-coach suddenly announced I'd be leading the swim team into the next world championships because he liked a couple of articles I'd written?"

"You think I got this job under false pretenses."

"Got a journalism degree?" he asked.

"No."

"Done an internship?"

"You know I haven't."

"Then, yes, I think you didn't earn this job."

She blinked. He spread his hands wide.

"You asked," he said.

"Actually, you offered—to the whole office."

"If you think some of them haven't thought the same thing…" He shrugged.

She glanced at the other journalists who were all eavesdropping shamelessly. Was it possible some of them shared Jake's opinion?

"Leonard came knocking on my door, not the other way around." She sounded defensive, but she couldn't help it.

"You accepted the offer," he said. "You could have said no."

"So I'm not allowed to have a career outside of swimming?" she asked.

"Sure you are. You're even allowed to have this career, since we all know the Australian public is so in love with its sporting heroes they'll probably eat up anything you write with a spoon, even if you can't string two words together. Just don't expect me to like it," he said. "I worked long hours on tin-pot newspapers across the country to get where I am. So has everyone else on this team. I'm not going to give Leonard a standing ovation for valuing my skills so lightly he's slotted a high school graduate into a leading commentator's role just because she looks good in Lycra and happens to swim a mean hundred-meter freestyle. Never going to happen."

Poppy stared at him. He stared back, no longer bored or cool.

"You might have come to this job by working your way through the ranks, but I've earned my chance, too." She hated that her voice quavered, but she wasn't about to retreat. "I'm not going to apologize for the fact that I have a public profile. I've represented this country. I've swum knowing that I'm holding other people's dreams in my hands, not just my own. You don't know what that's like, the kind of pressure that comes with it. And while you're on your high horse judging me, you might want to think about the fact that you wouldn't even have a job if it wasn't for people like me sweating it out every day, daring to dream and daring to try to make those dreams a reality. You'd just be a commentator with nothing to say."

She turned her back on him and walked away.

The other journalists were suddenly very busy, tapping away at their keyboards or shuffling through their papers. She sat at her desk and stared hard at her computer screen, hoping it looked as though she was reading, when in fact, she was trying very, very hard not to cry.

Not because she was upset but because she was *furious*. Her tear ducts always wanted to get involved when she got angry, but she would rather staple something to her forehead than give Jake the Snake the satisfaction of seeing her cry.

Ten minutes later, Macca approached.

"I was just in, speaking to Leonard. I'm going to work with you on your first few articles, until you find your feet," he said.

She stared at him, chin high. "What did he bribe you with?"

"Actually, I volunteered."

She blinked.

"What can I say? I've always had a thing for water sports."

She gave him a doubtful look.

"And I think Jake was out of line," he added. "So what if you haven't earned your stripes in the trenches? Welcome to the real world, pal. People get lucky breaks all the time for a bunch of different reasons. And even if he disagrees with Leonard's decision, being an asshole to you is not the way to deal with it."

"Hear, hear," she said under her breath.

He smiled at her. "So, we cool? You want to show me what you've got so far?"

"Thank you." She was more grateful for his offer—and support—than she cared to admit.

He pulled up a chair beside her. She shifted the computer screen so he could read her article more easily and sat in tense, twitchy silence while he did so. She'd spent a lot of time working on it—all of last night and most of this morning. She knew it wasn't great, but she hoped it was passable.

"Hey, this is pretty good," he said.

She tried not to show how much his opinion meant to her.

She'd already been nervous enough before The Snake had aired his feelings. Now she knew all eyes would be on her maiden effort.

"You can be honest. I'd rather know what's wrong so I can fix it than have you worry about my feelings," she said.

"Relax. Ask anyone, I'm a hard bastard. Open beer bottles with my teeth and everything," Macca said. "If this was utter crap, I'd tell you. I think we can work on a few things, make some of the language less formal and stiff, but otherwise there's not much that needs doing."

Poppy sank back in her seat and let her breath out slowly.

"And if you're free for lunch, I'll give you the lowdown on the office politics," Macca said.

She smiled. Maybe there was an upside to being savaged by an arrogant, know-it-all smart-ass after all—she'd just made her first new friend at the *Herald.*

THAT NIGHT POPPY HAD her second Factual Writing for the Media class at night school. She'd enrolled when Leonard had offered her the job. So far, she'd learned enough to know she had a lot to learn. But that was why she was there, after all.

There was a message from Uncle Charlie when she finally got home. She phoned him on his cell, knowing he'd be up till all hours since he was a notorious insomniac.

"Hey there, Poppy darlin'," he said when he picked up the phone. "I've been waiting for you to call and fill me in on your first day at work."

"Sorry. To be honest, it was a little sucky, and day two was both worse and better. I was kind of holding off on calling until I had something nice to report."

She filled him in on Jake and their argument and the way Macca had come to her aid.

"Bet this Jake idiot didn't know who he was taking on when he took on you," Uncle Charlie said.

She laughed ruefully. "I don't know. I don't think he was exactly cowed by my eloquence. It makes swimming look pretty tame, doesn't it, even with all the egos and rivalries?" she said a little wistfully.

"Missing it, Poppy girl?"

She swung her feet up onto the arm of her couch.

"I miss knowing what I'm good at," she said quietly, thinking over her day at work and how lost she'd felt in class tonight.

"You're good at lots of things."

"Oh, I know—eating, sleeping…"

"You forgot showering and breathing."

They both laughed.

"Just remember you're a champion." He was suddenly very serious. "The best of the best. Don't let some jumped-up pen pusher bring you down. You can do anything you put your mind to."

Uncle Charlie was her biggest fan, her greatest supporter, the only member of her family who'd watched every one of her races, cheered her wins and commiserated her losses.

"You still haven't told me what you want for your birthday," she said.

He turned seventy in a few weeks' time. She already had his present, but asking him what he wanted had become a bit of a ritual for the two of them.

"A pocketful of stardust," he said. "And one of them fancy new left-handed hammers."

She smiled. He had a different answer every time, the old bugger.

"Careful what you wish for."

"Just seeing you will make my day."

She couldn't wait to see his face when she gave him her present. She'd had her first gold medal mounted in a frame alongside a photograph of the two of them at the pool when she was six years old. It was her favorite shot of the two of them. He was in the water beside her, his face attentive and gentle as he guided her arms. She was looking up at him, laughing, trusting him to show her how to get it right.

He always had, too. He'd never let her down, not once.

"Love you, Uncle Charlie," she said.

"Poppy girl, don't go getting all sentimental on me. Nothing more pitiful than an old man sooking into the phone," he said gruffly.

They talked a little longer before she ended the call. She lay on the couch for a few minutes afterward, reviewing the day again.

She was proud of herself for standing her ground against Jake Stevens, but she wished she hadn't had to. The only place she'd ever been aggressive was in the pool. She couldn't remember the last time she'd had a stand-up argument with someone.

Just goes to show, you've led a sheltered life.

She stood and walked to her bedroom. She was pulling her shirt off when she caught sight of a familiar orange book cover on the bookcase beside her bed. The name Jake Stevens spanned the spine in thick black print.

"Uh-uh, not in my bedroom, buddy," she said. She picked up *The Coolabah Tree* with her thumb and forefinger and marched to the kitchen. She dumped the book in the trash can and brushed her hands together theatrically.

"Ha!"

She'd barely gone three paces before her conscience made her swing around. Before she'd met Jake, *The Coolabah Tree* had been one of her favorite books. His being a jerk didn't change any of that.

She fished out the book and walked into her living room. She looked around. Where to put it so it wouldn't bug the hell out of her?

She laughed loudly as an idea hit her. She crossed to the bathroom and put the book amongst the spare toilet-paper rolls she stored in a basket in the corner near her loo.

She was still smiling when she climbed into bed.

"ANYONE WANT A COFFEE?" Poppy asked.

Jake didn't bother looking up from his laptop. There was no way she would bring him a coffee, even if he was stupid enough to ask for one. The three weeks she'd been at the *Herald* hadn't changed a thing between them.

"I'm cool," Davo said.

"White for me," Hilary said.

Jake glanced over his shoulder as Poppy moved to the back of the press box. The room was buzzing with conversation and suppressed excitement. In ten minutes, the Brisbane Lions and the Hawthorn Hawks would duke it out for the Australian Football League Premiership.

Jake still couldn't believe that Leonard had assigned the newest, greenest writer on the staff to cover the AFL Grand Final. It was the biggest event in the Australian sporting calendar, bar none. Even The Melbourne Cup didn't come close. The *Herald* would dedicate over six pages to the game tomorrow—and Poppy hadn't even clocked a month with the paper and had only a handful of columns under her belt.

Granted, her articles had been a pleasant surprise. Warm, funny, smart. She needed to loosen up a little, relax into the role. Stop trying so hard. But in general the stories hadn't been the disaster he'd been anticipating. Which still didn't make her qualified to be here.

They'd flown into Brisbane two days ago to cover the teams' last training sessions and interview players before the big event, and he'd been keeping an eye on her. What he'd seen confirmed she was a rookie in every sense of the word. She interviewed players from a list of questions she'd prepared earlier, reading them off the page. She studiously wrote down every word they said. She was earnest, eager, diligent—and way out of her depth. Yesterday, Coach Dickens had brushed her off when she tried to ask him about an injured player. She'd been unable to hide her surprise and hurt at the man's rude rebuff.

Better toughen up, baby, Jake thought as he watched her wait patiently in the catering line for her chance at the coffee urn. Most journalists would eat their own young for a good story. As for common courtesies such as waiting in line…

As if to demonstrate his point, Michael Hague from the *Age* sauntered up to the line and slipped in ahead of her, chatting to a colleague already there as though the guy had been saving him a place. Poppy frowned but didn't say anything.

Jake shook his head. She was too nice. Too squeaky clean from all that swimming and wholesome food and exercise. Even if she developed the goods writingwise, she simply didn't have the killer instinct a journalist required to get the job done.

He was turning to his computer when she stepped out of line. Hague had just finished filling a cup with coffee and Poppy reached out and calmly took it from his hand. She flashed him a big smile and said something. Jake couldn't hear what it was, but he guessed she was thanking him for helping her out. Then she calmly filled a second cup for Hilary.

Jake laughed. He couldn't help it. The look on Hague's

face was priceless. Poppy made her way to their corner, her hard-won coffees in hand. Her gaze found his across the crowded box and he grinned at her and she smiled. Then the light in her eyes died and her mouth thinned into a straight, tight line.

Right. For a second there he'd almost forgotten.

He faced his computer.

He was on her shit list. Which was only fair, since she'd been on his ever since he'd learned about her appointment.

He shook the moment off and focused his attention on the field. The Lions and the Hawks had run through their banners and were lined up at the center of the ground. The Australian anthem began to play, the forty-thousand-strong crowd taking up the tune. The buzz of conversation in the press box didn't falter, journalists in general being a pack of unpatriotic heathens. On a hunch Jake glanced over his shoulder. As he'd suspected, Poppy's gaze was fixed on the field and her lips were moving subtly as she mouthed the words to the anthem.

It struck him that of all the journalists here, she was the only one who could even come close to understanding how the thirty-six players below were feeling right now. He had a sudden urge to lean across and ask her, to try and capture the immediate honesty of the moment.

He didn't. Even if she deigned to answer him, just asking the question indicated that he was softening his stance regarding her appointment. Which he wasn't.

The song finished and the crowd roared its excited approval as the two teams began to spread out across the field. Jake tensed, adrenaline quickening his blood. He loved the tribalism of football, the feats of reckless courage, the passion in the stands. It was impossible to watch and not be affected by it. Even after hundreds of kickoffs over many years, he still got excited at each and every game. The day he didn't was the day he would retire, absolutely.

The starting siren echoed and the umpire held the ball high and then bounced it hard into the center of the field. The ruckmen from both teams soared into the air, striving for possession of the ball.

Jake leaned forward, all his attention on the game. Behind him he heard the tap-tap of fingers on a keyboard. He didn't need to look to know it was Poppy. What in hell she had to write about after just ten seconds of play, he had no idea. Forcing his awareness of her out of his mind, he concentrated on the game.

POPPY CHECKED HER WATCH as she stepped into the hotel elevator and punched the button for her floor. By now, most of the players would be drunk or well on their way to it, and probably half of the press corps, too. She'd been too tired to take Macca up on his invitation to join him, Hilary and Jake for a postcoverage drink. Even if she hadn't been hours away from being ready to file her story by the time the others were packing up to go, she'd had enough of The Snake over the past few days to last a lifetime. She wasn't about to subject herself to his irritating presence over a meal. Not for love or money.

She scrubbed her face with her hands as the floor indicator climbed higher. She was officially exhausted. The lead-up to the game, the game itself, the challenging atmosphere of the press box, the awareness that she was part of a team and she needed to deliver—all of it had taken its toll on her over the past couple of days and she felt as though she'd staggered over the finish line of a marathon.

She was painfully aware that she'd been the last of the team to file her stories every day so far. She'd sweated over her introductions, agonized over what quotes to use, fretted over her sign-offs. Writing didn't come naturally to her, and she was beginning to suspect it was something she would always have to work at. No wonder her shoulders felt as though they were carved from marble at the end of each day.

She toed off her shoes as she entered her hotel room. She'd given up on high heels after the first week in her new job. Not only did they make her taller than most men, she couldn't walk in them worth a damn and they made her feet ache. She shed her navy tailored trousers and matching jacket, then her white shirt. Her underwear followed and she made her way to the bathroom and started the shower up. She felt ten different kinds of greasy after a day of being jostled by pushy journalists and fervent football fans and hovering over her laptop, sweating over every word and punctuation mark. She tested the water with her hand and rolled her eyes when it was still cold. Stupid hotel. No one had warned her that the *Herald* were a pack of tightwads when it came to travel expenses. It was like being on the national swim team again.

She glanced at her reflection while she waited for the water to warm. As always, the sight of her new, improved bustline made her frown. She'd never had boobs. Years of training had keep her lean and flat. But now that she'd stopped the weights and the strenuous training sessions and relaxed her strict diet, nature had reasserted itself with a vengeance over the past few months.

She slid her hands onto her breasts, feeling their smooth roundness, lifting them a little, studying the effect in the mirror. She shook her head and let her hands drop to her sides. It was too weird. She wasn't used to them. Kept brushing against things and people. And she'd had to throw out half her wardrobe. Then there was the attention from men. She didn't think she'd ever get used to that. Never in her life had she had so many conversations without eye contact. She'd quickly learned not to take her jacket off if she wanted to be taken seriously. Which meant she wore it pretty much all the time.

The water was warm at last and she stepped beneath the spray. Ten minutes later, she toweled herself off and went in search of food. The room service menu was uninspired. What she really felt like eating was chocolate chip ice cream and a packet of salty, crunchy potato chips. She eyed the minibar for a few seconds, but couldn't bring herself to pay five times the price for something that was readily available in the convenience store two doors down from the hotel.

She pulled on sweatpants and a tank top, decided against a bra since she was making just a quick pig-out run, then zipped up her old swim team sweat top. Her feet in flip-flops, she headed downstairs.

The latest James Bond movie was showing on the hotel's in-house movie service. She smiled to herself as she thought about Daniel Craig in his swim trunks. Sugar, salt and a buff man—not a bad night in.

She was still smiling contentedly when she returned to the hotel five minutes later, loaded down with snack food. She was in the elevator, the doors about to close, when Jake Stevens thrust his arm between them. She stood a little straighter as he stepped inside the car.

Damn it. Was it too much to ask for a few moments' reprieve from his knowing, sarcastic eyes and smug smile?

She moved closer to the corner so there wasn't even the remote chance of brushing shoulders with him.

His gaze flicked over her briefly. Suddenly she was very aware of her wet hair and the fact that she wasn't wearing a bra. She shifted uncomfortably and his gaze dropped to her carrier bag of goodies.

"Having a big night, I see," he said.

"Something like that."

He leaned closer. She fought the need to pull away as he hooked a finger into the top of the bag and peered inside.

"Chocolate-chip ice cream and nacho-cheese corn chips. Interesting combo."

Up close, his eyes were so blue and clear she felt as though she could see all the way through to his soul.

If he had one.

"Do you mind?" she said, jerking the bag away from him.

He raised his eyebrows. She raised hers and gave him a challenging look.

"Just trying to be friendly," he said.

"No, you weren't. You were being a smart-ass, at my expense, as usual. So don't expect me to lie down and take it."

His gaze dropped to her chest, then flicked back to her face. She waited for him to say something suitably smart-assy in response, but he didn't. The lift chimed as they hit her floor.

Thank God.

She stepped out into the corridor. He followed. She frowned, thrown. Then she started walking toward her room, keeping a watch out of the corner of her eye. As she'd feared, he was following her.

She stopped abruptly and he almost walked into her as she swung to face him.

"I don't need an escort to my door, if that's what you're doing," she said. "I don't need anything from you, which I know probably sticks in your craw since your ego is so massive and so fragile you can't handle having a rookie on the team."

Jake cocked his head to one side. Then he smiled sweetly

and pulled a key from his pocket. The number 647 dangled from it. Two rooms up from hers.

Right.

She could feel embarrassed heat rising into her face. Why did this man always make her so self-conscious? It wasn't as though she cared what he thought of her.

She started walking again. She had her key in her hand well before her door was in sight. She shoved it into the lock and pushed her door open as quickly as she could. She caught a last glimpse of his smiling face as she shut the door.

Smug bastard.

She grabbed a spoon from the minibar and ripped the top off the ice cream. She needed to keep an eye on her temper around him. And she had to stop letting him get under her skin. That, or she had to somehow develop Zen-like mind-body control so she could stop herself from blushing in front of him.

Large quantities of chocolate-chip ice cream went a long way to calming her. She turned on the TV and opened the corn chips. An hour into the movie, she was blinking and yawning. When the movie cut to a love scene, she decided to call it quits for the night. She liked watching James run and jump and beat people up, but she wasn't so wild about the mandatory sex scenes. She knew other people liked them, even got disappointed when they didn't get enough of them, but she so didn't get it.

She contemplated the issue as she brushed her teeth.

Sex, in her opinion, was one of the most overrated activities under the sun. She figured she was experienced enough to know—she'd had three lovers in her thirty-one years, and none of them had come even close to being as satisfying as George, her battery-operated, intriguingly shaped friend. Disappointing, but true.

Of course, it was possible that she'd had three dud lovers in a row, but she thought it far more likely that sex, like most anti-aging products and lose-weight-now remedies, was not all it was cracked up to be.

But that was only her opinion.

She spat out toothpaste and rinsed her mouth. Then she climbed into bed. Just before she drifted off, she remembered that moment in the hallway again. Next time she came face-to-face with The Snake, she was going to make sure she was the one who came out on top. Definitely.

THE NEXT DAY SHE CAUGHT A CAB to the airport for her flight home and discovered that while she and the bulk of Australia had been focused on the ups and downs, ins and outs of a red leather ball, the baggage handlers union had decided to go on strike.

The mammoth lines of irate and desperate-looking people winding through the terminal were her first clue that something was up. She collared a passing airport official and he filled her in. The strike was expected to run for at least three days. Most flights had been canceled.

"Damn it," she said.

He held up his hands. "Not my fault, lady."

"I know. Sorry. It's just my uncle's birthday is on Wednesday."

She'd planned to drive to her parents' place in Ballarat, about an hour north of Melbourne, for the party. But at this rate it didn't look as though she was even going to be in the same state come Wednesday.

"Lots of weddings and funerals and births, too," the official said with a shrug. "Nobody likes an airline strike."

He moved off and Poppy stared glumly at his back. This

was not the first time she'd been left stranded by an airline. As a swimmer, she'd been at the mercy of more than her fair share of strikes, bad weather and mechanical failures. Once, the swim team had almost missed an important meet in Sydney thanks to an airline strike, but their coach had had the foresight to hire a minibus and had driven them the thousand kilometers overnight.

A lightbulb went on in Poppy's mind. If it was good enough for Coach Wellington, it was good enough for her. She turned in a circle, looking for the signs for the car rental agencies. She spotted the glowing yellow Hertz sign. Then she spotted the lineup in front of it. Well, she could only try.

Fingers crossed, she headed over to join the masses.

JAKE WOKE, FEELING LIKE CRAP. Headache, furry mouth, seedy stomach—standard hangover material. He groaned as he rolled out of bed and blessed his own foresight in ensuring he had an afternoon flight out of Brisbane and not a morning one. He'd played this game before, after all, and he'd known last night would be a big one. And it had been. He'd lost track of which bar he'd wound up in, and who he'd been drinking with. There had definitely been some disappointed Bears players in the mix, drowning their sorrows. And he could distinctly remember someone singing the Hawk's club song at one stage.

Whatever. A fine time was had by all.

Well, not *quite* all. Some people had chosen to forgo the festivities and hole up in their room with chocolate-chip ice cream and nacho-cheese corn chips.

He rinsed his mouth out as the memory of Poppy's uptight little "I don't need an escort" speech filtered into his mind.

He didn't know what it was about her, but he couldn't seem to resist poking her with a stick. Maybe it was the way her chin came up. Or the martial gleam that came into her eyes. Or maybe it was the pink flush that colored her cheeks when he bested her.

He stepped beneath the shower and lifted his face to the spray. Oh, man, but he needed some grease and some salt and some aspirin. Big-time.

Of course, Ms. Birmingham wouldn't be in search of saturated animal fats this morning. She'd had hers last night, in the quiet privacy of her room.

Someone needed to tell her that road trips were a good opportunity to bond with her colleagues. Especially when you were a newcomer to the team.

He shrugged. Not his problem. And she was unlikely to take advice from him, anyway.

He recalled the way she'd looked last night, hair wet, face devoid of makeup. Sans bra, too, if he made any guess. She had more up top than he'd expected. Definitely a generous handful.

He soaped his belly and wondered again what she'd look like naked. She wasn't his type, but he supposed he could understand why Macca followed her with his eyes whenever he thought no one was watching. She was striking. She could almost look Jake in the eye, she was so tall. He bet she liked to be on top, too.

He stared down at his hard-on.

Okay, maybe she *was* his type. But only because it had been a while since he'd gotten naked with anyone. Four...no, five months. That was when he'd decided that his fledgling relationship with Rachel-from-the-gym was too much of a distraction from the book he still hadn't written.

He turned the water to cold. Brutal, but effective—his erection sank without a trace.

He dressed and packed his luggage. Then he checked out.

"We hope you enjoyed your stay with us, Mr. Stevens," the woman on the reservation desk said. "And we hope the strike doesn't inconvenience you too much."

He lifted his head from signing his credit card slip. "Strike? What strike?"

"The baggage handlers' strike. It looks like it'll last three days minimum at this point. We've had a lot of people coming back from the airport to check in again."

Shit. He had ten days vacation starting tomorrow. He had plans to go fishing with an old college buddy. No way was he going to kick his heels in Brisbane when there were rainbow trout going begging.

He grabbed his bags and headed to the taxi stand. He'd been caught out like this before and he knew that even during a strike there were still planes in the air. He might be able to talk his way onto one of them. And there was always the bus, God forbid, or a rental.

The moment he hit the airport he nixed the idea of talking himself onto a flight. Lines spilled out the door and every person and his dog was on a cell, trying to hustle some other way home.

He turned for the rental desks. No lines there. Bonus. Maybe no one else had thought of driving home yet.

He dropped his bags in front of the counter and smiled at the pretty blonde behind the desk.

"Hey, there. I need to rent a car," he said.

She rolled her eyes. "You and the rest of the country. Sorry, sir, as we announced five minutes ago, we're all sold out."

He kept smiling.

"There must be something. A car due back later today? Something that didn't pass inspection?"

"Many of our cars didn't come in when our customers

heard about the strike. We've been pulling cars in from our other branches, but there's no stock left. I'm very sorry, sir."

She didn't sound very sorry. She sounded as though she'd had a long and stressful day and was privately wishing him to hell.

"There must be something," he said.

"Where are you traveling to?"

He waited for her to start tapping away at her keyboard to find him a car, but she didn't.

"Melbourne."

"The only thing I can suggest is that you hook up with someone else who is driving your way. I know that blond woman over there is going to Melbourne. She got our last car—maybe she'll take pity on you."

Jake turned his head to follow the woman's finger. He stared in disbelief at the back of Poppy Birmingham's head.

"Shit."

"Excuse me, sir?"

There was no way Poppy was going to take pity on him. She'd more than likely laugh in his face—if he gave her the opportunity.

"Is there a bus counter around here?" he asked. He hated bus travel with a passion, but desperate times called for desperate measures. There were trout swimming in the Cobungra River with his name on them, and he intended to be there to catch them.

"They're on the west side of the airport. Just follow the crowd."

"Thanks."

He hefted his bags and started walking. He could see Poppy up ahead, talking on her cell phone. If it were anyone else— a complete stranger—he'd throw himself on her mercy in a split second. But Poppy didn't like him. Admittedly, he'd given her plenty of reasons to feel that way, but the fact remained that she was far more likely to drive over him in her rental car than offer him a lift in it.

He walked past her, wondering how she'd react if he snatched the keys from her hand and made a bolt for it. But she was probably pretty fast on her feet. She had those long legs and hadn't been out all night swilling beer and red wine the way he had.

He kept walking. Then he started thinking about sitting on a bus with seventy-odd other angry travelers, sucking in diesel fumes and reliving horror flashbacks from half a dozen high school excursions.

Man.

He stopped in his tracks. He lowered his chin to his chest. He thought about the bus, then he thought about his pride. Then he turned around and walked to where Poppy was finishing her phone call.

He stopped in front of her. She stared at him blankly. Then her gaze dropped to his luggage. A slow smile curved her mouth. He waited for her to say something, but she didn't.

She was going to make him ask.

Shit.

He took a deep breath. "Going my way?"

Her smile broadened. "I'm sorry, but you're going to have to do much better than that."

She crossed her arms over her chest and waited. He stared at her for a long moment.

Then he braced himself for some heavy-duty sucking up.

3

POPPY STILL COULDN'T BELIEVE she'd let Jake into her car. Even if she drove nonstop like a bat out of hell, she'd sentenced herself to twenty-four hours in The Snake's company in a small enclosed space. Had she been on drugs twenty minutes ago?

She slid him a look. His eyes were hidden behind dark sunglasses but he appeared to be staring out the windshield, his expression unreadable. He hadn't shaved and his face was dark with stubble. He hadn't said a word since they argued over who was driving the first leg and which route out of the city to take.

He resented having to kiss her ass, but she didn't regret making him do it. It was nice to have a bit of power for a change, even if it was only temporary.

She focused on the road. If he wanted to play it strong and silent, that was fine with her. She'd had more than enough of his smart mouth over the past three weeks.

"Do you mind if I turn the air-conditioning on?" he asked ten minutes later.

It was an unseasonably warm day for September and she was starting to feel a little sticky herself.

"Sure."

He fiddled with the controls. "Hmph." He sat back in his seat. "It's broken."

"It can't be."

He turned his head toward her. She didn't need to see his eyes to know he was giving her a look.

"Feel free to check for yourself."

She did, flicking the switch on and off several times. He didn't say a word as the seconds ticked by and no cool air emerged from the air vents.

"Fine. It's broken," she said after a few minutes.

"No shit."

She cracked the window on her side to let some fresh air into the car. He did the same on his side. The road noise was loud, the equivalent of being inside a wind tunnel.

Great. Jake the Snake beside me, and a bloody hurricane roaring in my ear. This is going to be the road trip from hell.

After half an hour she couldn't stand the noise any longer. She shut her window. A short while later, so did Jake.

The temperature in the car rose steadily as the sun moved across the sky. Jake shrugged out of his jacket and so did she. By the time they'd been on the road for two hours, her shirt was sticking to her and sweat was running down her rib cage.

Poppy spotted a sign for a rest area and turned into it when it came up on their left.

Jake stirred and she realized he'd been dozing behind his glasses and not simply staring out the windshield ignoring her.

"You ready to swap?" he asked, pushing his sunglasses up onto his forehead and rubbing his eyes.

"Nope," she said. "I'm changing into something cooler."

She got out of the car and unlocked the trunk. Jake got out, too, stretching his arms high over his head and arching his back. His T-shirt rode up, treating her to a flash of flat belly, complete with a dark-haired happy trail that disappeared beneath the waistband of his jeans. She frowned and looked away, concentrating on digging through her bag in search of her sports tank. When she found it, she gave him a pointed look.

"Do you mind?"

He stared at her.

"What?"

"A little privacy, please." She spun her finger in the air to indicate she wanted him to turn his back.

He snorted. "Lady, we're on a state highway, in case you hadn't noticed. Everyone who drives past is going to cop an eyeful unless you hunker down in the backseat."

"I don't care about everyone else. I have to work with you."

She didn't care if he thought she was prudish or stupid—she was not stripping down to her bra in front of him. She absolutely did not want him knowing what she looked like in her underwear. It was way too personal a piece of information for him to have about her. She wasn't exactly sure how he could turn it to his advantage, but that was beside the point.

He sighed heavily and turned his back.

"If I see anything, I promise to poke an eye out," he said.

She unbuttoned her shirt and shrugged out of it. She checked he still had his back turned. He hadn't moved. Her tank top got tangled in her haste to pull it over her head. She twisted it around the right way and tugged it on. She glanced at him again. This time his face was in quarter profile as he gazed over the acres of grassland running alongside the freeway.

Had he sneaked a look? She stared at him suspiciously, but he didn't so much as blink.

"I'm ready," she said.

He turned and his gaze flicked down her body briefly before returning to her face. She was acutely aware that her tank top was small and tight and a far cry from the business shirts and jackets she'd been wearing to work to date.

She slammed the trunk shut and moved to the driver's side door. He met her there, his hand held out expectantly.

"I'll drive," he said.

"No, you won't."

If he'd asked, maybe she would have considered it. But there was no way she was taking orders from him. They'd be serving ice cream in hell before that happened.

"There's no way you're driving all the way to Melbourne," he said.

"I'm not an idiot. When I'm tired, I'll let you know."

His stared at her, his blue eyes dark with frustration. Then he turned on his heel and returned to his side of the car.

She waited till he had his seat belt on before pulling back onto the highway. Immediately he leaned across and turned the radio on. Static hissed and he fooled around with the dials until he found some music.

Johnny Cash's deep voice filled the car. Poppy forced her shoulders to relax. Jake Stevens got on her nerves. She wished he didn't, but he did. As she'd already acknowledged, she needed to get a grip on her temper when he was around.

It would also be good if she wasn't quite so aware of him physically. Her gaze kept sliding across to where his long legs were stretched out into the footwell. And she kept remembering that flash of flat male belly. It was highly annoying and disconcerting. She didn't like him. She didn't want to be aware of him.

She slid another surreptitious glance his way and tensed when she caught him looking at her. More specifically, at her breasts.

She glared at him until he lifted his gaze and met hers. He had the gall to shrug a shoulder and give her a cocky little smile.

"Hey, what can I say? I'm only human."

"Subhuman, you mean."

"Staring at a woman's breasts is not a capital offense, last time I checked," he said.

"Maybe I don't want you looking at my breasts. Ever think about that?"

"Don't worry, I won't make a habit of it."

She stiffened. What was he saying? That he didn't like her breasts? That he didn't consider them ogleworthy? She glanced down at herself and frowned.

"What's wrong with them?" she asked.

She could have bitten her tongue off the moment the words were out of her mouth. She could feel the mother of all blushes working its way up her neck.

She kept her eyes front and center as he looked at her.

"Relax," he said. "I didn't mean anything by it. Men check out women all the time. It's basic biology."

"I *am* relaxed," she said through her teeth. "And I didn't think you were about to propose because you checked out my rack. I might not be used to having boobs, but I know that much."

She didn't think it was possible, but her blush intensified. She couldn't believe she'd made such a revealing confession to The Snake.

There was a short silence before he spoke.

"I wondered about that," he said. "All the photos I ever saw, you looked about an A cup."

"You made a note of my *cup size?*" she asked, her voice rising.

"Sure. I'm not blind. So, what, you stopped training and puberty kicked in, is that it?"

He spoke conversationally, as though they were talking about the weather. As though it was perfectly natural for him to go around guessing women's breast size. And maybe it was—but not *hers*. She didn't want him looking at her and thinking about her like that. It made her feel distinctly…edgy.

She clenched her hands on the wheel. "We are not talking about my breasts."

"You brought it up."

"I did not! You were staring at me!"

"Because you changed into that teeny, tiny tank. I could hardly pretend I didn't notice."

"The air-conditioning is broken and I was hot and you could have tried. A gentleman would have," she said.

He laughed. "A gentleman? Baby, I'm a journalist. I wouldn't have a job if I was a gentleman. Something you better learn pretty quick if you want to survive in this game."

She held up a hand. "Spare me your sage advice, Yoda. You're about three weeks too late to apply for the position of mentor."

He shrugged. "Suit yourself."

"I will, thank you."

"Always have to have the last word, don't you?"

"Look who's talking."

"Thank you for proving my point."

She pressed her lips together, even though she was aching to fire back at him.

He angled his seat back and stretched out, his arms crooked behind his head. "Do you miss it?"

"I beg your pardon?"

"Swimming. Training. Being on the team. Do you miss it?"

She made a rude noise in the back of her throat. "Just because we're stuck in a car for a few hours doesn't mean we have to talk."

"It's a long drive."

"I'm not here to entertain you."

He was silent for a moment. She flipped the visor to the side to block the sun as it began its descent into the west.

"Okay, what about this? I get a question, then you get one. Quid pro quo."

"Thank you, Dr. Lecter, but I don't want to play."

"Why? What are you scared of?"

She shifted in her seat. He was goading her, daring her. She knew it was childish, but she didn't want him thinking he could best her so easily.

"Fine," she said. "Yes, I miss swimming. It was my life for twenty-five years. Of course I miss it."

"What do you miss the most?"

"You think I can't count? It's my turn. Why haven't you published a follow-up to *The Coolabah Tree?*"

She could feel him bristle.

"I'm working on one now," he said stiffly.

"What's it called?"

"Nice try. Why do you want to be a journalist?"

"Because it's not swimming. And because I feel I have something to offer. How long did it take you to write your first book?"

"Two years, working weekends and nights."

"How many drafts did you do?"

"Three. And that was two questions."

"You answered them."

He shrugged. "Do you ever think about the four-hundred-meter final at Beijing? Wish you could go back again?"

She should have known he'd bring that up. The lowest point in her swimming career—of course he'd want to stick his finger in the sore spot and see if she squirmed.

She put the indicator on and pulled into the approaching rest stop.

"What's wrong?" he asked.

"I'm tired."

"Right."

She got out and stretched her back. She was aware of Jake doing the same thing on the other side of the car. Dusk was falling and the world around them was muted in the fading light. They crossed in front of the car as they swapped sides.

She waited until he was on the highway again before answering his question.

"I used to think about it all the time, but not so much now. I had my chance and I missed it and I came home with silver instead of gold. I had a bunch of excuses for myself at the time, but the fact is that I simply didn't bring my best game on the day. It happens. If you can't live with your own mistakes, competing for a living will kill you."

"You're very philosophical."

"Like I said, I used to think about it a lot. But you can't live in the past."

He reached up and adjusted the rearview mirror. "Your turn."

She studied his profile. He was a good-looking man. Charming and interesting—when he wanted to be. Not that she'd experienced any of that firsthand, but she had eyes in her head. He'd cut a swath through the female contingent in the press box with his boyish grin and quick wit.

"Why aren't you married?" she asked before she could censor herself.

He frowned at the road. "I was. We divorced five years ago."

"Oh." She hadn't expected that. Watching him at work, the way he came in early and left late, she'd figured him for a loner, one of those men who had dodged commitment so many times it had become a way of life. But he'd been married. And he sounded unhappy that he wasn't still married.

"What about you? Why aren't you married?"

She smiled ruefully. Quid pro quo, indeed. "No one's ever asked me."

He glanced at her, a half smile on his mouth. "That's a cop-out."

She shrugged. "Maybe, but that's all you're going to get."

They lapsed into silence, even though it was her turn to ask a question.

"We should stop for food soon. And start thinking about where we're going to stay the night," he said.

They wound up at McDonald's since it was the only thing on offer. They studied the road map as they ate, deciding on Tamworth as their destination for the evening.

"There'll be a decent motel there, and a few places to eat," Jake said.

She pushed the remains of her burger and fries away.

"You going to eat those?" Jake asked, eyeing her fries.

"Go nuts."

He polished them off then went back to the counter to order an apple pie for the road.

She waited outside in the cold night air, looking up at the dark sky, listening to the rush of cars on the highway and marveling that she and Jake Stevens had spent several hours in a car together and no blood had been spilled.

Yet.

"Okay, let's hit the road," he said as he joined her in the parking lot.

She glanced at him, straight into his blue eyes. They stared at each other a moment too long before she turned away. He walked ahead of her as they crossed to the car. She found herself staring at his butt. She'd always had a thing for backsides and he had a nice one. Okay—a *very* nice one.

Why am I noticing Jake the Snake's butt?

She frowned and looked away. Must be the car equivalent of Stockholm Syndrome. At least she hoped that was what it was.

POPPY WAS DRIVING AGAIN when they pulled into Tamworth just before eight o'clock. Apart from one small disagreement over radio stations, their unofficial cease-fire was still in effect. Jake craned his head to read the brightly illuminated signs of the various motels as they cruised Tamworth's busy main street.

"That place, over there," he said, pointing to a blue-and-white neon sign in front of a brown-brick, two-story motel. "They've got spa baths."

She rolled her eyes but pulled over, since she didn't have a better suggestion.

"Park the car and I'll get us some rooms," he said.

Before she could say anything, he was out of the car and striding toward reception.

"Yes, sir," she said to herself. "Three bags full, sir. Have you any wool, sir?"

Because it would rankle too much to obey him to the letter, she joined him in reception as he was handing over his credit card to the middle-aged clerk.

"Hang on a minute," she said. "I'll pay for my own room."

"You got the car. I'll get this."

It was a perfectly reasonable argument but she opened her mouth to dispute it anyway.

"We can argue after dinner," he said. "You can arm wrestle me to the floor and pound me into submission."

"What makes you think I'm having dinner with you?"

"Because you can't sit in your room and eat ice cream and chips two nights in a row. You'll get scurvy. You need vitamin C."

The desk clerk was watching their interplay curiously. Poppy took her room key.

"This doesn't mean I'm having dinner with you," she said.

But after she'd had a long shower and changed into fresh clothes, the sterile cleanliness of the room started to get to her. Plus she was hungry. When Jake knocked on her door ten minutes later, she pocketed her room key and stepped outside.

"There's a steak place up the road," he said.

He hadn't doubted her for a moment, the smug bastard.

"This is only because I'm hungry and they don't have room service," she said.

"It's all right. I didn't think you were about to propose because you agreed to have dinner with me."

He was deliberately echoing her words from during their ill-fated breast discussion. She couldn't help it—she cracked a smile.

"You are such a smart-ass," she said.

"You're no slouch yourself."

"No, I'm strictly amateur hour compared to you. You're world-class."

They started walking toward the glowing roadside sign for Lou's Steakhouse.

"Now you've made me nervous," he said.

"Sure I have."

"You have. World-class—that's a lot to live up to. You've given me performance anxiety."

"I bet you've never had performance anxiety in your life."

"That was before I met you."

She became aware that she was still smiling and slowing her steps, dawdling to prolong their short walk to the restaurant. She frowned, suddenly uneasy. She looked at him and saw that he was watching her, an arrested expression on his face. As though, like her, he'd just realized that they were enjoying each other's company.

Good Lord. Next thing you know, the moon will be blue and a pig will fly by.

She lengthened her stride and fixed her gaze on the steak house. The sooner this evening—this *drive*—was over, the better.

"YOU ARE SO WRONG. He meant to get busted. Why else would he volunteer to do a second drug test when he'd already been cleared?"

Poppy leaned across the table as she spoke, one elbow propped on the red-and-white tablecloth. Jake tried not to smile at the earnest determination in her expression. She was pretty cute when she got all passionate about something.

They were the only customers left in the restaurant, even though it was barely ten. They'd been talking sports throughout the meal, their current topic being the recent drug scandal involving a well-known British cyclist.

"There's no way anyone would throw away their career like that. He's banned from cycling for life. He's lost his sponsors. He's screwed," he said.

She nodded enthusiastically. "Exactly, and that's what he wanted. Why else would he take that second test?"

The neck of her shirt gaped. Not for the first time that evening he noticed the lacy edge of her bra and wondered if she knew her underwear was on display. He suspected not— Poppy didn't strike him as the kind of woman who seduced with glimpses of lace and skin. She probably had no idea one of her buttons had slipped free.

Maybe it made him an opportunist, but he wasn't about to tell her. Not when the view was so rewarding.

He returned his attention to her face, aware that his jeans were a little snug around the crotch all of a sudden.

"No way. I just don't buy that anyone would throw it all away like that."

"You don't know what it's like," she said darkly. "Everyone looking at you, pinning their hopes on you, channeling all their ambitions and dreams into your life, your career, your achievements. Maybe he self-destructed rather than risk failing on the track."

He studied her. She looked so sunny and uncomplicated, even after several glasses of wine and a long day on the road. He couldn't imagine her ever wanting to throw her career in.

"Is this a confession? Did you injure your shoulder on purpose so you'd miss the World Championships?" he asked lightly.

She reached for her wine and took a big swallow. "You're joking, I know, but there were definitely times when I thought it would be easier if I simply couldn't swim anymore. Not because I decided not to, you know, but because I just *couldn't* and the decision was taken out of my hands."

"And then you got injured."

"Yep, I did. And I discovered that the grass is always greener." She laughed, then shrugged self-deprecatingly. "It's not like I could keep swimming forever. There are girls coming up now who are so strong and fast…. I would have been a dinosaur wallowing around the pool in a few more years."

She picked up the dessert menu and studied it. He took the opportunity to study her. She looked like everybody's idea of a poster girl for Australian swimming, the kind of athlete you'd find smiling from the back of a cereal box: the blond hair, the clear skin, the frank way she had of meeting his eye whenever she spoke. But she was more complicated than that. She was funny. She was honest. She was smart. She questioned things, was curious about the world.

He liked her.

"How have things been going with Macca?" he asked. "He been helping you out with your columns okay?"

She'd been about to take another mouthful of wine but she froze with the glass halfway to her mouth. She stared at him for a long moment, then put her glass down.

"Dear Lord. Someone pinch me—Jake Stevens has got a conscience."

He shifted in his chair. "I might be a smart-ass, but I'm not an asshole."

She raised an eyebrow. For some reason it seemed very important to him that she not believe the worst of him.

"I owe you an apology." The words came out a little stiffly but he was determined to set things right. "I shouldn't have taken my frustration with Leonard out on you."

"No, you shouldn't have."

"It's not your fault he turned into a publicity whore. And you've done a good job."

She raised a hand to her forehead and blinked rapidly. "Wow. Is there a gas leak in the room or did you just pay me a compliment?"

He poured himself more wine. They were both a little tipsy, which was no bad thing given the turn the conversation had taken.

"Okay, maybe I have been an asshole," he admitted.

"It's okay. You gave me something to worry about other than my writing. And you were entitled to be pissed about the situation—just not at me."

She smiled. He smiled back.

"You're being very generous," he said.

"I think I'm a little drunk. No doubt I'll regret not making you grovel more in the morning."

"That wasn't groveling. That was an apology."

"You say tomato…"

She was laughing at him, her gray eyes alight with humor. He raised his glass.

"To starting again."

She clinked glasses with him.

"To learning from the best," she said.

He frowned, then shook his head ruefully as he took her meaning. "You don't want me mentoring you. I'm a smart-ass, remember?"

"You're right, I don't. But I want your advice sometimes. I want to know when I'm screwing up and haven't realized it yet. You're the best writer on the paper. I'd be an idiot not to learn from you if I can."

She held his eye as she said it. There was no denying he was flattered. And a little embarrassed by her unflinching assessment.

"Macca's pretty good. And Hilary's up for a Walkley Award this year."

"Modesty, Mr. Stevens? I'm surprised." She propped her elbow on the table again and leaned her chin on her hand. "Come on, hit me with your next hot tip for the day. What do I need to know? Where have I gone wrong so far?"

He winced at the reminder of his comment regarding her reference books. Not his kindest act. He owed her.

"You should have come out with us last night," he said. "Everyone's tired after a long haul like the Grand Final, but you missed out on a chance to be part of the team."

She frowned, processing what he'd said.

"Okay, fair enough. Next time, I'll come out to play. What else?"

He poured her more wine and topped up his own glass. The waitstaff were standing at the counter looking bored, but he figured if they wanted Poppy and him to leave they could say so.

"You need to be tougher. When Coach Dickens ignored you the other day when you asked for a comment, you backed off. You should have tried again, said something to get his attention, made him stop and engage with you."

"I didn't want to alienate him. I know what it's like when the press get in your face."

"That's our job. He gets paid a lot of money to do what he does. If he didn't want the fame and glory, he'd be at home watching it on TV like everyone else."

She nodded. "I'll try to be pushier. Even if it does make my toes curl."

He settled back in his chair and let his gaze dip below her face again. He'd been thinking about her breasts on and off ever since their conversation in the car. He wondered if they were as firm as they looked. And if her skin was as warm and smooth as he imagined.

"One thing you should think about," he said. "The players. Football, tennis, cricket, it doesn't matter—they're hound dogs, even a lot of the married ones. No matter what, don't go there. Shortest route to trashing your career."

She waved a hand dismissively. "Not a problem. Next."

"I'm serious. Remember Joanne Hendricks? She would have been in line for Leonard's job by now if she was still around."

He didn't need to say more. He could see from Poppy's expression that she remembered the furor that had erupted when the high-profile journalist's affair with a married rugby player had gone public. She'd subsequently been forced to resign from the *Herald*.

"I take your point, but it's not an issue."

"You say that now, but I've seen some of those guys go to

work on a woman. They can be bloody charming when they want something."

Poppy made a frustrated sound. "As if I'm going to jeopardize my career for a bunch of pointless fumbling and huffing and puffing. I'm not a *man*." She drained her wineglass.

"*Huffing and puffing?* And what does being a man have to do with it?"

"Sex is for men," she said simply. "You get off on it more, therefore you're more likely to be idiots about it."

She said it as though reporting proven medical fact. He raised his eyebrows and leaned toward her.

"Let me get this straight—women don't enjoy sex? Is that your contention?"

"I can't speak for all women. But I bet I'm not the only one who thinks it's overrated."

She was drunk. That was the only reason she would ever say something so personal and revealing to him. If he were a gentleman, he'd ignore it and move on.

"You think sex is overrated?"

"In a word, yes."

"Baby, you're *so* doing something wrong."

She shook her head. "No. I've done it enough to know. Sex is like an Easter egg—big and impressive on the outside, but empty on the inside. All promise, no delivery."

"You've never had an orgasm," he said with absolute certainty.

"On the contrary. I have had many, thanks to the marvels of modern technology. Which is more than I can say for sex."

Oh, man, was she going to regret this conversation in the morning.

"There's no way a piece of plastic and silicone can match the satisfaction of real sex," he said.

"Your opinion. I'd take twenty minutes with George over

twenty minutes with a man any day. He never talks back, he always does what I want and he always delivers at least once."

"George? Your vibrator is called George?"

"After George Clooney."

He shook his head.

"You can't handle it because male egos like to think that women get off as much as they do during sex. It's a prowess thing."

"I don't *think* anything. I *know* women have a good time in bed with me."

She shook her head slowly.

"Remember the diner scene from *When Harry Met Sally?*" She thumped her fists on the table a couple of times. "Oh, yes. *Yesss. Yesss!*" She slumped in her chair languorously, ran a hand through her hair and looked at him with heavy, smoky eyes.

He had to admit, it was a pretty damn convincing impersonation of a woman having an orgasm.

She sat up straight and smiled at him. "I rest my case."

He narrowed his eyes at her. "Why do women have sex then if they don't enjoy it as much?"

"Because they want to keep men happy. Because they want them to put the garbage out and catch spiders and change the oil in the car and they understand sex is the currency of choice when dealing with the male of the species."

Jake simply couldn't believe a woman could be so messed up about something so simple.

"Come on," he said, standing. He threw some money on the table to cover their bill.

"It's not your fault. It's biology. You scored the penis. Every time you put it inside something, it feels good. We scored the clitoris. If they'd really known what they were doing, whoever designed human beings would have put it *inside* the vagina."

She was talking loudly and the staff were exchanging looks. He grabbed her hand and towed her out of the restaurant.

"The clitoris works just fine where it is," he said, leading her back toward the motel.

"With George on the job it does."

She stumbled and he steadied her. She rambled some more about the differences between men's and women's bodies as they completed the short walk to the motel. He was too busy focusing on reaching his room ASAP to pay much attention. Finally he opened his door and led her inside.

She blinked as she looked around. "This isn't my room."

"Nope. It's mine."

He kicked off his shoes. She blinked at that, too.

"What are you doing?"

"Setting you straight." He glanced over his shoulder at the clock on the bedstand. "Does the twenty minutes start from now or when we get naked?"

She stared at him for a long moment.

"You're drunk."

"So are you."

"Not that drunk."

"Me, either. So what are you waiting for?"

She hesitated another beat. Then her gaze dropped to his crotch where he was already hard for her. Her mouth opened. He swore her pupils dilated. Then she started shrugging out of her jacket.

"I hope your ego can handle this," she said.

"I hope your body can handle this," he said.

She pulled her shirt off and he stared at her full, lush breasts, covered in white lace. He was already hard, but he got a whole lot harder.

"Your time starts now," she said.

4

POPPY REACHED BEHIND HERSELF to unclasp her bra. If she stopped to think about it, she knew she'd lose her nerve. This was nuts. Absolutely bonkers.

For starters, until a few hours ago she'd loathed Jake Stevens, and she was pretty sure the feeling had been mutual. Then there was the small fact that she worked with him.

So why was she sliding her straps off her shoulders and letting her bra fall to the carpet?

Jake made a small, satisfied sound as he saw her breasts. Heat swept through her.

That was why—the rush of hot, sticky sensation that had hit her every time she'd caught Jake staring at her breasts over dinner.

He was attracted to her. He wanted to get her naked, touch her breasts, slide inside her.

And even though she was almost certain the buildup would be more fun than the actual main event, she wanted to do all those things, too.

"For the record, in case you have any doubts at all, you have great breasts," Jake said, his gaze intent on her. "Really, really great."

He stripped off his T-shirt and she stared at his broad shoulders and lean belly. He was tall and rangy but still firm and lean with muscle. Dark hair covered his pectoral muscles before trailing south. Her gaze dropped to his thighs where his erection was clearly visible against the denim of his jeans.

She imagined what he would look like—long and thick and hard. Need throbbed between her thighs.

She undid her belt and unzipped her fly, then worked her jeans over her hips. She hesitated, unsure whether to take her panties off at the same time. She shrugged; they were on the clock, after all. Might as well give him a fighting chance. She slid her thumbs into the side elastic of her underwear and tugged them off with her jeans. She kicked the lot to one side and looked at him.

He was pushing his jeans and underwear down his legs and his erection bounced free. Her eyes widened as she saw how big he was, how hard.

Oh, boy.

He looked up from kicking his clothes to one side and grinned when he saw her face. Then his gaze dropped to study her legs, her hips, the neat curls between her thighs.

"Come here," he said, crooking his finger.

She took a small step forward, all her doubts clamoring for attention. This was a bad idea. Really, really bad.

Jake closed the remaining distance between them. She opened her mouth to tell him she'd made a mistake, that she was sober now and this was a crazy. He reached out and slid both hands onto her breasts. His hands were warm and firm, and he locked eyes with her as he cupped her in his palms, then swept a thumb over each nipple. She bit her lip. He squeezed her nipples between his fingers, rolling them gently.

"Nice?" he said, his breath warm on her face.

"Yes."

"Good."

He lowered his head. She closed her eyes as his mouth covered hers, soft yet firm, his tongue sweeping into her mouth. He brought his body against hers, her breasts pressing against his chest, his erection jutting into her belly. His skin felt incredibly hot where it touched hers, his body hard where hers was soft.

He tasted of wine. His tongue teased hers, wet and hot. She shivered as his hand slid across her lower belly.

"Normally, we'd fool around a little more than this before I made a play for third base," he murmured as he kissed his way across to her ear. "But my honor's at stake here. So if you don't mind, I'm going to go for it."

She let her head drop back as he slid his tongue into her ear.

"I think I can make an exception this once," she said.

The truth was, she didn't know if it was the wine or the situation or Jake himself, but she could feel how wet she was for him already. Tension had been building between them all night. His clear blue eyes watching her across the table. The way he'd teased her. The way he'd looked at her body. It had all been leading to this moment. Why else had she issued her challenge?

And it *had* been a challenge. Definitely.

She shivered as he slid a single finger into the folds of her sex. Her hands gripped his shoulders as his finger slicked over her clitoris and then slid farther still until he was at her entrance.

Slowly, he circled his finger. She widened her stance, clenching her muscles in anticipation of his penetration. And then he slid his finger inside her. She tightened around him and he gave an encouraging groan.

"You're very tight, Poppy," he said near her ear.

She gasped as his thumb slid onto her clitoris and began to work her while his single, long finger remained inside her.

His other hand toyed with her breasts, plucking at her nipples, squeezing them, teasing them.

She ran her hands across his back and slid her hands onto his ass. It was every bit as firm and hard as she'd imagined it would be. She squeezed it, imagining holding him just like this as he stroked himself inside her.

Her legs started to tremble. She realized she was panting.

Jake walked her backward a few steps, his thumb still circling her clitoris. She felt the mattress behind her knees and sat willingly, lying backward and spreading her legs as he followed her down.

"Yes," he said as began to work his finger inside her, sliding in and out. She lifted her hips, wanting more. He lowered his head and drew a nipple into his mouth.

Men had touched her breasts before. They'd sucked on her nipples, bitten them. But none of them had made her moan the way Jake did. He alternated between licking and sucking and rasping the flat of his tongue over her, and it drove her crazy. She spread her legs wider, wanting more than just his hand between her thighs.

That was new, too—the need to be full, to have his erection inside her.

"I want you," she panted. "I want you inside me."

"Not yet."

She reached between their bodies to find his cock. It was very hard and she found a single bead of moisture on the head of it as she wrapped her fingers around him.

"Now," she said, stroking her hand up and down his shaft.

"Not yet," he repeated.

He slid another finger inside her and his thumb began to pluck at her clitoris, as well as circle it.

"Ohhh," she moaned, letting her head drop back.

Tension built inside her. She realized with surprise that she was close to coming.

Unbelievable. She gripped his shoulders, her whole body tensing.

He slid his hand from between her thighs. Her eyes snapped open and she saw that he was smiling and looking very pleased with himself.

"Don't you dare stop," she said.

He glanced at the bedside unit.

"There's still seven minutes on the clock. Just wanted to check in. How am I faring compared to George?"

She frowned and reached for his hand, placing it back between her thighs.

"Badly. George never stops before I say so."

He laughed. "You're not nearly ready yet, baby."

Then he lowered his head and licked first one nipple, then the other. Then he began kissing his way down her belly.

"Oh," she said.

She couldn't see his face, but she knew he was smiling again as he settled himself between her widespread thighs. Her hands fisted in the sheets as he opened his mouth and pressed a wet, juicy kiss to her sex. He pulled her clitoris into his mouth and began to trill his tongue against it, the sensation so intense, so erotic she gasped.

"Oh!" she moaned.

He slid a finger inside her, then another. Her whole body was trembling. She held her breath as her climax rose inside her.

And again Jake pulled away.

She opened her eyes and stared at him in disbelief. "You have got to be kidding."

She was ready to kill him—but not before she'd jumped him and taken what he refused to give her.

"Two minutes left on the clock," he said. "I'm a man on a mission."

He reached for his jeans pocket and pulled out a condom. She propped herself up on her elbows and watched as he stroked the latex onto himself. For some reason, it turned her on even more, watching him touch himself so intimately.

He caught her eye as he moved over her. Her breasts flattened against his chest and her hips accepted his weight as she felt the tip of his erection probing her wet entrance.

She tilted her hips greedily, and he obliged her by sliding inside her with one powerful stroke.

She forgot to breathe. He was big. Almost too big. She could feel herself stretch to accommodate him. He flexed his hips and stroked out of her. She clutched at his ass and dragged him back inside.

"That. Feels. Amazing," she said.

"Damn straight." He sounded as surprised as she felt.

He began to pump into her, long, smooth strokes that made her gasp and cry out and circle her hips. And then suddenly, at last, her whole body was shaking and she let out a long, low moan as she came and came and came.

She'd barely floated down to earth before Jake kissed her, his mouth hard on hers. He tensed. His breath came out in a rush. Then he thrust into her one last time and stayed there, his cock buried to the hilt. His body shuddered for long moments, then softened. After a few seconds he opened his eyes and stared down into hers.

"Want me to go get George from your room?" he asked.

He was so smug, so sure of the answer. But she was too blown away to care.

"No." She felt dazed, overwhelmed.

He withdrew from her and rolled away, disappearing into

the bathroom. She pressed a hand between her legs. Every-thing felt hot down there, hot and throbbing and wet. And su-premely, hugely satisfied.

Jake's eyebrows rose when he stepped back into the room and saw where she had her hand, but he didn't say anything.

"Just making sure it's all still there," she said.

He smiled. "Want a bath?"

She registered the sound of running water. Right. He'd chosen the motel with the spa baths.

"Okay."

She moved to the edge of the bed and stood. Ridiculously, her legs faltered as she took her first step, as though her knees had forgotten how to do their thing. Jake's smile widened into a grin.

"Wow. I've never crippled a woman before."

"It could have been a fluke, you know. A one-off. A freak occurrence, never to be repeated."

He stepped close and slid a hand between her thighs where she was still tender and throbbing from his ministrations. He kept his fingers flat, exerting the faintest of pressures on her sensitized flesh.

"You should probably know that I do my best work over long distances," he said, his voice very low, his eyes holding hers. "So if you're issuing another challenge, you better make sure you're up to it."

Despite the fact that she'd just had an orgasm that rocked her world, a shiver of anticipation tightened her body.

"I'm going to take that as a yes," he said.

She reached for him, sliding her hands over his shoulders, his chest, his flat belly, until finally she found his cock, already growing thick and hard again.

"Bring it on," she said.

SHE WAS INCREDIBLE. Jake wanted to be inside Poppy again, wanted to feel the tight grip of her heat around him. But first he wanted to drive her crazy once more, watch her eyes grow cloudy with need, listen to her pant and gasp and beg for him.

He led her into the bathroom where the tub was already half full. Bubbles foamed on top of the water. She followed him into the tub and he experienced a small moment of regret as her breasts disappeared beneath the foam.

They were way too good to hide. Twin works of art. Silky smooth. So responsive he'd almost lost it just playing with her nipples.

Which begged the question, what the hell had the other guys she'd slept with been doing that she'd had to resort to a battery-operated substitute to get off? She wasn't remotely frigid or unresponsive or prudish. She'd been so wet and hot for it, he simply couldn't understand how she could have gone unsatisfied for so long.

She settled against the edge of the tub, her arms spread along the rim. He sat opposite her, letting his legs tangle with hers beneath the water. She was still flushed, her eyes smoky. His gaze found her nipples as they broke the surface of the water.

"So, these other guys you slept with—were they swimmers?" he asked.

She eyed him warily. "Why? You planning on writing an exposé?"

"Just working on a theory. Were they all swimmers?"

"Yes."

"Ah."

He sank deeper into the water.

"*Ah* what? You can't just say *ah* then not explain."

"I'm not surprised things were tepid in the sack. You

trained together, ate together, hung out together. Kind of like brothers and sisters."

"Nothing like brothers and sisters. Not even close."

"Then maybe it was all the training. Maybe they were so beat from all those laps they didn't have anything extra to give."

She thought for a minute. "Maybe."

"Plus, I'm pretty good in bed," he said, to get a rise out of her. "We should definitely not overlook my awesome technique."

She laughed. "You want a medal? A badge of honor?"

He eyed the rosy peaks of her breasts. "How about an encore? Come here."

She hesitated a moment, the way she had earlier when he'd invited her to step closer. He hooked his foot behind her hip and tried to pull her toward him. "I'll make it worth your while."

Her mouth quirked into a smile. "Yeah? How so?"

"Come here and I'll show you."

She pushed away from the edge of the tub and floated toward him. He slid his arms around her and pulled her close for a kiss.

She had a great mouth. He couldn't get enough of it. He shifted in the water until she was straddling him. He deepened their kiss, his hands roaming over her breasts. She tensed slightly every time he plucked her nipples, a shiver of need rippling through her. It drove him wild.

He slid a hand between her thighs to where she was spread wide for him. She was slick and silky beneath his hands. He took his time exploring her, playing with her clitoris, teasing her inner lips, sliding one finger, then two inside her.

"Jake," she whispered, reaching for his cock.

He wanted it, too, but they couldn't use a condom in the water. She seemed to understand as he continued to work her with his fingers. She stroked her hand up and down his length as he stroked his fingers between her thighs. Soon she was shuddering, close to coming again. He was too greedy to let her climax without him.

"Let's go," he said, his voice very low.

She stood and stepped from the spa. She didn't bother toweling herself dry, simply strode straight into the bedroom and reached for his jeans.

"You'd better have another condom," she said.

She smiled triumphantly as she pulled the foil square from his back pocket.

"That's it, though," he said.

"Then we'd better make it count."

She climbed onto the bed on all fours, offering him a heart-stopping view of her slick heat and her firm, toned ass. She looked over her shoulder at him, her skin still glistening from the bath.

"What are you waiting for?"

"Excellent question."

He sheathed himself and moved to the bed. She arched her back and pressed into his hips as he came up behind her. He steadied his cock with his hand and slid it along the slick seam of her sex. She sighed and pressed back some more.

"Stop teasing," she said.

"Stop being so impatient."

But he loved how much she wanted it. He especially loved how wet she was. He pressed forward, the head of his penis sliding just inside her entrance. She arched her spine and took all of him. He closed his eyes as she clenched her muscles around him.

So good. So damned good.

He began to move, withdrawing until just the tip of his cock remained inside her then resheathing himself. She rocked to his rhythm, her body very warm and tight around him. Slowly the tension increased. He slid a hand over her hip and between her thighs. Her clit was swollen and slick and he'd barely touched it before she started to shudder around him.

"Yes. Oh, yes!" she panted.

Man, but she was hot. Tight, wet, her body firm and strong. He closed his eyes as his climax hit him, his hands gripping her hips as he pumped into her once, twice, then one last time.

They were both breathing heavily afterward. He withdrew from her and stepped into the bathroom to dispose of the condom. When he returned, she was lying on her side, the same dazed, slightly lost expression on her face she'd had the first time.

"You okay?" he asked.

"I think so. I feel like I just found out the earth is round after years of thinking it was flat."

He dropped onto the bed beside her. She rolled onto her back and his gaze traveled over her body. She was all woman, incredibly sexy. He remembered how round and firm her ass had been as he pounded into her from behind.

"Give me a few minutes and I'll give you another geography lesson," he said.

She shifted her head to look at him.

"I thought we were out of condoms."

"We are. But we've still got this." He leaned across and licked one of her nipples.

Her eyelids dropped to half-mast.

"And there's always this." He pressed a kiss to her belly, then the plump rise of her mound.

She held her breath and he glanced up at her. She wanted him again. Just like he wanted her.

"George would have run out of batteries by now. You realize that, don't you?"

She laughed and fisted a hand in his hair, using her grip to draw him back up her body.

"You win. Hands down. Happy?"

"Satisfied, I think you mean."

"Okay, are you satisfied?"

He looked at her body, remembering the too-brief taste he'd had of her earlier.

"Not yet," he said. "But I'm working on it."

POPPY WOKE TO THE SOUND of running water. She opened her eyes and frowned at the unfamiliar ceiling. Then memories from last night washed over her like a tsunami.

Right. She'd come to Jake's room. She'd challenged him and he'd taken her up on it and they'd spent the next several hours going to town on each other.

"Oh, God," she whispered, pressing her fingers against her closed eyes.

The things she'd done last night. The things he'd done. The way her body had responded.

What had she been thinking?

But there had been precious little thinking going on. From the moment she'd met him she'd been too aware of him physically. Then she'd caught him looking at her yesterday and understood she could have him. If she wanted him. And she had.

He'd given her more pleasure in one night than all of her other lovers combined. Hell, he even made George look average. She shifted restlessly as she remembered the feel of his hard cock sliding inside her.

The shower shut off and she sat up in bed.

Shit. She didn't know what to say to him. And he was going to be showered and fresh and possibly dressed, and she was lying here, naked and drowsy and stupid.

She scrambled from the bed and grabbed her jeans. Her panties were tangled in one leg. She didn't bother trying to get them on, simply dragged her jeans on and stuffed her panties into her pocket. Her bra was on the floor. She'd just fastened the clasp when the bathroom door opened and Jake entered. His dark hair was wet and sticking up in spikes. A towel rode low on his hips.

The sight of him made her mouth water.

He stopped in his tracks and they stared at each other for a beat. Then she bent and picked up her shirt.

"Sorry. I didn't mean to oversleep. We should probably be on the road by now," she said.

There was a short pause before he answered.

"No worries. We can make up the time during the day. I took a look at the map. What do you say we aim for Gundagai today?" he said, naming a town roughly halfway between Sydney and Melbourne.

"Sure. That sounds good. I'll, um, I'll grab a shower and meet you at the car."

She buttoned her shirt enough for modesty, picked up her shoes and jacket and headed for the door. She didn't breathe easily until she was outside. Then she closed her eyes and groaned.

"You idiot."

She'd never had a one-night stand in her life. Not that she thought sex was a sacred act that could only occur between two people who loved each other or anything like that. It just hadn't ever come up. She'd been so busy training, concentrating on her swimming, that huge aspects of her life had gone unexplored. Like good sex, apparently. And casual sex. Consequently, she was woefully ill-informed on how she should handle herself the morning after. Her bare toes curled into the concrete as she remembered the awkward pause when Jake had emerged from the bathroom. Was she supposed to have been gone? Was that what the shower had been about—to signal to her that the night was over and it was time for her to skedaddle back to her own room?

Good Lord, maybe she shouldn't have even fallen asleep. Maybe she should have gotten dressed and returned to her room at two or three in the morning, whatever time it had been when they'd finally given in to fatigue and stopped having at each other.

She let herself into her room and stripped. Her body felt strange under the shower, oddly sensitive and tender.

She dressed quickly in a pair of black linen drawstring pants and a white T-shirt. She finger combed her hair, then took a moment to study her face in the mirror.

She didn't look any different, but she felt it. Last night had been a revelation, pure and simple. She felt as though she'd been granted membership to a secret club. For years she'd read books and watched movies where people did crazy, hurtful, risky things for love and lust. She'd never understood why. Until now.

She could understand why a woman would risk a lot for another night in Jake Stevens's arms. The pleasure he'd given her last night was like a drug. She'd never felt more alive, more sensual, more passionate, more beautiful.

And it's never going to happen again.

She knew the practical voice in her head was right. Not for a second did she believe that what had happened between her and Jake was the beginning of something and not the sum total of it. She only hoped she could remember that for the next however many hours she was stuck in the car with him because thinking about him, about what had happened between them last night, made her want him all over again.

He was leaning against the car when she exited her room

with her overnight bag in hand. His arms were crossed over his chest and he had his sunglasses on. Her gaze dropped to his thighs for a second and she remembered the power of him as he'd thrust into her last night.

Never going to happen.

She had to keep reminding herself. She pulled her own sunglasses from her coat pocket and slid them on.

"Ready to go?" he asked.

"Yeah. We can grab breakfast on the road."

"Good idea."

He took the first turn behind the wheel. She cranked the passenger seat back and pretended to be getting a little extra shut-eye. Anything to avoid looking at him and remembering.

He spoke after an hour. "There's a truck stop coming up. You hungry?"

"Sure," she said.

They parked between two huge rigs and made their way inside the Do Drop In Tasty Stop. Jake slid into one side of a booth, she the other. The table was so narrow their knees bumped beneath it.

"Sorry," they both said at the same time.

Poppy studied Jake from beneath her eyelashes. She didn't know how to deal with him now. Before last night, he'd been her enemy and it had been easy to keep her guard up. Yesterday, they'd brokered a peace deal during the long hours on the road. And last night…well, last night they'd crossed the line, and she had no idea how to uncross it.

Right now, for example, she couldn't seem to stop herself from eyeing his broad shoulders and the firm, curved muscles of his pecs as he sat opposite her. He'd felt so hot and hard pressed against her. His skin was smooth and golden and she'd licked and kissed and sucked him all over until he'd—

"What are you having?" Jake asked.

She tore her eyes from his chest and saw that a waitress was hovering beside their booth, pen poised over her pad.

"Um, scrambled eggs on toast. Bacon. Coffee," she said.

"Same." Jake handed his menu to the waitress.

His blue eyes settled on her once they were alone. She remembered the way he'd looked into her eyes, his nose just an inch from her own last night after he'd made her lose her mind the first time.

"Looks like it's going to be another hot day," he said.

"Yep."

"Should grab some water for the road."

"Good idea."

Silence fell. She ran her thumbnail along the edge of the Formica table. If she was more experienced in the ways of the world, she'd know how to handle this situation.

But she wasn't, and she didn't.

They ate in silence, both of them staring out the window at the unexciting panorama of freeway, gas station and dry scrubland.

"I'll get this. You got dinner," she said when the waitress presented their bill.

"If that's what you want," he said.

She stared at him for a moment, frustration twisting inside her. What she wanted was for things to not be so awkward. She frowned as she registered the dishonesty of her thoughts. Okay, that wasn't what she *really* wanted. What she really wanted was for Jake to kiss her again and slide his hand between her legs and make her feel as liquid and hot as she had last night. But she would settle for not feeling stiff and uncomfortable and self-conscious around him.

It was just sex, she reminded herself. *Two adults enjoying*

*each other's bodies. No big deal. Nothing to get your knickers
in a knot over.*

She settled the bill and joined Jake at the car.

He'd bought a couple of bottles of water from the gas
station and he handed her one. She settled in her seat and
closed her eyes once they were on the highway again. If she
could doze, it would help pass the time. And maybe a miracle
would occur while she slept and she'd wake up and the tension
in the car would be gone.

Her thoughts were too chaotic to be restful, however. She
could smell Jake's aftershave, could remember washing it
from her skin this morning. From her neck and her breasts.
From between her thighs.

She pushed the memory away, deliberately focusing instead on Uncle Charlie's upcoming birthday. She thought
about her present, tried to work out what to say when she gave
it to him. More than anyone else in her life, he'd shaped her
to be the person she was today. She didn't have the words to
tell him how important he was to her, but somehow she had
to find them.

She woke to the sensation of the car slowing.

"Ready to swap?" she asked, sitting up and stretching.

"Pit stop," Jake said. He indicated the toilet block in the
rest area they'd pulled into.

She got out of the car and shoved her sunglasses into her
pocket. She cracked the seal on her bottle of water as he
walked across the gravel to the facilities. She took a mouthful
and shielded her eyes to look out across the plains. The land
looked brown and dry, unwelcoming.

Gravel crunched as Jake returned. He stopped in front of
her and she offered him the water.

"Thanks."

He pushed his sunglasses on top of his head and took a long pull. She let her eyes slide over his chest and belly and thighs. She was gripped with a sudden urge to put her hand on his chest so she could feel the warm, strong resilience of his muscles.

Stop it. She curled her hands into fists, but she couldn't make herself look away.

He took the bottle from his mouth and a single drop of water slid over his lower lip and down his chin. She stared at his mouth, remembering what he'd done to her with his lips and his tongue and his hands last night.

She could feel her nipples hardening. From a look, a single small moment. She met his eyes. For a long beat, neither of them moved. She held her breath.

"Better hit the road." His voice sounded rough.

She climbed into the car and fastened her seat belt. She took a deep breath, then another. She'd never had to fight lust before. She wasn't quite sure how to do it. She was so damned aware of him, couldn't stop remembering small, breathless moments from last night: his harsh breathing near her ear as he pumped into her; the feel of his firm, muscular butt beneath her hands; the skilled flick of his tongue between her legs.

Stop it, she told herself again. She was practically panting. She had to get a grip.

The car dipped as Jake got in beside her and slid his sunglasses onto his face. He started the car and stepped on the gas. Almost immediately he slammed on the brakes. She looked across at him, surprised. He was staring straight ahead, his forehead creased into a frown.

"What's wrong?" she asked.

He turned to look at her. She couldn't see his eyes behind his dark glasses, but something—some instinct—made her look down.

He had a hard-on. The ridge of it was unmistakable beneath his jeans.

"Oh." She let her breath out in a rush, hugely relieved that the need throbbing low in her belly was not one-sided.

"Why didn't you say so?" she said. "I've never done it in a car before."

A slow smile curved his mouth. "Another first. We're really clocking them up."

He leaned across the hand brake and she met him halfway. His lips, his tongue, his heat—just the taste of him sent her pulse through the roof. Within minutes they were pulling at each other's clothes and breathing heavily.

"You stay where you are," she said when they both tried to clamber across the center console at once. She wriggled out of her trousers and underwear while he cranked his seat back. She climbed across the hand brake and into his lap. His erection sat hard and proud beneath her. She shifted her hips, rubbing herself against his length.

"Damn it," she said suddenly. "No protection."

How could she have forgotten something so fundamental?

Jake gave her a wicked smile and reached for the glove box. She shook her head when he pulled out a pack of twelve condoms.

"A little cocky, don't you think?" she said, arching an eyebrow.

"A lot cocky," he said. He grinned and she found herself laughing.

She pulled a condom from the pack and tilted her hips to access his erection. The latex went on smoothly, all the way to his thick base. She held him there and rubbed herself back and forth across the plump head of his cock.

"That feels so good," she said, eyes half shut.

He grabbed her hips and pulled her down impatiently, thrusting upward at the same time. She bit her lip as he filled her. And then she was riding him, his hands on her breasts, his eyes on hers as she drove them both wild.

They came together, bodies shuddering. Poppy braced her arms on the seat on either side of his body afterward, her breath coming in gasps as she stared down at him.

Every time was better than the last. She wasn't sure how that was possible, but it was.

A semitrailer drove past and gave a long blast on its airhorn. They both startled, then laughed.

"Guess we're lucky he wasn't a few minutes earlier," she said, even as she was wondering at her own audacity.

Last night she'd had her first one-night stand and today she'd graduated to sex in a public highway rest stop. She felt as though she'd taken a crash course in sexual desire. Lust 101.

She slid off him and back to her side of the car. Jake took care of the condom, exiting the car to walk back to the toilet block. She struggled into her clothes, bumping elbows and knees in the cramped quarters.

It occurred to her then that, technically, what had just happened between them meant last night had not been a one-night stand.

She tightened the drawstring on her linen pants, frowning. She wasn't sure how to feel about the realization. Clearly, she and Jake had some pretty serious sexual chemistry going on. And they were stuck with each other for at least another day. Her thoughts raced ahead to tonight, to what might happen when they stopped and checked in to yet another motel. Would they pay for one room, or two?

Movement caught the corner of her eye and she turned to watch Jake walk back to the car.

It might be foolish, but she wanted more of him, more of how she felt when she was with him. If he asked—and she hoped he did—she'd opt for one room.

Jake slid behind the wheel. She smiled. He looked at her for a moment, his expression unreadable, then he reached for the ignition key. He didn't turn it. Instead, he took a deep breath and twisted to face her.

"We should probably talk," he said.

"Okay." Suddenly she felt incredibly transparent, as though he knew exactly what she'd been thinking as she watched him walk to the car.

"I'm not really sure how to say this…so I'll just say it. I'm not looking for a relationship right now," he said.

She took a deep breath. Wow. Talk about straight to the point.

"Sure. I know that," she said.

And she did. Just because she'd been thinking about sharing a room with him tonight didn't mean she thought this thing had a future. It was just sex. Nothing more.

"I wanted to be clear. I like you, Poppy. I don't want things to get messy between us, given the way we started out."

"I'm not going to start stalking you and stewing small animals on your stove, if that's what you're worried about," she said. "I had fun last night. But I know exactly what it was."

He studied her face for a long moment, as though he was trying to gauge the truth of her words. She smiled, then punched him on the arm. "Relax. I didn't think you were about to propose because you gave me a bunch of orgasms."

Finally he smiled. "Okay. Good. Great."

He started the car. She put her sunglasses on and made a big deal about getting comfortable in her seat. She stared out the side window as he accelerated onto the highway.

She could punch him on the arm and play it cool however much she liked, but she couldn't lie to herself.

She was disappointed.

It's the sex. You're disappointed there won't be any more of the amazing sex when you stop tonight.

It was true, but it was also a lie. She liked him. She hadn't realized how much until thirty seconds ago.

She crossed her arms over her chest. The sooner they got to Melbourne, the better.

5

JAKE'S CONSCIENCE WAS CLEAR. He'd looked Poppy in the eye and been honest. Admittedly, that had happened *after* he'd had the best quickie of his life with her, but he'd never claimed to be perfect.

Jake reached for his bottle of water and took a mouthful.

He had no idea why he was feeling guilty. She'd wanted it, too. She'd been more than ready to meet him halfway. And she'd been fast to acknowledge that what had happened last night and five minutes ago didn't have a future. No matter how spectacular the sex was.

So why did he feel like a horny teenager desperately trying to justify bad behavior to himself?

There were many solid, rational reasons why nothing beyond sex was ever going to happen between them. They worked together, for starters. And he'd made himself a promise not to get involved with anyone until he'd finished his second novel. The last thing he needed right now was the distraction of a new relationship, especially one with a woman like Poppy.

She'd expect things from him. Commitment being at the top of the list. His thoughts turned to Marly and the mess of their marriage. No way did he want to go there again. Ever. Which didn't leave a man and a woman much room to maneuver, at the end of the day.

He rolled his shoulders and eased his grip on the steering wheel. How in the hell had he gotten from vague guilt about a rest-stop quickie to thoughts of marriage and monogamy?

He slid a glance Poppy's way. She was staring out the window, her face angled away from him.

He thought about the dazed look in her eyes after they'd had sex last night. He remembered her laughter in the bath, and the way he'd caught her scrambling into her clothes this morning.

He was a moron.

He should never have touched her. He should have taken a deep breath last night and walked away instead of letting his hard-on do the thinking for him.

He reached out and punched the radio on, frustrated with himself. Dolly Parton's voice filled the car, wailing about eyes of green and someone stealing her man.

He sighed. What was with rural Australia and country music? Hadn't anyone heard of good old-fashioned rock'n'roll out here in the back of beyond?

The electronic ring of a cell phone cut into Dolly's refrain. Poppy stirred and reached into the backseat to pull her phone from her coat pocket. He tried not to notice the fact that her breast brushed his shoulder or that she smelled good, like sunshine and fresh air.

"Hey, Mom, what's up?" she said into the phone.

He punched off the stereo to make it easier for her to hear.

"What? No!"

He glanced across at her. She'd gone pale and her hand clutched the cell. He eased off the gas.

Something was wrong.

"No! He was fine when I spoke to him on Saturday. He was fine!" she said. Her voice broke on the last word.

Something was definitely wrong. Her eyes were squeezed

tightly shut and she bowed her head forward, pressing a hand to her forehead.

"Did they say… Did they say if he was in any pain? Was it quick?"

Jesus. A death.

He glanced around, but there was no rest area in sight. He pulled off the highway anyway, as far over on the gravel shoulder as he could go.

She didn't seem to notice. All her attention was focused on the bad news coming down the line.

"I understand. Yes. I'll be there as soon as I can. No, I'll drive myself. No. Yes. Okay, I'll…I'll see you soon."

She ended the call and simply sat there, shoulders hunched forward, hands loose between her legs. For a long moment there was nothing but the sound of her breathing and the tick, tick of the engine cooling. A truck sped past and their rental car rocked in its wake.

"Poppy. Is there anything I can do?" he asked quietly.

She didn't say a word, just reached for the door handle and shot from the car. She struck out into the drought-browned pasture alongside the highway as though she could outrun the reality of what she'd learned. Then she stopped suddenly, doubling over. He didn't need to hear her or see her face to know she was crying. She sank to the ground, her shoulders shaking.

Damn.

He had no clue what to do or say. No idea who had died. Her mother had called. Had her father died? Or a brother?

He shook his head and climbed out of the car. He walked slowly toward her, his gut tensing as he saw how tightly she had folded into herself, her arms wrapped tightly around her pulled-up legs, her face pressed into her knees.

He crouched down beside her and placed a hand in the middle of her back.

"Poppy."

She didn't lift her head. He sat down properly, keeping his hand on her back. After a few minutes, she shifted a little and her head came up.

Her eyes were puffy and red, her face streaked with tears. She looked gutted, utterly stricken.

"Uncle Charlie," she said. "Uncle Charlie died."

"I'm sorry."

Talk about inadequate. But there were no words that could take away her pain.

"It was his seventieth on Wednesday. That was why I wanted to get home so badly. He had a heart attack, Mom said."

"Sounds like it was quick."

Her face crumpled. "I should have been there. He was always there for me."

She started crying again. He gave in to his instincts and slid his arm all the way around her shoulders, pulling her against his chest. She let her head flop onto his shoulder and one of her hands curled into his T-shirt and fisted into the fabric. He held her as her body shook.

She was heartbroken. He didn't know what to do for her.

A few minutes later, she loosened her grip on his T-shirt and pulled away from him. He let his arm fall from her shoulders. She used her hands to wipe the tears from her cheeks, not looking at him. She took a couple of long, shuddering breaths. Then she stood.

"I need to get home," she said, still not looking at him.

"Okay. We're nearly to Sydney. We can cut around the city, be in Melbourne in about eleven hours."

He'd already done the math in his head, worked out the best route.

She nodded and started toward the car. She got in and stared straight ahead as he walked to the driver's side. He could almost feel her sucking her emotions back in, building a wall around herself until she could find a safe place to give vent to her grief.

She didn't say a word as they drove around the outskirts of Sydney. She lay on the half-reclined seat facing the window, her back to him. He had no idea if she was crying or sleeping or simply grieving.

He stopped in Goulburn, two hours south of Sydney, for food. She didn't touch her cheeseburger and he wrapped it up and put it aside in case she wanted it later. He stopped again in Albury for gas and coffee. She left the car and walked slowly toward the restrooms, her head down. When she returned her hair was wet and he guessed she'd splashed her face with water.

"I'll drive if you're tired," she offered. Her eyes were bloodshot and blank.

"I'm fine. Three more hours and we'll be home."

She nodded. "Thanks. I appreciate it."

He shrugged off her gratitude. He only wished there was more he could do or say, but they hardly knew each other. Sad, but true.

IT WAS DARK WHEN Jake pulled into the rental car return lot at Melbourne airport. Poppy had been sitting upright and staring grimly out the windshield for the last hour. He could almost hear her making plans in her head.

"Where's home? Can I drop you anywhere?" he asked as they collected their things from the trunk.

"My car's in long-term parking, and my parents are in Ballarat. Uncle Charlie lives— His house is down the road from them."

"Okay. I'll take care of the car return. You get going."

"Thank you. I owe you."

"No, you don't."

Even though he figured she probably didn't want him to, he pulled her close for a quick hug. She was hurting. He felt for her. Surely even a one-night stand and a work colleague was allowed to care that much?

She didn't meet his eyes when the embrace ended, just nodded her head and turned away. He watched her walk toward the pickup point for the courtesy bus to long-term parking.

For the first time since he'd met her, she looked small and fragile.

He turned away. She'd be with her family soon. She'd be okay.

POPPY THREW HER OVERNIGHT bag into the back of her Honda. At least the airport was on the right side of the city; she'd be in Ballarat within an hour. Her eyes filled with tears as she climbed behind the wheel.

Uncle Charlie was dead. She still couldn't comprehend it. It was too big. Too hard. She didn't want it to be true. Didn't want to accept that she would never hear his voice or hold his hand or feel the rasp of his stubble on her cheek when she embraced him.

She blinked the tears away. She couldn't give in and cry yet. She needed to get home. Then she could curl up in a ball and howl the way she wanted to.

She slid her key into the ignition and turned it. Instead of the reassuring roar of the engine starting, she heard a faint click. She frowned and tried the ignition a second time. Again she heard nothing but a faint click.

She stared at her dash and saw that the battery indicator light was shining.

She sat back in her seat. Her battery was dead.

Shit.

Tears came again. She swiped them away with the back of her hand and pulled her cell phone from her pocket. The auto club people could jump-start her. Or if worse came to worst, she could rent another car.

She got out of the car while she was waiting for the phone to connect to the auto club. Might as well look under the hood in case one of the clamps had slipped off a battery terminal or something.

She knew it was a faint hope. She listened to cheery hold music as she peered at her engine. It was hard to tell in the dark, but everything looked the way it should.

"Thank you for calling the Royal Auto Club of Victoria. How can we help you?"

Poppy leaned against the side of her car and explained her situation to the woman. Her eyes were sore and she rubbed them wearily.

"We'll have someone out to take a look at your car as soon as possible," the woman said.

"How long will that be?"

She wanted to be home. She *needed* to be home.

"At this stage, the system is telling me there's a two-hour wait. Our nearest mechanic is on the other side of the city, I'm afraid."

Poppy closed her eyes. Two hours.

"Forget about it. I'll take care of it myself." She ended the call.

She'd go and rent a vehicle. She didn't care about anything else. Her car could sit here until the end of time for all she cared.

A low, dark sports car cruised past, its engine a muted rumble. She grabbed her bag from the backseat and walked around to the front of her car to close the hood.

"What's wrong?"

She slammed the hood down. Jake was standing in the open doorway of the sports car, a frown on his face.

"Dead battery."

"Right." He checked his watch. "What are you going to do?"

She shouldered her bag and used her remote to lock her car.

"The auto club wait is two hours. I'm going to rent a car."

He frowned. "They're pretty busy in there. The strike's still on."

She shrugged. She'd get a freaking taxi all the way if she had to.

"Get in," he said.

She stared at him. "What?"

"I'll take you. Get in."

"It's an hour's drive out of the city."

"So what? You need to get home, right?"

She stared at him.

He was offering only because he felt sorry for her. And things were awkward between them.

But she really needed to get home.

"Okay." Pride was a luxury she couldn't afford right now.

He took her bag and put it in the trunk. She slid into the passenger seat.

"You've been driving for hours," she said when he got in beside her.

"One more hour won't make a difference. If I look like I'm dozing off, feel free to slap me."

She studied his profile as he navigated his way out of the parking lot.

"You didn't have to do this," she said after a short silence.

"I know. I'm a saint."

"Well, I appreciate it. And the fact that you did all the driving today," she said.

"If you're about to thank me for sleeping with you, you can get out now."

It was so unexpected she laughed.

"What's the best route out of the city?" he asked.

She gave him directions. He hit a switch and the mellow sounds of Coldplay eased into the car.

He didn't talk for the next half hour. She was grateful, just as she'd been grateful for his silence earlier today. She wasn't up to polite chitchat, and she wasn't ready to talk about Uncle Charlie. Certainly not to Jake Stevens. He was a virtual stranger, despite how intimate they'd been. There was no way she could share her pain and grief with him.

The exit for Ballarat came up quickly and she gave Jake directions to her parents' house. They lived on the outskirts of the rural center of Ballarat in a big, rambling farmhouse at the end of a long gravel drive. Jake's car dipped and rocked over the uneven ground as they covered the last few yards to the house. The porch light came on as she climbed out of the car. Her parents stood silhouetted in the light.

"You made good time," her mom said.

"We weren't expecting you for a while yet," her father said.

Poppy stood at the bottom of the steps, staring up at them. All the grief she'd held on to for so many hours rose up the back of her throat. She started to cry.

"Oh, Poppy. I knew you'd take it hard," her mother said.

Her mother embraced her with the awkward stiffness that characterized all their physical contact. Vaguely, Poppy was aware of her father introducing himself to Jake and of her mother shuffling her into the house. Then she was sitting at the kitchen table, a cup of sweet tea in her hands, tears still coursing down her face.

"He went the way he always wanted to go—quickly, not hanging around," her father said. "You know he dreaded having a stroke and lingering."

Her parents stood at the end of the table, concern and confusion on their faces. They didn't know what to do. They never did when it came to the world of the emotions.

Never had Poppy needed Uncle Charlie more.

She ducked her head, the tears falling from her chin to plop onto the tabletop.

"She's exhausted. We've been driving for hours," someone said, and she realized Jake was standing behind her.

For some reason it made the tears flow faster and she hunched further into herself.

"Sweetheart. I hate to see you so upset. Uncle Charlie had a good life. We're all going to miss him, but we all have to die sometime. Human beings are mortal creatures, after all," her mother said.

Poppy lifted her head, trying to articulate the gaping sense of loss she felt. "He was my best f-friend."

"I know. And he was my brother and it's very sad but you'll make yourself sick getting so wound up like this," her father said.

Poppy pressed the heels of her hands into her eyes. They didn't understand. They never had.

"What about a shower?" her mother suggested. "What about a shower and some sleep?"

"That's a good idea. What do you say, Poppy?" her father said heartily.

"Sure." Poppy stood and made her way to the bathroom

at the rear of the house. Her mother pressed a fresh towel into her hands.

"I'll turn down your bed," she said, patting Poppy's arm.

Poppy nodded. Then she was alone, the towel clutched to her chest.

She undressed slowly and leaned against the shower wall as the water ran over her, lifting her face into the spray so that she had to gasp through her mouth to breathe. A hundred memories flashed across the movie screen of her mind as the water beat down on her.

Uncle Charlie hooting and hollering from the stands at her first Commonwealth Games. Uncle Charlie sitting patiently beside the pool during her early-morning practice sessions, day after day after day. Uncle Charlie holding her hand in the specialist's office when she was waiting to hear the verdict on her shoulder injury.

She didn't bother drying herself off when she stepped out of the shower. She simply pulled on her old terry-cloth bathrobe and wrapped the towel around her wet hair.

The light was on in her old bedroom and she walked slowly toward it. She pulled up short when she heard her mother talking to someone.

"Don't be ridiculous. It's late, you've been driving for hours. I won't have an accident on my conscience."

Poppy moved to the doorway. Jake stood beside her old bed, watching her mother fluff the pillows. He looked bemused, like a man who didn't quite know what had hit him.

"I'm insisting that Jake stay the night," her mother said when she saw Poppy.

Jake's expression was a masterpiece of tortured middle-class politeness.

"I've just been explaining to your mother that my fishing buddy is expecting me. And that the last thing you probably want is me in your bed after the day you've had." He widened his eyes meaningfully.

"And I've been telling Jake that Allan and I aren't old-fashioned about these kinds of things."

Poppy stared at her mother, not quite getting it. Then her slow brain caught up—her mother thought Jake was her boyfriend.

No wonder he was looking so hunted.

"Jake and I aren't together."

"Oh!" Her mother blushed, one hand pressed to her chest. "I'm so sorry! I just assumed…"

"Jake was helping me out," Poppy said. She turned to him. "She's right, though. You should stay. You must be exhausted after all that driving. There are plenty of other bedrooms."

"Yes! Of course there are! Adam's room is right next door, and the bed is already made up." Her mother nodded effusively, eager to make up for her gaffe.

"I'm fine. Really," Jake said.

Poppy's mother looked to her, clearly expecting her to intervene.

Poppy shrugged. "It's your decision," she said, turning away.

He was a grown-up. If he thought he was okay to drive, it was up to him. She sat on the side of the bed and stared at her feet. She was numb and exhausted and so empty it hurt.

There was a short silence.

"Maybe I should get a few hours' shut-eye before I hit the road again," Jake said.

Poppy pulled the quilt back and crawled beneath the covers. She didn't look at either of them, just rolled onto her side and closed her eyes.

She wanted to wipe the day out, strike it from the record as though it had never happened. She wanted to turn back the clock to a time when Uncle Charlie was still a part of her world.

"I'll show you Adam's room," she heard her mother say.

There was the scuff of shoes on floorboards, then Poppy was alone. She opened her eyes and stared blindly at the far wall.

"Uncle Charlie," she whispered.

JAKE LAY IN POPPY'S brother's bed and stared at the ceiling. By rights he should be halfway to Melbourne by now, Poppy and her grief left far behind. Instead he was lying here, listening to the sounds of a strange house settling for the night.

The truth was, he hadn't been able to leave her.

Which was nuts. Even if she was devastated by grief, the last person Poppy would turn to was him. They'd been thrown together by circumstances, nothing else. Even the sex had been about availability and proximity. At least initially, anyway. And yet here he was in her parents' house, unable to abandon her to her family's distant, entirely inadequate sympathy.

His chest got tight every time he remembered the empty, sad look on Poppy's face as she sat at her parent's kitchen table, shoulders hunched forward as though making herself smaller could diminish her grief, protect her from it somehow. And her parents had simply stood there and let her ache.

His own family were far from perfect. His father had a temper and his mother wasn't above playing the martyr to get her own way. His brothers and sisters all had their fair share of flaws and foibles. And yet if someone close to them had died, if one of them was hurting or needy or in trouble, the Stevens family would not hesitate to circle the wagons and pull up the drawbridge. Hugs would be the order of the day, along with kisses and tears and laughter. It would be messy and loud and warm and real.

By contrast, Yvonne Birmingham had looked so uncomfortable embracing her daughter that she might as well have been undergoing root canal, while Allan had offered his grief-stricken daughter rational words and philosophy and precious little else. Jake had waited in vain for someone to offer Poppy the simple comfort of another warm body to cling to. Hell, even a hand on the shoulder and a sympathetic handkerchief or tissue would have done the trick. But the Birminghams were not huggers, he'd quickly realized.

Allan had given Jake their bona fides while Poppy was in the shower—they were both academics, tenured professors at Ballarat University. Allan taught history, Yvonne English literature. Jake had detected a faint accent in both their speeches and he guessed from the photographs on the wall that they had emigrated to Australia from England some years ago.

He couldn't think of a more unlikely pair to have produced a larger-than-life, earthy woman like Poppy. In fact, the more he thought about it, the more impossible it seemed. They were so self-contained and cerebral, and Poppy was so physical and full of energy and honesty.

Staring into the dark, he pondered what it must have been like for Poppy, growing up with parents who lived in their minds when she was a person who lived in her belly and heart. He might not know all the ins and outs of Poppy's world, but he knew that much about her.

Lonely, he guessed. Hence her close relationship with Uncle Charlie.

The second cup of tea Yvonne had pressed on him before bed made its presence felt and he swung his legs over the side of the mattress and went in search of the bathroom. He made a deal with himself as he shuffled up the darkened hallway. He'd try to grab a few hours' sleep when he got back to bed, but if sleep didn't come he'd dress and slip out the back door and head for Melbourne.

It wasn't as though he was serving any purpose here, after all.

He was passing Poppy's bedroom door on the way back to Adam's room when a low sound made him pause. He gritted his teeth; she was crying. He hesitated for only a second. He could be a stubborn bastard and a self-confessed smart-ass, but it simply wasn't in him to walk away from someone in so much pain.

He pushed her door open. "Poppy."

She didn't respond but he could hear her breathing.

Again he hesitated. Then he entered the room and closed the door. His shin found her bed before his outstretched hands did and he swore under his breath.

"Don't freak out, I'm getting into the bed," he said.

She didn't say a word as he pulled back the covers. It was only a double bed, but she was curled up on the far side. He slid across the cool sheets until his chest was pressed against her back. He wrapped an arm around her waist and pulled her tightly against his body. She was rigid with tension and as unresponsive as a lump of wood.

"It's okay, Poppy," he said very quietly.

She started to shake. He pulled her closer, curling his legs behind hers so that they were tightly spooned. He could feel her grief, her pain, vibrating through her.

"It's okay," he said again.

"No, it isn't."

Her chest heaved as she sucked in a breath, then she was shuddering, sniffing back tears, gulping for air. He held her tightly, not saying a word. It wasn't as though there was anything to say, anyway. There wasn't a well-formed phrase in the world that made losing someone less sad.

Slowly the crying jag passed. Poppy sniffed noisily and moved restlessly in his arms. He eased away from her and released his grip.

"I'm sorry," she said.

"For what?"

"All of this. My mom forcing you to stay the night. Taking more time away from your fishing trip. This wasn't exactly what you signed on for when you offered me a lift home."

"Your mom didn't force me to stay. I wanted to make sure you were okay."

Her head turned toward him on the pillow. In the faint light from the window he could see the dampness on her cheeks.

"Noble of you."

"Don't worry, I'm sure it won't last."

She managed a faint smile, then she used the sleeve of her robe to wipe her eyes. It was a child's gesture and it made her seem even more vulnerable.

"You want to talk?" he asked. His ex-wife would keel over in shock at hearing those four words leave his mouth, but he didn't know what other comfort to offer.

She shrugged and dabbed at her face again with her sleeve.

"Not much to say. He was my best friend. He taught me how to swim. Came to every major meet and most of the minor ones. And now he's gone."

"He was your father's brother, yeah?"

"Yes. But Charlie was older by twelve years. There was less money when he was born, so he didn't get the same education as my father. He was a house painter. He was the one who decided to emigrate to Australia. Mom and Dad followed him a few years later."

"I wondered about the accent."

"Cambridge."

"Right."

He thought about what she'd said about her uncle coming to every meet and what it implied about her parents—they hadn't. And for the first time it occurred to him that while he'd seen plenty of books piled all over the place and black-and-white photographs of England on the walls of her parents' home, there hadn't been a single shot of Poppy. No photos on the winner's dais. No newspaper clippings. No framed medals or ribbons. No indication at all that the Birminghams had a world-record-holding, gold-medal-winning daughter.

"You know what the crazy thing is?" Poppy asked after a short silence. "All I could think about when we were on the road is getting home. And once I got here, I realized that the thing I'd been holding out for was Uncle Charlie. And he's not here anymore." She tried to keep her voice light, as though she was telling a joke on herself, but there was a telltale quaver in it.

"It was his birthday on Wednesday, too. I'd been teasing him for months about what I was going to get him. And now he'll never know…" She was crying again, tears sliding down her face and onto the pillow.

"What did you get him?"

"I had a frame made for my first gold medal. And there was this picture of the two of us when I was a kid… I wanted him to know that I couldn't have done any of it without him."

"It sounds great. I bet he would have loved it."

She shifted, sitting upright then leaning over the side of the bed. He heard the rustle of paper as she fumbled in the dark, then she lifted a large, flat box from beneath the bed. The weight of it landed heavily on his legs as she placed it in his lap.

"Open it," she said.

He stilled. "Are you sure?"

"Yes. I want someone to see it."

There was an undercurrent to her words. Then he remembered the lack of photos in the house and thought he understood.

She flicked on the bedside lamp. They both blinked in the sudden light, even though it wasn't terribly bright. He glanced at her. Her eyes were puffy, her cheeks damp. Her hair had dried into messy spikes. She looked about fifteen years old.

"Open it," she said.

He pulled himself into a sitting position. She'd wrapped the box in shiny black paper with a bright yellow ribbon. He felt as though he was trespassing as he tugged the bow loose and slid his thumb under the flap of the paper.

"Tear it. I don't care," she said when he tried to ease the tape off neatly.

When he continued to be careful, she reached across and ripped the paper for him, shoving it unceremoniously to one side. Then she found the tab that released the lid on the plain packing box beneath and pushed it open. Jake eased a double layer of tissue paper aside to stare at Poppy's gift to her late uncle.

The frame was dark wood—walnut, he guessed—and deep, creating a three-inch recess behind the glass. Poppy's first gold medal was fixed to a dark green mount. A black-and-white photograph sat alongside it. The middle-aged man in the photograph had big shoulders and a craggy face. His dark eyes were gentle as he looked at the little girl standing beside him in the shallow end of the pool. She had short blond hair and two teeth missing from the front of her smile. And she looked up at him with absolute trust and adoration as he guided her arms into position.

Poppy sniffed loudly.

"He was so patient with me. He never got angry with me, except when I doubted myself," she said. "He loved swimming, couldn't get enough of it. Knew all the coaches, all my competitors' stats."

She shook her head. "I can't explain it."

"You don't need to. You loved him. And he loved you."

"Yes. He did."

Her chin wobbled as she reached out to press her fingers to the glass over her uncle Charlie's face.

"I'm going to miss him so much."

Jake slid his arm around her shoulders and pulled her against his chest. She didn't resist, didn't try to be strong. Her hands curled into the muscles of his shoulders and she pressed her face into his chest. Her breath came in choppy bursts and her tears were warm on his skin.

He eased against the pillows, one hand smoothing circles on her back. With the light on he could see more of her room. The far wall was covered in ragged posters of past Australian swimming greats—Dawn Fraser, Shane Gould, Kieren Perkins. A fistful of old swimming carnival ribbons were pinned together in the corner. All blue for first place, naturally. To the side of the bed was a battered dressing table. He couldn't help smiling to himself as he saw the earplugs, goggles, swim caps and other swimming paraphernalia strewn across it. Any other teenager would have loaded it with makeup, perfume and pictures of the latest teen heartthrob, but not Poppy.

"You must be tired," Poppy said after a few minutes. "You've been driving all day. Now you've got me sooking all over you."

"I'm fine."

"Still. You should try to get some sleep. You're going to be on the road again tomorrow, aren't you, driving to hook up with your fishing buddy?"

"Yeah."

She pushed herself away from his chest and reached for the frame. He watched as she set it beside the bed, leaning it against her bedside table. He pushed back the covers and swung his legs over the side of the bed, preparing to return to her brother's room. She frowned.

"What's wrong?" he asked.

"Nothing."

"Poppy."

She lifted a shoulder in a self-conscious shrug. "Would you mind sleeping in here with me? It makes it easier, not being alone."

"Not a problem."

She gave him a watery smile. "Thanks. I appreciate it."

She sat on the edge of the bed and shrugged out of the bathrobe. Then she strode naked across to the dressing table and tugged a drawer open. He told himself to look away, but it was too late—he'd seen the full swing of her naked breasts and the mysterious shadow between her thighs as she bent to pull an old T-shirt from the drawer. He'd traced the firm curve of her ass and the strong lines of her back with his eyes as she tugged the T-shirt over her head.

Only when she was walking back to the bed did he manage to make himself look away. Too late. Way too late.

Despite the fact that he knew it made him a cad of the highest order, he couldn't help responding to what he'd just seen. She had a great body and he'd enjoyed many hours of pleasure with her last night. He told himself she was grieving, in shock, sad. His penis didn't care. It remembered only too well the feel of her skin against his, the slick tightness of her body, the rush of her heated breathing in his ear.

The bed dipped as she got in beside him and flicked off the light. He closed his eyes. There was no way he was going to get any sleep lying here with a hard-on. He resigned himself to a long night.

"Jake. I know this is beyond the call of duty, but would you mind…would you mind holding me?"

Right.

"Um, sure. Not a problem. How do you want me to…?"

"Like you did before was nice." He could hear the shyness in her voice, knew how much it was costing her to ask him for comfort.

"Cool."

She rolled onto her side, her back to him. He reached down and adjusted his hard-on in his boxer briefs in a futile attempt to minimize the obviousness of his arousal. Careful to keep his hips away from her rear, he slid his arm around her torso and pressed his chest against her back.

Funny how last time he'd done this it hadn't been even remotely erotic. But then she'd been wearing the robe and he'd been too focused on how upset she was to register the warmth of her skin and the brush of the lower curve of her breasts against the back of his hand. He hadn't noticed the clean, fresh smell of her or thought for a minute about any of the things they'd done to each other last night. The way she'd taken him in her mouth. The way her eyes had widened when he'd found her sweet spot and touched it just right. The greedy, hungry way she'd reached for his cock and guided him inside her.

He gritted his teeth and forced his mind to something else. The stats for the top five teams on the AFL ladder. The chances of Roger Federer winning both Wimbledon and the U.S. Open again this year. His agent's recent phone message requesting a meeting with him.

Poppy sighed. Jake felt some of the tension leave her body as she relaxed into the bed.

"I really appreciate this, Jake," she said again.

He tightened his grip around her waist in response and she wriggled her backside more closely into the cradle of his hips. She stilled.

So much for his playing the chivalrous knight.

"Is that what I think it is?" she asked.

"Yes. But I would like to point out that sometimes it has a mind of its own. And you have a great body."

She rolled away from him, and he waited for her to kick him out of bed and tell him what an insensitive jerk he was.

"Where are the condoms?" she asked instead.

In the dim light from the partially open curtain he could see her pulling her T-shirt over her head. Any blood that wasn't already there rushed south and his cock grew rock hard. It got even harder when she slid a hand over his belly and into his underwear to wrap her palm around him.

"In the car."

"Huh. We'll have to be careful, then," she said.

Her hand was working up and down his shaft. He closed his eyes. Then his conscience came calling, tap-tapping persistently in the back of his mind.

"Are you sure you want to do this? I mean, you're upset. I don't want you doing anything you might regret."

She pressed a wet, openmouthed kiss to his chest.

"I want to feel alive right now. Do you mind?"

"Do I feel like I mind?"

"No. You feel good." She practically purred the last word.

She slid a leg over both of his and shifted so that she was straddling his hips. She pushed his underwear down and he shoved it the rest of the way down his legs. Then she slid his cock into her wet heat and bore down on him.

"Oh, yeah." He sighed as her body enveloped him.

She started to rock her hips. He could see her breasts swaying in the dim light, pale and full. He slid his hands up her rib cage and took the weight of her in his hands, sliding his thumbs over her nipples. They hardened instantly. She let her head drop back.

She felt so good. Soft yet firm. Silky and smooth. He drew her down so he could pull a nipple into his mouth. She shuddered and began to circle her hips. He slid a hand between their bodies to where they were joined. Her curls were wet and warm and she was swollen with need. He teased her with his thumb, working her gently. She started to pant. He felt her tense around him.

He thrust up into her and wished he could see her face properly. He had to settle for the fierce throb of her muscles tightening around him as she came and the low moan she made in the back of her throat. He closed his eyes and thrust up into her rhythmically, chasing his own release. Then he remembered they didn't have a condom.

Damn.

He stilled, his hands finding her hips to stop her from moving on him.

"No condom," he reminded her. She stilled.

"Right."

She slid off him, one last torturous stroke of her body against his. Before he could feel true regret, she shifted down his body and lowered her head. The wet heat of her mouth encompassed him and he groaned his approval.

She used her hand and her mouth and soon had him bowed with tension. He drove his fingers into her hair and held her head as he came. Afterward, she pressed a kiss onto his belly and rested her cheek on his hip.

"Come back here," he said.

Her body slid along his as she joined him on the pillow. He peered into her face, trying to see her eyes.

"You okay?"

"If you keep asking questions like that, you're going to ruin my image of you as a gifted-yet-emotionally-shallow pants man."

"I'd hate to do that. Not when I've spent so many years perpetuating that image. It's not something that happens overnight, you know."

She smiled. He looked at her and wondered if that was really how she thought of him—a pants man, out for what he could get, when he could get it. Then he thought over the past few years of his life and wondered how inaccurate the description was, at the end of the day.

As a teenager, the idea of being a celebrated swordsman had held enormous appeal. Lots of women, lots of sex, lots of variety. The Errol Flynn myth, basically. But as an adult man, he knew there was more to life than sex.

For a moment he was filled with a bittersweet regret for the early years of his marriage. For moments like these when he and Marly had laughed and talked while their bodies cooled. For the comfort and joy and familiarity of coming home to find the lights on, cooking smells in the kitchen and off-key singing coming from somewhere in the house. For shared jokes and favorite movies and the sense of achievement that came from finding the right birthday or Christmas gift.

But it was impossible to remember the good times without the bad memories crowding in. The bitter fights, the recriminations. The tears, the misery. The fury. The helplessness. And, finally, the emptiness when it was all over.

So, yeah, maybe being described as a pants man wasn't the

highlight of his life, but it beat the hell out of his marriage and his divorce. Hands down.

Poppy's head was heavy on his shoulder and her breathing had deepened. He peered down at her. She was asleep. Exhausted, no doubt, after the trials of the day. Slowly, he eased her head off his shoulder and onto the pillow.

He'd done his bit. He'd offered her all that he had to give. She would wake tomorrow and remember all over again that her uncle Charlie was gone. But she'd gotten through the first night, and she'd get through the rest, too.

His boxer briefs were lost somewhere beneath the quilt. He didn't bother looking for them, just slipped out of bed and back to Poppy's brother's room. He dressed in the dark and let himself out the back door. His car engine sounded loud in the quiet of the country night. He rolled down the driveway, then hit the gas when he reached the road. Before long he was turning onto the freeway toward town.

He spared a thought for how Poppy would feel when she woke. Then he remembered her pants man comment. She'd understand.

6

HE WAS GONE. POPPY REGISTERED the cool sheets and the absence of warm male body and lifted her head to confirm that Jake had left her bed.

She rolled onto her back, her forearm draped over her eyes to block out the sunlight shining between the half-open curtains. After a long moment she lifted her arm and squinted at the clock on her bed stand. It was nearly eight. She'd slept all the way through the night, exhausted by grief and a heart-pounding climax courtesy of Jake's clever hands and hard body.

He must have gone back to his own bed. She wished he hadn't. His warmth, the low timbre of his voice, the simple sound of another human being breathing next to her—he'd helped her get through the night.

He'd been kind to her. Very kind. He'd stayed overnight when he hadn't wanted to, he'd sought her out when he'd heard her crying. And he'd held her, offering her the reassurance of his body. And, later, he'd offered her his desire and a few precious moments of forgetfulness and release, too.

She'd called him a pants man afterward. It wasn't true. Men who were just after sex didn't take the time to offer comfort to someone in need.

Jake Stevens was a nice man. It was a surprising discovery, given the way they'd started out.

She pushed her hair off her forehead. It was time to get up. Time to face the day ahead. Her parents. Her brother and sister, most likely. The funeral arrangements.

Her belly tightened at the thought and she took a steadying breath. It was tempting to hide away and grieve. But putting Charlie to rest was the last thing she could do for him.

She rolled out of bed. She kept some old clothes at her parents' place for the weekends when she stayed the night and she pulled on a pair of worn jeans and the T-shirt she'd worn for just a few minutes last night before she'd felt the unmistakable hardness of Jake's erection against the curve of her backside.

Even now, hours later, the memory sent a wash of heat through her. She eyed herself in the dressing table mirror as she finger combed her hair. That was the thing about death—life went on despite it. People ate and slept and fought and laughed and cried and lusted and had sex, same as they always had.

Life went on.

"Uncle Charlie," she said quietly.

The world had not stopped because he was dead, but it had changed for her, irrevocably.

She could hear low conversation as she walked toward the kitchen. She recognized the pitch and rhythms of her sister's speech and the low bass of her brother's. They'd come up from the city, then, as she'd guessed they would.

"I still can't believe I missed him. All this way and he's gone already." This from her sister, sounding aggrieved.

"I thought you came all this way for Uncle Charlie?" Adam said.

Poppy stopped in the doorway. Her mother was at the sink, filling the kettle. Her father hovered over the toaster, eyeing the glowing slots like a cat at a mouse hole. Adam and Gillian sat at the table, the morning papers spread wide before them.

"Poppy. You're up," her mother said too brightly. "I hope you had a good night's sleep."

"It was okay."

Poppy stepped forward to kiss her brother and sister hello. Gillian patted her arm briefly as Poppy pressed a kiss to her cheek.

"How are you holding up?" Gillian asked.

"You know." Poppy shrugged. "Did you two come up together?"

"Yes. I'm due back in the afternoon, but I thought I could help out with the funeral arrangements this morning."

"And meet a certain much-lauded author," Adam said with a dry smile.

Poppy frowned. "Sorry?"

Adam nudged Gillian's chair with the toe of his shoe. They were both small and dark-haired like their parents, dressed expensively and conservatively in dark business suits.

"Mom told Gill that Jake Stevens was here when she called early this morning and she was in the car like a shot," Adam said.

Gillian flushed a little. "Thank you for making me sound like a juvenile delinquent with a crush. I happen to be a great admirer of his work. *The Coolabah Tree* is a modern Australian classic."

Poppy crossed to the cupboard to grab a coffee mug. She should have known her family would be excited about meeting Jake. Her mother had taught a seminar on him a few years ago and her sister worked for a small feminist publishing house in the city.

"I didn't put two and two together until this morning, Poppy," her mother said. "You should have told me who Jake was. I'm so embarrassed I didn't recognize him."

"It wasn't exactly at the top of my mind last night."

"I know, but still…"

Poppy spooned instant coffee into her mug.

"I should go wake him. He probably wants to hit the road."

"Oh, but he's gone already," her mother said. "His car was gone this morning when I let the cats out."

The teaspoon clanged loudly against the side of the mug.

Not just gone from her bed, but gone from the house? Gone in the early hours of the morning?

"It was good of him to drive you up here when your car broke down," her father said.

"Yes," Poppy said. She stared at the brown granules in the bottom of the cup. It was ridiculous, but she felt abandoned. As though Jake had offered her something in the dark of the night that he'd reneged on this morning.

"I still can't believe you made that gaffe over the rooms, Mom," Gillian said. She shook her head, a wry smile on her lips.

Adam made a joke at their mother's expense, then her mother asked something about Gillian's work and her father asked who wanted more toast.

A great wave of sadness and loneliness and grief washed over Poppy as she watched her family. She'd never felt like one of them, had always felt like an outsider in the face of their collective academic and professional achievements. It had always been her and Uncle Charlie against the rest of them.

Her vision blurred and her shoulders slumped. Without saying a word, she moved to the back door and pushed her way out into the sunlight.

"Poppy," her mother called after her.

"Let her go," she heard Adam say. "She obviously wants to be alone."

Head down, she walked out into the backyard. She didn't know where she was going. She just knew that it would be easier to be on her own than to be with her family right now. They had loved Charlie, but they had never understood him. Just as they had never understood her.

A WEEK LATER, ALL THE LITTLE hairs on the back of Poppy's neck stood on end as she sat at her desk, working on her latest article. She didn't need to look up to know that Jake had walked into the department.

He was back from holidays. She told herself she didn't care and clicked to a new screen on her computer. Then, without her permission, her gaze flicked across to where he was shrugging out of his jacket.

Fishing obviously agreed with him. He was golden-brown and dark stubble covered his cheeks. He looked lean and a little dangerous and wild.

She returned her attention to the computer screen. She didn't care how he looked or whether he was dangerous or not. Sleeping with him had been a big mistake. As for allowing him to comfort her in her grief… Words were inadequate to describe the wholehearted chagrin she felt for ever allowing herself to turn to him.

She was more angry with herself than him. She'd known exactly what he was before she slept with him—a cynical, smart-mouthed pants man. She'd even told him so straight to his face while they were still basking in the afterglow of yet another round of spectacular sex. And yet she'd still allowed herself to hope. Not for long—only for those few almost-conscious seconds between sleeping and waking—but for long enough. She'd reached out a hand to touch him, to make sure he was real, to reassure herself that he had actually held her in his arms and said all the right things and been so…*human* and generous. And all she'd found was cold, empty sheets.

Stupid. He'd told her up front, hadn't he? He wasn't interested in a relationship. And yet for those few foolish seconds she'd imagined that he would be there for her when she woke. That he liked her. That there was more than great sex between them.

More fool her.

A shadow fell over her desk. She kept her attention on the computer screen and her fingers moving on the keyboard.

"Hey. How did your uncle's funeral go?" Jake asked.

"Fine. Thank you."

"I guess you took a few days off?"

"That's right."

Still she didn't look at him. She had no idea what she was typing. She was too busy concentrating on keeping her face impassive.

"What about your car? Did you get that sorted out?"

"Yes, thank you."

For a long moment there was nothing but the sound of her fingers tapping on the keyboard. She could feel him watching her, but she refused to look at him. Finally he turned and walked away. Poppy let her breath out and her shoulders drop.

What on earth had possessed her to get naked and sweaty with a colleague? She must have been sniffing glue that night in Tamworth. And in the car after that. And at her parents' place.

She risked a glance at his retreating back. Her eyes gravitated to his perfect ass, then dropped down his long legs.

Right. That was why. He was sexy as all get out.

She dragged her gaze away. She had no business being attracted to a man who'd proven himself so unworthy.

Poppy girl, just because you can sometimes see the bus crash coming doesn't mean you can always avoid it.

Uncle Charlie's voice sounded in her head as clearly as

though he was sitting beside her. An increasingly familiar pang of loneliness and sadness pierced her.

His funeral had been exhausting, a day of shaking hands and accepting hugs and condolences, of trying not to cry too much or too loudly. She had been surprised by the turnout, particularly by the number of people from the swimming community who came to pay their respects. Her old coach. Some of her former competitors. Former swimmers from the high school squad Charlie had coached way back in the day. His warmth and wisdom had touched a lot of lives. He'd been valued. He would be missed. And he would be remembered. At the end of the day, that knowledge had given her some solace.

Getting on with the plod of everyday life was hard, however. He had been her mentor, counselor and friend, and she picked up the phone countless times a day to call him and tell him some joke or small story she knew he'd relish, only to remember all over again that he was gone, that there would be no more phone calls or shared laughter.

Her mouth grim, Poppy deleted the paragraph she'd written while Jake hovered over her shoulder. Not gibberish, thank God, but not something she wanted her boss to read, that was for sure. She pushed her hair off her forehead and rolled her shoulders. Then she put her fingers to the keyboard again. This article was due by midday and she still wasn't happy with the intro and the conclusion. She'd sweated over both until late last night, staying at her desk until the cleaners came and began emptying trash and vacuuming around her.

It worried her that the writing wasn't getting any easier. If anything, it felt harder. The more she learned in her night classes, the more she could see the failings in her own work. And the worse thing was, she didn't know how to fix them.

Even though she and Jake were the only people in the department this early, Poppy glanced up as she eased her desk drawer open. It wasn't as though she'd care too much if someone else saw what she was doing, but if Jake caught sight of the underlined, annotated article in her drawer she didn't think she would ever recover from the humiliation.

He was busy checking his e-mail, one hand idly clicking away at the mouse. The glow from his desk lamp gave his dark hair golden highlights. She switched her attention to the article in her hand.

It had been her class assignment this week—select a piece of journalism she admired and analyze its structure and content. She'd agonized over her choice and then forced herself to admit that the only reason she wasn't selecting one of Jake's articles was because of what had happened between them. Dumb. He was the best writer in the department, one of the most awarded on the paper. And she'd admired him for years. She might feel foolish and naive and exposed because she'd slept with him and allowed herself to hope for more, but it didn't change the fact that he was one of the best. And if she was going to learn, she wanted to learn from the best.

She read his opening paragraph again, admiring the deceptively easy flow of it. It was impossible to stop at those few sentences, though—inevitably she wanted to keep reading, even though she'd gone over and over the damned thing many times already. He was a master of the hook, superb at delivering information in fresh and interesting ways and drawing the reader in. His observations were insightful, his judgments crisp and unapologetic.

She turned to her own opening paragraph, frowning at the stiffness of her phrasing. No matter what she tried—chatty and informal, choppy and succinct or somewhere in between—

she wound up sounding like a high school student laboring over an end-of-term paper.

The tap-tap of Jake's keyboard had her lifting her head again. Words filled the screen as his fingers flew. For a moment she simply stared at him, envying him his easy gift. He was in his element, utterly confident. She knew what that felt like. At least, she used to know.

She shoved the annotated article into her drawer and pulled her keyboard toward herself. She might not have natural talent, but she was smart and she learned fast. She would conquer this if it killed her.

Just as she would live down making the rookie's mistake of sleeping with a coworker.

LATER THAT AFTERNOON during the department meeting, Jake leaned back in his chair and studied the woman sitting diagonally opposite him. Poppy sat ramrod straight, a pad and pen at the ready in front of her like a good little schoolgirl, just in case Leonard said anything she needed to jot down. Her gaze was resolutely focused on their boss as he droned on and on about circulation figures.

She'd made a point of being everywhere he wasn't since their nonconversation this morning. If he entered the kitchen, she left. If he was collecting something from the printer, she gave it a wide berth. So much for hoping there would be no repercussions from their road-trip fling.

She was pale, he noted, her eyes large in her face. A tuft of hair stuck up on her crown as though she'd been running her fingers through her hair. Her lipstick had worn off, but her lower lip was wet from where she'd just licked it.

She looked sad. And sexy. A disturbing combination at the best of times.

He frowned.

As if she could sense his regard, her gaze flicked up to lock with his. Her face remained expressionless, utterly still for a long five seconds. Then she coolly returned her attention to their boss.

Jake shifted in his seat. He told himself that there was no rational justification for her anger, that he had no reason to feel guilty. He didn't owe her anything, after all. He'd gone beyond the call of duty, driving her home when her car had broken down, hanging around at her parents' place to make sure she was okay.

Yeah, and then you crawled into her bed in the middle of the night when she was at her most vulnerable and threw the leg over.

He would swear on a stack of Bibles that sex had been the last thing on his mind when he'd heard her crying. Absolutely. And yet somehow he'd still ended up shagging her again.

Never screw the crew.

Don't dip your pen in the office ink.

Don't shit in your own nest.

There was a reason there were half a dozen colloquial warnings against sleeping with a coworker—the aftermath sucked.

I was honest with her. I told her I wasn't looking for a relationship.

Which gave him the perfect get-out-of-jail-free card—in theory. Things got a little muddy once he factored in her grief and the way he'd felt compelled to comfort her and the truths they'd shared in the small hours of the morning. Oh, and the sex. The postcomforting, postsharing sex.

He should have said no. Should have ignored his hard-on, rolled out of bed and gone back to her brother's room. Instead, he'd gotten lost in the warmth of her body then bailed without saying goodbye.

He waited until she was filing out of the meeting room with the others before approaching her.

"Poppy, can I have a word?"

Several sets of eyes turned their way and she had no choice but to agree. She hovered near the door as the last person exited.

"What?" she asked.

She crossed her arms over her chest and set her jaw stubbornly. Clearly, she wasn't about to make this easy.

"Look, I would have woken you but I thought you needed the sleep more," he said.

"No, you didn't. You didn't wake me because you were worried I would take what had happened the wrong way."

"Yeah, and I was right, wasn't I?" he said, gesturing to indicate the discussion they were having, their mutually closed-off body language, the tension in the room.

"You're so arrogant it blows my mind," she said, shaking her head. "For your information, you are not God's gift to women. A handful of decent orgasms doesn't even come close to making you irresistible."

He crossed his arms over his chest and leaned his hip against the table. For the first time all day she had some color in her cheeks and there was life in her eyes. He wasn't sure if he should be pleased or not. And whether he should be worried about noticing in the first place.

"Why are you so pissed with me, then?"

"I don't know. Maybe because you sneaked out of my parents' house like a thief in the night?"

"So? You knew I needed to get going, that I wanted to catch up with my buddy. What was the big deal if I left early or not?"

She opened her mouth then shut it without saying anything. Her gaze slid over his shoulder and her jaw tensed. Her eyes were angry when they met his again.

"Fine, I admit it. You're right. I was surprised when you weren't there in the morning. I thought at the very least that we were friends after everything that had happened. That you cared enough to say goodbye. I felt stupid when I realized you were gone."

He stared at her. Her confronting honesty left him nowhere to go. It was his turn to look away. "We both agreed that it was just sex."

"I know."

And they both knew it had become more than sex when he slid into her bed and wrapped his arms around her.

"I'm sorry," he said after a long silence. "I only wanted to help. I didn't mean to hurt you."

"I'm not crying myself to sleep over you, Stevens," she said drily. "Get over yourself."

He shrugged. "For what it's worth, I'm a shit prospect anyway. Workaholic. Messy. Hopeless with birthdays and anniversaries. Cranky in the mornings."

She simply looked at him, her big gray eyes depthless. "Are we done here?"

"Yeah, we're done."

She walked away, her spine very straight. He watched till she turned the corner, aware that he still felt dissatisfied, as though they had unfinished business.

What had he expected from their confrontation, anyway? What exactly had he been trying to achieve?

He remembered the way they'd sparred in the car, the push and pull of their conversation over dinner at the steak house. He remembered her laugh, the deep throaty pleasure of it.

And he remembered the utter vulnerability of her as she wept in his arms.

He liked Poppy Birmingham. Hell, he even admired her, especially after meeting her parents and gaining a small glimpse into the indifference she'd had to fight against to rise to the top of her sport. If he hadn't messed things up by sleeping with her, he'd like to think they could have been friends.

But he had. And, worse yet, he still wanted her, even though he knew he was never going to have her again.

JAKE LEFT THE DEPARTMENT earlier than usual that night. His agent had called to set up a meeting, and Jake had been unable to put him off any longer. Poppy was still at her desk, bent over her keyboard, one hand absently combing her hair into spikes. She worked long hours. He wondered if journalism was living up to her expectations.

His agent was waiting for him at the wine bar in the nearby restaurant precinct of Southgate when Jake arrived. Dean Mannix waved a hand when he spotted Jake but didn't bother standing. Nearly sixty years old, he had bad knees and walked with the aid of a cane. His improbably black hair gleamed with hair oil and Jake pretended not to notice the discreet touch of eyeliner around the other man's eyes.

"Where's Rambo?" he asked, glancing around for his agent's much-cosseted Chihuahua.

"Spa day," Dean said with the flick of a limp wrist.

"Ah. What are you drinking?" Jake asked, seeing Dean's glass was almost empty.

"Surprise me with something sweet and sticky."

Jake suppressed a smile and crossed to the bar. It had been nearly twelve months since he and Dean had spoken face-to-face. In the early days, his agent had practically lived on his doorstep. Marly had called him "that little man" and rolled her eyes every time he called. But there hadn't been much need for Dean to make contact recently.

Jake scanned the cocktail menu and ordered a Fluffy Duck and a glass of merlot. Dean's mouth quirked into a smile when he saw the umbrella poking out the side of his drink.

"Fabulous." He took a long pull from the straw. "And absolutely disgusting."

He said it with such relish Jake could only take it as high praise.

"So, what's up?" Jake asked.

He waited for Dean to ask him about his writing, when Jake might have something for him. That was usually why Dean requested a face-to-face.

"Did I mention I saw Bryce Courtney the other day?" Dean said instead. He went on to tell an anecdote about the other author. Jake listened and made the appropriate noises, growing more and more tense with every passing minute. Finally Dean drank the last of his cocktail and sat back in his chair.

"Isn't this the part where you ask me what I've been working on and I lie and tell you I've got a good start on something?" Jake joked.

Dean smiled but his eyes were sad.

"Jake, I'm going to let you off the hook," he said. "Make it official and tear up our agreement."

Jake let his breath out on a rush. This was the last thing he'd been expecting. "You're cutting me loose? You don't want to represent me anymore?"

"I'd love to represent you. I think you're a wonderful, talented writer and you've made me a lot of money. I've been proud to have your name on my books for the past seven years. But the truth is that you aren't writing anything for me to represent."

"So I'm a little blocked. I've got the second book outlined, the broad strokes are there. I just need a clean run at it."

"Jake, it's been seven years. And, yes, I know things with Marly were messy for the first two years, but you've had five years since the divorce and you haven't brought me anything."

Jake stared at him, unable to refute his words. "So I'm deadwood now? You're just going to cut me off?"

Dean sighed heavily. "No. Like I said, I'm letting you off the hook. No expectations. No guilt. No niggle in the back of your mind. You're free to write or not write as you choose. No pressure from anyone but yourself."

"Wow. I feel so free. What a gift you've given me."

Dean didn't flinch at his sarcasm and Jake immediately felt like an asshole. It wasn't as though Dean hadn't been patient. Seven years was a long leash by anyone's standards. Jake rubbed a hand over his face.

"Sorry. I just…I understand. You've been very patient."

"You start writing again, call me. Call me anyway, let me know how you're doing," Dean said.

Jake forced a smile. "Sure."

Dean leaned forward. "I know you've got another book in you, Jake, but you need to give yourself permission to write it."

Jake frowned. "What the hell is that supposed to mean?"

"Why do you think you haven't been able to get the words down?"

"I've been busy. I've let other things get in the way. No discipline."

"You know what I think? I think Marly spent so much time blaming you for being away on a book tour when she miscarried that you couldn't help but absorb some of it. And now you won't let yourself write again because giving up something you loved is your way of punishing yourself."

Jake flinched. "Didn't realize you'd hung up your shingle as a headshrinker since we last saw each other, mate. Or have you just been watching too much *Dr. Phil?*"

"Something has held you back all these years."

"I don't need counseling, for Christ's sake. I need an agent."

Dean braced his arms on the table and pushed himself to his feet.

"When you need an agent, you'll have one," he said. He grabbed his cane. "Look after yourself. Call me every now and then, let me know how you're doing."

Jake watched Dean walk away, anger and shame and regret burning in the pit of his belly. Then Jake downed the last of his wine and walked slowly to his apartment, squinting against the last rays of the setting sun.

He dumped his bag and coat by the front door and went straight into the kitchen to grab a bottle of wine and a glass.

So, it was official—he was no longer a writer. Just another journalist. He walked to the living room and stared at the half a dozen copies of *The Coolabah Tree* on his bookcase. First editions, foreign translations, international editions. Jesus, he'd been so proud when he'd held his book in his hands for the first time. He and Marly had danced around the apartment and spilled champagne and gotten in trouble with the neighbors for making too much noise. He'd imagined half a dozen books filling the bookcase alongside his debut work.

Swearing, he crossed to his desk and powered up his computer. He pulled up a chair in front of a blank screen. He placed his fingers on the keyboard, his mind going over the story he'd outlined all those years ago, the story that was supposed to be the spine of his second novel.

Words formed in his mind, sentences. He began to type. But after a few minutes, his hands fell into his lap.

It wasn't right. Maybe he'd been out of the habit of writing fiction for so long, he'd forgotten how. Maybe the story was stale. Or maybe it really was over.

He stared at the screen.

I know you've got another book in you, Jake, but you need to give yourself permission to write it.

"What a load of bollocks."

Angry, he pushed away from the desk and reached for the wine bottle again. Dean could get stuffed. As for his amateur-hour theories about Marly and the baby… It was probably as well the old man wasn't representing him anymore.

7

A WEEK LATER, JAKE WAS making notes on an article in the café in the foyer of the *Herald* building when Macca and Jonesy pulled up chairs at the adjacent table. Jake exchanged a few words of greeting then returned to his work. He must have been listening to the other men's conversation on some level, however, because his ears pricked up when he heard Poppy's name. His pen stilled on the page but he didn't look up as he waited to hear more.

Macca had been mentoring Poppy since her first week on the job. In Jake's opinion, the other man was way too smitten to be objective. The way he followed Poppy around with his eyes was becoming the office joke.

"You're never going to know if you don't sling your hook, mate," Jonesy was saying, taking a huge bite out of a chicken schnitzel sandwich.

"There's no way she's single." Macca spoke with the resigned hopefulness of the truly besotted.

"Won't know till you ask. She's never mentioned anyone. Give it a go, see what she says."

Macca made a noncommittal noise.

"Up to you, buddy, but you're not the only one who wouldn't mind going for a bit of gold." Jonesy laughed at his own joke. "Saw Patrick from advertising sales doing the old smoothie routine on her the other day."

Jake frowned. Patrick Larson was a slick dickhead in an expensive suit. The thought of him smarming all over Poppy made Jake's neck itch.

"Matter of fact, if you're not going to make your move, I might just ask her out myself," Jonesy said.

Jake's head came up at that. Jonesy was leaning back in his chair, his belly pouring over his belt, crumbs from his lunch scattered over his shirtfront.

In your dreams, pal. Poppy is way too fine for you.

The flash of territorialism was disturbing. Poppy was nothing to him. They were barely on speaking terms, despite having cleared the air last week.

He must have been glaring because Jonesy glanced at him, offering a just-between-the-boys grin. Jake frowned and the other man's smile faded.

"Anyway. Better get back to it," Jonesy said, standing and brushing debris from his shirt.

Jake sat staring at his notes after they'd left. Someone should say something to Poppy. Warn her. Because it was obvious what was going to happen—Macca would ask her out. Or Patrick. Or—God forbid—Jonesy. And before she knew it, guys would be nudging each other all over the building. It wasn't only male athletes a female reporter had to worry about in this profession. Like it or not, journalism was still a boys' club.

He grabbed his notes and crossed to the elevator. As he exited on the fifth floor, he saw Poppy shuffling papers together near the printer and diverted from his course to his desk to stop in front of her.

"Got a minute?" he asked.

She flicked a look at him. He'd never noticed before, but she had very long lashes. So long that they swept her cheekbones when she glanced down at the papers in her hands.

"It depends," she said.

"What on?"

"What it's about."

"Right." He'd walked into that one. "It's, uh, private."

One of her eyebrows rose. "Please don't tell me you've got a nasty rash."

It was so unexpected he laughed. He'd forgotten how dry she could be. How fast on her feet.

"No rash. Everything's in tip-top working order," he said.

"So did you just want to give me a status report or was there something else?" she asked.

"It's about Macca."

"Right."

"And Jonesy. And that Patrick dickhead from sales."

"He's not a dickhead. He was very helpful when I was looking for some information the other day."

Jake stabbed a finger at her. "Exactly. He wants to get you into bed. Along with Macca and Jonesy."

"You mean like a…a foursome?" she asked, incredulous.

She looked so appalled he had to laugh.

"No. Separately. Every man for himself."

"Right. Very funny." She shook her head and turned to walk away.

He grabbed her arm. "Don't you believe me?"

She gave him a withering look. "I'm not an idiot. Despite recent behavior that might indicate otherwise."

She glanced pointedly at his fingers circling her arm, but he didn't let go. Partly because he hadn't finished talking to her, and partly because she felt good and it had been too long since he'd touched her.

"Trust me. Macca has a crush on you. And Patrick collects scalps like baseball cards. As for Jonesy…well, he's not blind."

She shook her head again. She had no idea how attractive she was. Tall and strong and supple. Curvy in all the right places, with a pretty, open face that hinted at an enjoyment of the simple things in life. Like food and wine and sex.

"Why are we even having this conversation, Stevens?"

She'd started calling him by his last name since their road trip. He didn't like it. He'd been inside her. He'd pressed his face into the soft, silken skin of her inner thighs. He'd made her purr with pleasure. He figured at the very least that put them on a first-name basis.

"A while back you asked me to step in if I thought you were putting a foot wrong. One pro to another," he said.

"And?"

"I just wanted to warn you that sleeping with one of the guys from the department would definitely fall under that category."

She stared at him. She opened her mouth, closed it, then shook her head. "Are you *seriously* warning me against screwing one of my coworkers?"

"You asked me to give you a heads-up if you needed it."

She huffed out a laugh, but he didn't think she was amused. More incredulous, if he didn't miss his guess.

"Unbelievable," she muttered under her breath. Then she turned away from him.

"Hang on a minute." She had no idea how gossipy a bunch of guys could get over a few beers. He grabbed her arm again.

"Do you mind?" she said coolly.

"I don't think you're taking this very seriously," he said.

She stared at him. They were standing so close he could see her nostrils flare. He could smell her deodorant and whatever soap she washed her clothes in, could feel the warmth of her body.

"Do you honestly think I need another lesson on why screwing someone I work with is a sucky idea, Stevens? Really?"

For a moment he saw clear through to her soul, saw the regret and the embarrassment she felt over their few sweaty, hot encounters.

She wished it had never happened. It was there as plain as day in her eyes. If she could, she'd wind back the clock and reclaim the hours they'd lost in each other's arms. Even though it had been the best sex he'd ever had. Even though he couldn't stop thinking about it, about her, she wished it out of existence.

He let her go. She strode to her desk. He crossed to his own desk and dumped his jacket and notes. His wine club order had been delivered while he was at lunch and he shoved the carton to one side as he sat and called up his e-mail in-box. Then he stared at it unseeingly.

He didn't regret sleeping with her. Not for a second. Even though it had made things weird at work. It had been worth it—that was how good it had been.

But to Poppy, he was just some guy she worked with who she'd slipped up with on the road. She'd filed him under the same heading as Macca and Patrick and Jonesy. Despite the many moan-inducing orgasms he'd given her. Despite the fact that he'd left George, her battery-operated friend, for dead. Despite the laughter they'd shared and the challenge of their conversations.

It was a humbling realization. And an uncomfortable one.

You should be thanking your lucky stars. She could be crying all over the place, blabbing to the other women on the floor. You could be getting dirty looks from everyone with two X chromosomes within a one-mile radius.

He didn't feel grateful, however. He felt pissed. Dissatisfied. Frustrated.

A phone rang across the office and he came out of his daze. He reached for his mouse. What was it Poppy had said to him last week?

Get over yourself.

Maybe she had a point. He had no right demanding anything from her, including recognition that what had happened between them had been out of the ordinary. Not when he had nothing to offer in exchange. He wasn't looking to start something up with someone. Not now, not ever.

He concentrated on proofing his article with new resolve. So what if he was too aware of everything Poppy said or did, every move she made? So what if he only had to think of touching her breasts, sliding his hand between her legs and he had a hard-on that wouldn't quit? It didn't matter. It meant nothing. It was over.

THE NOTICING-POPPY'S-every-move thing came back to haunt Jake later that evening as he worked at his desk. Slowly the department emptied until only the hard-core workaholics were left. Which meant it was down to him and Poppy, essentially. He was aware of her crossing back and forth between the printer and her desk, then going in to talk to Leonard before hitting her computer again. Leonard left at seven, but Poppy remained at her desk. He glanced at her as he headed for the kitchen to forage for something to keep him going for a few more hours. She was kneading her forehead as she frowned at a page, red pen in hand. The page was covered in little notes to herself, lines and arrows, deletions and insertions. Tension radiated from her in palpable waves.

He poured himself a tall glass of water in the kitchen and unearthed a stash of muesli bars someone thought they'd hidden at the back of the cupboard. He grabbed one for himself, then went back for a second. He dropped it on her desk as he walked past.

"Can't think without food," he said over his shoulder.

She didn't say a word, but he heard the rustle as she tore open the package. She was still working away with the red pen when he shrugged into his jacket and picked up the carton of wine. He hovered for a beat, watching her. She looked tired, but he knew there was no way she was leaving her desk until she was satisfied.

She'd probably tell him to take a long walk off a short pier, but he couldn't help himself. Which was becoming a bit of a recurring theme where she was concerned. Couldn't stop himself from poking her with a stick. Couldn't stop himself from wanting her. Couldn't stop himself from having her. Couldn't stop himself from feeling for her.

She slid the printout she was working on under today's edition of the paper when he stopped beside her desk. She sat back in her chair and looked up at him, one eyebrow raised.

"What?" she asked as though he was a pesky kid annoying her in the playground.

"You want some help?"

Her expression immediately became guarded. "I'm fine."

"Yeah? How late were you planning on working? How many red pens you planning on running through?"

Her mouth tightened. "I'll work it out."

"Anyone ever told you you're stubborn?"

Before she could react, he snatched her article out from beneath the newspaper.

"Hey!" She was on her feet in a second, trying to grab the paper from his hands.

He held it out high from his side. If she wanted to get it, she was going to have to wrestle him for it. She seemed to be considering doing just that for a moment, then her shoulders slumped.

"Fine. I'm sure you could do with a good laugh after a long day."

He frowned at her defeated posture and lowered his hand so he could read what she'd written. The page was so crossed and marked with red it was almost impossible to decipher the original text.

"Move over," he said, nudging her to one side.

Without asking, he took her seat and used the mouse to take him back to the top of her article on the computer screen. He could feel her nervousness as she hovered behind him while he read. It took him thirty seconds to see where the problem lay.

"This isn't as bad as you think it is," he said.

"Thanks," she said drily.

He shot her a look. "Pull up a chair."

She eyed him for a long moment, then slowly pulled over the chair from a nearby desk.

He pointed to the screen.

"You're overthinking this too much, overwriting. It's an interview. People will read it because it's about David Hannam and he's the country's number one tennis star, not because you're being clever. You just need to feed them some of what they expect, then throw in a few little surprises. Make them feel they've found out something they didn't know before."

"Easy for you to say."

He could hear the tiredness in her voice. She was running on empty.

"What's the most interesting thing he said to you when you interviewed him?" he asked suddenly.

She blinked, then frowned.

"No, don't think about it—just say the first thing that comes into your head."

"Okay. When he was a kid, he wanted to be an astronaut. He didn't discover tennis until he was fifteen."

"Great. There's your opener."

He rolled his chair to one side and gestured for her to take his place at the keyboard. She did so slowly, warily.

He watched as she placed her fingers on the keys. Then she sighed and let them drop into her lap.

"I can't do this with you watching."

"Yeah, you can. They're just words, Poppy. Words and ideas."

"Not by the time I'm finished with them," she said ruefully.

"Pretend you're having a beer with some mates and telling them about the interview. You're not going to bother with any of the boring crap up front. Who cares what his stats are? Bury that stuff toward the end for the nerds. Tell a story."

She put her fingers to the keyboard again and started writing.

When David Hannam was a kid, he wanted to be an astronaut. He figured that flying through space and looking at the earth would be about the coolest thing ever. Of course, that was before he discovered the thrill of standing in a packed stadium with the winner's trophy in his hands…

She wrote for twenty minutes, stopping and starting. Every time she went to press the delete key he caught her hand.

"Just write what comes to you. You can edit later."

Finally she stopped typing.

"Good. Now cut and paste this paragraph. And this one. And those two," he said, pointing out the material from her previous draft.

He sat beside her for another hour as she finalized the interview. Finally she hit the key to send it to the subeditor for tomorrow's edition.

She let out a sigh, then scrubbed her face with her hands.

"Thank you," she said.

"It was no big deal."

"To you, maybe. This stuff is second nature to you."

"I've been doing it for fifteen years, Poppy."

She shrugged. She was a perfectionist, that was her problem. And she was used to being the best.

"If it makes you feel any better, I can't dive worth shit. And my backstroke is laughable."

She gave him a dry look.

"It's true." He stood and grabbed her elbow to encourage her to stand, also. He passed her her jacket.

"Go home. Eat. Sleep. Stop thinking."

"Easy for you to say," she said for the second time that night.

He laughed. "You think I don't think?"

"I have my doubts sometimes. Like this afternoon when you warned me not to screw the crew." She was smiling. He felt an absurd sense of achievement.

"I was protecting your honor."

"Is that what you call it? I thought you were pissing in the corners."

Startled, he looked at her face. She cocked an eyebrow at him and he realized she was right—he *had* been pissing in the corners, marking his territory. Making sure she didn't hook up with one of the other guys from work.

"Well, I never said *I* was honorable," he said.

They walked toward the elevator. The cleaners had come and gone and the lights were dim, only the glow from various computers and electrical devices and the occasional desk lamp illuminating the newsroom. He stood to one side to let Poppy enter the elevator before him. He didn't mean to, but somehow his eyes sought out the shadowy V at the neckline of her shirt as she moved past him. He could see a thin line of black lace and his mind filled with images of Poppy's full, creamy breasts spilling out of black satin.

He reined in his libido in time to note that she hit the button for the foyer rather than the basement parking garage. There was only one reason for her to be getting out at ground level— she planned to walk across to Flinders Street station and catch the train home.

"Car still in the shop?" he guessed.

She gave him a startled look. "How did you—"

"I'm a journalist. We notice things."

"Right."

"You want a lift?"

Given the black lace fantasy that he'd just beaten back with a stick, it wasn't such a smart idea. But he had a long track record of not being smart around Poppy.

"It's out of your way."

"You don't know that. Where do you live?"

"Malvern. Miles away from South Yarra."

She kept her eyes on the floor indicator but a small frown appeared between her eyebrows. He smiled. Poppy had looked up his home address. Interesting.

"I'll drive you. Might as well—I've got the car tonight, since I knew this was coming." He indicated the carton of wine in his arms.

"I'll be fine."

"It's past nine, Poppy. Don't be stupid."

"That's why I'm saying no—I'm not being stupid."

She met his eyes then and he knew that she'd noticed him

looking at her breasts. She was probably aware that he was half-hard, too, in the same way that he was aware that she was breathing a little too quickly and her pupils had dilated with desire.

"It's just a lift home."

He wasn't sure if that was a lie or not. All he knew was that he wanted to spend more time with her.

She looked at the floor. The lift pinged open at the foyer level. She didn't move. He reached out and hit the door closed button.

"Nothing is going to happen," she said.

"I know."

But he was fully hard now, every inch of him craving her. He wanted to duck his head and inhale the scent from the nape of her neck. He wanted to slide his hands beneath her shirt and cup her breasts. He wanted to watch her face as she moaned and pleaded and came.

He couldn't sleep with her again. Not after the conversation they'd had last week where she'd more or less confirmed that she wasn't the kind of woman who did casual sex.

It was a pity his body hadn't gotten the memo yet. Forcing his mind to thoughts of frolicking puppies and old ladies with canes, he led Poppy to his car.

POPPY SLID INTO THE SMOOTH embrace of butter-soft leather upholstery and reached for her seat belt.

Was she *nuts?* What on earth was she doing letting Jake Stevens drive her home?

And how had she not noticed last time she'd been in his car that he drove a Porsche? She'd been so numb she'd barely registered the color, let alone the make, but now she was fully aware that he drove the kind of sleek and sexy car that screamed sex and power and lots of other things that weren't doing anything to slow the pulse beating low in her belly.

You idiot.

Self-abuse wasn't going to help, either. She'd been a goner the moment Jake had stopped beside her desk and leaned close enough for her to smell the unique scent that was aftershave, soap, laundry detergent and hot male skin. Heady at the best of times, but absolutely deadly when her dreams had been haunted by long, liquid moments from her two nights with Jake.

She wasn't sure what it said for her psyche that even though she wasn't sure she liked him much, she still craved his body.

She winced and stared out the passenger side window. Who was she kidding? She liked him. She liked him plenty. She thought he was funny and clever. And he'd proven himself to be kind, in action if not in word. Just because he wasn't interested in having a relationship with her didn't negate any of that. Even if he had embarrassed her and made her feel gauche and foolish with his midnight flight. And even if he'd had the outrageous gall to point out to her that sleeping with a work colleague was a dumb idea—as though she hadn't worked that one out about five seconds after discovering the other side of the bed was empty.

At the end of the day, he'd never promised her anything. And she was aware that her grief and upset over Uncle Charlie probably didn't put her in the best position to judge this situation rationally. But she was also aware that only a very, very foolish and self-destructive person would put her head in the lion's mouth twice. Especially when said person had a weakness for said lion, and said lion was licking his chops and had a speculative gleam in his eye.

"Whereabouts in Malvern are you?" he asked. He held up a hand. "Wait, let me guess. Near the pool, right?"

She hated giving him the satisfaction of being right, but he was.

"Yes. How did you know?" she asked, irony heavy in her tone.

"I'm a journalist. We—"

"Notice things. Thank you, I got that the first time."

He was grinning, and the corners of her own mouth were curling upward.

"Do you still swim?"

"Every day." She felt a little stupid admitting it. She was retired, after all. She was supposed to be getting a life outside of the pool. But ever since losing Uncle Charlie, she'd craved the comfort of the familiar and she'd given in to the urge to swim every day, either before or after work.

"Not today, though, right?" he asked. "Surely even you aren't going to do laps after nine at night?"

"The pool is closed," she said. "Plus I swam this morning."

"Better be careful, Birmingham. You're gonna lose that spectacular rack if you keep training so hard."

She shot him a startled look. His attention was on the road but he was grinning hugely.

"I think the less attention you pay to my rack the better."

"Wise words. Would you consider wearing a burlap bag as your part of the bargain?"

She laughed. As always with him, she couldn't help it. He was just so damned cocky and incorrigible. If someone had asked her beforehand if such a combination would appeal to her, she would have laughed in their face. Which went to show how well she knew herself.

Another disturbing thought.

"Do you have these kinds of conversations with Hilary or Mary? Because it's not going to be long before you're up on sexual harassment charges if you do."

"I haven't slept with Hilary or Mary," he said.

"Very restrained of you."

"I've never slept with anyone from the paper before."

He was still watching the road. She eyed his profile for a long moment.

"Wow. I guess I should feel flattered."

He smiled faintly. "But you don't?"

"It was a stupid thing to do."

"Maybe."

She frowned, wondering what he meant by that. There was no doubt in her mind that she'd screwed up monumentally when she'd let him lay hands on her. Amazing orgasms aside.

The sustained gurgle of her hungry stomach cut through the silence in the car. She pressed a hand to her belly.

"Sorry."

"I'm starving, too. Maybe we should stop for a burger. There's a drive-through on High Street, isn't there?"

She made a face. "Plastic food. Disgusting."

"Says Ms. Chocolate Chip and Nacho Cheese."

She blinked. He remembered what she'd had in her shopping bag up in Queensland. Either he had an amazing memory, or… She didn't allow herself to complete the thought. No doubt, if she questioned him under bright lights, he'd tell her he was a journalist, and he noticed things.

"At least it's made from real cream and real sugar and real fat," she said. "Haven't you seen that documentary about fast food?"

"No. Why on earth would I voluntarily rule out one of the major food groups from my diet by learning a bunch of stuff that would make it impossible for me to ever eat it again?"

She shook her head. "So bad for you."

"Lots of things are. Doesn't stop most of us from indulging."

There was something about the way he said *indulging* that made her want to squirm in her seat. Damn him. Only Jake Stevens could make a single word sound so…provocative.

"There's an Indian takeout a little farther up. If you must eat crap."

"I must. And so must you. I have it on good authority that your body requires sustenance."

She was about to argue but her stomach growled again. "See?"

She rolled her eyes but still ordered chicken tikka masala, vegetable korma and a plain naan bread when they stopped at the Indian restaurant. Ten minutes later they were back in Jake's car, the heady smell of spicy food rising around them. She directed him to her street and he stopped outside her apartment block. She opened the car door before she turned to thank him.

"I appreciate the lift. I know it was out of your way."

"Not a problem," he said.

His face was cast in shadows, but she could see the gleam of his eyes in the soft light from the dash. She felt a ridiculous impulse to lean forward and press a kiss to the angle of his jaw. Just to see if he felt and tasted as good as she remembered.

Hunger was clearly making her light-headed. She swung her legs out of the car and stood.

"Anyway. See you tomorrow," she said. Then she remembered it was Friday. "I mean, Monday," she quickly amended.

"Have a good weekend, Poppy."

She pushed the car door closed and turned away, but she couldn't help thinking that he was a good fifteen minutes from home and by the time he got there his naan bread would be more soggy than light and fluffy and his samosas more spongy than crunchy. Before she could edit herself, she turned on her heel and rapped on the side window of his car.

The glass lowered with a discreet hum and Jake looked out at her, eyebrows raised questioningly. She studied his mouth before she spoke. If there was even a hint of that knowing, smug smile of his… But he wasn't smiling. He was watching her, his expression unreadable.

She swallowed a sudden lump of nervousness.

"If you want to come up and eat your food before it gets cold, that would be okay."

As invitations went, it wasn't the most gracious she'd ever issued. But maybe that was for the best. Maybe her awkwardness would make him say no and she could put this moment of madness behind her.

"That would be great. If you don't mind."

"Of course not."

They sounded like two scrupulously polite old ladies. She waited for him to exit his car and lock it. Then she led him upstairs to her second-floor apartment. Her gaze immediately went to the stack of newspapers piled on the dining room table, then to the tower of dirty cereal bowls on the kitchen counter, then to the basket full of laundry on her armchair. If she'd known she'd be entertaining guests, she'd have cleaned up a little this morning instead of gulping down her breakfast and racing for the bus.

"Um, sorry about the mess," she said. She dumped her bag of food on the counter and began clearing up.

"Relax. I'm not about to whip out my white gloves. My place is a pigsty."

"Really?"

"Hell, yeah. Who has time to clean? I thought about hiring someone to come in once a week, but it seems pretty shameful when I live in a two-bedroom apartment."

"Ditto." She forced herself to relax and dumped the cereal bowls in the sink instead of stacking them in the dishwasher. She pulled out two plates and some cutlery, then gestured for him to take a seat at the table. "Your food's getting cold."

He sat at the end of the table and she sat on one of the sides, facing the window. For a moment there was only the rustle of plastic bags and the snap of containers being opened as they loaded up their plates.

She stole a glance at him as she tore off a chunk of her naan bread. Jake Stevens, in her apartment. She couldn't quite believe it. After the way he'd treated her when she first started at the paper, then the way she'd felt when he'd pulled his midnight disappearing act... Well, she hadn't exactly anticipated this moment.

"You own this place or rent?" Jake asked as he dipped one of his samosas into yogurt sauce.

"Own. Uncle Charlie insisted I do something sensible when I started getting sponsorship money."

"Smart man."

"Yeah. What about you? Own or rent?"

Good grief. Could this conversation be any more stilted? Jake smiled at her as though he could hear her thoughts.

"Own. Same deal—I decided to do something a little more long-term than buy a hot car when *The Coolabah Tree* was a surprise success."

"Then you went ahead and bought the car anyway."

"I'm only human. I believe Tom Cruise said it best in *Risky Business*—'Porsche. There is no substitute.'"

"Wow. You sure know your Tom Cruise. I'm...disturbed. Which is your favorite scene in *Top Gun?* The topless volleyball game or the topless shower scene?"

He grinned and scooped up a spoonful of rice. "And you think I'm a smart-ass."

She smiled down at her plate. She liked sparring with

him. A little more than was healthy, if she was being honest with herself.

His gaze wandered to the pile of newspapers. He frowned slightly, then tugged the top paper toward himself. It was opened to the sports section and she realized too late what he was looking at—the notes she'd made in the margin when she read his article this morning. She'd gotten into the habit of analyzing his writing, trying to deconstruct it so she could pick up some clues for her own work.

She leaned across the table, ready to snatch it from his hands. Jake threw her a curious look and she retreated to her chair.

"It's nothing. Just some notes for school," she said.

"School?"

"I'm taking a journalism course at night school."

She waited for him to say something mocking but he didn't. He simply returned his attention to the newspaper and her penciled-in notes. She tried to remember what she'd written.

Please, nothing about how much I admire his writing. Anything but that.

"You enjoying it?" he asked after a long moment. He put the paper down and slid it away from himself.

"Um, school, you mean?" she asked, her attention on the newspaper. She desperately wanted to grab it and check that she hadn't written anything too revealing, but she knew that would only make her look even more foolish.

"School, the paper. The whole thing."

"Sure. It's a challenge, but that's only because it's new. And I feel like I'm slowly starting to find my feet."

Okay, that was a lie, but she wasn't about to admit the truth.

He nodded, using his bread to wipe sauce off his plate. "You were right—this is good stuff. Much better than a burger."

She watched as he licked a smudge of sauce off his bottom

lip. Between anxiety about what he might have read in the margins of the paper and her hyperawareness of him physically, her appetite had completely deserted her. She pushed her half-finished plate away and used a paper napkin to wipe her own mouth.

"You don't do anything by halves, do you?" Jake asked suddenly. Her startled gaze found his. They stared at each other for a long moment.

"No. Sometimes I wish I could. But I can't. It's just the way I'm built."

He reached across and caught her hand in his. His thumb stroked the back of hers as he cradled her palm.

"You have beautiful eyes, Poppy Birmingham, you know that? Someone should have written about them when they were mentioning all those gold medals you won."

She forgot to breathe for a moment. His hand slipped from hers and he pushed back his chair. He started shoving empty take-out containers into one of the bags.

She felt very uncertain all of a sudden. She didn't understand him. Every now and then she thought she had a reading on him, but he kept taking her by surprise.

"Leave it. I have to clean in the morning, anyway."

"Do you mind if I use your bathroom before I go?" he asked.

She nodded. "Down the hall, to the right."

He'd have to pass her bedroom on the way. She resigned herself to the fact that he'd see her wildly messed bed, the clothes strewn everywhere, her underwear kicked into the corner, the books piled beside her bed. So much for keeping her distance from him. By the time he left her apartment there wouldn't be a single one of her shortcomings and foibles he wouldn't be aware of.

Which reminded her...

She grabbed the newspaper he'd abandoned and reviewed her notes. She'd underlined a couple of phrases, passages that had really appealed to her. Nothing too incriminating— except for the two words she'd scribbled in the margin: *talented bastard.*

Great. Now he knew she admired him professionally, as well as desired him personally.

She heard footsteps in the hallway and hastily dropped the newspaper onto the table. She tried to look casual and at ease, but her shoulders felt as though they were up around her earlobes.

Jake was holding something in his hand when he entered. It took her a moment to recognize the copy of his book that she'd exiled to the toilet-paper basket.

She closed her eyes. This evening was getting better and better.

"I'm curious. If I look through this, are there going to be any pages missing?"

"Oh. Um. No. Of course not. I'm not even sure what that was doing in the bathroom…."

Jake cocked his head to one side and the lie died in her throat.

They stared at each other, then his mouth stretched into a grin.

"Just how long have I been gracing the smallest room in the house, anyway?"

"Since my first day on the paper." He'd surprised her again. His writing was not something she'd expected him to have a sense of humor about.

"That long. Did it make you feel better, putting me in there?" he asked, weighing the book in his hand.

"Yes."

"Good."

He turned to leave the room and she realized he was going to put the book back where he'd found it.

"No. Don't," she said. "I don't think I want it in there any-more."

He stilled. "It's not a bad place for it."

"Maybe."

Jake turned to face her. Their eyes met across the space that separated them, and suddenly they were at the point they'd both been dancing around all night. Poppy could feel her heart kicking in her chest, feel the flood of adrenaline racing through her body. Deep inside, her body throbbed in anticipation.

She wanted him. And she knew he wanted her. Could prac-tically smell it in the air.

"Where do you want it, then?" he asked.

"I used to keep it in my bedroom."

His eyes darkened. "I don't think that's the best place for it."

"Why not?" She held her breath, waiting for his answer. They both knew they weren't talking about his book or her apartment.

"Because it's your space. It's too personal," he said quietly.

So.

She nodded to let him know she understood his message. She hoped her disappointment didn't show on her face. Maybe this time she'd learn her lesson where he was concerned.

She held her hand out for the book.

"Okay. I guess I'll have to find a new home for it. Some-where between the toilet and the bedroom."

He passed the book over. They both turned toward the hall. She moved ahead of him to open the front door. She kept her hand on the lock, gripping the cool metal tightly as he hesi-tated in the doorway.

"It's not you, Poppy. I really like you."

She shrugged. "I get it. We work with each other. Things have already been awkward. I get it."

"It's not about work." He ran a hand through his hair, stared at the floor for a long beat. "I don't want to hurt you."

"Then don't," she said simply.

He lifted his head to meet her eyes. "It's not that simple."

"Yeah, it is. I'm not asking for a marriage proposal, Jake. I just want you to be there when I wake in the morning. Or to at least say goodbye before you go."

He searched her face. She could feel the tension in him. "I don't have anything to offer you."

Right now she was focused on only one thing—the rush of blood in her ears, the spread of warmth in the pit of her stomach.

"Can you be here in the morning?" she asked. "That's all I want from you right now."

He closed his eyes. "Do you have any idea how much I've thought about you over the past few weeks?" His voice was rough and low. It scraped along her senses and sent a shiver through her.

"It's not like I've been counting sheep at night, either."

His eyes opened. "What have you been counting, then?"

She smiled slowly. "What do you think?"

By slow degrees his smile grew to match hers. He took a step forward and she met him halfway. The press of her breasts against his chest was almost a relief.

His eyes glinted as he lowered his head toward hers. She opened her mouth to him and closed her eyes as his tongue swept into her mouth. He sipped at her lips, stroked her tongue with his, murmured something deep in his throat. She let go of the door and reached for his hips, pulling him closer. He was already hard, his erection straining the fine cord of his pants. She slid a hand onto his butt and held him against her, savoring the heat and hardness of him.

After a long moment he lifted his head. She stared into his face, drugged with need.

"Yes. The answer is yes. I can be here in the morning," he said.

Just as well, because she wasn't sure she had the willpower to push him away if his answer had been anything different.

"Then what are you waiting for?"

Taking his hand, she shut the door behind them and led him to her bedroom.

8

POPPY'S ROOM LOOKED AS THOUGH a bomb had hit it. Clothes and shoes everywhere, books stacked beside the bed, her chest of drawers strewn with papers and toiletries. About the only space that was clear was the bed. Which was good, since that was Jake's destination.

"Sorry about the mess," she said.

Jake grunted to let her know he didn't give a damn about the cleanliness or otherwise of her bedroom and pulled her down onto the mattress, eager to feel the warmth of her beneath him. Every night she'd slipped into his dreams, taunting him with remembered passion. He wasn't sure where he wanted to touch first, which part of her he needed to taste the most. He tugged at her clothes, yanking off her jacket then fumbling with her shirt.

"Slow down." She laughed.

"Can't."

And it was true, he couldn't. He'd been convinced he'd never slide his hands over her breasts again, and yet here they were, warm and full and soft in his hands, her nipples hard beneath the silk and lace of her bra. He'd been certain he'd never feel the greedy press of her hips against his again, or the firm strength of her long legs tangling with his. And yet she was even now rubbing herself against him, one leg wrapped around his waist as she sought satisfaction.

It was too much. She was too much. He sucked a nipple, lace and all, into his mouth, laving her with his tongue. She moaned and he slid a hand down her belly and into the waistband of her tailored pants. The button gave way easily, the zipper hissed down, then he was sliding his hand over the plumpness of her mound, his fingers gliding into damp curls then into hot, slick flesh. He slid a finger inside her, felt the instinctive tightening of her muscles as she clenched them around him. She was so hot, so tight. He wanted to be there, needed to be there. He pushed her trousers down, as clumsy and urgent as a schoolboy. She laughed, the sound low and sultry, as he freed himself from his pants. A moment to protect them both, then he was inside her, his pace already wild, his whole body taut with need.

No laughter from her then, just a dreamy, distant look in her eyes as she bit her lip and tilted her head back and thrust her hips in rhythm with his.

He ducked his head to her breasts again, using his teeth to pull the silk of her bra cup down so he could bite her dusky nipple before tugging it into his mouth. Her hips bucked beneath him as he flicked his tongue over and over her. He slid his hands beneath her hips and drove himself to the hilt again and again. She felt so good. Everything about her. Her skin. The softness of her breasts. The plumpness of her mound. The slick tightness between her thighs.

"Poppy," he whispered against her skin.

"I know," she whispered.

Then he was coming, his climax squeezing his chest, his belly, his thighs. He ground himself against her, feeling her own climax pulse around him. For long seconds he remained tautly above her and inside her. And then he collapsed on top of her, his breath coming in choppy gasps.

"Pinch me," she said after a short while.

"Is this a kinky thing or…?"

"I just want to make sure this is real."

He lifted his head to look into her face. Man, he loved the slightly bewildered look she got on her face after he'd made her come. As though she wasn't one hundred percent certain which way was up or down.

He withdrew from her and rolled to the edge of the bed.

"Come on," he said, reaching for her hand. "Let's have a shower. I couldn't help noticing you have this handy bench tiled into the wall in there."

"For when I was training, to help loosen me up. Back when we weren't on water restrictions because of the drought."

"Ah, the good old days," he said. His trousers and boxer briefs were still tangled around his ankles and he kicked them off. He tugged her pants the rest of the way off, too, then ran a hand from her knee up her thigh, over her hip, stopping on the flat plane of her belly. He felt her muscles contract beneath his hand, watched as her nipples hardened all over again. Her lips parted and she watched him through half-lowered lids.

"Come have a shower," he said.

"Okay."

She led the way up the short hallway. He watched the sway of her hips, the tight flex of her butt. He couldn't resist sliding his hands onto it, cupping it in his palms.

"Just out of curiosity, you ever tried to crack a walnut with these suckers?" he asked, squeezing the twin cheeks of her derriere firmly.

She gave him a look over her shoulder. He grinned and shrugged.

"Just curious."

"Hmm," she said. "I'm not sure I want to know what other questions you have floating in that brain of yours."

He stood back and watched some more as she reached to turn on the shower. Even in winter she had a light tan from her hours in the pool. He eyed the lines on her ass from her swimsuit and remembered how creamy and smooth her breasts were in comparison with her golden arms and legs.

He was hard again. More than anything he wanted to press her against the shower wall and slide inside her again, but there were other, more pressing issues to attend to. Like the fact that he'd been craving another taste of her for weeks now.

"You coming?" she asked as she stepped beneath the water.

He smiled and stepped in after her. "Definitely."

He reached for the soap and the washcloth hanging from her shower organizer. She watched as he worked up a good lather on the cloth.

"Now," he said, drawing her toward him. Slowly he washed her from head to toe. He traced the whorls of her ears, mapped the elegance of her long neck. Paid loving, intimate attention to her breasts and her armpits and the curve of her hip. Dipped between her thighs, washed behind her knees. Then he knelt and lifted her feet, one by one, and washed her toes and her soles and her heels, his fingers massaging the washcloth against her skin.

When he was finished, he looked up at her.

"Sit down," he said.

Poppy's eyes widened as she guessed his intention. Then her focus dropped to his erection where it pressed, hard and ready, against his belly.

"I want—"

"Later."

She sat on the tiled bench behind her. He moved between

her legs, pushing them apart. The air was thick with steam and moisture and warm water pounded down on both of them. He parted the pinkness of her folds. She sucked in an anticipatory breath. He glanced up at her, taking in the flush on her cheeks, the heaviness of her eyelids.

Then he lowered his head and tasted her.

Better than he'd remembered. Slick, silky flesh, the gentle musk of her sex, the freshness of her arousal. He used his hands to keep her open, circling his thumbs around and around her entrance as he teased her clitoris with his mouth. She was very turned on, the bud stiff against his tongue and he sucked her into his mouth again and again. Her hips bucked and one of her hands slid into his hair and fisted there. She lifted a leg to brace it on the seat beside her, offering him greater access. He slid a finger inside her and stroked her inner walls. He knew the moment he found the spot he was looking for—her whole body tensed as though she'd been shocked.

"Jake," she panted.

He smiled against her sex and renewed his assault, stroking her clitoris with his tongue, stroking her G-spot with his finger. It didn't take long. She sucked in a deep breath, her hips lifting. He clamped a hand onto her thigh to hold her in place. He stayed with her as her body convulsed with pleasure, her inner muscles vibrating around his finger.

He lifted his head at last and looked up at her, savoring the abandoned, provocative picture she made, her head dropped back against the shower wall, water streaming down her peaked breasts and her flat belly.

He'd meant to wait, to dry her and take her to bed, but he couldn't hold off a second longer. Standing, he took himself in hand and nudged her folds with his erection.

"Yes," she said, lifting her hips.

He was inside her, gritting his teeth at how wet she was, how good she felt. She shuddered, a whole body ripple of need.

He withdrew until just the tip of his cock remained inside her then watched as he pressed forward and his cock disappeared into her body once more. He repeated the move, reveling in the greedy clutch of her body, savoring the glide into tightness as he drove into her. He glanced at her face, saw she was watching the place where they were joined, too, and that her breasts were rising and falling rapidly. They locked gazes and suddenly he was on the verge, just like that, pleasure rushing through his body. Swiftly, he withdrew from her, stroking himself once, twice with his hand until he came on her belly, his body shuddering.

"I think maybe I just died," she said.

He laughed. He'd never met a woman so open about her own pleasure. With Poppy there had never been any games, no pretense that she didn't want him, that she didn't enjoy the sex, that it wasn't important to her.

She was equally honest about her feelings, too. Another thing he found attractive. He couldn't ever imagine Poppy sulking or punishing him with silence. If she wanted something, she either asked for it or dealt with her need in some other way.

They made love again when they returned to the bedroom. He honestly hadn't thought he was up to it—he wasn't a perpetually horny teenager anymore—but watching her crawl on all fours to the far side of the mattress had his cock flooding to life again. He slid into her from behind this time while they both lay on their sides, her backside cradled by his hips. They rocked together for long, lazy minutes until desire took over. Then Poppy moved onto her hands and knees and he slammed himself into her until they both came yet again.

Poppy dragged the quilt up over their bodies afterward,

shaking her head and laughing ruefully when he slid a hand onto her breast.

"Give me five minutes," she said.

They fell asleep, his hand on her breast, his body curved against hers. His thoughts drifted to the way they fit as he slipped into sleep. She was so tall, he felt all of her against all of him. A good feeling. Complete.

JAKE WOKE WITH SUNLIGHT warm against his face. He turned his head, and there Poppy was, golden light streaming in her bedroom window, gilding her breasts. She was awake, too, her hair was mussed, her eyes heavy.

She smiled faintly when she caught his eye. "You're here."

"Yep."

"A minor miracle."

He smoothed the sole of his foot down the side of her smooth calf. "Hardly." He held her gaze when he said it, wanting her to know that if it was only about her, her honesty and funniness and desirability, he would never have left her bed. Her gaze slid away, but her smile remained.

She didn't know where she stood with him. Which was fair enough—he had no idea where he stood, either.

"There's cereal and bread if you're hungry, but I usually have breakfast at the pool on the weekends. There's a cute little café, and they make great pancakes." She said the words carefully, not quite issuing an invitation.

"Does a person have to swim laps to qualify for breakfast? Or can a person just sit back like a fat bastard and watch other people exercise?"

Her eyebrows rose, then a smile spread across her face. She tried to get it under control, to tame it, but he could still see her pleasure in her eyes even after she'd reined in her mouth.

A moment of doubt bit him. She was so damned open, the way she broadcast everything via her big gray eyes and her expressive face.

He didn't want to hurt her. He remembered what she'd said last night—*then don't*. She'd been asking him to be honest with her. To commit to a night. To one moment at a time.

Could it really be that easy?

Poppy made him walk the two blocks to the pool, claiming it was a good warm-up. The sky was a pale blue, but the sun was shining. The Harold Holt Memorial Pool had two offerings for patrons to choose from: a smaller, heated indoor pool and a competition-length beast outside. The indoor pool was frothing with bodies, since it was September and the tail end of winter was still in the air outside. Only the serious swimmers were prepared to brave the elements for a more challenging swim. Predictably, Poppy led him outside.

She shucked her tracksuit pants immediately and started swinging her arms in broad circles. He frowned and eyed the swimmers churning up the lanes.

"Come on, scaredy cat," she said.

She'd talked him into borrowing a pair of board shorts a "friend" had left behind in her apartment, promising him that while he could still have his pancake breakfast without doing some laps, it would be that much more delicious once he'd earned it.

He'd always been skeptical of that argument—he'd enjoyed plenty of things in his lifetime that he hadn't strictly earned. But he could see she wanted him to swim with her. And it seemed like a small, simple sacrifice to make to bring that slow smile to her lips again.

"I wasn't joking when I said I can't dive for shit," he said.

She shrugged. "So use the steps or jump in."

"I'm not that hopeless."

"Come on, stop stalling and get undressed."

She moved to the diving block at the head of the fast lane while he undressed. He watched her tug her goggles into place and step onto the block. Despite the cold wind and the gooseflesh prickling his arms, he felt a thrill as he watched her bend into position. She looked magnificent, all muscle and long legs and coiled potential. For long seconds she hovered on the verge of exploding off the block, waiting for the lane to be clear. Then she dived, her body arching out over the water for what seemed an impossibly long time before she sliced cleanly into the blue of the pool. He watched her power her way up the lane, marveling at the precision and economy of her stroke.

A particularly chill gust of wind reminded him that he was freezing his proverbials off, and he crossed to the medium lane and dived into the water in his own messy, unaccomplished way.

He'd had enough after ten laps. Running kept him fit, but swimming made different demands on his body. He hauled himself out of the pool and dried off, searching for Poppy's blond head in the water. He found her at the far end of the pool, surrounded by half a dozen young swimmers. A middle-aged woman who he guessed was their coach squatted on the deck, her face intent as she listened to Poppy talk to the swimmers. Jake watched as Poppy lifted her arms, demonstrating a stroke technique. The children all imitated her, their small faces filled with reverent awe as they looked at her. Poppy reached out to correct the angle of one boy's arm, talking all the while. The boy laughed, but Jake saw he kept his elbow high as Poppy had shown him when he tried the stroke again.

Poppy looked up and caught Jake's eye. She signaled that she would be with him shortly, and he signaled back that she should take her time. He was almost fully dressed by the time she joined him on the wooden bleachers beside the pool.

"Sorry. I got caught up. Sally—that's the coach for the under-fourteens—keeps asking my advice when she sees me down here. It's becoming a bit of a habit."

"They like you."

She shrugged as she pulled on her sweatpants. "I've been on TV."

"You're a hero, Poppy. They probably have posters of you on their walls at home."

She looked startled at the thought, then she smiled the sweetest, shyest smile he'd ever seen. "Maybe. They're good kids. Some of them can really swim."

She led him to the café and they ate pancakes with berries, surrounded by the high-pitched squeals of children from the indoor pool and the warm, humid smell of chlorine.

They talked about work on the way back to her apartment block, their steps slowing as they approached his car.

"Well. Thanks for giving me the opportunity to freeze my ass off," he said.

"It wasn't that bad."

"You're only saying that because you didn't see my dive."

"I did, actually."

"And?"

She held her hand out palm down and seesawed it back and forth. "So-so. I've seen worse."

"Let me guess. In the five-year-old class?"

Her smile turned into a grin. "Seven-year-old, actually."

"Hmm."

They smiled at each other. Sunlight filtered through the bare branches overhead, brushing her cheek, setting her hair on fire. He didn't want to go home.

He pulled his car keys from his pocket. "Well. I guess I'd better get going."

He waited for her to say something, give him an excuse to come back upstairs with her.

"Yeah. Thanks for the lift home last night," she said. "And for the help with the Hannam article."

"Always so well mannered, Birmingham," he said, shaking his head.

"Always so rude, Stevens."

Even though he wasn't certain she'd welcome it, he ducked his head and kissed her. No tongue, just warm lips and a too-brief taste of her.

"I'll see you later, Poppy."

"Sure."

He got in his car, dumping his wet gear on the passenger side floor mat. Poppy waved once before turning to walk up the path to her apartment.

He pulled away from the curb, hands tight on the wheel.

This is already getting out of hand.

The thing was, after a night in her arms, he couldn't remember exactly why that was such a bad idea anymore.

9

POPPY SPENT SATURDAY tidying her apartment and catching up on her homework for school. Every time her phone rang her heart leaped, even though she told herself that there was no way she would hear from Jake again that weekend.

She was wrong. He called at six that night and they went out for dinner before going to his place. Sunday night they went to an Al Pacino double feature at an old Art Deco cinema near Jake's house and wound up necking in the back row and making love in Jake's car because they couldn't wait to make it home. She left his bed at two in the morning to get some sleep before starting the working week.

She had no idea what was going on between the two of them—great sex, definitely. But there was more to it than that, too.

She felt incredibly self-conscious when she entered the newsroom the next morning, late for the first time since she'd started at the *Herald*. She hadn't given much thought to work during the weekend, how things might play out, how she might feel. Perhaps she should have. She felt as though there was a flashing neon sign above her head announcing that she and Jake had spent the past two days skin to skin.

She kept her head down, but she couldn't resist shooting a quick glance toward Jake as she sat at her desk. He had his back to her as he wrote something in a notepad, one elbow braced on his desk. She studied the breadth of his shoulders, the subtle strength of his arms. His dark hair just brushed the collar of his shirt, the ends curling slightly. She knew exactly how soft that hair was, what it felt like in her hands, against her skin…

She was staring. She forced her gaze away and concentrated on unpacking her bag. The last thing she wanted or needed was people at work guessing what had happened between them. If this was a mistake—and despite how he made her feel, how drawn she was to him, she suspected it was—then she wanted it to be a private one, not a public debacle open to her colleagues' scrutiny and discussion.

She straightened her in-tray, untangled her phone cord. Dusted her computer monitor, culled the out-of-date sticky notes from her diary. Only then did she allow herself to look at Jake again.

He was still writing in his notebook. She wondered if he'd even noticed her arrival, if he was as acutely conscious of her as she was of him.

Stop staring and do some work. Because that's where you are: at work. Where people do stuff other than stare at their lovers.

This was new territory for her, all of it. The hot need he inspired in her. The nature of their relationship, if it could even be called that. The fact that they worked with each other. Her previous life of discipline and focus had left her woefully unprepared to deal with these kinds of situations. Which was probably why she felt so out of control.

She concentrated on calling up a new file and saving it. She had a profile on an up-and-coming runner to write, and she frowned over the notes she'd taken from the interview. Out of the corner of her eye, she registered movement. Her whole body tensed as Jake pushed back his chair and stood. He turned toward the kitchen, started walking. She held her breath, lifted her gaze as he passed her desk. Waited for him to make eye contact or smile, do something to acknowledge that the weekend had really happened.

He was almost past the point of no return when he turned his head toward her. He nodded once, briefly, his gaze glancing over her face.

"Hey," he said.

Then he was gone.

She stared after him.

Hey. That was it? That was all she got after half a dozen orgasms, two movies, dinner and some seriously funny pillow talk?

She turned to her article but all she did was frown at the screen.

What were you expecting? A declaration of love?

No. But she hadn't expected *Hey,* either.

It was a long day. She had to stop herself from staring at Jake in their department meeting. At lunchtime, she went down to the café and ate her lunch two tables away from him, pretending she didn't care that he was sitting and talking and laughing with Jonesy and Davo.

By the time Jake threw her a casual goodbye wave just after six and headed for the elevator, she understood why workplace romances were frowned upon. She'd been unfocused and distracted all day, had a headache that wouldn't quit and was so confused she didn't know where to put herself.

Then she stepped out of the elevator into the underground garage and saw the note folded under her windshield wiper and her stomach lurched with excitement.

Pathetic, Birmingham. Really, really sad.

She waited until she was in the relative privacy of her car before unfolding the note. She stared at the single line:

Dinner after your swim? J.

A more sophisticated woman would wait awhile before texting to accept such a last-minute invitation. Poppy dug her phone out of her bag and sent a quick confirmation.

It wasn't simply that he wanted to see her, despite his cool demeanor all day. He'd remembered that she swam every day. A small thing, perhaps, but it felt as though it meant something. At the very least, it meant he listened to what she said, remembered it.

Yes. That had to mean something.

THEY SAW EACH OTHER every night that week, even Tuesday night when Poppy had night school till nine. By Friday, she was growing used to Jake's cool friendliness at work. It still gave her pause when he treated her as casually as he did everyone else, but she knew it was smart to keep their private life private. After all, the odds were good this thing of theirs had only a finite lifespan. This way, she got to keep her dignity afterward.

Friday night, Jake took her to an out-of-the-way Malaysian restaurant he'd been hearing good things about. They both went into raptures over the pork in coffee sauce and tamarind prawns, and Jake insisted she try a Malaysian beer with their meal.

"It's what the locals drink. It makes the experience authentic," he said.

She obliged him by taking a mouthful from his glass.

"Okay, it's nice," she conceded. "Even though I am not a beer fan."

"And you call yourself an Australian."

"I know. It's my dirty little secret."

"What other dark truths lurk in your soul, Poppy Birmingham?" Jake asked, leaning toward her. "Hmm?"

His eyes were bright with laughter, his hair ruffled. He was smiling, one eyebrow quirked in expectation. She stared at him and knew that she'd never meet a more attractive man in her life.

"I don't think I have any dark truths."

"I refuse to accept that. There must be something."

"Sorry, my conscience is clean."

He grinned. "Well, maybe I should make it my mission to dirty it up a little."

"Yeah? How exactly do you plan on doing that?"

"Well, for starters—"

"Poppy! God, of all the places!"

Poppy's head came up at the sound of her sister's voice. Sure enough, Gillian stood beside the neighboring table, about to sit down with a large group of friends.

"Gill," Poppy said. For absolutely no reason, she felt acutely self-conscious. She never, ever ran into her sister or brother around town, mostly because they moved in very different circles. To run into Gillian while she was out with Jake felt…awkward. She wasn't quite sure why.

Gillian's gaze shifted to Jake, then back to Poppy again.

"I've been meaning to call you. How are you doing?" Gill asked. Her sister wiggled her eyebrows meaningfully. She wanted an introduction.

"I'm good. Work's been busy. Um, Gill, this is Jake. Jake, this is my sister, Gill," she said.

Gill turned the full force of her charm on Jake, smiling and offering her hand. "Jake, pleased to meet you. I'm going to be gauche and come right out and say I'm a big fan of your

book. I work in publishing and I still think it's one of the best
Australian novels of the last decade."

Jake sat back a little in his chair. "Nice of you to say so."

Even though his face was completely impassive, Poppy
could feel his discomfort. He didn't like talking about his
writing. She'd never really registered it before, but it was true.

"Well, I'm not the only one to say so. I was talking to
Robert Hughes the other day and he was raving about you,
wondering why we haven't seen a second novel yet," Gill
said, shamelessly dropping the name of Australia's foremost
art critic.

"You know how it is, life gets in the way," Jake said.

Gillian propped her hand on her hip and gave him an ap-
praising look, a half smile on her lips. Poppy could see her sister
was about to launch into a full interrogation, despite Jake's
patent reluctance. She did the only thing she could think of—
she reached across the table, took Jake's hand in hers and smiled
at her sister.

"Have you been here before? The food is really great.
Jake's friend recommended it to him, otherwise we never
would have heard about it. Which I'm glad we did, because,
honestly, the coffee pork is to die for." She was talking too
fast, had said too much, but her sister took the hint.

Gill's gaze rested on their joined hands for a moment before lifting to Poppy's face.

"No, I haven't. But I've heard a lot of good things." She
turned to Jake. "It was nice to meet you. We should do lunch
or something soon, Poppy."

"Sure," Poppy said easily.

Gill rejoined her friends, and Poppy tried to ease her hand
from Jake's. His fingers curled around hers, refusing to let go.
She met his eyes and saw he was smiling at her.

"Slaying my dragons for me, Poppy?"

She shrugged, embarrassed. "She can be a bit scary some-times. And I could tell you didn't want to talk about it."

He turned her hand over and lifted it to press a kiss into her palm. Her breath caught in her throat as he looked at her.

"Thank you."

Warmth expanded in her chest. When he looked at her like that…

Finally he let her hand go. She tucked it into her lap, still feeling the brush of his lips against her skin.

"So, where does the Amazonian gene come from? Is your brother blond like you?" he asked.

"Nope. He's small and dark, like the rest of them. Charlie said I was a throwback to our long-lost Viking heritage."

Jake smiled. "Poppy the Conqueror. Yeah, I can see you wearing a helmet with horns, waving a big sword around."

"Thank you. I think that's the nicest thing anyone's said to me all day," she said drily.

He laughed. She loved that he got her jokes. And she loved the way his gaze kept dropping to the neckline of her shirt, making her think of what would happen when they got home. She especially loved the way he'd looked at her just now, his gaze warm and intense.

"I'm going to go powder my nose," she said.

She wove her way through the crowded dining room to the restrooms. When she exited the cubicle to wash her hands, her sister was standing by the hand basin.

"Gill," Poppy said, not really surprised to see her. They weren't the closest of sisters, but she knew Gill was interested in Jake because of who he was.

"Poppy, you dark horse. I thought you and Jake were just friends."

"We were."

"But you're not anymore?"

"Um, no. I guess not." Poppy shuffled from one foot to the other. She'd never been the kind of woman who talked about her sex life with friends.

Gill eyed her speculatively as Poppy washed her hands. "He's much better looking in real life."

"Yes."

"Very sexy."

"Mmm."

"Well, Mom will be thrilled. She'll get to grill him properly now."

"Oh, no. It's not like that. We're just… It's very casual. Very," Poppy explained. The last thing she wanted was her mother on the phone, asking twenty questions about her literary boyfriend.

Gill frowned. "That doesn't sound like you."

"First time for everything." Poppy made a point of checking her watch. "Better get back to the table…"

Gill caught her arm before she could go. "Poppy, wait a minute." Gill searched Poppy's face, her eyes concerned. "Are you sure you know what you're doing?"

"Of course. I *have* had sex before, you know."

"In a relationship, though, right?"

"Honestly, Gill…"

"I'm only asking because I don't want you to get hurt."

"I won't. I know exactly what this is. Jake's not up for anything serious. He made that clear up front."

"And what about you? What are you up for?"

Poppy shrugged. "I'm going along for the ride."

Gill studied her face for a long moment. "Well, I hope that's true. Because if you're hanging in there, hoping your casual thing will turn into something less casual, you're setting yourself up to be hurt, Poppy. Believe me, I've been there, and if there's one piece of advice I can give you, it's to believe a man when he says he's not interested in having a relationship. Women always think they know better, or that once the guy gets to know them that rule won't apply to them, but it always does."

For a moment Poppy could see every one of her sister's thirty-five years in the lines around Gill's eyes and mouth. Then Gill patted her arm.

"Sorry—here endeth the lesson, I promise. Have fun with your sexy writer. And look after yourself, Poppy."

She kissed Poppy's cheek and gave her a brief hug, both enormously demonstrative gestures for her typically stand-offish sister.

"I will. You, too," Poppy said.

Jake was talking on his cell phone as she picked her way through the dining room to their table. She watched as he laughed at something his caller said, then started talking animatedly.

He was so damned *compelling,* it almost hurt her to look at him.

Her sister's words echoed in her mind: *you're setting yourself up to be hurt, Poppy.*

She lifted her chin. She wasn't stupid. She knew the score. As long as she kept reminding herself that what was happening between her and Jake was about sex and nothing else, she would be fine.

Absolutely. And in the meantime, she would have fun. After years of swimming drills and discipline, she figured she'd earned a little.

THE FOLLOWING SATURDAY, Jake poured himself a cup of strong black coffee and walked to the living room to sit at his desk. He'd just returned from Poppy's. She'd been headed for the pool as he left, a towel slung over her shoulder, long legs eating up the sidewalk.

He'd been tempted to join her, but he had to polish a feature on Australian cricketing greats that was due on Monday. For the first time in a long time, he resented the fact that his work often bled into his personal life. Maybe because for the first time in a long time he actually had a personal life. Today, for example, it would have been nice to swim with Poppy, then take her to the old Abbotsford Convent, where he'd heard there was an organic bakery and a vegetarian restaurant. Poppy would get off on the healthy food, and afterward they could walk around and look at the old buildings. Instead, he was writing about Donald Bradman and Dennis Lillee.

Jake frowned and took a mouthful of coffee. He was thinking about Poppy way too much. Making plans in his head, coming up with new places to take her, things she might enjoy. For a casual thing, their relationship had quickly taken on a life of its own.

He had no idea what he was doing. Every day he told himself to back off, take it easy with her. And every day he found an excuse to touch her, to be with her. He wasn't ready to give her up yet. He knew he would have to, eventually, but right now he didn't have it in him to walk away.

He forced himself to focus and two hours later he hit Save for the last time. According to his complaining belly, it was well past lunchtime. He stood and stretched, then walked into the kitchen in search of food. He hadn't been shopping all week, so it was probably going to have to be cereal or toast. He opened the freezer to make sure he had no frozen pizzas left and barked out a laugh when he saw what was in there—

a neat stack of frozen meals, a sticky note stuck to one of the boxes. He smiled as he read Poppy's sloping, messy scrawl:

In case of nutritional emergency, break box and heat contents. Then get your pitiful bachelor ass to the supermarket to buy some real food.

He wondered when she'd sneaked the meals into his freezer, then remembered he'd jumped into the shower to wash off the sweat from his run shortly after she arrived on Wednesday night.

"Sneaky," he said into the depths of his freezer.

He chose a stir-fry dish, pierced the top and popped it into the microwave. Then he reached for the phone and dialed her number.

She answered on the third ring.

"Hey," she said.

"Hey, yourself. Ask me what I'm having for lunch."

He leaned a hip against the door frame and slid his free hand into the front pocket of his jeans.

"Lunch? Oh, right. You found the meals."

"Pretty sneaky, getting them into my freezer without me noticing. Ever thought about a career in industrial espionage?"

"Every other day."

"Worried about me starving to death, Poppy?"

"Just making sure you keep your strength up. For entirely selfish purposes. Don't want you passing out at a vital moment or anything."

"Hmm. I guess I should probably return the favor. Keep your strength up, blah blah."

"Well, you know my great love of frozen food," she said with heavy irony.

He grinned. He could imagine the exact look she had in her eyes, the tilt to her head.

"You've been ruined by years of good nutrition, that's your problem."

"Yeah, it's a killer."

"Come to dinner," he said. "I'll cook you something nice."

There was a short pause. He frowned.

"If you have other plans, we can do it another night," he said, even though what he really wanted to ask was what she was doing and who she was doing it with.

"What time do you want me?"

His shoulders relaxed. "Seven. How does that sound?"

"Okay. I'd better get out of this wet swimsuit. Wash the chlorine off."

"Sure. I'll see you later."

He ended the call and stared at the receiver for a few minutes. He hadn't planned on seeing her tonight, but now he was. He shrugged. Poppy was a big girl, she could take care of herself. If she didn't want to see him, she'd say so.

HE SPENT THE REST OF THE afternoon doing some much-needed laundry. At four he went out for groceries. It was close to seven and the kitchen was rich with the smell of baking lasagna when the phone rang. He wiped his hands on a tea towel before taking the call.

"Jake Stevens."

"Jake."

One word was all it took for him to recognize his ex-wife's voice, even though it had been four years since they last spoke. Slowly, he put down the tea towel.

"Marly."

"How are you?"

"I'm good."

"I've been reading your columns. I liked that piece you did on retiring footballers."

"Thanks." He took a deep breath. "Listen, Marly, did you want something?"

There was a small silence on the other end of the line.

"Wow. That's certainly straight to the point."

"Sorry." He pinched the bridge of his nose. It had been five years since the divorce, and he still couldn't talk to her without feeling the old tension in his chest.

"It's all right. We haven't exactly been on talking terms, have we?"

"No."

"That's kind of why I'm calling, actually. I know you still see Marian and Paul sometimes, and I didn't want you hearing it from them." She paused. "I'm pregnant."

He should have expected it. What other reason would she have for calling, after all? She and Gavin had been married for two years now, they'd probably been trying for a while. It was only natural that having a baby together would be high on their list of priorities.

But still he felt winded.

"Jake? Hello?"

He took a deep breath and pulled himself together.

"Congratulations. When are you due?"

That was what he was supposed to ask, right? There was no way he could ask the other questions crowding his mind. Are you still going to call the baby Emma if it's a girl and Harry if it's a boy? Do you still want a natural birth?

Will it make you forget the baby we lost?

"I'm twenty weeks. Halfway."

Four weeks past the point when she'd miscarried last time.

"That's great. Everything good? Mother and baby both well?" he asked.

"Yes."

"Well. I'm happy for you."

"Gavin's taken some time off work and we're going to take it easy for the last few months. Just to make sure everything is okay this time," Marly said.

He closed his eyes, hearing the implied criticism in her tone. Even now, she couldn't let it go.

"Should give you plenty of time to prepare for the baby," he said neutrally.

She was silent for a beat. He could hear her breathing on the other end of the line.

"Do you ever think about her?" she finally asked.

"Yes. Of course I do."

"She'd be six years old. In grade one at school." She was crying, her voice breaking.

"Marly…"

"I'm sorry. It's just been on my mind a lot lately. For obvious reasons."

"Sure."

"Anyway, I'll let you go. Stay well, Jake."

"I'll keep an eye out in the paper for the announcement," he said.

He ended the call. For a long moment he simply stood there, trying to keep a lid on all the shit she'd stirred up.

It was amazing, but even after five years he still felt the tug of responsibility toward her. The tears in her voice, the thread of misery—like Pavlov's dogs, all the old instincts roared to life inside him. The need to make her happy, to heal her, to somehow find the one magic thing that would make it all okay.

The old anger was there, too. Anger at himself, for not being around when she needed him. Anger at her for not being stronger. Anger at life for throwing more misery at them than they'd been able to handle.

Memories he'd thought long buried rose: the emptiness in Marly's eyes when he'd finally arrived at the hospital after she'd lost their baby; the oppressive darkness of their bedroom for months afterward, Marly curled on the bed day after day. And finally Marly's body stretched on the bathroom floor, pale and lifeless.

He swore under his breath and strode to the living room. He didn't know where to put himself. He didn't want to relive this shit. He wanted it gone, forgotten. But all the old stuff was welling up inside him.

Why the hell had she called? He didn't need to know she was having another baby. It was none of his business. Nothing to do with him.

His movements jerky, he grabbed a bottle of wine and pulled the cork. He was taking his first mouthful when the doorbell rang.

It took him a moment to remember that he'd invited Poppy over.

Shit.

He passed a hand over his face and took a deep breath. Then he went to open the door.

"Hey," she said brightly. She held up a supermarket bag. "I brought ice cream for dessert."

He forced a smile.

"Great. Come on in. The lasagna's almost done."

She followed him into the kitchen and unloaded a tub of chocolate-chip ice cream onto the counter. He shoved it into the freezer and grabbed another wineglass. All the while he avoided her eyes. If he looked at her, he was afraid it would all come tumbling out—all the misery, all the grief, all the anger.

"Did you get your article finished?" she asked as he poured her a drink.

"Yes."

He slid her glass across the counter. The wine slopped dangerously close to the rim.

"Is there anything I can do to help?" She looked expectantly around the kitchen.

"You know what, why don't you go to the living room and find something to put on the stereo while I make the salad?"

He felt as though his skin was too tight, as though one wrong word or gesture would shred what little control he had.

She hesitated for a moment.

"Sure, no worries. I'll leave you to it."

Once she was gone, he braced his arms against the counter and hung his head.

It's the past. It's gone. It doesn't mean anything.

"Jake, is everything okay?" Poppy asked quietly from behind him.

He straightened. She was standing in the doorway, a wrinkle of concern on her forehead.

"Did you find something you want to listen to?"

He reached for his wine and took a good swallow. Poppy watched him, her eyes wary.

"If you need to talk… I mean, it's not as though I don't owe you on that front, after Uncle Charlie and everything."

"I'm fine," he said. It came out a little more curtly than he'd meant it to and she flinched.

"Okay." She gave him a small, uncertain smile and returned to the living room.

The timer sounded and he grabbed the oven mitts. He'd

barely got a grip on the stoneware lasagna dish when his wrist contacted one of the hot wire shelves. He jerked away from the pain, and the dish slid from his hands and hit the tiled floor with a crack. Lasagna went everywhere.

"Shit. Bloody hell."

He threw the oven mitts to one side and sucked on the burn on his wrist. Couldn't he catch one freaking break tonight? Was that too much to ask?

"You've hurt yourself. Let me see."

Poppy was in the room, reaching for his arm. He pulled away, unable to tolerate her gentle sympathy.

For a moment they were both very quiet. Then she took a step backward.

"Listen, Jake. If this is a bad time for you, I can always go home."

He stared at the mess on the floor. His chest ached with guilt and anger and grief.

"Yeah. Maybe that's a good idea."

She blinked and he realized she hadn't expected him to take her up on her offer.

"Okay. I guess I'll see you at work, then."

He moved to walk her to the door. She held up a hand.

"It's fine. I know the way out," she said.

She was gone then, the front door closing behind her with a decisive click.

He swore again and closed his eyes.

He'd hurt her feelings. Again.

Grim, he squatted and used the tea towel to scoop the bulk of the ruined lasagna into the two halves of the dish. He dumped the lot in the sink then decided the rest could wait till morning. He needed to get out of the house.

He grabbed his car keys and his wallet and took the

stairs to the back of the building where his Porsche was parked.

He shot out into the street and wove through the traffic, working his way north and east until he was turning into the darkened road leading into Studley Park. Just four kilometers from the city center, the park sprawled over more than six hundred acres and featured one of Melbourne's most challenging roads. Jake put his foot down and took the first corner hard. The Porsche growled beneath him as he changed down a gear and punched the accelerator.

By the time he roared to a stop at the lookout point, he'd wrestled his way around enough corners to take the edge off. The engine quieted to a low rumble, then fell silent as he switched it off.

He walked to the lone picnic bench at the lookout, cold wind biting through his sweater. He sat on the table, feet on the bench seat, elbows braced on his knees. He stared out at the city spread below—the towering skyscrapers, the many twinkling lights of the sprawling suburbs, the constantly moving red-and-white dots of cars on the roads.

Marly had caught him off guard with her news, but it scared him how quickly the old shit had come up at him. He'd thought he'd put it all behind him. Wanted to, more than anything. He'd taken what lessons he could from the experience and moved on.

So why was he sitting up here alone, tears burning at the back of his eyes as he thought about the child he'd lost and his broken marriage?

He stood and walked to the very edge of the lookout, right to the safety barrier where the land fell away abruptly.

Shit happens, man. Deal with it.

It had been his motto for the long months of Marly's depression. Deal with her silence. Deal with her tears. Deal with her accusations and blame. Deal with her attempt to take her own life.

The truth was, he'd spent so much time looking after her, he'd barely had time to feel anything for himself. But someone had had to be the strong one.

Slowly the churning in his gut settled. He returned to the picnic table and sat, breathing in the cool night air. Inevitably, his thoughts turned to Poppy.

He'd hurt her, the way he'd pushed her away. He scrubbed his face with his hands. Maybe it was for the best. The past few weeks had been crazy, but maybe now was the time to start being smart. Before great sex turned into something more than it was ever meant to be.

He stared at the night sky and thought about cutting Poppy out of his life. About never touching her again. Never laughing with her, never teasing her.

Letting her go, before she got hurt.

He turned and went back to his car.

HE'D LET HER WALK OUT the door so easily. That was what killed her the most.

Poppy pushed away the untouched bowl of pasta she'd made for herself and stared at the worn spot on the arm of her couch.

He'd been upset, wounded in some way. She'd seen it in his eyes, his face, the moment he'd opened the door to her. And instead of seeking comfort from her, instead of sharing or taking solace, he'd blocked her out. Literally kicked her out of his kitchen, then let her walk away when she offered to give him space.

Shouldn't have offered to leave if you didn't mean it, her cynical self said.

She'd wanted him to talk to her—that was why she'd offered to leave. She hadn't expected him to let her go.

Which said a lot about the dynamics of their relationship.

Time to face the music, Poppy.

She took a deep breath and then let it out again.

She wanted more from Jake than he was willing to give. This wasn't casual for her. Maybe it never had been.

And she knew, absolutely, that Jake did not feel the same way. Even though things had been pretty damn intense between them the past few weeks, even though when they were together they laughed and had great sex and interesting discussions about everything under the sun, there was always a part of Jake that was constantly checking the exits, in case he had to leave in a hurry. He was drawn to her despite himself, a reluctant recruit to their mutual attraction.

What was it her sister had said?

If there's one piece of advice I can give you, it's to believe a man when he says he's not interested in having a relationship.

Good advice. Pity Poppy had already been too far gone by then to take it.

Poppy pulled her legs tight to her chest and rested her chin on her knees. This was new territory for her, this aching vulnerability, this tenderness. It scared her, because she knew there was a part of her that wanted Jake so much that she'd take whatever scraps of himself he was willing to throw her way. And she might not be an expert on relationships or love, but she knew that that way lay great heartache.

The doorbell rang. She stared down the hallway. It was Jake. It had to be—it was nearly ten and she couldn't think of anyone else who'd come calling unannounced at this time of night.

Plus, her heart was racing. Usually a reliable sign he was somewhere in the vicinity.

All the same, she checked the peephole before opening the door, just in case. Jake stood in profile to her, his head down. He was holding flowers. His expression was unreadable, utterly neutral.

She rested her forehead against the cool surface of the door for a second, love for him washing over her. She wanted to open the door and cling to him, press her face into his neck and inhale his smell, wrap her body around his, get as close as it was humanly possible for two people to be.

She was such an idiot.

It had crept up on her when she wasn't looking, but it had probably been inevitable from the moment she asked him to stay the night. She wasn't the kind of woman who could be casual with her body or her feelings. Her sister had seen it—and deep in her heart, Poppy had known, too.

She took a deep breath. Then she opened the door. Jake swung to face her. Up close his eyes were watchful, wary. He offered her the flowers.

"I'm a dick. I was having a bad day. I shouldn't have taken it out on you," he said simply.

She stared at the flowers, then his face, wanting more. Some small sign that he trusted her. That this was about more than sex for him. That the ache in her chest was not about to become a permanent fixture.

His mouth quirked into a half smile. "If you're interested, there's a little café in Fitzroy that serves great lasagna. Even better than the stuff I scraped off my kitchen floor."

She waited, but there was nothing more.

So.

He wasn't going to give her a reason why.

He wasn't going to share his pain with her, the way she'd shared hers with him.

It's early days yet. He's wary. He's obviously had a bad divorce. Give him time.

Of course, it was also entirely possible that the only part of himself that Jake would ever willingly share with her was his penis, and that holding out for more would only make the inevitable that much more painful.

"Can I come in?" Jake asked.

She realized she'd been standing staring at him for a long time. Slowly, she stepped to one side.

She followed him to the living room and watched him take in the abandoned bowl of spaghetti on her coffee table.

"You've eaten already," he said.

"Yes."

End it. End it now. Save yourself a world of disappointment. End it while you can still look him in the eye and be his friend and work with him.

Her sensible self, speaking with her sister's voice.

She stared at the flowers in her hand. They were something, right? He'd gone to the trouble of finding a florist that was open at this time of night. He could have shown up empty-handed, or gotten some nasty, limp bouquet from the gas station.

She looked at him.

"There's some spaghetti left, if you want it. I could heat it in the microwave."

"Yeah? To be honest, I'm starving," he said. He looked tired. She wanted to cup his face in her hands and draw the pain out of him.

Instead, she went into the kitchen and took the bowl of left-over pasta from the fridge. She could feel him watching her as she put cling film over the bowl and set the microwave timer, but she deliberately didn't look at him. She needed a few seconds to get her game face on. The last thing she wanted was for him to look into her eyes and understand she'd fallen in love with him.

He was studying the dancing monkeys on her baggy old pajamas when she turned around.

"I'm not exactly dressed for company," she said.

His eyes were warm on her from across the small room. "Come here."

When she didn't move, he reached out and caught her elbow, tugging her toward him.

"The spaghetti…"

"I came here for you, not for food."

He kissed her then, his hands cradling her head, and she closed her eyes against the tide of longing and need that rose inside her. One kiss, one caress was all it ever took with Jake.

"I'm sorry, okay?" he said against her mouth. "I was an asshole. It won't happen again, I promise."

He held her eyes until she nodded.

"I'll hold you to it," she said.

"Good."

They kissed again and he slid his hands down her back and beneath the waistband of her pajamas. She shivered as his hands cupped her bare backside, his fingers curving beneath her cheeks.

"No underwear, Ms. Birmingham?"

"As I said, I wasn't expecting company."

"So this is what you get up to when you're on your own, swan around the apartment commando?"

"George likes it that way."

He grinned and backed her against the kitchen counter. "George. I was kind of hoping he was off the scene."

He was, but she wasn't about to tell Jake that he'd ruined her for all other forms of pleasure.

He slid his knee between her legs, nudging them apart. One of his hands found the buttons on her pajama top and he slid them free while he kissed the tender skin beneath her ear, his tongue sending prickles of desire racing through her body.

He murmured his appreciation as he bared her breasts, then he lowered his head and she let her head drop back as he pulled a nipple into his mouth.

He felt so good. She was so ready for him it hurt.

She fumbled with his belt, then his fly. He took care of protection while she kicked her pajama pants off, then she lifted her leg over his hip and he pushed inside her, big and thick and long.

She clutched his bare ass, holding him still inside her for a few precious seconds, savoring the moment. Then he started to move, his cock stroking her, the friction exquisite. His backside flexed and contracted beneath her hands. His breathing became ragged. She could hear the sounds of their bodies meeting and parting, could feel the hot wetness of her own desire.

She pressed her face close to his chest and inhaled, consciously absorbing his smell, the feel of his skin against hers, the power of his body as he pressed himself into her.

I love you, she told him in her mind as she pulled his hips closer, urging him inside her. *I love you, Jake Stevens.*

He kissed her, his tongue sweeping her mouth, his lips teasing hers. She held her breath. Tensed. Closed her eyes.

Then her body was pulsing with pleasure, wave after wave washing over her. She clutched him to her, calling his name over and over. She felt him tense. His body stroked into hers one last time. He shuddered, his body as hard as granite as he came.

For a moment there was only the sound of their harsh breathing. Then Jake drew back a little so he could look down into her face.

"I think the spaghetti is done," he said.

She hadn't even heard the timer sound. Amusement danced in his eyes, along with something else. Something warm and real. Something that made her fiercely glad that she'd let him in, despite the lack of explanation and her realization that she was far more invested in their relationship than he was.

He cares. He may not love me yet, but he cares.

He smoothed her hair from her forehead with his thumb. Then he kissed the corner of her mouth and withdrew from her. She listened to the heavy tread of his footsteps as he headed for the bathroom.

She closed her eyes for a moment, savoring the satisfied pulse of her body. Maybe she was stupid. Maybe she was going to get hurt, but so be it. Right now, right this minute, she'd take what she could get of Jake Stevens and hope like hell that the warmth she saw sometimes when he looked at her was not wishful thinking and self-delusion.

And maybe next time he was troubled or his demons came calling, he would turn *to* her instead of away.

10

THE NEXT MORNING, JAKE woke with words in his head. Poppy was breathing deeply beside him, still asleep, and he kept his eyes closed as images and ideas swirled in his mind. Slowly, the words became phrases, then sentences. He shuffled them in his head like a deck of cards. More words came to him. His fingers itched to pick up a pen and find some paper.

It had been so long since he'd woken like this, he was almost afraid. Once, it had been commonplace, a part of his world. But he hadn't wanted to write, needed to write, for a long time.

Finally the urge to put it down on paper became too much for him. He eased out of bed, tugged on his boxer briefs and went to the living room. Poppy kept scrap paper by the phone to take down messages and he helped himself to a few pages. He sat at her dining room table and started to write. After a few minutes, he stood and grabbed more paper. A few sheets wasn't going to be enough. He felt as though a floodgate had opened inside him. The words and images were flowing fast, and he needed to get them down.

His hand flew across the page. Twenty minutes in, his fingers began to cramp. He shook them out and kept writing.

"Hey. You're up early."

Poppy stood in the doorway, a T-shirt barely skimming the

tops of her thighs. Her hair was ruffled and there was a crease on her face from the pillow.

"Couldn't sleep," he said.

Her gaze dropped to the pages of closely written script in front of him. There was a question in her eyes when she raised them to his face. He shrugged self-consciously.

"An idea for work," he said.

"Ah. I was wondering what had you so fired up so early."

He felt bad for lying to her, but the truth was that he didn't know what this was yet. He started gathering the pages together.

"You want cereal or toast?" she asked as she moved toward the kitchen.

He shook his head, standing. "I'm all right, thanks." He went to the bedroom and began pulling on his clothes.

Poppy looked surprised when he stepped into the living room, fully dressed, pages folded into his back pocket.

"You're going?"

"I've got some things I need to do," he said. "But I'll call you this afternoon, okay?"

She nodded. "Sure."

He kissed her goodbye, savoring the cool softness of her cheek against his. Then he was heading down the stairs, his mind full of more words, more ideas.

He spent the day writing. A story was starting to emerge from the conversations and scenes he'd woken with. The man in his story took on flesh, found his voice. The woman, too. It wasn't until she became pregnant that Jake understood what he was doing. His fingers slowed on the keyboard then stopped. He stared at the screen.

He couldn't write this. Could he?

But already he knew where he wanted to go next, what he needed to put on the page. He wanted to tell it all, every ugly, sad, messy moment of it. He wanted to lay it all out on clean white paper and sweep it out of the dark corners of his mind.

No one need ever read it. Certainly he would never publish it—it was too raw, too personal. But maybe it was something he needed to do. And since it was the first time he'd felt the urge to write in years, it didn't feel as though he had a choice. Not if he ever wanted to reclaim his life.

He took a deep breath. Then he started to write.

TWO WEEKS LATER, POPPY LAY on her bed and watched the morning sun paint patterns on the far wall.

Her body was warm and languid from Jake's lovemaking, her blood still thrumming through her veins. She turned her head and stared at the hollow his head had left in the pillow. She could hear him in the bathroom down the hall, singing his version of Madonna's "Like a Virgin" while he showered. She smiled as he reached for a high note.

That was the thing about Jake. He could always make her laugh, be it with an arrogant comment, a smart-ass quip or boyish stupidity. It was one of the things she loved about him.

The list was growing longer by the day.

Don't start, Birmingham.

She pulled the sheet up to cover her breasts and grabbed his pillow, piling it behind herself before reaching for the book she was reading. It was a Saturday and she didn't have to be anywhere in a hurry. In the bathroom, Jake switched to Nina Simone.

Two weeks ago, she would have been in there with him, but staying in bed this morning and letting him shower alone was today's proof to herself that she could live without Jake Stevens in her life. She made a point of doing something every day to reassure herself that she could. She might love him, but she could live without him. And she would. If she had to.

Loving Jake was like riding a roller coaster. Sometimes when he looked at her, she was so sure she saw something more than lust in his eyes. She had no doubt that he liked her, that he enjoyed spending time with her. He cared about her feelings. And he wanted her. If all of that didn't add up to love, it came pretty damn close.

She could almost let herself believe the fantasy. Almost. But she still had no idea what had cut him so deeply the night of their disastrous dinner. And he still hadn't told her what he was working on. A new book, she guessed. But that was only a guess, because he hadn't shared it with her.

She ached to ask him. Just as she ached for him to confide his pain in her. She wanted to share his life, in every sense of the word. But Jake had to want to share it with her, he had to offer himself up—his trust wasn't something she could demand.

The water shut off and she opened her book and started reading. She was doing a credible impression of an engaged reader when Jake came into the room, a towel slung low on his waist. She tried to keep herself from following him with her eyes as he dressed, but she was powerless against her desire for him.

He had a beautiful body, long and strong and lean. Her gaze swept the width of his torso then ran down his spine. He had a great ass, round and firm from running. And his legs were corded with muscle and dusted with crisp, dark hair. He pulled on boxer-briefs and she watched as he adjusted himself.

Man, it got her hot when he touched himself like that.

She shifted in the bed and he glanced at her.

"Good book?" he asked.

She had to flick a look at the cover to remember what she was reading.

"Yeah. It's funny. He's a good writer," she said.

"When are you going to your parents' place?" he asked as he tugged on jeans.

"Early afternoon. Mom and Dad's party isn't till tonight, but I promised I'd help out."

Jake finished buckling his belt and crossed to sit on the side of the bed.

"Drive carefully, okay?" he said.

He took her hand, his thumb running across the top of her knuckles. Her heart swelled in her chest as she looked into his face. He cared. Definitely he cared.

"I've driven that road about a million times," she said.

"Still." He leaned forward and kissed her gently. Then he stood and grabbed his T-shirt from the top of her chest of drawers.

"When do you think you'll be back?"

"I'll probably leave after breakfast tomorrow, be back midmorning. Don't worry, I haven't forgotten your precious Martin Scorsese double feature."

Jake had been eyeing the Sunday matinee all week.

"This is for your edification, not mine. I can't believe you haven't seen *Goodfellas*. It's a classic."

"I'm prepared to be moved."

He grinned. "Oh, you will be."

He finished tying his shoes and straightened. She put down her book.

"Well. I guess I'll see you tomorrow," he said.

"Yep."

This would be the first Saturday night they'd spent apart in four weeks. She wondered if he'd even noticed.

He leaned down to kiss her. She slid her hand around his neck for just a second, holding him close, then she forced herself to let him go.

"See you," she said.

She made herself stay in bed, supremely casual, as he let himself out. Once she'd heard the door close behind him she fell back against the pillows and closed her eyes. She could still smell his deodorant hanging in the air.

"I love you," she told the empty room.

Before she could start thinking things to death, she threw the covers back and hit the shower. If she went to the pool now, she could get her laps done and spend some time helping Sally with the under-fourteens. At least that was one area where she felt on solid ground.

She spent an hour cutting through the water, losing herself in the rhythm of the pool. Sally was teaching her kids tumble turns, and Poppy showed them a few tricks of the trade before showering and hitting the road.

It was nearly midday when she pulled into her parents' driveway. She spent the afternoon helping prepare for their anniversary party. Gill arrived at four with her new boyfriend, Daniel, followed shortly by Adam with his long-term partner, Wendy. Poppy was acutely aware that Uncle Charlie was missing from the family circle as they all stood in the kitchen talking and laughing. For a moment she was overwhelmed with sadness. Then her mother asked for help stirring the gravy and she didn't have time to think until it was time to file into the dining room.

It wasn't until they were all seated that Poppy registered she was the only person without a partner. Normally, Uncle Charlie sat beside her, so she wasn't as aware of her single status. Certainly it had never bothered her before. But tonight she looked around the table and felt her aloneness acutely.

Her sister must have noticed the same thing because she cornered Poppy in the kitchen after dessert.

"I was kind of thinking Jake might be here," she said.

"No."

"Family dinner too dull for him, huh?" Gill asked. She was joking, her attention more than half-focused on cutting herself a second slice of cake.

"I didn't ask him. I figured mentioning a family gathering would be a surefire way to send him running for the hills."

Poppy closed her mouth with a click. Where the hell had that come from?

Gill's face was an advertisement for sisterly concern.

"Oh, Poppy," she said.

Suddenly Poppy was blinking away tears. "I'm fine. It's all good. We're having a good time, no strings."

"Except you want there to be strings."

It wasn't a question. Poppy nodded miserably. It was almost a relief to admit it to someone.

Gill shook her head. "Men are such assholes sometimes."

"I'm the one who broke the rules," Poppy said. "This was supposed to be a casual thing."

"Yeah, right. I told you, didn't I? It always gets messy. If you like a man enough to spend that much time with him, to share your body with him, what the hell is going to stop you from falling all the way in love with him?"

"Excellent question," Poppy said with a watery smile.

Gill grabbed her forearm, very earnest. "Tell him how you feel, Poppy. Don't do what I did. I hung on and hung on with Nathan, hoping and hoping he'd realize he cared. I wasted a year eating my heart out for him, going alone to parties because we weren't a couple despite the fact that we slept with each other all the time, turning away other men because I was always holding out hope that Nathan would get it. And he never did."

Poppy stared at her sister. She remembered Nathan. He was a senior executive at the publishing house where Gill worked.

Poppy had been introduced to him once when she'd dropped into the office to pick up her sister for a lunch date.

"I always thought Nathan was only a work colleague," Poppy said.

Gill's smile was tight. "You were right. It just took me a while to work that out."

"I'm sorry things didn't work out for you."

"Hey, it's old news. And Daniel is a sweetie, don't you think?"

"Yeah, he seems great."

Gill squeezed Poppy's arm. "Do yourself a favor—tell Jake how you feel, what you want. At least that way you'll know now, rather than waiting and waiting and finding out down the line that you'll never get what you want."

Poppy shook her head. Even the thought of telling Jake made her belly tense. "It's too soon. It's only been a few weeks."

"It was long enough for *you* to fall in love with *him,* wasn't it?" Gill asked.

Poppy stared at her sister, utterly arrested. She knew Gill was right. In her bones she knew.

Their mother entered, a stack of plates in her hands.

"Your dad's pulling out the liqueur glasses. I think it's going to be one of those nights."

Without giving herself time to stop and think, Poppy turned to her mother.

"Mom, I think I'm going to head back into town," she said.

Her mother frowned. "I thought you were staying the night? And haven't you been drinking?"

"I've had one glass. And there's something I need to do," Poppy said.

Gill met her eyes and gave her an encouraging nod.

Ten minutes later Poppy was on the freeway to Melbourne, her gut churning with nerves. She went over and over what she wanted to say in her head, imagining what Jake might say in response. By the time she hit the city she was half nervous, half terrified.

She had no idea how Jake would react. She was very, very afraid that he would reject her. But there was also a flicker of hope in her heart.

She found a parking spot right in front of his apartment building. She told herself it was a good omen. She figured she needed every scrap of luck she could get right now. Her boots rapped sharply against the marble stairs of his building as she climbed to the second floor. She paused outside his door, her hand fisted, ready to knock.

He wasn't expecting her. She probably should have called, warned him she was on the way.

She knocked. There was a short silence, then she heard the sound of footsteps on the other side of the door.

"Jake," she said.

But it wasn't Jake standing in front of her, it was a tall, elegantly dressed woman in a white silk blouse and tailored black pants. About thirty-five, maybe a little older, her hair long, dark and smooth, her makeup flawless.

Poppy stared. She didn't have it in her to do anything else.

Another woman. God, why hadn't she even considered it? It wasn't as though she and Jake had ever discussed being exclusive, after all. She had just assumed...

Which, clearly, had been a stupid, naive thing to do.

"Sorry, Jake's not here right now," the woman said. "But he shouldn't be long, if you want to come in and wait?"

Poppy took a step backward.

"No, no. Um, it's okay, I can talk to Jake later. At—at work. I didn't mean to barge in. I should have called."

Dinner burned the back of her throat. While she'd been falling in love with Jake, he'd been…what? Romancing this other woman on the side? Sleeping with her the few nights he hadn't been with Poppy?

"Seriously, he just ducked out. Gerome wouldn't quit whining about there being no beer."

"Hey! I made one comment. Hardly whining," a male voice said, then a dark-haired man in his early forties stepped into view and rested a hand on the woman's shoulder.

Poppy stared at him. Then she stared at his hand. Some of the panicked urgency left her body.

The woman stuck her hand out. "I just realized, I should have introduced myself. You probably think we're breaking into Jake's place or something. I'm Fiona, Jake's sister."

Somehow Poppy managed to clasp Fiona's hand and shake it.

"I'm Poppy. Um, I work with Jake," she said.

"When you're not whipping ass for Australia. I'm Gerome, Fiona's whining, beer-loving husband." He smiled. "I've got to say this, even though you probably hear it all the time, but that was an amazing final in the relay you guys pulled off in Beijing. I nearly wet my pants when you outtouched the Poms to come home with the gold."

Fiona rolled her eyes. "Can't take him anywhere." She waved Poppy forward. "Come in, please. Jake will be angry with us if we let you go before he gets back."

Before Poppy could protest, she was drawn into Jake's apartment. It was only when she followed Fiona into the living room that she saw his sister and husband weren't the only visitors. An older couple sat on the couch, wineglasses on the coffee table in front of them.

"Poppy, these are my parents, Harriet and Bernard Stevens. Guys, this is Poppy Birmingham."

"You don't need to tell us that," Jake's dad said. He stood and offered her his hand. "An honor to meet you. My wife and I are big fans."

Poppy smiled and said something appropriate. At least she hoped it was appropriate—she was too busy trying not to stare at the half-eaten birthday cake on the coffee table. She could just make out the words that had been iced on the cake before someone had cut into it: Happy Birthday, Jake. Her gaze shifted to the crumpled wrapping paper on the floor, then to the stack of obviously new books on one arm of the couch.

It was Jake's birthday. And he hadn't told her. He had his family over from Adelaide, and he hadn't told her.

Why would he? a cynical little voice said in the back of her mind. *You're just the warm body he screws. You're not part of his life. Why would he share his family with you?*

His mom was saying something. Poppy shook her head, tried to focus.

It was too much. She'd come here, ready to bare her soul to him, and he hadn't even bothered to let her know it was his birthday.

"I'm sorry. I—I have to go," she said suddenly, interrupting Jake's mother. The other woman looked startled, but Poppy didn't care. She had to get out of there before she burst into tears in front of a roomful of strangers.

"I'm sure Jake will be here any minute. He said the liquor shop was around the corner. I'll call him," Fiona said, pulling out her cell phone.

"No!" Poppy practically yelled it. They all stared at her. "I'll catch up with Jake another time. There's nothing I need to say that can't wait."

She headed for the door and took the stairs two at a time, desperate to avoid bumping into Jake. If she saw him right now, there was no way she'd be able to stop herself from breaking into big, blubbering, self-pitying tears. She hit the foyer at speed and barreled into the street. Relief hit her as she slid behind the wheel.

She'd made it.

Now she just had to do what needed to be done and learn to live with the consequences of her own foolishness.

THE SIX-PACK OF BEER SWUNG heavily in the bag as Jake climbed the stairs to his apartment. At least now his brother-in-law could stop looking so hangdog about the lack of malt-and-hops-based beverages in the house. He'd have to warn his family that if they planned to ambush him on his birthday again they needed to bring their own drinks or possibly end up disappointed.

He smiled to himself as he pulled his keys from his pocket. He still couldn't believe his sister and his parents had flown all the way from Adelaide to Melbourne to surprise him. Although the "casual" phone call he'd had from his sister during the week was now explained. Crafty bastards.

He let himself into the apartment and shrugged out of his coat.

"Okay, Gerome, you fussy bugger—it's beer o'clock," he said as he walked to the living room.

"See, I told you he'd walk in the door the moment she'd gone," Fiona said. She sounded frustrated. "Your timing has always sucked, Jake."

"Sorry?"

"You just missed your friend," his mother said.

Jake frowned.

"Poppy Birmingham," Gerome explained. "She of the long legs and many gold medals."

"Yeah? Poppy was here? She's supposed to be in Ballarat at her folks' place."

"We told her to wait for you, but she wouldn't stay," his mother said.

"Huh." He pulled his cell phone from his back pocket and dialed her cell. She wouldn't have had time to drive far; she could turn around and come back to meet his family.

He frowned as the call went to voice mail.

"Poppy, it's me," he said. "Give me a call when you get this." He thought for a second. She hadn't said anything, but he'd been very aware that this was her first family occasion without Uncle Charlie being around. Maybe it had been too tough and she'd bailed. "Hope everything went okay tonight."

"She said she'd speak to you tomorrow," Fiona said when he'd ended the call.

"And in the meantime, I believe there are six perfectly good beers calling my name," Gerome said.

Jake handed the bag over, still thinking about Poppy.

"She's very striking," his mother said. "I've only ever seen her on TV but she's got a real presence, hasn't she?"

"Yeah," Jake said. He'd wait until she was home then call her to check everything was okay.

"Why don't I make us some coffee?" his mother said, standing and starting to collect wineglasses.

"I'll get it. What does everyone want?" he asked.

He took orders and his mother followed him into the kitchen, clearly determined to help out. He pulled coffee mugs from the cupboard while she filled the kettle, and all the while his mind was on Poppy. Ten more minutes and he would go into his bedroom and call her, make sure she was all right.

"Jake, I know this makes me the worst sort of interfering mother, but I have to ask. Are you seeing Poppy? Is she your girlfriend?"

He pulled the coffee out of the freezer. "You're right, it does."

His mother gave him a dry look. "Well, tough. I'm your mother and I've been worried about you, so I get a free pass now and then."

"I'm fine," he said.

His mom crossed her arms over her chest and leaned against the sink. "Are you?"

"Yes."

"It seems to me that all you do these days is work. That's all you ever seem to talk about when I call."

"Well, you know, unless I win the lottery that's the way it's probably going to be until I retire."

"Jake, stop bullshitting me. I'm serious here."

He stared at her. His mom never swore.

"Ever since the divorce I feel as though you've forgotten how to really live."

"Mom, I'm fine. I swear. I go out, I do stuff. It's not like I'm some bitter divorcé holed up in my apartment, living off canned food."

His mother walked to the freezer and opened the door like a lawyer inviting the jury to examine exhibit A. Jake stared at the neat stack of frozen meals and pizzas filling the small space.

"Okay, maybe I could eat a little better," he conceded.

His mother looked at him sadly. "I wish I could show you how much you've changed. The look in your eyes, the way you carry yourself—it's as though you're always braced, ready to defend yourself in case someone gets too close."

He didn't know how to respond. What his mother was saying was probably true. His marriage had changed him. Made him wary. Worn him down.

"I'm doing okay, Mom," he said.

"I want you to be doing more than okay. I want you to find someone you can love again, someone who loves you.

I want you to have children and write more beautiful books and live a full life instead of this frozen-dinner existence you've been enduring."

"I'm not getting married again, Mom." He said it very seriously, so she'd know it wasn't open to debate. "I don't want to go through any of that crap ever again."

"But what about love? Companionship? What about having a warm body to wake up next to and someone to share jokes with and someone to rub your feet at night?"

His thoughts flew to Poppy, to the way they'd laughed and kissed and fooled around for an hour in her bed this morning before he'd finally got his ass into the shower.

"Never say never," he heard himself say.

His mother blinked. She didn't look any less surprised than he felt himself. When had his strict no involvement, no commitment policy gotten so ragged around the edges?

"Well. I guess I'm going to have to settle for that, aren't I?" his mother said. She was looking rather pleased with herself. And why not? He'd pretty much confirmed her guess about Poppy.

She left him to finish making the coffee alone. He set out sugar and milk on a tray, his thoughts circling.

So much for keeping Poppy at arm's length. She'd crept into his life a moment at a time, even though he'd been telling himself to back off, to be careful. And now it was too late. He cared. He didn't want their relationship to have an expiry date. He was hooked, well and truly.

He rolled his eyes.

Hell, might as well admit it, while he was being honest with himself: he was probably even in love. Wait until his mother worked that one out. She'd be skipping and singing.

He waited for the old tension to grip him as he faced his

feelings at last. Loving Marly had been a burden in the end, a weight that he carried with him every minute of every day. He'd been driven by the need to help her, heal her, protect her. And in the end he'd had to let her go. He'd never wanted to go there again.

And yet here he was. Poppy had sneaked under his guard and into his heart while he wasn't looking. He'd thought he was indulging in hot sex and a bit of fun, but all the while he'd been falling for her honesty and earthiness and warmth.

He touched a hand to his chest, but there was no band of tension there, no sense of heaviness in his body. He didn't feel burdened by his feelings for Poppy.

He felt…warm. Grateful. Relieved.

A smile spread across his face.

For the first time in years, he felt hope.

"Damn," he said softly.

He wanted to jump in his car and go find her, but he settled for calling her house. He wasn't about to blurt out his feelings over the phone, but he really needed to hear her voice.

The phone rang and rang before her answering machine picked up. Disappointed, he left another message asking her to call him when she got in.

She didn't. He was half tempted to call her after another hour had passed, but it was late. And there was always tomorrow. His feelings weren't going anywhere, right? They'd still be there when he woke. And so would Poppy, even if he felt a ridiculous, adolescent urge to stand beneath her window and serenade her and make absolutely certain that she was his.

HE TRIED PHONING POPPY again first thing the next morning and got her answering machine once more. He wanted to go straight over to her place, but his parents and Gerome and Fiona had flown all the way from Adelaide to see him. Swallowing his impatience, he took them for breakfast at the café in the nearby Royal Botanic Gardens. His gaze constantly strayed to his cell phone throughout, but still Poppy didn't call. To his great relief, his family decided to check out the galleries and shops after breakfast. Jake walked to his apartment alone, planning to try Poppy one last time before heading over to her place.

He spotted her car in front of his apartment block when he turned the corner. A smile curved his mouth. It had never occurred to him before, but he was always smiling when she was around. She was sunshine in human form—strong and proud and beautiful, and he couldn't believe it had taken him so long to see what was right under his nose.

She got out of her car as he approached. By the time he'd reached her side, she'd removed a bag from the trunk.

"Hey," he said. "I was worried about you."

He leaned in to kiss her, but she turned her cheek so that his lips landed on the side of her jaw. He pulled back to look at her. She met his eyes, her expression utterly impassive.

Something was wrong.

"I came over to return the things you left at my place," she said. "Some underwear and a book or two."

She offered him the bag. He looked at it but didn't take it. "What's going on?"

"I don't want to do this anymore. Sleep with you, I mean."

He felt as though she'd sucker punched him. For a long moment he just stared at her.

"Where is this coming from?" he finally asked. His voice sounded rough, as though he'd forgotten how to use it all of a sudden. "I thought we were having a good time together."

Her gaze slid over his shoulder. "It was always a casual thing, right? I figure it's run its course."

He shook his head. "No. Something happened." He reached for her arm. "Let's go upstairs, grab some coffee, talk properly."

She shrugged away from him. "There's nothing much to say, is there? We were always only about the sex. Once that got old, this was pretty much inevitable. I'm calling it before it gets messy."

She was so damned matter-of-fact. Utterly unmoved, unemotional.

"I wasn't aware that the sex *had* gotten old," he said. He'd meant to provoke her into something, some sign that she felt something as she stood there, kissing goodbye to the most intense four weeks of his life.

She simply lifted a shoulder. "I wanted to tell you to your face."

She offered the bag again. When he still didn't take it, she placed it by his feet.

"It's been a lot of fun. I hope we can still be friends," she said.

Then she offered him her hand. He stared at it. A handshake. She wanted to shake his hand after all the things they'd done together. After he'd made her sob with pleasure. After he'd kissed and caressed and tasted her all over. After he'd fallen in love with her.

"This is bullshit, Poppy. Tell me what's really going on."

"I'm being smart." She turned toward her car.

"Hang on. You can't just drop your little bombshell and drive off."

She kept walking. "You made the rules, Jake." She sounded resigned and sad.

"Poppy."

"I'll see you tomorrow at work."

She got into her car. He swore and reached for the passenger side door, but it was locked. She pulled out into the street. He started after her, then realized what he was doing. He couldn't chase her car down. And even if he could, it wasn't going to get him anywhere. Poppy had made up her mind. She'd cut him loose.

"Shit."

He stood staring after her, his body tight with frustration. There had been no sign that this was coming, not a hint. Yesterday morning, she'd clawed at his back as he made love to her. She'd laughed with him and promised to call the moment she was back from Ballarat. She'd teased him about the Scorsese double feature.

"Shit."

He walked to the sidewalk and picked up his belongings, staring at his neatly folded boxer-briefs and T-shirts in the bottom of the bag. She'd even cleaned him out of her apartment.

By the time he'd climbed the stairs to his apartment his temper was firing on all cylinders. He kept remembering the distance in her voice, the way she'd offered him her hand as if she was some goddamned business associate or something.

"Bullshit, Poppy. This is bullshit," he said as he threw the shopping bag onto the couch.

She'd said that they'd always been only about the sex, but that wasn't true—that hadn't been true from the first time they slept with each other. They were friends. At the very damned least they were friends, and friends owed each other a little more explanation than a handshake and a casual "so long and thanks for all the orgasms."

He was pretty sure that if he didn't feel like hitting something, he'd almost be able to laugh at the irony of the situation. For over a month she'd been his and he hadn't appreciated her, hadn't understood exactly how freaking lucky he'd gotten when those baggage handlers had gone on strike and he'd been trapped in a car with her. And now he knew, and it was over. She was walking away.

Images flashed across his mind: Poppy smiling at him sleepily when she opened her eyes first thing in the morning; Poppy giving herself a shampoo Mohawk in the shower and insisting that he have one, too; Poppy standing in his kitchen, folding pizza boxes for recycling and reprimanding him for his crappy eating habits.

For five years he'd been sandbagged inside his own life, too exhausted, too goddamned weary and wary to risk feeling anything for anyone. Then he'd met Poppy, and she'd burned her way into his heart with her warmth and her spirit.

He stood.

"No way is this over. No freaking way."

He grabbed his car keys and headed for the door.

11

POPPY MADE IT AROUND the corner from Jake's apartment before she had to pull over. The ache in her chest was so painful she rubbed the heel of her hand over her sternum, over and over. Tears slid down her face.

She'd done it. And she'd done it without crying or breaking down and asking him if he loved her or felt anything for her beyond desire. A small victory, but an important one.

She stared out the windshield of her car. Who was she kidding? There was no upside to this situation. She'd fallen in love with a man who wasn't interested in anything other than sex. She'd done it with her eyes wide-open, telling herself every step of the way that she could handle it, that she was in control.

Hah.

She was so tired. She'd had a terrible night tossing and turning then finally pacing as she came to the inevitable, painful conclusion that she needed to end things with Jake.

She kept thinking of the previous day, the moment when she'd understood that he'd celebrated his birthday without her. She'd let him into her heart and her life, confided her fears, cried out her grief, shared her secrets. And he hadn't even been able to let her know it was his *birthday,* or that his family were in town to celebrate it. That was how little she meant to him. How compartmentalized she was in his life—Poppy Birmingham, slotted neatly away in the pigeonhole marked "sex, when you like it, how you like it, no strings attached."

Well, not anymore.

Poppy took a deep, shuddering breath and started the car again. She knew that on one level it was unfair of her to be angry with Jake. He hadn't promised her anything, after all. Not a single word regarding the future, his feelings, their relationship had ever passed his lips. In fact, he'd warned her that he was a poor prospect, that he didn't want to settle down or commit. Yet their relationship had quickly gone beyond the bounds of what anyone would define as casual. It had become intense and all-consuming and both of them had been a party to that. Except she was pretty sure she'd have to hold a gun to Jake's head before he admitted as much. God forbid he ever trust someone enough to talk about his feelings. God forbid he ever let his guard down for one second.

She made an impatient noise as she signaled and turned onto her street. She was hurt, and she was angry with him for being so damn stubborn and obtuse and disinterested that he'd let that happen, but she also knew that Jake couldn't help being the way he was. He was damaged. Someone—his ex-wife, probably, but how would Poppy know since he hadn't seen fit to confide in her?—had hurt him and he was determined not to let the same thing happen again. It was a pity she hadn't understood all of that before she'd lost her heart to him.

She thought she was going home until she found herself turning into the parking lot at the pool. She smiled a little grimly as she grabbed her swim bag from the backseat. It wasn't as though she had anywhere else to go to seek comfort. Uncle Charlie was gone, and her parents had never been her confidantes.

She changed into her swimsuit with brisk economy. The fast lane was empty when she made her way to the outdoor pool. She performed a racing start even though she hadn't taken the time to warm up, exploding out of the block with everything she had. The water rose up to meet her and she closed her eyes for a second as she felt its familiar, all-encompassing embrace. She started to swim, powering up the pool with a length-eating freestyle stroke. The end of the lane arrived quickly and she did a tumble turn, surging away from the wall. Her shoulders were tense, her stroke choppy. If Uncle Charlie or her coach were watching, they'd tell her she needed to pace herself, that she'd burn out well before the race was done.

She didn't care. She wanted to not feel and not hurt and the only way she knew how was to push herself to the limit. She swam faster and faster, her muscles screaming, her lungs on fire. And then somehow she was swimming and crying at the same time and she was swallowing water and choking. She stopped midstroke, reaching blindly for the line-marker. The plastic dug into her armpits as she threw her arms over it and tried to breathe.

It hurt. It physically hurt to love Jake Stevens and know he didn't love her back.

For the first time in her life, the pool failed to offer the sanctuary she craved. Go figure. Just when she needed it the most, the comfort of the familiar deserted her.

Her arms and legs heavy, she swam slowly to the end of the pool. It wasn't until she'd pulled herself up the ladder that she saw Jake waiting for her where she'd left her towel on the bleachers. She stiffened, wondering how much he'd seen. Her thrashing up and down the pool? Her crying and holding the lane marker?

She squared her shoulders. It didn't matter. She felt the way she felt. There wasn't anything she could do about it, and it suddenly seemed supremely foolish to pretend she didn't care. Besides, telling Jake she loved him was probably the one surefire way to get him to keep his distance.

Face set, she walked toward him.

SHE'D BEEN CRYING. Jake fought the urge to haul Poppy into his arms and instead offered her her towel.

"Can we talk?" he asked as she patted her face dry.

"Why?"

"Because I want to know what happened. Why one minute we were okay, and then the next you were gone."

"There is no *we*. There never has been." She pushed past him and walked toward the change rooms.

"That's bullshit, Poppy. We've practically lived in each other's pockets for the past month. What the hell was that about?"

"Sex, apparently."

He grabbed her elbow before she could disappear inside the women's change room.

"You can't bail on me like this. At the very least I deserve an explanation," he said, fear and confusion getting the better of him. She was so adamant, so damned determined.

What on earth had happened?

She stiffened then jerked her arm away from him. "Why should I tell you anything about how I'm feeling or what I'm thinking? Why should I bare my freaking soul to you when you can't even bother to let me know it's your *birthday?*"

He stared at her, the pieces falling into place. Damn. It hadn't even occurred to him.

He almost laughed with relief as he understood why she was upset. This he could fix. Definitely.

"My family surprised me, Poppy. They turned up on my doorstep Saturday afternoon. I had no idea they were coming over from Adelaide. I swear, if I'd known, you would have been there," he said.

He reached for her, needing to touch her, but she took a step away from him.

"So you had no idea it was your birthday? Is that what you're telling me?"

He frowned. "It wasn't exactly a red-letter celebration, Poppy. I'm thirty-six. It's no big deal."

"You don't get it, do you? You know everything about me. You've met my sister and my parents, you know about Uncle Charlie. You know how hard it's been for me to adjust to working at the paper. You know I'm messy and that before I met you I had no idea about sex. I've cried on your goddamned shoulder, Jake. And you can't even tell me it's your birthday."

"Poppy…"

"No. No more. I'm sick of being on the outside of your life. I'm sick of being someone you sleep with but don't share with. I deserve more."

"You're not on the outside of my life. Not by a long shot. There's no one else but you, Poppy."

"If that's true, then what happened the night you sent me home, Jake? What made you so upset that you couldn't stand being near me?"

He stared at her. His past with Marly had nothing to do with this. Poppy was a clean slate, a fresh start. He didn't want any of the past clinging to his future.

"It was nothing to do with you, I swear it," he said.

"See? You don't trust me. You can't even tell me that you've started writing your next book. You think I don't notice when you shut me out, Jake? You think it doesn't mean anything?" Her face crumpled for a moment. She pressed her fingers against her closed eyes, took a deep breath as she tried to regain control.

He couldn't stand seeing her like this. He pulled her into his arms. Her body felt cold against his chest.

"Poppy. Please," he said. He wasn't sure what he was asking for.

She rested her forehead against his chest for a few seconds, then she pushed away from him, shaking her head.

"No. I can't live like this. I can't give you all of me and accept a part of you. I can't love you and take the crumbs from your table."

He stilled. Poppy loved him? He closed his eyes. Of course Poppy loved him. He was the biggest freaking idiot under the sun.

When he opened his eyes again, she was about to disappear into the change rooms.

"Wait!"

"There's nothing more to say, Jake," she said sadly.

She turned the corner. He lunged after her, only to pull up short when a middle-aged woman and her grandchildren emerged from the change rooms. The woman gave him an outraged look.

"This is women only!" she said.

"Sorry," Jake said, grinding his teeth with impatience.

He needed to go after Poppy, to explain to her that he loved her, too. He needed to convince her that he did trust her, that the only reason he hadn't told her about Marly and the baby and all that mess was because it didn't matter. It wasn't a part of his life anymore. As for his writing... Surely once he'd explained that it wasn't a book he was working on, that he didn't really know what it was himself, she'd understand why he hadn't mentioned it, why he'd kept it so close to his chest?

Jake closed his eyes as he realized what he was doing: making excuses, coming up with ways to convince her to give him another chance on his terms.

She was right. He'd shut her out.

He'd been so busy fooling himself he wasn't falling in love with her. He'd given ground by slow degrees—first admitting he found her desirable, then giving in to the need to spend more time with her, get to know her. And all the while he'd been quarantining the parts of himself that held his saddest, ugliest truths.

He remembered something his mother said last night: *the look in your eyes, the way you carry yourself—it's as though you're always braced, ready to defend yourself in case someone gets too close.*

Loving Marly had just about finished him. She'd needed so much from him, been so vulnerable. By the time it was over, he'd been empty. Exhausted. Loving someone who was in so much pain and being unable to help her had been the hardest, saddest thing he'd ever done. He'd been determined to never, ever put himself in a position of caring that much again. Of being that vulnerable.

But Poppy was not Marly. She was her own person. Strong, determined, disciplined. Funny, wise, honest. He loved her. Irrevocably. Even though he'd resisted his feelings every step of the way.

And he'd hurt her, time after time.

He ran his hand over his face, thinking of all the times he'd kept her at arm's length. She was right—she deserved more. She deserved everything he had to give.

He started walking.

Suddenly he knew exactly what he needed to do to make things right.

IT WAS NEARLY DARK by the time Poppy returned to her apartment. She'd been reluctant to go home after her swim, afraid that Jake would be there waiting for her, so she'd driven into the city and drifted through the shops. She didn't want to face him again, not today. It would be bad enough tomorrow and for all the days after tomorrow when she'd have to work with him and try not to blubber every time she saw him.

Her steps slowed when she approached her front door. Jake was sitting there, his head leaning against the door. His eyes opened when he heard her and he stood.

"I wanted to give you this," he said.

For the first time she saw that he had a sheaf of papers in his hand.

"This is what I've been working on," he said. "It's not a new book, it's something else. A record, maybe. Of my marriage. Of what went wrong."

She stared at him.

"Will you read it?" he asked.

"If that's what you want."

"It is." He frowned, looked away for a moment. "It's pretty sad and small, but it's what happened. It's part of me. And I want you to know." His voice was thick with emotion.

"Jake—"

"There's more, but it can wait," he said. "I know I've hurt you, Poppy. I'm more sorry than you'll ever know. But I want to try and make it up to you."

He handed her the papers then turned away. Poppy opened

her mouth to call him back, but then she glanced down at the top page of his story.

> He wasn't sure when it ended. It wasn't as though a light switched on or off inside him, or he woke one day and the world had changed. It just…happened. She was still his wife. He still loved her. But it hurt him to look at her sometimes. So much pain. Leaking out of her, all the time. And he'd run out of fingers to plug the holes….

When she looked up again, Jake was gone. She stood frozen for a moment, half-afraid of what she held in her hands. Then she unlocked her front door and entered her apartment. She shed her coat and sat at the dining room table, Jake's story in front of her. She smoothed her hands over the crisp white pages with their neat lines of print.

A record, he'd called it. He wanted her to know.

It felt like a huge step forward. It felt like everything.

Lowering her head, she started to read.

It took her nearly three hours to reach the final page. She felt drained. She pushed the manuscript away from herself and used the sleeve of her sweatshirt to wipe the tears from her face.

As Jake had said, it was small and sad, the kind of every-day tragedy that happened to many, many people. The loss of a much-anticipated baby. Marly's subsequent depression. Jake's guilt for being on a book tour when it happened. The counseling. The terrible day when he came home from work to find Marly unconscious in the bathroom, an empty bottle of sleeping tablets beside her. Her first words on waking: *I hate you.* Jake's pain and rage and guilt and love and hate.

It was all there, captured as only Jake could capture it—

honestly, vividly, emotionally. It made her want to howl for him. And it helped her understand.

Why he'd locked himself away. Why he'd denied what was happening between them. And how much it must have cost him to hand over his intensely personal, revealing story to her.

She reached for a tissue and blew her nose. Then she grabbed her car keys and headed for the door. Her feet were a blur on the stairs and she broke into a run as she exited her building. She needed to see him, right now. She needed to tell him—

"Poppy."

She stopped in her tracks. Jake was leaning against her car, his arms crossed over his chest. He straightened, arms dropping to his sides. She frowned, then she understood: he'd waited for her. He'd hand-delivered his story and waited out front of her apartment in the dark for three hours while she read it.

She walked toward him. He met her halfway.

"I'm sorry," she said.

He shook his head. "You don't need to apologize to me."

"I'm not. I'm just sorry." She reached out and cupped his face. "I know it must have been incredibly hard for you to let me read this."

"I trust you, Poppy. I never didn't trust you. I think it was myself I didn't trust."

"It doesn't matter."

"It does. I pushed you away so many times. You're the best thing that has ever happened to me and I almost lost you."

"It doesn't matter."

To prove it to him, she pressed a kiss to his mouth. She broke the kiss and rested her cheek against his, her hand still cupping the side of his jaw.

"I love you, Jake."

His hand came up to hold her face and they stood cheek to cheek, holding one another close for long moments.

"I love you, too, Poppy. More than I can say."

She closed her eyes. It was nice to hear the words at last, but she didn't need them. Not now.

Jake's hand slid from her cheek, and he wrapped both arms around her and held her so tightly it almost hurt. He pressed his face into her neck and she could hear him breathing, struggling for control.

"Thank you," he said, his voice muffled. "Thank you for giving me another chance."

He was crying. She held him tightly, fiercely. She'd wanted to share his pain, and here it was. She closed her eyes, pulled him closer.

"I'm not going anywhere," she said quietly. "I love you and I'm not going anywhere and no matter what happens we'll always work it out."

He pulled back so he could look into her face. Her heart squeezed in her chest as she looked into his eyes. There was so much raw vulnerability there, and so much determination. And, finally, at last, so much love.

"Poppy Birmingham, you are the most amazing person I've ever met. Freaking courageous. So bloody determined you put me to shame. Sexy as all get out." He shook his head, made a frustrated noise. "There are no words. I adore you. I don't know what I did to deserve you, but I've got you and I'm not letting you go."

"No words, my ass."

He smiled. Then he looked into her eyes and the smile slowly faded.

"Forgive me for being the stupidest man on the planet?"

"Careful. You're talking about the man I love."

"Poppy."

She kissed him. "We both made mistakes. Ever heard the saying it takes two to tango?"

"You're always letting me off the hook."

"I know. Kind of makes you wonder what's in it for me, doesn't it?"

As she'd hoped, he laughed. Then he slid his hand into hers and began to lead her up the path toward her apartment.

"Where are we going?" she asked, even though she knew. It had been a whole twenty-four hours since they'd been naked, after all.

"I'm going to show you what's in it for you. It may take a while. How does fifty or sixty years sound?"

He glanced at her over his shoulder. Warmth unfolded in her chest at the look in his eyes.

"Wow. That's a lot of showing. You sure you're up to it?"

"The question is, are you?"

She was grinning. She couldn't help herself. Jake loved her. He'd let her in, finally.

He smiled back at her and used their joined hands to tug her close.

"Answer the question, Birmingham," he said, his mouth just inches from her own.

"Yes," she said. "Yes. Yes to the moon. Yes to infinity. Yes."

He smiled into her face.

"Correct answer."